S

"How long has it be[...] [...]
you anywhere, even [...]

Anywhere?

His breath flowed softly over her lips, making her head spin and her blood race. "A good number of years, I think. What a sinful waste." His presence wrapped her, then his arms did too.

A kiss, careful but confident. She resisted the impulse to close her eyes and float away on the intimacy, but she was tempted far more than she ever expected to be. Within her shock she struggled to hold back the dreamy tide of pleasure that threatened to inundate her and drown her very sense of herself.

But, oh, it was too sweet, and so poignant that she wanted to weep. The warmth wrenched her heart. A part of her long denied, long buried and ignored, ached to break free and sing. She was a girl again within that embrace, and painfully alive.

PRAISE FOR
MADELINE HUNTER'S NOVELS

"A writer whose novels every reader will adore."
—*Romantic Times* (Top Pick)

"Richly spiced with wicked wit and masterfully threaded with danger and desire, the superbly sexy first book in Hunter's new Regency historical quartet is irresistible and wonderfully entertaining." —*Booklist* (starred review)

Berkley titles by Madeline Hunter

RAVISHING IN RED
PROVOCATIVE IN PEARLS
SINFUL IN SATIN
DANGEROUS IN DIAMONDS

Dangerous in Diamonds

MADELINE HUNTER

JOVE BOOKS, NEW YORK

THE BERKLEY PUBLISHING GROUP
Published by the Penguin Group
Penguin Group (USA) Inc.
375 Hudson Street, New York, New York 10014, USA
Penguin Group (Canada), 90 Eglinton Avenue East, Suite 700, Toronto, Ontario M4P 2Y3, Canada
(a division of Pearson Penguin Canada Inc.)
Penguin Books Ltd., 80 Strand, London WC2R 0RL, England
Penguin Group Ireland, 25 St. Stephen's Green, Dublin 2, Ireland (a division of Penguin Books Ltd.)
Penguin Group (Australia), 250 Camberwell Road, Camberwell, Victoria 3124, Australia
(a division of Pearson Australia Group Pty. Ltd.)
Penguin Books India Pvt. Ltd., 11 Community Centre, Panchsheel Park, New Delhi—110 017, India
Penguin Group (NZ), 67 Apollo Drive, Rosedale, Auckland 0632, New Zealand
(a division of Pearson New Zealand Ltd.)
Penguin Books (South Africa) (Pty.) Ltd., 24 Sturdee Avenue, Rosebank, Johannesburg 2196,
South Africa

Penguin Books Ltd., Registered Offices: 80 Strand, London WC2R 0RL, England

This is a work of fiction. Names, characters, places, and incidents either are the product of the author's imagination or are used fictitiously, and any resemblance to actual persons, living or dead, business establishments, events, or locales is entirely coincidental. The publisher does not have control over and does not have any responsibility for author or third-party websites or their content.

DANGEROUS IN DIAMONDS

A Jove Book / published by arrangement with the author

PRINTING HISTORY
Jove mass-market edition / May 2011

Copyright © 2011 by Madeline Hunter.
Cover photography by Claudio Marinesco.
Cover design by Rita Frangie.
Text design by Laura K. Corless.

ISBN: 978-0-515-14934-0

JOVE®
Jove Books are published by The Berkley Publishing Group,
a division of Penguin Group (USA) Inc.,
375 Hudson Street, New York, New York 10014.
JOVE® is a registered trademark of Penguin Group (USA) Inc.
The "J" design is a trademark of Penguin Group (USA) Inc.

PRINTED IN THE UNITED STATES OF AMERICA

10 9 8 7 6 5 4 3 2 1

Chapter One

The death of a duke is cause for many people to mourn, but none so much as those dependent on his patronage. So it was that the passing of the fourth Duke of Becksbridge left many a relative and retainer in tears. A few had to swallow the inappropriate inclination to smile, however, in particular several persons named in his testament as recipients of gifts or pensions.

One such beneficiary neither wept nor rejoiced. Rather, on the Tuesday following the duke's funeral, he finally attended to the oddity that he had received any gift at all.

"I hope he did not expect me to maintain the mourning rituals in his memory because of this," Tristan, Duke of Castleford, muttered.

He examined the deeds of the properties he had just inherited. If his head did not ache from the sobriety he adopted once a week on Tuesdays, he might muster some grief or nostalgia for this recently departed fellow peer. It would take considerable effort on the best of days, however.

Becksbridge had been a collateral relative, some distance removed, and most of the bequeathed holdings appeared to be distant as well. Also small. So small and insignificant as to hardly be worth the ink used to record the gift in the will.

"You do not intend to mourn? He was an important man and much esteemed." Mr. Edwards, his bespectacled secretary, spoke from his paper-covered desk in the study where together they labored on Castleford's business affairs.

"He was an ass. Worse, a boring, self-righteous ass. The boring part was only tiresome, but the self-righteous part unforgivable."

The latter had been an inherited turn of character, but in Castleford's opinion, that hardly absolved Becksbridge from being tedious in executing the tendency. That entire side of their complex family tree was so smug in their goodness that it made one want to puke. All the same, if Becksbridge had lived and let live, he might have been tolerable.

But, of course, he couldn't "let live." The Becksbridges of the world believed it was the duty of paragons of virtue to remind others they should strive for equal dreariness. In fact, in anticipation of his inheritance, Becksbridge's son and heir, Gerome, Earl of Latham, had been publishing popular screeds on morality. The next Duke of Becksbridge had already taken his scolds to the world through print and had forged a reputation as an arbiter of morals with his damned essays.

Castleford was inclined to sneer at the irony, but thinking much on the topic would only make his head hurt worse. Still, he knew Latham better than anyone else in the world did. Of similar age, they had raised hell together in years past. Even perfectly tended branches of family trees produce a few wormy fruit. The boring ass was about to be succeeded by a dangerous hypocrite.

"You have that sniveling expression you wear when you are choking on swallowed words, Edwards. Do you disapprove that I speak ill of the dead?"

Edwards flushed. Only twenty-five years of age, he had not yet learned to keep his own counsel on Tuesdays, especially when his employer invited him to speak freely. "The duke was unparalleled, and he was very generous. It is said he endowed an orphanage in his will."

"Unparalleled? Are you saying outright, to my face, that I am not his equal? That is ungrateful for a secretary who may have to labor on the one day a week when I tend to my estate, but who otherwise has more freedom of movement than any servant ought."

"I—that is, you are unparalleled as well, Your Grace. Everyone says so, and—"

"I do not hold with the notion that asses should be fondly remembered just because they have the means to spread around gifts to make others beholden. As for his generosity to *me*, I neither need nor want these small landholdings. The man has managed to be a nuisance beyond the grave."

"The properties all have tenants. Managing them will not create more trouble."

Castleford peered at the deeds. "It is too peculiar that he gave them to me at all. We were not fond of each other. We had not spoken civil words in years." That was an understatement. Their few meetings had been marked by reproaches on Becksbridge's part and ridicule on Castleford's.

A letter had been delivered with the deeds. Castleford tore it open.

Castleford,

You are no doubt surprised by the legacy that I left you, since you of all men need nothing from me. Neither the lands nor the money would form more than a tiny drop in your ocean of wealth. Therefore I assume that you will not care that it was never my intention for you to enjoy the fruits of either. Rather, I am depending on what little is left of the better side of your character, and requesting that you discreetly handle a matter for me that I prefer not to address through my testament.

The landholdings that I left you are currently used by tenants in whose welfare I have a committed interest. It is my wish that the tenants be allowed to remain indefinitely at the current rent of one pound a year. Furthermore, the money left to you should be used to ensure that the tenants' families are never in want of the basics of life.

I trust this is a small matter that your stewards can execute without troubling you. It should in no way interfere with the inebriated fornications that normally occupy your time. (And which, I am obligated to remind you, bring disrepute to your name and blood, a likely early death to your person, and inevitable damnation to your everlasting soul.)

Becksbridge

Castleford shook his head. Even in this letter—in which he placed an unwelcomed obligation on a distant relative with no fond memories of him—Becksbridge could not resist scolding.

"I suppose I will have to visit these spots of land soon, or I might forget about them entirely. Get maps and mark them, Edwards. I will deal with it before summer ends."

"That might not be possible, sir. There are not enough Tuesdays left for such journeys along with attending to your usual affairs."

"Calm yourself, Edwards. I do not have to be sober to visit my estates."

D aphne Joyes flipped through the mail that Katherine had brought to her. She masked her disappointment when it became apparent that the letter she awaited had not arrived.

Foreboding sickened her. If that letter had not come by now, it probably never would. She would have to turn her mind to what that meant about the future. Plans had already begun forming. None of them were pleasant to contemplate. Worse, goals that she had thought herself finally close to achieving would now be put off indefinitely. Perhaps forever.

That possibility pained her heart. She held her composure and mourned privately, secretly, the way she had done for years now.

Katherine took a chair facing the large window in the back sitting room where they shared some coffee. Dark hair neatly dressed and apron crisp despite a morning tending to plants, Katherine waited patiently to hear any news in today's letters that Daphne chose to share.

She appeared a little foreign, Daphne thought, not for the first time. Katherine's high cheekbones and dark, almond-shaped eyes were not typically English in appearance, but it was the light brown of her skin, caused by the summer's sun, that really created the impression. Even the biggest-brimmed bonnet could not entirely protect a woman's complexion if she spent hours every day in a garden.

"Audrianna writes to say that she and Lord Sebastian will be going to the coast today, to escape the town's summer heat," Daphne offered.

"That is probably wise, in her condition. Will she remain there for her lying in?" Katherine said.

"I expect so, although she does not say."

Daphne opened and read the next letter. Katherine sipped her coffee and did not ask after this letter's sender either, even though Katherine had a special bond with the dear friend who had written it.

Katherine held strictly to the rules of the house. The most important rule was that the women living there were never to pry into each other's lives or personal business, past or present. In the years that Daphne had been sharing her home with women alone in the world like herself, that rule had served its purpose of ensuring harmony. However, some of the women who had lived here also found relief and safety in the right to keep their own counsel. Katherine was one of them.

The members of the household had fallen into two groups, Daphne thought, her mind distracted from the letter by the notion. They either belonged to the haunted or the hunted. A few seemed to suffer both afflictions. Like Katherine.

It was hard not to be curious. Hard not to believe that

if one learned the history and the truth, one could help. Daphne knew better, however. After all, she was a bit haunted and hunted herself, in ways that no one could ever change.

"Verity mostly writes about the doings at her home in Oldbury," she said, passing the letter to Katherine. "Lord Hawkeswell journeyed north to assess whether the trouble up there will affect her iron mill."

Katherine frowned over the letter while she read it. "I am glad that she did not go with the earl. The papers are full of dire predictions and warnings about violence."

"They often exaggerate. As you can see, her husband did not think there is any danger to their property or people."

"It could be different come August. There is that big demonstration planned."

"Plans are not certainties." However, it *could* be very different come August. One more thing to contemplate while reassessing the future.

Daphne turned to the paper itself. In addition to news about all those doings up north, the *Times* had other political stories, as well as correspondent letters from the Continent. One caught her eye. The new Duke of Becksbridge had been honored at a dinner a fortnight ago, attended by the best of Parisian society. It was, from the telling, a party to say good-bye prior to his imminent departure for London to take up the duties of his inheritance.

Would he live in England now? Or would he, hopefully, do as some other peers had since the war ended, and return to the Continent to make his home permanently in France?

"Who is that?" Katherine said.

Daphne looked over to see Katherine sitting upright, peering out the window behind Daphne's sofa.

Daphne turned around. "I see no one."

Katherine stood and moved closer. She squinted at the tapestry of flowers and plants outside. "A man just walked through the garden, not fifty feet from this window. He is near the rose arbor now."

Daphne's sight followed Katherine's pointing finger. She glimpsed the movement of a dark form near the arbor.

Just then their housekeeper, Mrs. Hill, entered the sitting room with a frown on her birdlike face. "There is a horse in front. I did not hear it approach on the lane, but there it is, with its rider gone."

"The rider is in the garden." Daphne could not see him any longer. She removed her apron. "I will go out and invite him to leave."

"Will you be wanting the pistol?" Katherine asked.

"I am sure that this person was only curious about a property named The Rarest Blooms that he found himself passing. He probably ventured up the lane to see just how rare the flowers might be."

Katherine remained tense, staring at the garden. Hunted, Daphne thought again.

"I suggest you watch from the greenhouse, Katherine. If our trespasser behaves in a threatening manner when I address him, you come out and brandish the pistol. Just try not to shoot him unless it is absolutely necessary."

D aphne left the house as if going for a midday turn on the property. She strolled past the kitchen garden, then followed paths through beds displaying summer flowers.

The greenhouse flanked the plantings on her right, and a brick wall with espaliered fruit trees hemmed in the garden on her left. Two portals on either side of the house gave entry to the gardens. The intruder must have come through one of them.

She meandered left, toward the arbor near the wall. The climbing rose that provided shelter from the sun there had not yet blossomed, but its leaves created a dense, shadowed sanctuary. As she approached, she saw the man sitting on the bench within.

He saw her too. He cocked his head a little, as if her presence fascinated him. He did not appear the least disconcerted at being found trespassing like this. He remained sitting there—sprawled, really—his shoulders resting against the arbor's back slats and one leg fully extended, so the sun shone on the foot of his boot.

A very nice boot, she noted as she drew near. Expensive. Expertly crafted of superior leather and polished within an inch of its life.

Her intruder was a gentleman.

She came to a halt about twenty feet from the arbor. She waited for him to speak. An apology, perhaps. Or an expression of interest in the gardens. Instead he silently regarded her as if he studied a painting in which, unaccountably, a figure had moved through the oiled colors.

The moment grew awkward. She looked back at the greenhouse, scanning its small panes of glass for Katherine's dark head. Not that there would be any trouble, of course. Yet she experienced a surprising amount of relief when she spotted Katherine.

Deciding that grace would achieve more than accusations when it came to boots like that, she smiled in acknowledgment of his presence. "Welcome to The Rarest

Blooms, sir. Did you come to admire the gardens? Do you have a particular interest in horticulture?"

"I know nothing about horticulture, although this garden is worthy of admiration." He stood, as etiquette required. He did not leave the arbor but remained within its dappled shadows.

He was tall. Taller than she was, and her own unfashionable stature often left her nose-to-nose with men or even looking down from an elevated prospect. He had dark hair and dark eyes and appeared quite handsome from what she could see. Young, but not very young. Thirty years of age, thereabouts, she guessed.

"Perhaps you seek to purchase a selection of special blooms for a favored lady?"

"It never entered my mind."

He did not appear inclined to share what *had* entered his mind and led him to intrude like this. He behaved, in fact, as if she had no right to know. She was beginning to dislike this man. She found his manner conceited and his relaxed attitude condescending.

"Perhaps you should consider it. Ladies consider flowers romantic. They love receiving them as gifts."

"They only pretend that they do. They are actually disappointed. They prefer jewels to flowers, no matter how rare the blooms might be. I daresay the thinnest silver chain would be favored over the most exotic plant."

"You speak with secure authority, as if you know the mind of every woman on earth."

"I have sampled enough to speak with confidence."

She was very sure that she did not like him now. "I am very fond of flowers, as you might surmise from the quantity here. It appears that your experience with women's minds has been incomplete."

That amused him. "If given a choice between the rarest bloom in the world or a diamond of good clarity, you would choose the latter. Only a fool would not, and you do not impress me as being a fool."

"If the choice was exquisite transience or exquisite permanence, if the diamond were of the first water, I would take the jewel. But if the diamond were second rate, I would not. Now, since you have no interest in procuring flowers, and only a passing interest in gardens, perhaps it is time for you to resume your journey to wherever you were headed when you detoured down our lane."

"I did not detour. This was my destination. I arrived earlier than I expected, and have been passing the time here to avoid calling at an uncivilized hour." He pulled out his pocket watch. "Still too early, but perhaps you will tell Mrs. Joyes that I am here, if you think she would not mind receiving me now."

"Mrs. Joyes? Are you a friend of hers?"

"We have friends in common, but she and I have never met to my knowledge."

"If you have never met, you have never been introduced. I doubt she would receive you under those circumstances."

"She is strict that way, is she?"

"Fairly so, yes." *Especially today, with you.*

"Damn. That is a boring nuisance."

Being called boring hardly endeared him to her. "Perhaps you should return with a letter of introduction from one of those mutual friends."

"I would like to meet with her today, since I am here."

Irritation colored his words. So did a note of command, as if his preference was paramount. She decided that Mrs. Joyes would definitely not oblige his conceit.

"I know her very well, and she will not see you without an introduction. How inconvenient for you that she is a woman consumed by all that boring strictness."

"Inconvenient for us both. Mine is not a social call. I have come about the Duke of Becksbridge's estate."

Relief replaced irritation. She instantly looked more favorably on this visitor. No wonder there had been no letter. She was close enough to London for a personal meeting to be held. And of course this man would be curious about the property, if he had a hand in executing the duke's will.

"Ah . . . under those circumstances, perhaps Mrs. Joyes can be convinced to receive you."

"It would be in her interest to do so. If we must stand on ceremony, I will go out the portal, to the front door, and present myself. Otherwise, perhaps you might go in and inform her of my presence in the garden."

"Neither will be necessary." She tried what she hoped was a conciliatory smile. "As it happens, I am Mrs. Joyes."

He gave her a good examination, from crown to toe. "Are you indeed."

"Forgive my small deception. For all I knew you might have been a dangerous trespasser. In fact, another member of our household has had a pistol trained on you, just in case."

"Ah, yes, the pistol. I have heard about the pistol from our mutual friends." He examined the house, probably looking for a gun barrel at a window. "It was a good thing that I did not succumb to my initial impulse to drag you into this arbor and kiss you, then."

She laughed politely at his inappropriate little joke.

His vague smile suggested she found more humor in the comment than intended.

"Are you the executor? A lawyer? When I did not hear anything after the funeral, I feared—"

"I am no lawyer, and old Becksbridge would not dare make me his executor. Heaven forbid he should have saddled me with that burden too."

He finally stepped out of the arbor, into the sunlight. The perfection of those boots became visible again, and also that of his frock coat and other garments, and the artistic cut of his tousled hair. Brown eyes, with golden lights that flickered like devilish fire, surveyed her from head to toe once more. A touch of gold streaked through his brown hair too.

He was a handsome man, that was certain, made more compelling by a sartorial style that appeared both costly and effortless. A lithe strength marked his posture. He made an impressive figure, in part by appearing utterly indifferent to whether he did or not.

She had no idea who their common friends might be, but he did appear vaguely familiar, as if she had seen him once from a distance at least. She searched her mind, trying to place the memory that nibbled at her. Not so much his face pricked her recollection—more the way he carried himself and his air of arrogance and bored indifference that probably could be felt from the other side of the garden.

"I had no idea Mrs. Joyes was so young," he said, coming toward her on the path, bemused and curious. "I pictured a woman of more mature years, with a reformer's severe expression."

"I am mature enough and can be severe when warranted."

"I am sure you can be." He flashed a smile. A rather familiar one. Almost flirtatious. He acted as if they shared a special secret. She could not imagine what he thought that secret might be.

Slowly, languidly, as if he had all day for the tour, he strolled around her as if she were a statue set amid the flowers for viewing.

She wished she could pretend that she did not know what he was thinking as he took his little circular turn. Unfortunately, it flowed through the air. She did not turn to keep an eye on him, but she did not have to. She felt his every step and change in location, and his gaze all but burned through her clothing.

"If you are not a lawyer involved with the estate, just whom am I addressing, sir?"

His casual path brought him to where he faced her again. "I am Castleford."

Castleford? Dear heavens—the *Duke of Castleford*?

"Are you unwell, Mrs. Joyes? You have been extraordinarily composed thus far, but now you appear close to fainting. If my failure to identify myself earlier has distressed you, I will be undone."

His devilish eyes belied his smooth tongue. He was delighted to have flustered her. She prided herself on the composure he mentioned and on an even temper that permitted her to always maintain her poise. All three, she had learned, kept one from being at a disadvantage with others in the world.

She swallowed her surprise. "I am not distressed or even discomposed, so do not concern yourself. I am merely confused as to what connection you could have with the settlement of the estate, Your Grace."

"Ah." He scratched his head and tried to appear confused too. "Well, it appears I am the new owner of this property. For reasons unknown, Becksbridge left it to me."

For a moment her mind refused to comprehend what he said. Then his words settled in, and composure, poise, and good temperament truly deserted her. For the first time in years, in *memory*, an unholy wrath broke like a storm in her head.

Becksbridge had left this property to *him*? To *Castleford*? To a man so rich he had no use for anything more? To a besotted, notorious libertine who did not give a damn about anyone or anything?

Becksbridge, you insufferable, lying scoundrel.

Chapter Two

M rs. Joyes was in high color now. Her gray eyes, as cool as an overcast winter sky mere minutes ago, fairly blazed. Castleford thought it probably a good thing that the pistol she owned was not nearby.

Not that these fires were directed at him. Pity, that. He wondered if she ever released them in bed, to a different purpose.

She was a stunning woman, so he had begun erotic speculations about her almost immediately. Tall and elegant, with a pale beauty of a sort rarely seen, she appeared a palette of whites tinged slightly with color. A touch of yellow in her very fair hair. A drop of ochre, no more, in her ivory skin. Gray in those intelligent eyes. The pale blue dress she wore completed the composition. He had seen porcelain figurines colored that way.

She was not a woman he would fail to notice or forget seeing or not want. And so, as she had approached on the garden walk, he was sure he had seen her before. He could not place where. Perhaps they had only passed on a London street.

Now, of course, there was a good deal of pink on her cheeks too, and countless dark glints flickered in her eyes. He welcomed the evidence that she was not as cold as the palette and her manner implied. Passion became her. She did not seem to know what to do with the rage flexing through her, however, so he doubted she permitted herself high emotion of any kind very often.

He gestured to the arbor. "Perhaps you should sit, Mrs. Joyes, while you accommodate yourself to this revelation."

She strode over, sat on the bench like an iron rod held her back, and grasped its edge on either side of her hips with tight, beautifully tapered fingers. She stared at the ground. He could see her trying to force calm on herself. It did not work well. He could almost hear the thunder.

He stayed at the arbor's edge, where the climbing rose's leaves fluttered over the last slat of wood. He noticed that the breeze was bringing in storm clouds from the west, just in time to match her mood.

"You expected Becksbridge to give you this property, didn't you?" he asked when some of the tenseness left her posture.

She looked up with a withering glare.

"Did he promise he would?"

She hesitated, stared back down at the ground, then, almost imperceptibly, shook her head.

Castleford suddenly remembered where he had seen her before. Years ago, at a garden party at Becksbridge's London house. It was before he had broken with Latham.

Late in the party, Becksbridge's daughters by his second wife had come out on the terrace with their governess.

He looked into the arbor and saw Mrs. Joyes laughing with those girls. Not so cool back then. Not much more than a girl herself.

She had been in service to Becksbridge, and now she lived on his property for nominal rent. She was a tenant in whom he claimed a "committed interest" but whom he did not want to name in his testament or reveal to the other paragons hanging from his branch of the family tree.

She had expected to receive the property for good in the will. And, unless his eyes failed him, the color in her face now came less from anger and more from embarrassment.

Well, well. *Becksbridge, you unbearable, hypocritical ass.*

"If it offers any relief to your distress—"

"I am not distressed. I am only surprised, Your Grace."

"I can perhaps alleviate this *extreme* surprise by explaining that the duke did indicate his wish that you remain here as in the past, as long as you choose."

That was something, at least. Not what she had expected. Not what had been implied. And at least the new Becksbridge would not be getting this property.

Counting her blessings did not help as much as she wished. She still battled the almost uncontrollable urge to hit something. Castleford, for example. Not only was he bearing sorry news, but he also seemed to be enjoying her *extreme surprise* to an unseemly degree. For all of his solicitous concern, he watched her the way the eyes in a crowd watch a burning building.

She calmed enough that the precise words of his last statement sorted themselves out in her head.

"You say the duke expressed the wish for all to remain as it was. Is it your intention to honor that wish?"

Castleford ruminated on the question. "I have not decided."

"You can have little use for a small bit of land like this, with all your other holdings."

"One never knows."

Was he teasing her? Goading her to more extreme surprise? "If you regret the loss of income, I could pay a higher rent. I would want a proper lease, however."

"Mrs. Joyes, I am not looking to negotiate by delaying matters. I have not decided only because I have a way of making decisions that serves me well. I save all the boring ones for one day a week. This is not that day."

"You intend to leave me dangling simply because it is not Tuesday?"

He strolled the few steps to the bench and sat. He made himself comfortable in the extreme. Back angled and shoulders propped as before, legs extended and arms crossed, he lounged beside her. She had to turn to see his face.

"You know about that, do you? About Tuesdays?"

"We do have those mutual friends. I have been treated to a few Castleford stories."

"How indiscreet of them."

"I do not think you mind. If you did, you would have long ago reformed your reputation."

"And become as boring as our reformed mutual friends? I hope I die first."

"From what I hear, that is likely. Which is why I would like that lease no matter what the rent. A very long one."

"I see you are feeling better. I hope that when you are more yourself you do not have a tendency to be a scold."

"It is not for me to scold you, sir. My interest is not with your behavior or health but with my future and with how your drinking and brawls and duels might cause trouble for that."

"Did they tell you anything else about me? Besides the drinking, brawling, and dueling?"

They had told her plenty, and the scandal sheets had added many salacious details. "That you delight in being incorrigible."

"Well put, and the telling of it explains me well enough. After all, have you ever heard it said that someone delights in being an epitome of virtue? There is little fun in that, and no delight at all. Just repetitive goodness."

"Is your badness so varied that it is still delightful? I expect anything gets boring after a while."

He looked at her with interest. "How perceptive you are. It takes a good deal of effort to keep badness from being boring. One must seek out new experiences and challenges. Our mutual friends may think I have an easy life, but being notorious is grueling work after a few years."

She had to laugh. That seemed to please him.

"What a delightful visit this is proving to be, Mrs. Joyes. Good country air, a lovely woman overcome by surprise, and pleasant conversation. If I had known what waited, I would have come down sooner. I hope my visits to the other properties are as enjoyable."

"Other properties?"

"Four in all."

She barely resisted the impulse to query him further about those other bequests. Their existence troubled her, however. They suggested that Becksbridge's arrangement with her had not been unique. She had long suspected as much. She doubted she could quiz Castleford on it without him finding her curiosity peculiar, unfortunately.

"Why would you bother with such a small matter? You must have servants who could learn all that you have."

"I doubt that. I decided to see to it myself because the bequest piqued my interest. Becksbridge disliked me heartily and disapproved even more. So I thought to see what it was all about. And now I know."

There was no accusation in that last sentence, but she understood his assumption about why Becksbridge had allowed her to live here, and that he now believed he would find the same thing on the other spots of land.

The sky had darkened considerably. In the distance beyond the greenhouse roof, a flash of lightning heralded the approaching storm. She stood.

"I have kept you too long, Your Grace. You risk a drenching if you ride back to town. The inn at Cumberworth might be a wise choice for the night. I will await word from you, regarding your decision, after next Tuesday."

He pulled himself to his feet and stepped out of the arbor. He checked the sky and dark clouds. A few large drops of rain splashed down on the path.

"Hawkeswell says the inn at Cumberworth has bedbugs. I clearly remember that warning, although I'll be damned if I recall when or why he gave it."

"Two miles east there is the town of—"

"I think that I will stay here instead."

She searched his expression, wondering if this was another odd and inappropriate joke. He merely gazed up at the house with curiosity.

"We are a household of women, Your Grace. It would be—"

"—generous and gracious of you to offer hospitality. I know you have allowed male guests before. Our mutual friends have told me a few stories too. Besides, it is not shocking for a man to stay in his own property."

Now, that was pointed. His blithe tone indicated that he assumed he would have his way on this and most everything.

"If you are going to insist on your property rights, I would be foolish to refuse you."

"And, as I saw at first glance, Mrs. Joyes, you are not a fool."

"I hope not. However, if we extend the hospitality that you expect, let us have a right understanding on one point, sir."

"How stern you sound." Again, that too-familiar gaze and slow smile. He possessed a talent for crossing lines without overtly taking any steps. "It must be a significant point."

She tried to sound very stern indeed. "There is a young woman living here. If you in any way importune her in your ongoing efforts toward varied badness, if you even flirt with her, I will shoot you."

The splats of rain picked up their rhythm while she spoke. One hit her nose, as nature conspired to undermine the authority she tried to convey.

He smiled, far too amused for her purpose. He reached over and flicked the little bubble of rain off her nose. "If I die, they will hang you."

"No, they will not. My lawyer will pack the courtroom with other women you have seduced, and every father on the jury will vote to acquit me."

He placed his hand over his heart. "I give my word as a gentleman that I will treat this young woman like she is my sister."

He seemed sincere, even if naughty lights danced in his eyes.

"Then you are welcome inside to share our simple dinner and make use of one of the spare chambers."

The rain began falling in earnest now. He joined her as she hurried to the garden door. He followed her into the house, peering this way and that at the new surroundings.

Katherine came in from the greenhouse, and Daphne introduced her. Katherine bobbed a curtsy and fled.

"I doubt you will see Miss Johnson again," she said. "It was probably unnecessary to require your word."

"I promise that it was. I have no interest in Miss Johnson. The fact is, Mrs. Joyes, if I were of a mind to seduce any female in this house, it would be you."

By eight that evening, Castleford was concluding that someone putting a gun to his temple would be a mercy.

The exquisite Mrs. Joyes had dodged him all afternoon. First he saw to his horse—a chore he had not performed in more years than he could count. By the time he finished he was in a sour mood and grousing privately that Mrs. Joyes had better be worth all the trouble that his impulsive and determined desire for her was causing.

After that, he was left to his own devices in her small, feminine library. The presence of women all but drenched this house, and their light steps and quiet voices just out of sight and just out of hearing hardly helped his concentration on the tome he chose to pass the time.

Finally, the housekeeper, a scowling little woman named Mrs. Hill, dark of eye and sharp of beak beneath her cap's lace edge, showed him to a bedchamber decorated in feminine yellows and blues. He prepared for a casual dinner.

To his delight, Katherine did not attend, so he was alone with his hostess. He settled down, anticipating a lively exchange while he lured Mrs. Joyes into more high color and, once all progressed as he intended, another outburst of passion. One that he would ensure went on a good long while.

He politely asked early on after the gardens and this business called The Rarest Blooms. A mistake, that. He had listened to the ensuing detailed explanations for two hours now, barely managing not to yawn. Mrs. Hill served a simple meal of soup, cold ham, and finally a trifle probably whipped up just because he had intruded.

Mrs. Joyes remained a chilled column of winter composure the whole time. Etiquette impeccable and expression serene, she entertained him with grace, speaking in a slow monotone that made his eyes want to cross. The result was that he found himself imprisoned in exactly the kind of tediously proper congress that he loathed. It was so unbearable that he even gave up wondering what the woman looked like naked.

It was time to take matters in hand and make things more interesting. Since Mrs. Joyes was of considerable interest, he forced the conversation onto her.

"I am told that you are a widow," he said when she finally paused after naming every damned variety of verbena grown in her greenhouse.

"My husband died in the war." She lowered her eyes as she replied, to signal that this topic should be avoided.

Perhaps it should be, but he never learned anything useful if he obeyed such cues. "Were you married long?"

"Less than two years."

"He was at war most of that time, I assume."

"I followed the drum, so we were at least together."

"Still, how unfair for you, to be made a widow before you barely had time to enjoy the pleasures of marriage."

She gazed at him so blandly that one might think she had missed the sensual allusion and the way it pushed a door ajar just a tad. She was good, he had to give her that. She wore her composure like a shield. Getting her to drop it, even for an instant, was turning into a challenge.

He in turn gazed around the chamber. "Did none of our mutual friends ever think it odd that an army captain left you a property like this? That is what they assume, isn't it? That this came to you through your husband."

"I suppose they might assume that. I was never asked about it."

Vague memories regarding references to Mrs. Joyes had been emerging since he learned her identity outside. "Is that why you have that peculiar rule here, that no one pry into anyone's past? So no one would ask, and you would not have to explain?"

A few of those dark glints sparked in her eyes. She did not favor this topic. On the other hand, he was not being bored by lists of flowers anymore, itemized by their Latin names, no less. That had not been an accident, he decided. She had deliberately tried to numb him senseless. His reference to seduction must have put her on her guard. Careless, that.

"Lady Sebastian Summerhays lived here briefly and is your cousin, is she not?" he pressed. "One would expect a relative to inquire about the particulars of an inheritance."

"I did not establish that rule to hide the duke's generosity regarding this property from Audrianna or anyone else, but to protect the women themselves. There were a few who required privacy in such matters. Sometimes a woman has good cause to leave the past completely behind." She spoke with tense emphasis, clarifying an important point.

"You do your sex proud in your lack of curiosity. I doubt I could be so restrained."

"I never said I was never curious. One is not obligated to pry as a result, however."

"I always pry if I am curious. It breaks up the ennui."

He drank some of the sweet punch provided with the dinner. It tasted of berries and was probably made from the garden's own products. It was the sort of drink of which his physician would approve.

"This is delicious. It would be even better with a splash of brandy in it," he said.

"We only have a small amount of spirits here, kept strictly for medicinal purposes."

He had a flask with him, but it would be rude to retrieve it to improve the punch. Unless she invited him to use one if he had it. Which it appeared she was taking some pleasure in not suggesting.

"I knew that you would be more comfortable at the inn," she said with pointed satisfaction. "Hence my suggestion that you stay there."

"Is this another rule? None of you ever imbibe, even secretly? Not even sherry or wine?"

"Wine is permitted, when we have it. We do not have it now."

"Pity."

"Yes. I am so sorry."

The hell she was sorry. Mrs. Joyes was turning this into a Tuesday on purpose. It was his punishment for forcing this intrusion on their convent.

The meal was finished. She looked poised to take her leave and pleased at how well she had handled him. Well, being a duke had its privileges. He settled back in his chair to indicate she did not have permission to escape just yet.

The dining room's window faced north, and the heavily overcast evening light coming through flattered her and made her eyes very dark gray.

"I recognized you," he said. "As you approached in the garden, I knew I had seen you before. You were governess to Becksbridge's two daughters nine years ago. I saw you at a garden party."

A bit of color tinted her ivory cheeks. Not extreme surprise, but surprise all the same.

"You have an excellent memory for a man said to be drowning his brain in drink, Your Grace."

She had not forgotten herself again, but she was angry enough under that cool exterior to speak bluntly. He was glad to see a bit of spirit emerge despite her determination to bore him to death.

"My brain swims quite well, Mrs. Joyes. Especially when I turn my mind to a question that piques my curiosity, as I said."

"Does that happen often? I expect stroking against the tide requires some effort."

"Admittedly not often. A beautiful woman can prod my curiosity when otherwise it might remain dormant, however. And you are an exceedingly beautiful woman."

Her fingers rested on the hilt of her dinner knife, and now they absently fingered the silver surface. She did not appear aware of that nervous tiny action.

He liked that she did not disagree with his assessment of her beauty or feign ignorance of a quality that had to have been commented upon her whole life. He hated false modesty in women, whether in response to praise for wit, intelligence, or looks.

"How came you to be at that garden party? I would not have expected that family to welcome a man with your reputation," she said.

"My reputation was still in its infancy. Back then I practiced a good deal of discretion in enjoying my sins. Hence, I was invited as a friend of Latham and as a relative."

Her fingers froze on the silver. "You are Latham's friend? Considering his essays, that must be uncomfortable for your varied badness. Saints and sinners rarely get along well with each other."

Latham, now the new Becksbridge, was no saint. He never had been. He had only been sly and secretive instead of honest in his hedonism. "We have not been friends for a good long while."

"I am relieved to hear it." That slipped out with a sigh. It was possibly the first uncalculated sentence she had uttered all evening.

"Relieved for his sake? Do you fear I will corrupt him?"

She hesitated, to calculate once again. "I remember him as capricious and untrustworthy. I do not care for him. I would not like to think he might influence your Tuesday decision."

Now, *that* was interesting. Almost everyone loved

Latham. Vicars quoted his damned essays from the pulpit. The papers were currently full of irritating anticipation of him taking his father's place and heralding his return to England as the salvation of the world. One rarely heard a bad word about him.

Yet it appeared Mrs. Joyes held little admiration. Quite the opposite, from the way the subject darkened her expression. Perhaps she knew about Latham's worst sins. If she had lived in that house, she well might have heard the servants talk about the master's heir.

A memory forced itself into his mind. An ugly one in which he saw Latham going too far and crossing lines that no man should cross. The images stirred a visceral disgust, with himself as well as Latham.

He looked at the glass of punch with resentment while he conquered the thoughts and the reaction they provoked. He had not thought about that long-ago day for years. He probably would not have now either, if this woman had not made this a damned Tuesday.

"We are of like mind regarding him, Mrs. Joyes. I promise he is incapable of influencing me, or I him, unless pistols are involved." He angled toward the table and her. "Now, about the questions I find here—"

"There are no questions to consider here, so you can cease straining your mind," she said.

"There are many questions to consider. This legacy was odd enough. Finding you here now compels my attention. So little does these days that I am wont to seek explanations when puzzles taunt me."

"You already know why and how I live here. All that remains to clarify the situation is this: My father was a gentleman in Becksbridge's county and a friend of the duke. When he died and my relatives did not give me a home and support, the duke kindly accepted me into his household as a governess. Since the duke had known my father, I was treated better than other women in that situation might expect. I stayed a little less than a year before I left."

"To marry Captain Joyes."

She inclined her head in half a nod. "When I was left to my own devices once more, the duke kindly allowed me the use of this property. In his goodness he tried to help me again and ensure that I was not left destitute."

"You expected the title to this land, however."

"That was a silly hope, not an expectation. I had no claim on it or on anything at all."

It was a good explanation. Possibly the true one. Nor was it one that would require retreat on his part. She was a widow, in her late twenties he estimated, and certainly no innocent. He could still seduce her if he had a mind to. Which he did.

He could not shake the suspicion, however, that this whole arrangement spoke of the duke under moral obligation to care for a woman for reasons less noble than friendship with her father.

He still thought she had been Becksbridge's mistress while in that house. Then again, perhaps he only wanted to believe it of the self-righteous ass.

Well, he would know for certain once he visited the other little properties and saw if they also were now homes to other women like Mrs. Joyes.

In the meantime . . .

He stood. "I thank you for the hospitality and for the pleasure of your company at this dinner, Mrs. Joyes. I see the rain is well gone, and I think that I will take a ride through the area and see the lay of the land while there is still some light. Perhaps when I return, you will be kind enough to give me a tour of your very rare blooms."

A glance from those gray eyes. Direct. Knowing. She saw his game. Which did not mean he would not win the match.

"We retire early, Your Grace."

"I will not be gone long."

"Perhaps in the morning . . ."

"I expect to leave early. This evening would suit me far better."

"It will be too dark to see much."

"We will bring a lantern."

An exasperated frown marred her brow. "I can see that you are accustomed to having your way."

"Having my way is the best thing about being a duke."

"Then, once again, I would be foolish to refuse you."

He bowed to take his leave. "You may refuse me whatever you choose, Mrs. Joyes. I will not hold it against you."

Chapter Three

He had beautiful hands. That was what Daphne kept noticing about Castleford at dinner.

Thoroughly masculine but also undeniably elegant, those hands had compelled her attention. She had seen many gentlemen's hands, but none so flawless, she was sure. They were far smoother than her own, she judged at once. All the gloves and creams in the world could not maintain a lady's hands if a woman used hoes and shovels more than any lady should.

She probably should have given him some brandy or wine. She might have erred in refusing to. That was the question with a man who imbibed to the extent Castleford did. Would spirits dull his senses or make him rash?

She did not know. So she had relied on those stories, told by their mutual friends, of his whoring and drinking.

The two seemed to go together, and she had thought it best not to stoke any fires. But if they did go together, then perhaps if he drank he only bothered with whores and left such as her alone.

She paced the library after he left. She could simply retire and not be here when he returned. He had said she could refuse him anything. Only she did not think he meant the tour of the gardens. She suspected he only referred to what he would try to do once in the gardens.

The scoundrel expected to seduce her after knowing her less than a full day! The conceited man assumed she would just fall at his command, yield at his whim, give herself to a drunkard who was practically a stranger, and who did not come well recommended by the little she knew of him. His unfounded confidence was unparalleled.

Did he count on her not believing him about being able to refuse? Did he anticipate compliance because of this property? That would be just plain evil. And he *had* given that reassurance, hadn't he? Still, it worried her that perhaps he would take offense, and things would take a bad turn when he made his decision come Tuesday.

After fretting over the question, she realized there was no choice here. She would have to take him at his word. If he put them all out because she rejected his intentions, she would make sure those mutual friends learned the truth of it.

Indeed, that possibility might be her most formidable protection. Hopefully Castleford cared about his long friendships with the Earl of Hawkeswell, Verity's husband, and Lord Sebastian Summerhays, who had married her cousin Audrianna.

She heard the horse outside and froze in place. Her stomach lurched. At least it would be dark in the garden.

She would not see his expressions or his eyes with those golden lights.

She would be less likely to be charmed by his alluring combination of insouciance, with its air of carefree indifference to everything, and that undercurrent of intensity that implied quite the opposite.

He was dangerously handsome, and that always gave a man an unfair advantage. But she wasn't some girl anymore whose head could be turned by the seductive flatteries of dashing men.

Then it occurred to her that some light might be a good idea. He might be less bold if it were not totally dark. If she chose their path carefully, they would be visible from the house if they carried a light.

She hurried to the back sitting room and fussed with a lantern while he dealt with his horse again. He probably did not like doing that himself, but they did not have a groom or any male servant here. She handled her gig's horse herself, after all. It had not been too much to expect him to do the same.

She heard his boot steps enter the house and come toward her. Measured. Firm. Confident. This house so rarely had men inside it that his footfalls seemed to make it shake. Much like she was shaking, she realized.

She sat and pretended to read by the lantern, feeling nervous and unsteady and more fearful than her mind believed was warranted. It embarrassed her to admit that a rare excitement permeated her fluster, one that provoked sensations that were not unpleasant. It had been years since she had felt that kind of stimulation. Forever.

Perhaps he would just forget about his turn in the garden and leave her to her book, and she could—

"I expect we will need that lantern soon enough on

our stroll, but there is the slightest bit of twilight left now, Mrs. Joyes."

She managed to maintain her mask of disinterest despite the way he looked. The lantern's illumination barely reached him where he filled the doorway, but the way it did made her pulse pound.

Shadows and highlights cast his form and coat into an assemblage of crisp planes. Even his smile appeared hard. His ride had mussed his hair, so he looked more reckless than before. His eyes told the worst part of the story, however. Teasing glints revealed more interest in this stroll than she wanted to see.

Dear heavens. She was out of her depths. This man was a notorious libertine and she was—well, she was hardly an expert in these matters.

She stood. She swung a knitted shawl around her shoulders. Whatever games he hoped to play, nothing would happen unless she permitted it, and she intended to permit nothing at all.

"It is impressive," Castleford said, while he surveyed the plants in the greenhouse. "It is clearly not a decorative appendage to the house but a place of business."

Daphne heard no mockery in his voice. Her pride glowed at his praise.

She had been stupid to be so worried. He had been a perfect gentleman while they strolled the paths outside. He had even held the lantern in a way that made them very visible from the house's back windows. It appeared that he truly wanted to see how she was using the property and supporting the household with The Rarest Blooms.

Now the lantern rested on the stones in front of the

fireplace used to warm the greenhouse on the coldest nights. Castleford poked at some planting pots and admired the largest orange tree. The open glass panes in the walls and the ceiling allowed a sweet breeze to flow around them.

"It is all very fragrant here. A little intoxicating," he said.

"One gets used to it." She pointed to a massing of plants in a corner. "Those will be taken to town in two days. Wagons bring them to a friend who then will deliver them to homes that have ordered them. A good number of cut flowers from outside will go too. And look here—we are experimenting with plum trees, and this cherry. If they thrive, we intend to build another greenhouse just for fruit. One of the new kind, with pipes underneath to bring steam to heat the space evenly."

"Did Lady Hawkeswell begin her horticultural experiments while she lived here, or did you learn from her?"

He referred to Verity, the Earl of Hawkeswell's wife, who had stayed two years in this house. Daphne had not thought Castleford would bother to notice or remember the histories of the women married to his friends. "She began here. We all help with the plants, but Verity developed a passion for them."

"When did you develop your own passion?"

"It is not the same. I enjoy this labor, but it was always a means to an end for me, not a fascination as it became with her. One of the first women to share my house taught me."

He rested his hips against a worktable and looked at her. The lantern seemed far away suddenly. More moonlight veiled him than the illumination from that one distant candle.

"You speak as though that teacher is no longer here.

Nor is Lady Hawkeswell nor Lady Sebastian. I believe that Mrs. Albrighton also once lived here."

"I am surprised that you absorbed such small details about lives so removed from your own."

"I remember everything when I choose to." He cocked his head and regarded her. "How many have come and gone while you remained?"

"A few more, before the ones you know about."

The question induced nostalgia and, deep inside her, a tiny, cringing, recurrent fear that the day would come when there were no longer any transient sisters seeking sanctuary in her home, and she would be all alone.

"You must envy them at times," he said. "Envy their return to the world and the families they are building."

His words pierced her heart, and she could not deny their truth. Then, for the second time today, her temper spiked abruptly.

How *dare* he be so rude. Fending off a seduction would be preferable to these intrusive queries.

"I am happy for them." She heard her voice sound crisp with her annoyance. "They are my friends still, and as close to my heart as sisters."

"I did not say you were not happy for them. I merely observed that—"

"I know what you said. And what you implied. I am not some sad little woman pining on a shelf, dreaming about parties and morning calls, Lord Castleford. As for marriage, I am mature enough to know that there are so few men worthy of the effort that I am relieved such a future is out of the question."

He just looked at her for a long moment. Then she saw those mischievous lights appear in the dark of his eyes. "I fear that I have distressed you again."

"Not at all."

"You appear in high color once more."

"Oh, tosh. You can't even see my color in this vague light."

"I can hear it, however." Suddenly he pushed away from the table and was standing right in front of her. To her shock he placed his palm against her cheek. "And I can feel it."

He astonished her, *stunned* her not only with his boldness but also with the sensation of that hand against her face. Its skin felt as perfect as it had looked. Like warm velvet.

He moved closer, until his face hovered right above hers. "Perhaps it is not distress at all but only more extreme surprise. You are dazzling when in this state. Strong emotion becomes you."

It did not become her. It confused her. It weakened her. It left her gaping at a handsome man taking inexcusable liberties, when she should better remain calm enough to put him in his place.

She groped for her self-possession, but it kept sliding out of grasp. He was deliberately mesmerizing her. Absorbing her.

A series of furious denials and insults filled her head but refused to find her voice. *You are no gentleman, sir.—I am not one of your bawdy doves.—Unhand me, you scoundrel.* She could actually feel the heat of his body with him standing this closely. His hand on her cheek lured scandalous reactions out of her. Tingles and shivers and delicious, sly excitements. *You are too bold.— How dare you be so familiar.—This insult is not to be borne.* The man was a devil, and she needed to collect herself and—

"How long has it been, Mrs. Joyes? Since a man kissed you anywhere, even on the mouth?"

Anywhere?

His breath flowed softly over her lips, making her head spin and her blood race. "A good number of years, I think. What a sinful waste." His presence wrapped her, then his arms did too.

A kiss, careful but confident. She resisted the impulse to close her eyes and float away on the intimacy, but she was tempted far more than she ever expected to be. Within her shock she struggled to hold back the dreamy tide of pleasure that threatened to inundate her and drown her very sense of herself.

But, oh, it was too sweet, and so poignant that she wanted to weep. The warmth wrenched her heart. A part of her long denied, long buried and ignored, ached to break free and sing. She was a girl again within that embrace, and painfully alive.

You are nothing but a plaything to him. You of all women know that is true. The thought finally found its voice in her mind, after trying too long. She saw what was happening as if looking in through the nearby glass panes of the greenhouse wall.

She had responded to that kiss, and it had become two kisses, then many, each more dominating and hot. She was now pliant and accepting in his embrace, and he held her tighter against his body. His hands moved, tempting her with scandalous caresses that smoothed firmly over her hips and side, her back, and now, dear heavens, her thighs.

She heard her own sighs and gasps as tantalizing sensations cascaded through her, each more powerful. She noted how his caresses rose higher now, close to her breasts, and how her nipples tingled, waiting for the touch that would obliterate the last of her reserve.

She saw herself falling fast, like the pathetic, lonely widow he thought her to be.

You must end this at once, or he will ignore your attempts to do so later. The warning screamed in her head, an ugly truth and an unwelcome reminder of all the devastating vulnerabilities a woman faced in the world.

Stopping it was hard. As hard as he probably knew it would be once she allowed the first liberty. Harder than she believed possible, considering she hardly knew him and did not need the costs of such passion explained.

Somehow, she found the strength and forced her body to stiffen, then her mouth to as well.

He noticed at once. He stopped the kiss. She knew not all men would under the circumstances. She refused to meet his eyes in the long, searching gaze he gave her. Then his arms fell away. He stepped back.

In the taut silence that followed, she pieced together some composure. She could hardly upbraid him for insulting her. Considering how she had behaved, that would be comical. She would not give him the satisfaction of watching her run away like a frightened mouse, though.

She turned away and pointed airily to the far wall of the greenhouse. "Allow me to show you the grapevine we grow here, Lord Castleford. It always amazes visitors to find one flourishing inside. We are very proud of it."

She spoke nonstop as they strolled toward the passage that connected the greenhouse to the back sitting room. She explained the grapevine and encouraged him to admire a huge pot of camellias. He paced silently, a tall, dark presence exuding sensual danger.

She trusted he would take his leave gracefully, and they would pretend the kisses had never happened. He did not. Instead he subjected her to a gaze that ignored all social niceties. It was the gaze of a man debating his options and the strength of her will.

Heaven help her, he managed to revive some of those sensations in her while he looked too deeply into her eyes.

"I may have to devote the next year to seeing you in high color again, Mrs. Joyes."

What an outrageous thing to threaten. Vexed, she curtsied and turned to make good her escape. "Since drunkards are beyond my interest, I expect that my composure is safe for a year of Tuesdays, Your Grace."

*H*ell and Damnation.

Castleford downed another good swallow of brandy from his flask. It warmed his blood but did not help his mood one bit.

He cursed again more colorfully. Out loud. If Daphne Joyes heard, he really would not care. Nor, he assumed, would she.

He cursed Becksbridge and his stupid testament and letter. And his cowardice in not seeing matters through with his prior mistresses and instead leaving it to another man. *I am depending on what little is left of the better side of your character.* There was almost nothing left, damn it. Becksbridge had often pointed out as much.

Maybe it had all been a final joke to the old man. Perhaps he chuckled while he wrote that damned letter. The self-righteous ass—no, the self-righteous *hypocrite*— would throw his hated relative in the path of Mrs. Joyes, and Mrs. Joyes would show him what for.

Castleford took another swallow and looked around his chamber. Flowers covered every surface, it seemed. Damned yellow ones and damned blue ones made up repetitive sprigs that showered the bed drapes, curtains, pillows—the whole damned place. He had seen enough flowers today to carpet the realm. He would probably never see another one without remembering tonight.

She had thoroughly yielded. He knew she had. She had been all softness and sighs and sensual pliability, and he had been debating whether to lure her to a bed or take her right there. Then, suddenly, nothing. *Nothing.* Where in hell had she found the presence of mind to turn to stone like that?

Women never did that with him. *Never.* He knew women, and he knew what he was about with them, damn it, and this was *not normal.* And not even a stammer afterwards. Nary a blush. She had simply turned, as if he had not been about to start stripping her naked in the prior minute. With utter composure, she had talked about some damned grapevine while he suffered the effects of a desire well encouraged then painfully thwarted.

He began to raise the flask again but thought better of it. Hell only knew what he might do if he got raving drunk while fuming over the unfinished business with Daphne Joyes. He had never had a woman yield then retreat before, but it would not do to create a scene about it. Dignity required that he retreat himself and prepare to battle another day.

He rose and stripped off his clothes, then tossed back the damned flowered coverlet. He washed, then dropped onto the bed. He forced his mind to think about something besides the infuriating, desirable woman sleeping somewhere else in this house, when she was supposed to be naked beside him.

There was only one consolation about the entire matter. Except for those two deadly hours at dinner, he had not been bored much at all today.

Chapter Four

Pleasantly lighthearted and comfortably light-headed, Castleford hopped out of his coach and entered Brooks's. He surveyed the reading room until his gaze lit on a deep chair where a dark crown rose above an open newspaper. He strolled over.

"You are becoming predictable, Hawkeswell," he said. "A man of routine. Not even domesticated a year, and look at you, haunting the clubs in the afternoon, but not having fun with the diversions they offer."

The newspaper lowered. Sharp blue eyes speared with annoyance. A sigh of deep forbearance sounded.

"Castleford. How very good to see you, and so early in the day too. It is not even four o'clock. Did last night's soiled dove lose interest before dawn?"

Castleford dragged another thickly upholstered chair

over and sat down. Hawkeswell raised one eyebrow, indicating he had not invited company.

Castleford ignored that. The way he saw it, Hawkeswell was an old friend, and friends had responsibilities to each other. His own these days was to make sure that Hawkeswell did not follow his natural inclinations to allow sobriety and love to remove all of the fun in his life. It was becoming a hell of a chore, though.

"My women never lose interest before dawn, Hawkeswell. Even when we pay for pleasure, it is incumbent upon gentlemen to ensure their bed partners do not get bored. Lady Hawkeswell will be very grateful if you remember that our duty applies to the good women far more than the bad."

Hawkeswell slapped the paper down on his knee, piqued. The man really did adore his little wife, and not only for her considerable fortune. Being the old-fashioned, chivalrous sort, he did not take well any references to her that sounded in the least inappropriate.

"If you are here, half-sober from the looks of it too, I assume there is a reason," Hawkeswell said. "Our meetings are rarely accidental."

"There might be a reason. I am still deciding."

The paper rose again. "Inform me when you make up your mind."

"I would prefer to learn what I want by seeking Summerhays's counsel, you see, but he has gone to the coast. So I am left with you, even though I expect you to get tedious on me."

"Counsel? The great, omnipotent Castleford, the man who assumes his judgment surpasses all others', and who rises above ennui only to meddle in men's affairs like Zeus on a holiday, would seek another's counsel? I am delighted Summerhays is out of reach, if it means I am treated to this honor. I am all ears."

"It would be counsel from Summerhays alone. With you, I would only need the answer to a question."

"Ask away."

Castleford called for some wine first. He made sure to get Hawkeswell's favorite. He trusted the claret would inspire some gossip and also soothe Hawkeswell's tendency to a quick temper. After it was brought and poured, he angled toward the other chair for a tête-à-tête.

"I have met her, finally, despite your attempts to deny me the pleasure."

Hawkeswell frowned, perplexed the way he often was. The man at times had trouble understanding plain talk. Since it only happened with Castleford, it made no sense, but there it was. "Met her? Who is she?"

"Daphne Joyes, of course. I understand all your speeches now. About how it would distress your wife if I did anything untoward with anyone in that house, and how I was not allowed to enter it, et cetera, et cetera."

"I meant every word. I trust you behaved when you met her?"

Castleford ignored the prompt. "She was not what I expected. Not an aging harpy, the way you made her sound."

"No one ever said she was a harpy or old." Hawkeswell shrugged. "Formidable, yes. Strong-willed too. But not a harpy."

"No one ever said she was stunningly beautiful either."

"There was no reason to." Hawkeswell was all innocence while he drank his wine.

No, there was no reason to, but it had not been an accident. "It is a wonder you are so protective of her, after the role she played in your wife's history. If I were you, I would find it hard to reconcile myself to the woman at all, let alone endeavor to keep her a secret from the likes of me."

"I endeavored at nothing of the kind. Not every word uttered and every idea thought has you at its center, Castleford. I know that is a shocking notion, but you would be more bearable if you accepted its truth. As for Mrs. Joyes, I confess that I found her irritating at first meeting, especially after she threatened to shoot me. No doubt you found her somewhat annoying too."

Annoying did not quite fit his reaction that night, but Castleford just smiled and let Hawkeswell take it for whatever response he might.

"And, if one wants to be frank about it, I initially found the woman a bit suspicious too," Hawkeswell said, setting the newspaper aside and warming to the wine and the subject. "There is a vagueness to her. For example, that is a very nice property for the widow of an army captain. I mentioned it to Verity, and it only provoked an argument between us."

"But no explanation?"

"They have that odd rule and know little of one another's pasts as a result. Something else I suggested to Verity as perhaps self-serving on Mrs. Joyes's part. That caused another argument. They are all very defensive of one another."

"So, like a good, well-trained husband, you mentioned no more suspicions and had no more arguments."

"I simply ceased thinking about it, being distracted by domestic bliss. Something you will never understand or even know."

"Did that bliss make you like Mrs. Joyes more too?"

"Perhaps. It is true that I favor her much more now. I am grateful for the friendship she extended to Verity when—well, when my wife felt she needed a friend."

Now they were down to it. "Do you favor her in an admired acquaintance sort of way, or favor her like she is the sister of your wife?"

Hawkeswell frowned deeply. "That is a deucedly odd question. What is this about?"

Castleford rearranged himself. Forearms on knees, he leaned close to his friend's chair. "Here is the thing. I am going to seduce Mrs. Joyes."

Hawkeswell jolted straight. "Are you indeed!"

"Most certainly." Decidedly. Thoroughly.

Hawkeswell conquered his astonishment. He chewed over the revelation. "I am not really surprised, just taken aback by your announcement. She is a lovely woman. But—"

"What a worthless word that is—lovely. Daphne Joyes is *exquisite*."

"She may be exquisite, but I find her a little . . . cold." He shrugged.

"Perhaps she does not take to your manner. I, on the other hand, have seen her much the opposite of cold."

"Really?" Hawkeswell was the one to angle closer now, truly all ears.

"Anyway, it is my intention to have her. However, first I need to know if you are feeling so protective that you would do something inconvenient, like call me out over it. You seem to have taken efforts to warn me off."

Hawkeswell's expression fell to one almost stunned. "I am touched, Castleford. I am not joking when I say that either. That you would pass on an exquisite woman if it meant we faced each other on the field of honor—"

Castleford decided not to clarify that he had not actually said that he would pass. "So?"

Hawkeswell thought it over for a good while. "She may be like a sister to my wife, but she is not one in fact. I have no standing to call you out," he said.

"I am happy you see it that way."

"I should try to talk you out of this, though."

"Consider it done and spare us both."

Hawkeswell opened his mouth to argue, thought better of it, and drank more wine. "When? I need to be prepared on the domestic front for when Verity hears of it."

"Soon. A week . . . ten days at most. I only need to get her up to London first."

"You are supremely confident. So confident that you have not asked for my word not to warn her through my wife."

"There is no need to warn her. She already knows."

Hawkeswell's eyebrows rose high. "You actually announced your intentions?"

"Not exactly. But she knows."

Hawkeswell scrutinized him, then grinned. "You already tried, didn't you? You tried *and failed*. Don't act exasperated by an absurd suggestion. I know you, and I have it right." He slapped his knee in frustration. "Damnation, it is hell that Summerhays is not in town. We could lay bets on this and have a fine time watching the week you predict turn into a year. Or *never*."

"It may take you a year to get an exquisite woman into bed, but I assure you it will be a week in my case." Or two, perhaps. Three at the outside. But a year was ridiculous, and never was out of the question.

"Then you must have an ace in your hand that I do not know about."

"Only my charm."

Hawkeswell thought that was hilarious. He laughed so rudely that he turned red. Wiping his eyes of tears, he poured himself more wine. "We shall see how far your sodden charm gets you with *this* woman, Castleford."

D aphne parted the carriage blinds a bit and looked out. She noted glumly that they were already passing Hyde Park.

Beside her Katherine angled her head just enough so the slice of light coming in would not find her face. Not that anything much would, with the bonnet Katherine had worn. Its deep brim obscured all views except one face on, and a lace cap beneath the bonnet hid a good deal of that prospect too.

Daphne closed the curtain again. "No one is going to see you, I promise. You will be in this hired coach right up to the door, then inside in a blink. The servants will all be strangers and not take any note of you."

"I am not afraid of being seen," Katherine said. "I do not care for towns, that is all."

"Then I am doubly sorry to have forced today's visit to London on you, Katherine. I had little choice, however. I know you see that."

Katherine remained a tense stone statue beside her. It had been cruel to insist she come, but Daphne really could not make this particular call alone, without another woman by her side. That would be stupid.

"I do not see why he did not come down to Cumberworth again," Katherine muttered resentfully. "It was rude to request that you make the journey to see him, and for such a small thing. He may be a duke, but if he desires a social call, he should be the one inconvenienced, not you, and certainly not me."

This was, Daphne decided, one of those times when their rule about not prying was very useful. Katherine had drawn erroneous conclusions about this visit to London all on her own. Daphne was under no obligation to explain that this was not a true social call, that this duke had not exactly *requested* this visit, and that more was at stake than Katherine could ever guess.

Castleford's odd invitation sat in Daphne's reticule. One paragraph, written in the flowing hand and formal voice of his secretary, Mr. Edwards, apologized in the duke's name for not communicating sooner about her situation. Mr. Edwards explained that some questions had arisen about the property when the matter had been addressed last Tuesday, and they would in turn be taken up again soon. He requested her further patience.

Below Mr. Edwards's signature, in another hand—one more individual and abrupt—a few more words had been penned. *You had best call Tuesday next, three o'clock. Castleford.*

She still had not decided what "you had best" meant. It could be interpreted as a busy man encouraging her to be present so her interests could have a voice in his deliberations. Read differently, however, the line sounded like a threat.

She did not expect it to be a pleasant meeting in either case. Since it was Tuesday he should be sober, so she doubted he would misbehave. However, the last time she had seen him they had been parting a scant fifteen minutes after she rejected his advances. Uncomfortable did not begin to describe that final quarter hour together. Nor, despite her clear preferences, had he truly stood down.

She saw him in her mind as he finally took his leave of her. Displeased. Annoyed. Watching her the way a hawk might a field mouse.

I may have to devote the next year to seeing you in high color again, Mrs. Joyes.

He left the property at dawn the next morning, before the household rose. She had listened to his horse on the lane and closed her eyes with a deep sigh of relief. Facing him might have been the smarter move, however, if he had allowed it. They possibly would have laughed about what happened in the greenhouse. He might even have apologized.

Instead, she had worried about his mood for the next three days. She had grown frantic when no word came on Wednesday about Tuesday's deliberations. Then this odd letter arrived Friday afternoon.

The carriage stopped. Daphne pushed open the blinds, angled her head, and looked out. The breadth and height of Castleford's house would impress anyone. There was nothing reserved, modest, or discreet about the structure. It possessed more exuberant decoration than had ever been fashionable in England and more windows than most manor houses. Its design spoke unapologetically of wealth, privilege, and lack of restraint.

Of course it did.

A host of servants in blue, braided, old-fashioned livery waited to serve her. Hose and pumps marched forward. White gloves handed her and Katherine down.

Two periwigs beneath tricornered hats escorted them to the door. An impressive butler, decorated in gold buttons and embroidery, took her card, placed it on a silver tray held by a duller version of himself, then immediately led the way up the curving ceremonial staircase beyond the reception hall.

Katherine paced alongside, wide-eyed, too overwhelmed to be afraid anymore. Daphne tried not to be equally awed by the luxurious appointments layering her view in every direction.

"Have you ever seen anything so fine?" Katherine whispered. "Do Audrianna and Verity live like this?"

"Both of their homes might be as large, but the effect is not so ancien régime in its ostentation." Of course, neither friend now lived in a duke's home, either. Not that all dukes dwelled in such excess. Becksbridge had not, but then there were stories that some of his ancestors were secretly Puritans.

"There are some scandalous doings in those paintings up there." Katherine pointed to the ceiling high above, where gods and goddesses frolicked in bucolic landscapes, their nude poses full of amorous insinuations.

"Such things are not considered scandalous if the Roman gods do them."

"What are they considered instead?"

"Allegorical. I have always thought that was just an excuse for men to look at naughty images, however."

They entered the public rooms and passed through two huge drawing rooms. Finally their escort brought them to a chamber of relative simplicity at the end of the house, one paneled in medium tones of woods. Windows lined three of its walls, giving prospects of the river and Hyde Park. A pleasant cross breeze stirred the drapes.

The butler explained the duke would join them soon. Two servants arrived with trays of tiny cakes and tea. After some fussing and serving, she and Katherine were left alone.

Daphne sat on a settee and nibbled on a little cake that tasted of lemon. Her stomach had been tightening with every moment since they passed the park, and she could barely swallow it.

She probably worried for no reason. Castleford was not a total scoundrel, from the talk. He had been kind to both Audrianna and Verity at times. He might spend six days a week whoring and drinking, he might not care what was said of him, and he might delight in being bad, but no one had ever painted him as evil or cruel.

Unfortunately, putting her off that land would not qualify as either of those things. It would only be the act of a man making the best use of an inheritance. Hardly evil. Expected, actually. Smart.

She remembered the look in his eyes during those horrible few minutes after he stopped embracing her. She heard again the dark, sardonic tone with which he took his leave at the greenhouse door.

Her heart sank, and she ceased trying to be optimistic about how this meeting would end.

She probably should have begun packing right after she heard his horse galloping away at dawn.

Soon, a little thunder of footsteps worked its way through the adjoining drawing room. Two footmen opened the doors to the airy chamber, then held them wide. A line of men walked in, led by Castleford.

He appeared less informal today, Daphne thought. Crisper. Tidier in indefinable ways. Harder.

He walked like a man striding through life with a purpose. His severe expression spoke of sharp attention to whatever matter was at hand.

It became quickly obvious that, for the moment, she was that matter.

He gave her a good look. His gaze reflected his elevated station in ways not seen before. A duke accustomed to always getting his way was examining a woman who had dared deny him that privilege.

He made introductions to her and Katherine of the two men who had entered behind him. The young one with blond hair, spectacles, an unexpectedly firm jaw, and an earnest expression was his secretary, Mr. Edwards. The older, portly, balding man was one of his solicitors, a Mr. Goodale. Mr. Goodale carried a large roll of paper under his arm.

"Mr. Edwards, please take Miss Johnson below and show her the garden," Castleford said briskly, once the formalities had been completed. "She is an expert in horticulture. She is here to instruct you on all the things our gardeners are doing wrong, and you are to take notes for reference and improvements."

Mr. Edwards pulled a little ledger book out of his coat for those notes. He bowed to Katherine. "Miss Johnson, if you would do me the honor?"

Clearly confused, Katherine allowed Mr. Edwards to remove her from the chamber.

Castleford settled into a chair facing the settee. Daphne hoped his relaxation in that chair heralded a similar relinquishment of the severity his face wore.

Another dark scrutiny came her way. This time she could see the devilish lights in his eyes, only today they made him appear more dangerous than mischievous. Castleford was not a different man today, but his temperament seemed to sharpen along with his wits when he remained cold sober.

"Forgive my removing Miss Johnson with that little deception regarding her purpose here, Mrs. Joyes. I thought you might not want your friend to hear our conversation. I did not know if you had confided in her," he said.

"I have not confided. It is best she is not here." She had counted on Castleford to be circumspect around Katherine during this visit and to communicate his decision without being explicit. She had not expected him to receive her with a little entourage in tow.

"Then let us discuss the business at hand. Goodale here has a talent for finding information quickly. He is much smarter than he looks and enjoys poring over documents and records. He did a bit of investigating, so that I would know what I required in order to make a decision last Tuesday."

Her blood pounded in hard, slow beats. "Investigating?" It was all she could do to get the word out in a calm voice.

She looked at Mr. Goodale cautiously. He in turn ignored the insult buried in Castleford's praise and beamed with pleasure at his master's expression of high regard.

"It is wise to research inherited property, to see just what is what," Mr. Goodale explained. "His Grace was inclined to move quickly, but I convinced him to be more measured, to ensure there were no unexpected elements that required consideration."

In other words, this solicitor had interfered with last

Tuesday's decision, whether it would have been good or bad for her. "How wise of you, sir."

He bowed his head. "I like to think that I serve my patrons well and give good counsel."

"Stop flattering yourself, Goodale," Castleford said. "It is already wearying. You are only here for one reason, so get on with it."

"Certainly. Of course." Mr. Goodale positioned himself in her clear view for his performance. He unrolled the paper he carried. He held it up so his nose, eyes, and balding pate rose above the top edge and his paunch became a prop for the bottom.

It was a map.

"I had this made just for our conversation, Mrs. Joyes," he explained, his voice muffled by the paper. "You can see that everything is enlarged and much more easily viewed than on normal-size maps."

He glanced to the duke, looking for praise. When none came, Daphne did her best to fill in. "How clever of you, sir. I confess that most maps are so small as to be illegible to me."

"Me too! Hence my inspiration to make this easier for us both. I drew it myself, and believe even the scale is approximately correct. I am particularly proud of how I—"

"Move on, Mr. Goodale."

"Of course, Your Grace. Now, look here, Mrs. Joyes. This is Cumberworth." He pointed to a collection of squares and rectangles on the map's lower right. "Here is your home." He pointed to the lane, house, and gardens of The Rarest Blooms to the town's northwest. "And, as I anticipated, there is indeed an unexpected element. Right—here." He pointed to a large plot of land north of the copse of trees that bordered her property.

"That is fallow ground, unworked by its owner. That holding has been uninhabited for years. It has some trees and brush. Nothing more," she said.

"You misunderstand, dear lady. This is not a separate holding north of you. It is part of the property on which you now live. The whole acreage came to Lord Becksbridge through his mother. Hence his freedom to dispose of it in his testament."

"It is all of a piece?" She held out her hands for the map. Mr. Goodale brought it over and draped it on her lap. She bent over the lines and markings, very surprised.

Becksbridge had not given her a map. He had only provided directions to the house where she now lived. The land in front and behind obviously belonged to it. That to the north, past the trees along the lane, seemed obviously not to.

"If there is some concern with this other section, and it being attached to my tenancy, let me say that I have no need of it. It can be leased to another."

"That is not the only concern," Castleford said. "Show Mrs. Joyes the rest, and be quick about it. You are taking up more of this afternoon than can be afforded you."

Mr. Goodale bent over her and pointed again. This time to an area some distance from her house but less so from that other section. "Mrs. Joyes, do you see these markings up here? They represent notations from surveyors."

"Regarding what?"

"Minerals. Underground and untouched still, for the most part, but very recently a small mine has begun to be dug . . . here."

She noted the spot under his fingertip, a few miles from Cumberworth.

Mr. Goodale sat himself in a chair to her left. He eyed

the cakes but thought better of it. "Mrs. Joyes, while you have lived in that house, has the property ever, to your knowledge, been examined? Have there ever been men about with maps and such? Tools and apparatus that might be used for digging and boring?"

"Never."

Mr. Goodale's lips folded in on themselves. He pondered that.

"You may go now, Goodale. That will be all," Castleford said.

Mr. Goodale jumped to his feet as if a puppeteer had jerked his strings. A bow to her, then a deeper one to the duke, and he was gone.

Leaving her alone with Castleford.

Chapter Five

Daphne and the duke sat facing each other for a good while. He appeared to be thinking about something, but she had no idea what.

"You really can lease that other part of the property to someone else. We have no use for it," she finally said.

"There is no cottage on it. The income would never justify the investment of building one."

There was a house on the entire holding, however. Hers.

"Did you summon me here to tell me that due to the unexpected size of the property, you do not want it wasted on a household of women who can never pay the rent a farming tenant might? Was Mr. Goodale here to set the stage for your announcing a decision that I will not like?"

"I did not summon you."

"You certainly did not *invite* me."

"Was my note too brief? I do not like to write letters at all, so perhaps it was. I have never understood the habit of spending hours, *days*, writing letters to people of the slightest acquaintance. I'll wager you only write letters when necessary, since you are not a fool, and even then only because you do not have a secretary like I do."

"Your note was brief in the extreme, and it summoned me here merely so you could—"

"Again, it was not a summons. Should I ever command you, Mrs. Joyes, you will know it without question."

She closed her eyes and collected herself. The man was a trial. "You brought me here, only to learn that you are not prepared to honor Becksbridge's intentions for that property, I think."

"How well you put it. Goodale was supposed to clarify why, but I think he made a muddle of it. He goes on and on in the most wearisome way, obscuring the facts with his chatter instead of illuminating them."

"Can you do better than he?"

He propped his elbow on the chair's arm and rested his chin against his fist. "I can give you the usual dull reasons. In the end, they are all there are. I have duties, Mrs. Joyes. To my station, my title, and to future Castlefords. They involve the estate I received and that I will pass on. I find these duties annoying in their demands, I will not let them rule my life, but I do not take them lightly. Your property is now one of these duties."

"What of Becksbridge's intentions?"

"To hell with his intentions. It is mine now and requires the same stewardship I give all my property."

He was going to put her off that land. She knew it now. The best she might do is negotiate a stay of execution so she had time to find some hovel to which to move.

"You were more sympathetic when you visited us. A different man, actually."

"Mrs. Joyes, the biggest difference between that day and this, the only difference but the essential difference, was that it was not a Tuesday, and today is."

She thought that she had prepared herself, but she could not believe how horrible it was to actually face the certainty of this change. Not only her business would be lost—her very means of supporting herself—but also her long-laid plans and desperate hopes for the future.

One such hope, a very private one, entered her mind on a memory, much like a specter, bringing anguished nostalgia. Her composure wobbled in response. She looked down and clenched her teeth so she would not submit to the sudden urge to weep.

"It appears that you permit yourself cruelty on Tuesdays, Your Grace. That is why you reserve all those boring decisions for these days, isn't it?"

She sensed a reaction in him, but she dared not look up to see it. It altered the air so much that she feared she would see the fires of Satan if she looked in his eyes right then.

It passed. Mostly. She felt him there, however. Watching her.

"All is not lost," he said. "It is accurate that I am not prepared to honor Becksbridge's preference today, but I have not ruled out the idea either."

"You haven't?" She looked at him, not daring to hope again, searching to see if he teased her for amusement.

He appeared placid. Indifferent. He looked as if he was losing interest and would gaze out the window for diversion soon. "I have not made any decision yet. Before I do, I must learn a few things so I know my decision is based on sound facts. Even if I choose to ignore those facts, I must have them first. We must estimate the income to be lost if I leave it with you, for example." He all but yawned. "It should not take long."

"It could take a year if you only tend to these things once a week."

"You exaggerate. After all, you said it would take a year of Tuesdays before your color rose with me again, and here it is less than a fortnight later, and it has happened several times today alone."

It rose again at his casual reference to that night in the greenhouse. It worried her that he could cause her to flush so easily and frequently. No one else could.

She moved the conversation back to what mattered. "I should like to know where I stand soon, if possible. If I must leave, it would be better for the plants if it were in the autumn, and it could take a while to find another suitable property."

"Mrs. Joyes, are you now insisting that I decide today, when you just upbraided me for doing so? You are a confusing woman."

"It is disconcerting to be unsure of one's abode and means of sustenance. I do not want to rush you to an impulsive judgment, of course, but would be grateful for a timely one."

He stood and paced around the chamber while her plea hung in the air. Finally, he crossed his arms and sighed deeply. He looked like a man about to say something that he already regretted. "I suppose, *just this once*, so you are not left to worry indefinitely, I could take up this one bit of business on other days besides Tuesdays."

"Oh, thank you, Your Grace."

"I do not want to waste my time or suffer more intrusions than necessary, however. If a question arises that requires your aid, I want a quick answer. If I am to be bothered on any random day by new developments, I should not like details left unsettled, following me around all week."

"I promise that if you or Mr. Goodale write, I will respond through return post."

"Return post? That will hardly do. It would be better if you just stayed in London while we are on it. Then you can respond immediately."

The demand caught her by surprise. He looked at her, the picture of a reasonable man assuming she would accommodate him, now that he had accommodated her.

"That is not possible. I have duties too. At The Rarest Blooms."

"Surely Miss Johnson could tend those flowers and plants while you are gone a short while. It is very much in your interests to take residence in town. This would get settled much more quickly that way. You would be here to influence my decision too. I am surprised you do not see the benefits for your position."

She searched his expression for some sign of humor in how he was cornering her. She only saw the face of a duke concluding she was stupid not to realize that he was making her victory easier.

"How long do you think this would be?"

"A week. Perhaps ten days. I can't imagine it being longer than that."

She could not help but be suspicious. Still, if it would settle this more quickly, and if she could influence his decision—"I suppose that I could ask Celia—Mrs. Albrighton—for a chamber in her home."

He returned to his chair and made himself very comfortable. "I doubt her new husband will appreciate the intrusion. Also, she lives near Bedford Square, does she not? That is too far away and inconvenient. Better if you stay here, as my guest."

His innocent expression did not fool her. She had guessed the game he might be playing, and with that last sentence he showed all his cards.

"If I care a shred for my reputation, best if I do not stay here, Your Grace."

He smiled devilishly and looked more like he had at her house than he had all afternoon. "I forgot that Mrs. Joyes is fairly strict about proprieties."

"Yes, she is boring and inconvenient that way."

Still smiling, he gazed over in that familiar, incisive way that subtly crossed inappropriate lines. "And if I insist?"

So, there it was. This call was not only about that property and his decision. Perhaps it was not about either at all. She felt as if, rather suddenly, she had come under a predator's examination. It would help enormously if the caution he raised in her was not heavily tinged with alarming, warm stimulations.

"If you insist, I will question your motives, which are already suspicious, sir. I will also remind you that you said I could refuse you anything, and you would not hold it against me. I assume that as a gentleman you meant it."

"I don't remember saying that. I am sure you are mistaken. It doesn't sound like me at all."

"You remember well enough when you choose. It was the last thing you said at the end of our dinner."

"How careless of me. I am never so rashly generous."

The air was getting thick with words unspoken and implications layering high. She prayed that she would not blush again, but his long, knowing gaze provoked scandalous little thrills that dismayed her.

"I will write to Celia this evening and arrange to visit with her. New husband notwithstanding, she will be agreeable."

He dismissed her intention with an irritated flip of his hand. "I have a better solution, one to which you can not object. Summerhays has offered the use of his family house on Park Lane. Since he and his wife have gone to the coast and his mother has gone down to the country, you will have both comfort and privacy there, with all necessary proprieties in place."

He had planned this thoroughly, she realized. Perhaps plotted it for days. He had been leading her to this exact spot with the entire conversation. "I doubt that Lord Sebastian made this offer on impulse. What did you do to encourage him?"

"I may have written and mentioned I had met you and that I thought that you would be coming up to town for a fortnight."

"A week, you said."

"In my letter I expressed concern, since London in summer can be unhealthy. He responded that you must use their house. Since it faces the park, the air is quite cool and always fresh. He said Lady Sebastian would write to you and extend the invitation." He leaned forward to take a little cake. "Her letter probably arrived in Cumberworth today." He popped the cake in his mouth.

He looked pleased with himself and content that he had arranged her next week to his liking. Which he had. She did not have the confidence in his character to believe that, if she thwarted his plans, he would still be generous. He knew it too. He counted on his reputation leaving her unsure of him.

"You promise that you will turn your mind to this matter with discipline if I come to town?"

"I count on you permitting me to think about little else while you are here. Now, since you sound agreeable, let us go find Miss Johnson. I need to return to the hell where I suffer the tortures of the damned."

He escorted her out of the breezy chamber, through the luxurious public rooms, down the stairs, and out to the terrace. In the garden, Katherine was pointing to a rosebush while she spoke, and earnest Mr. Edwards was scribbling in his little ledger book.

He saw his employer and brought Katherine back to the terrace. Katherine appeared quite calm. The garden had soothed her misgivings, it seemed.

Castleford took Mr. Edwards aside for a few words. Katherine sidled close to Daphne. "Why did you not tell me that you brought me so I could have my first chance to advise on gardens and plants for a grand house? I am grateful that you have such confidence in me already."

Daphne noticed how Mr. Edwards was showing his garden notes to Castleford, who appeared bored to death. "I wanted to surprise you."

Castleford came over and took his leave of them. Then Mr. Edwards approached. "I have the honor to ensure that both you ladies are seen safely to your respective homes. His Grace instructed that we first go to Park Lane, Mrs. Joyes, and leave you there."

"I have a carriage. Nor will I take residence on Park Lane for a day or so. Your escort will not be necessary. You may return to His Grace."

The young man's face fell in dismay. "Your carriage was released an hour ago, Mrs. Joyes. On the duke's command." He consulted his little ledger and ticked off his orders. "Before we joined you, His Grace explained my duties. I am to take you to Park Lane, then Miss Johnson to Cumberworth—I am to ride alongside His Grace's coach, of course, and not accompany her inside. Then I must return to Park Lane with baggage Miss Johnson is going to pack for you."

Mr. Edwards had received these instructions before Castleford even entered that breezy chamber.

"I see that the duke intends your evening to be very full, Mr. Edwards. Unfortunately, His Grace did not take into account our preferences regarding our own plans when he made yours."

Mr. Edwards's face flushed. "Did he neglect to explain it all to you? My sincere apologies. That happens sometimes, I am sorry to say. Dukes have much on their minds, however."

This duke mostly seemed to have a game of seduction on his mind, Daphne suspected. He had taken efforts to make sure she remained conveniently nearby too, until he bothered to amuse himself by making the next move.

Chapter Six

The house on Park Lane was elegant and massive, as befitted the townhome of a lord. Daphne had visited Audrianna on occasion in the past and even knew some of the servants. She could not ask for a better situation if she wanted to spend a week—or ten days—in London in summer. Even with the household moved to the coast, enough retainers remained to ensure her safety and security along with her comfort and peace.

Nonetheless, from her first hour there she felt vulnerable. Perhaps the mere size of the place caused that. There was nothing cozy about the expansive library or towering dining room. Her presence created echoes wherever she went when she left her chamber.

That chamber became her sanctuary. She took her dinner there after Mr. Edwards deposited her in the reception hall. She was sitting at the window, observing how dark transformed the park, when he returned that night with her baggage.

Its arrival in her chamber involved a bit of ceremony, while the maid assigned to her hung out the dresses. Daphne noticed that her two best ones, the ones that would be presentable for dinner parties, had found their way here. She had not instructed Katherine to pack them.

Mr. Edwards had received rather detailed orders from his master, it appeared, and had interfered with Katherine's choice of wardrobe.

And that, she realized, was why she felt vulnerable. The duke had arranged for her to inhabit a huge town house with acres of chambers that the sparse staff never would enter. He had ensured she did not have any of her friends living with her, or any woman at all as a companion. His plotting indicated he was taking far more interest in her than any decent woman would welcome from such a notorious man.

She debated how to end his game as she fell asleep, and took up the matter again when she woke. Just as she admitted that she was only vulnerable because she did not find him as repulsive as she should, a maid brought her breakfast.

There was no mail, of course, but the day's *Times* came up with the tray. She read it while she ate at a table set near the window.

An article that reported the growing unrest among workers in the north captured her attention. She looked for familiar names of towns up there to see if violence threatened people that she knew. She prayed that those she loved would be safe, and also the others she knew in that region.

Toward the end of the article, however, another reference arrested her gaze.

The paper noted that Lord Latham, now the new Duke of Becksbridge, was expected to come up to London soon. It speculated that the prime minister would make it a point to meet with him, and proffered the opinion that Latham's recently published essay, in which he preached that a return to obedience to civil and natural law was critical to England's future, had found great favor within the government and army.

The article dimmed her mood. Thinking about Latham usually did. Fortunately, she had not had much cause to for years. Clearly that respite was over.

She would have to obtain this new essay of his. It would be comical to read. A return to civil and natural law, indeed. As she remembered it, this man had little conscience and thought himself above all laws. No doubt he believed that only the lower orders of society should be obedient.

The maid came to take her tray. A footman accompanied her and presented a calling card.

Lady Hawkeswell was down below.

Ten minutes later Verity breezed into the bedchamber, threw her silk reticule on the bed, and removed her bonnet to reveal the artful curls into which her dark hair had been dressed.

Verity possessed the most fashionable kind of beauty— ivory skin, red lips, dark hair—to a degree that annoyed certain ladies of society who did not think nature, let alone Lord Hawkeswell, should have favored a woman with Verity's common background.

"You should have chosen one of the other chambers,"

Verity said. "This one may face the park, but it also faces west and will be very warm on a summer afternoon. There is no sitting room attached either."

"Its size suited me, as did its prospects and its light colors." She took Verity's hand and urged her to sit. "How did you learn so quickly that I was here?"

Verity moved the chair up the wall so the sun, already pouring in as she had warned, did not blind her. "Celia sent me a note this morning. She in turn learned from her husband, who had learned of it while in the City."

"I don't suppose you know how Mr. Albrighton in turn learned of it."

"Castleford told him. They were at one of Mr. Albrighton's meetings regarding his inheritance early this morning. Since Castleford has found those conferences boring and no longer joins them, his presence today surprised Mr. Albrighton." Verity spoke casually. She looked around, examining the room's appointments. She strove to appear normal, but her blue eyes carried a lot of curiosity.

Daphne hated lying to her friends. She could not confide about Becksbridge's bequest, however, without telling far more than she had ever told anyone. None of it was a story for Verity's ears.

"I decided to take advantage of Audrianna's offer to use her house, to enjoy a few diversions while I meet with some families who have expressed interest in contracting with The Rarest Blooms." It was all true, just a bit out of order, and the reference to furthering her trade an inspired impulse.

Verity looked at her blandly. She knew it was not the whole story, but, Daphne was sure, she would not pry to learn more.

Verity fingered the lace that edged her gloves. "I did not realize you knew him. Castleford, that is. He was not at Celia's wedding in the spring. He rarely attends weddings, since they are in the mornings and most mornings he is . . . well, his schedules are reported to be other than most people's."

"We made each other's acquaintance recently."

"You must have impressed him. He is planning a dinner party, and it is all because of you."

He was?

"Celia mentioned it when she wrote. We are all to be invited. It will probably be in a fortnight or so."

"How kind of him."

"There is that side to him, but it is rarely seen and never predictable. Normally his every thought is selfish, and his rare activity is meddlesome. Despite that, I like him, perhaps because when he meddled in my direction it was one of those rare moments of kindness. Still, *woe unto someone who piques his curiosity*. That is what Hawkeswell says." Verity mimicked her husband's resonant voice, then dissolved into giggles.

Daphne wished she found it as humorous as her friend did. Castleford did have a habit of periodically rising out of his stupor to meddle, normally to great success. In Verity's case, he had made a rare effort to help the mill owner's daughter gain some acceptance when she entered society on her earl's arm. The meeting Castleford had attended this morning with Celia's husband Jonathan was the result of another time where he meddled in something not at all his business.

Unfortunately, this summer it appeared he was going to squander his brilliance on the curiosity named Daphne Joyes.

Woe unto her, indeed.

"I wonder if Audrianna and Lord Sebastian will return for the dinner," Verity said.

"I will write and advise she not make the journey. I may not even attend myself. It is not my intention to dally here very long."

"There would be no point in it at all if you did not attend. Castleford must have misunderstood the length of your visit."

Hardly.

"Well, we must find a way to all enjoy a diversion together while you are here," Verity said. "I will put my mind to it and consult with Celia. Town is quiet in summer, but we should be able to find something we can all do. A picnic, perhaps. Castleford would probably find that boring, however."

"There is no need to invite him, then. Is there?"

Verity shrugged and donned her bonnet again. "I must go. If you find it too lonely here, you are welcome to stay with us. I don't know why you did not write and ask to do so in the first place. You would not be an intrusion, Daphne. I know that you and Hawkeswell did not rub on well together at first, but he is very fond of you now. In fact, he asked for any news about you just two days ago."

Daphne saw her out. She wished she could believe that Hawkeswell would not mind a guest, but to say they had not rubbed on well together was being polite. She wanted to believe that as Castleford arranged this, he had been sensitive to that.

All the same, she guessed that she was not visiting with Verity mostly because Castleford did not want her visiting with Verity.

* * *

C astleford had his coach stop in the park. He alighted and strolled to the park's entrance, then walked up Park Lane.

His discretion was not only for Mrs. Joyes's sake. He did not mind gossip about himself if it was of the normal sort, but he did not want it reported that he pursued a woman. Wagging tongues would make too much of it, because it was generally known that he never bothered with such exertions.

He never had to. Usually all it took was an expression of interest and a few gifts, and soon the biggest challenge was how to free himself of the affair when he tired of it. The ends could be so complicated that he rarely bothered with the beginnings anymore. Life was easier if he restricted himself to professional women.

Yet here he was, making a social call on a woman in midday. He could not remember when he had last done so. The realization that he was about to break with his more sensible practices had annoyed him, until a bottle of good wine at his club put a better light on it.

He grudgingly admitted that Daphne Joyes and her cool composure had occupied his mind more than he liked the last ten days. It was all her fault too.

His interest in her might have passed quickly and normally if she had not thrown down a gauntlet. Several of them, to his mind. He was not a man to stand down from a challenge, and hers had provoked his mind even more than his pride. The only way to find peace when that happened was to follow where such fascinations led him and see them through to the end.

Usually that only meant cornering government lackeys

into answering his questions, to learn what cards some minister had up his sleeve. Sometimes the curiosity required more active investigations. On occasion the puzzles absorbed his attention for weeks.

He doubted that the object of his current stimulation would require much time to exorcise, however.

Most men might believe it demeaning to arrive at a woman's door on foot, but he did not care about such things because he, unlike most men, knew his worth. Well fortified with the wine that instilled a beatific sense of well-being, he presented his card to one very astonished servant.

Castleford amused himself with the paintings in the drawing room while he waited for Mrs. Joyes. He was lost in mentally improving the composition of an extravagant mythological scene by Le Sueur when the servant returned.

"Mrs. Joyes is not at home, Your Grace." The young man stammered it out, then flushed and averted his eyes. "I sincerely regret to inform you of that, sir. Most sincerely."

The footman looked young, green, and mortified to be delivering that message to a duke. As damned well he should be. Castleford did not hide his irritation and pointedly ignored how the footman positioned himself to escort the visitor out.

Women were never this bold. Even the ones afraid of him, even the ones who thought him the devil incarnate, did not dare this insult.

The footman appeared increasingly nervous and unsure what to do. Inappropriate flushes and fidgeting revealed his distress. Presumably the more experienced footmen had gone to the coast with Summerhays.

Castleford crossed his arms and gave the lad a good look. The footman's face got redder by the instant.

"What is your name?"

"P—" A strangled cough. "Perthy, sir. Your Grace. Horace Perthy. Sir."

"You seem an honest sort of person, Mr. Perthy."

"I try to be, sir."

"Then I am sure that you will tell me the truth now. Mrs. Joyes is indeed in this house, is she not? She sent down that message as women do at times, when they do not wish to see someone who has called. Am I correct?"

The fellow looked like he might faint. One could see him thinking hard to find some lesson on how he was supposed to handle such a blunt question from a visitor who refused to play by society's rules.

"Your silence speaks eloquently for you, Mr. Perthy. Now, find your tongue, and tell me just where in the house Mrs. Joyes resides."

"Oh, I cannot. . . . I mustn't. . . ."

"Mr. Perthy, there is no *cannot* or *mustn't* with me. Not even from the prime minister, and certainly not from you. Tell me where she resides, and no one will be the wiser. The alternative is that I will have to search the entire house to inform the lady of my displeasure."

Perthy's eyes bulged at the threat the house would be searched. He surrendered, relieved, forgetting that at least one woman would be the wiser in a few minutes. Whispering, he gave up the information.

Castleford favored him with a smile and sent him away. "Remember, Mr. Perthy, what you do not see, you cannot know."

A few moments later Castleford strode up the stairs. He must remember to tell Summerhays that the training of his servants lacked the requisite discipline. The boy had been intimidated too easily.

He found the apartment young Perthy had indicated. He opened the door to a bedchamber that did not even have an anteroom. It seemed fairly small for a house like this and was decorated in white with some green here and there. No flowers, he could not help but note. The park could be seen through the window, though.

A movement to his left stirred the air. A chilled little breeze wafted his way. Mrs. Joyes rose from a chair on the far side of the bed with a book in her hand.

She glared at him. "You are too bold, sir!"

Pride and insult stiffened her spine, and wonderful color marked her cheeks. Her fair hair had been dressed in the simplest way. It appeared only bound at her nape with a ribbon. He wondered how long it was. The bed spanned most of the space between them, and he imagined her kneeling on it, with that hair falling over her naked breasts.

He strolled into the chamber. "You refused to receive me, Mrs. Joyes. You sought to turn me away like some clerk or apprentice who forgot his place. And you think *I* am bold?"

Her nose rose. "A gentleman would have accepted my choice with grace, not invaded like a barbarian."

"I am no graceful gentleman, I am relieved to say. Being one forces the most stupid behavior on a man. However, I remind you that I am *Your Grace*."

He made his way to the window and checked its prospect. She could see Park Lane's length from it, which had probably been this small chamber's appeal.

He turned and faced her. "Do not do this again."

She did not like that. He did not care. She pressed the

wall behind her to put more distance between them. She made it a point never to allow her gaze to acknowledge that big bed beside her.

"I am not obligated to entertain you, Your Grace, especially when I have reason to believe you will not behave well."

"You had no reason to believe anything of the kind today."

"I saw you approach, while looking out that window. You appeared too happy."

"You hold it against a man that he is in a pleasant mood? Hell, you *are* strict."

"You were merely in a pleasant mood when you visited The Rarest Blooms. Today you exceeded that. I believe that you have been imbibing a good deal and are well in your cups."

"My cups are only half-filled at best. I am regretting my restraint more with each passing minute."

"You just ignored the proprieties of this house and intruded on my bedchamber. I would say that you are well beyond good sense. You would never do such a thing on Tuesday."

"I am a boring and hellishly bad company on Tuesdays. Also cruel. Remember?"

"And you are drunk other days. I do not receive men who are inebriated. I cannot receive your social calls if you are incapable of normal restraints with spirits."

She absolutely refused to back down and apologize. Unbelievable.

"I never said this was a social call. It is presumptuous for you to assume it is."

She sighed in a way that reminded him of Hawkeswell, when Hawkeswell was his most irritating. "I will not receive you for *any sort* of call when you are inebriated. When there is business to discuss, when you require information from me that influences your decision on that property, we will meet for that purpose, but not here." She squared her shoulders, lifted her damned invisible shield, and gazed over with her coolest regard. "Now, I must ask that you leave."

Damnation, she was *throwing him out.*

She was fortunate he was in such a pleasant mood. Her manner only prickled instead of inflamed. All the same, her hauteur goaded him. He'd go to hell before he stood down without goading a bit himself.

She held her poise so severely she might be one of those porcelain figurines. He looked right back, capturing her full attention, and he did not make any efforts to ignore the bed mere inches from her side.

He did not insinuate, he merely allowed his gaze to expand until the bed was in view along with the lady. He forced their mutual stare to acknowledge the intimacy of where they held this little contest and the possibilities of this privacy and the fact that he already had more familiarity with her than her manner today implied.

Her expression altered not at all. Her gaze did not waver. The slightest flush tinted her cheeks, however. He held her gaze until that tint darkened noticeably.

Finally, she looked away.

"We will do it the way you wish," he said. "I thought to spare you the inconvenience of formal meetings, but if they are your preference, far be it from me to inconvenience myself instead. Tomorrow at nine o'clock, call on me, and we will discuss the matter that brought me here today."

"Nine o'clock! That is uncivilized. As for where we meet—the park is preferable, I think."

"As I said, I thought to spare you, but I have only received your dreary scold for my generous efforts. Therefore, we will meet next time at my leisure, at an hour and place when this business will not interfere with my day and habits. That is nine o'clock tomorrow morning, at my house." He strolled to the door and bowed. "Until then, Mrs. Joyes."

Chapter Seven

It would be inaccurate to say that the servants on Park Lane considered Daphne's unexpected presence a nuisance. She suspected that she had disrupted their plans for an informal few weeks with no demands, however.

The best of them had traveled with Audrianna and Sebastian, and the ones who remained tended to be young and inexperienced. She was sure that Castleford would have never dared come up to the private chambers uninvited when the whole household was in residence, for example.

He had dared it, however, and now she found herself cornered again. There was nothing for it but to attend this business meeting in his house. She rose before dawn to prepare. Her maid yawned in her face when she arrived to help.

While washing and dressing, Daphne considered the

plans she had made yesterday for her week here, before Castleford intruded. She would, of course, see to influencing his decision on the property and hoped she acquitted herself better in the future than she had thus far. However, she had also seized on her inspired impulse during her conversation with Verity. It made sense to use her time to further her business. It might all come to naught within days, but if things went her way with Castleford, she could help The Rarest Blooms flourish even more.

Her gaze fell on yesterday's newspaper while her maid dressed her hair. That story about Latham had preyed on her mind ever since she read it. There would be no ignoring that man's presence in England now. It appeared that society would celebrate his every utterance and that his opinion would be sought at every turn. His role as moral philosopher would go unquestioned.

She snorted in derision so ungracefully that her maid's hands paused. She gestured for the girl to continue.

Latham was a fraud. Those essays were laughable coming from his hand. He might play the role of a good man, but there was nothing to recommend his character. Unfortunately, he had a talent for hiding his true nature beneath charm and eloquence. Even his own family did not comprehend how base he was and how he lacked the slightest sympathy for others.

Except Castleford, she reminded herself. He had endeared himself to her with his harsh judgment of Latham. It was the first time she had ever met another person of gentility who saw Latham as she did. Everyone else, it seemed, remained happily ignorant.

She looked in the mirror at her maid's handiwork. Then she averted her eyes so she would not meet her own gaze. Everyone remained ignorant because those who knew the truth never exposed him. He made sure that the only people who could denounce him were powerless to hurt him. He depended on their vulnerability making them confused and on their cowardice keeping them silent.

Of course, Castleford did not remain helpless or powerless. Yet, while he had broken with Latham, he had not exposed him.

They were relatives, of course, and two peas inhabiting the same extremely privileged pod. That probably accounted for it, and it made sense with the way the world worked. Still, realizing Castleford might have acted otherwise angered her. He might have spared some good people considerable grief.

She donned a discreet hat and accepted her gloves. She reached for her reticule and noted the newspaper again.

How much power would he have? How ambitious was he now? How many others who were vulnerable would he hurt? He really needed to be brought down. She would not mind being the agent of that.

While she was in London, she would learn what she could about the evidence of his sins and discover whether they were buried where she suspected. If she were clever enough, she might even learn a few things at this meeting today to aid her.

And if she succeeded, what then? She was not sure she was brave enough to reveal Latham's true face to the world. Worse, she did not think there would be any way to expose him without exposing others too.

She would decide what to do if she ever faced the choice. She would weigh the costs to herself and others after this little quest amounted to more than a righteous ambition.

* * *

The servant at Castleford's door this time lacked all that embroidery. Daphne assumed the captain of the guard had not taken his post yet. No normal house would have visitors at this ridiculously early hour.

Through the reception hall they went. Up the stairs where the Roman gods were up to no good on the ceiling. To her surprise, she was not led into the drawing rooms and back to that breezy chamber. Instead, the servant pivoted, crossed the landing, and continued up to the next level.

Most likely the duke had his study up here, near his apartment. He would have privacy then. She trusted that Mr. Edwards would be at his post. She would make sure Castleford did not find some pretext to send the young man away.

As she accompanied the servant, she girded her loins for battle. She would have to keep the duke on the topic at hand and not allow him to wander as he was wont to do when a word or observation distracted him hither and yon. Unless, of course, she led him yon through artful guidance.

She debated how to do that while she followed the wig to a set of doors. Her mind still contemplated the matter when he stood aside and ushered her in.

She froze. This was not a study. It was, from all appearances, a dressing room.

It bore a resemblance to a large sitting room, despite the wardrobes lining one wall, and the washbasin and dressing table near the windows. With all of its chairs and sofas, its tables and appointments, its dripping gilt moldings, it looked to be one of those dressing rooms

owned by the very best people and used as inner sanc-
tums where they might entertain their closest friends.

She held her temper in check with difficulty. If Castleford thought that she was going to attend a meeting
here, he was going to learn the meanings of *strict* and
scolding in new ways today.

"This way, ma'am," the servant encouraged. He stood
near another set of doors, waiting for her.

Relieved, she walked over. Of course the study was
part of the apartment. This was merely one way in. She
had reacted too strongly, but then Castleford warranted a
great deal of suspicion.

The doors swung open, and she saw at once that she
was correct on that point. If anything, she had underestimated him.

This was not a study either. It was the duke's bedchamber.

She peered in. The chamber had been redecorated
more recently than the others in the house. It did not sport
the same kinds of visual excess. The classical style domi-
nated, from the clean dentil moldings and sedate plaster
swags to the Roman styled chairs. The colors, mostly
creams and blues in a palette inspired by Mr. Wedgewood,
surprised her. She would have thought Castleford would
live among dark colors and reds. Lots of reds.

The duke sat at a writing table covered in papers. He
frowned over a letter he composed. Light from a nearby
window sliced across the table's surface, reflecting off the
metals of the inkwell and candleholders. It suffused his
distracted profile and found the few deep gold streaks
buried in his mussed hair.

She tore her attention away from that face and how
handsome and intelligent he looked. She then noticed

the rest of him: the deep blue of the loose, long silk coat he wore; the visibility of his neck above its collar; the absence of boots on his legs and the appearance of his bare feet.

He had not dressed yet. He still wore a morning robe. Unless she was mistaken—she prayed that she was—there was nothing under that blue silk except his body.

She inhaled sharply, shocked by his audacity.

He heard, and looked over. He set down his pen and stood. "Ah, Mrs. Joyes. You are punctual, I see."

"If you assumed I would not be, and require time to become presentable, I will gladly wait until you are ready for the day."

He looked down at himself, then shrugged. "There is no reason for you to wait. It isn't as if I am naked in bed."

She shook her head, exasperated. "You are unspeakable."

"Can I trust that means you will not speak? I much prefer that I talk. I think that I will find myself more interesting than I will find you this morning, if that expression of distress on your face—forgive me; expression of extreme surprise—is the warning signal of a tiresome scold waiting to pour out." He gestured to one of the Roman chairs. "Won't you sit?"

She did not want to sit. She did not want the intimacy of being with this man in his bedchamber, with him dressed like that. He had done this deliberately to punish her for trying to turn him away yesterday.

She thought about The Rarest Blooms and reminded herself why she tolerated him in the first place. She sat. He did not. He just gazed down at her, those sparks of mischief showing amusement at her discomfort.

Servants entered with trays and cloth. A table in the

center of the chamber turned into a small dining spot, full of silver, china, and glass.

Once the servants had withdrawn, Daphne looked pointedly at the duke's blue morning coat.

"If I could rise and dress, so could you," she said.

"I'll be damned. You have managed to scold anyway. I look forward to the day when the only complaint you have with me is that the pleasure ended too soon."

He stunned her speechless. He acted innocent, as if he had not just announced his goal in this contest.

"You had to leave a house and ride in a carriage, Mrs. Joyes. Dressing is obligatory then. I, on the other hand, intend to sleep once this is done, so dressing would be inconvenient."

His logic was not acceptable, even if it made an odd sort of practical sense. "You have not slept at all yet?"

"Not a wink, although I did have my valet get me out of my boots and such. For me, it is still yesterday."

He had been whoring and drinking all night was what he meant. She might have been ushered in when he was indeed naked in bed.

She stood. "Then I should come back when, for you, it is today."

He sighed dramatically and looked to heaven for patience. "Stop acting like a schoolgirl. I am hardly indecent. Sit and have some breakfast, and we will address the matter that brings you here. Unless, of course, you never want to talk about it. If I am never to call on you, and you are not going to call on me, I do not see how anything will progress, however."

Accepting that she would have to indulge him his outré behavior, up to a point, she sat at the table. He joined her and poured her some coffee.

"Do not worry about scandal," he said. "I promise that the servants who enter this apartment and who serve us today are rigidly discreet."

"It is good to know that your servants care about my reputation even if you do not."

"I care a great deal about it. That is why we are here. Even a meeting in my study would be more public. I have faith in the servants who saw to you this morning, but I cannot vouch for the others."

She leaned forward and looked him right in the eyes. "That is not why I am here. I would appreciate it if you remember your first impression of me—that I am not a fool." She straightened. "And if you think your dishabille in any way makes you more seductive, you are mistaken. It only reminds me what an inconstant, irresponsible hedonist you are."

He served himself some eggs and offered some to her. When she declined, he spooned some on her plate anyway. "Another scold. I am astonished that I don't mind more than I do. I am keeping count, however, should I ever be inclined to discipline you in return."

He ate his meal. She removed her gloves and picked at hers. The domesticity of the situation pressed on her. This private breakfast insinuated intimacy even more than his dishabille had.

Finally he set aside his silver. "I am sending men out to The Rarest Blooms to investigate what of value might be there besides pretty gardens. They will also look at the plot you never used."

"They will be looking for metals and such, you mean."

"Yes. It would be best if you had your housekeeper and that young woman Katherine come and stay with you in London. They may find the presence of these men intrusive."

"And what of those pretty gardens? And the income that derives from them? They require constant care. What you request is ruinous."

"Can you not hire some man for the time needed? I thought there was one already in your employ, who accompanies the plants that are brought to London."

"He drives a wagon. He is hardly fit to manage the entire business. If I could hire some man to tend the flowers and the plants without depleting the profit entirely, my hands would not look like this." She held one out. For all her care, its skin showed the labor over the years in subtle but noticeable ways.

He decided that her gesture invited him to examine her hand closely. He took it in his own. She barely managed not to jump in alarm as soft skin and tense strength enfolded her fingers. He turned her hand this way and that under his scrutiny. His thumb caressed both palm and back, checking the roughness.

She suffered it. She maintained her poise. She did not allow the way that stroking thumb affected her to show. But lively shivers worked their way up her arm from where he gazed and touched. They rose higher with every thoughtful stroke until they tingled her neck and began a downward path in her body.

Her breasts turned sensitive, ridiculously so. It was as if she could feel that thumb brushing them.

Did he know what he was doing to her? Was he so confident as that? She worried that he did, even if his expression showed no triumph but only thoughtful investigation of labor's effects on her.

She could hardly bear the way the tease seemed to affect all of her skin now. Her mind began betraying her badly, and she could not block speculations of other caresses and more direct sensations. Deep now, low and deep, prickles of desire began beckoning—

"You deserve better." He released her and sat back in his chair, oblivious to her arousal, it appeared. "If the women cannot come here, I will have to ensure their privacy there. I will send Mr. Edwards down with the others. He will make sure your household is in no way annoyed. He will stay at that inn in Cumberworth and accompany the men every day to the property."

She felt she should object, only she did not know why. He had been sly enough so far that she sensed that he must have some ulterior motive for this too. Of course, even his stated one—to discover if that land held hidden value—was hardly good news for her.

"How long do you think this will take? I should like to inform Katherine and Mrs. Hill."

He shrugged lazily. "If nothing is found, a fortnight. Somewhat longer if discoveries are made."

A fortnight. Apparently she would now remain in London at least that long.

"I will write to them and explain everything." She stood to make an escape before he made any other attempt to touch her. "I thank you for informing me."

He stood. As they faced each other, her composure returned.

"How did you know about the man who drives that wagon, Your Grace?"

"Damned if I remember. It must have been mentioned by one of our mutual friends."

Undoubtedly. But not in passing.

"Have you been asking questions about me?"

"Not beyond the normal sort regarding a tenant I have inherited."

"Are you also asking about the other ones, then? The tenants on those other bits of land you received from Becksbridge?"

"I have not met them, so they are not yet of enough interest to provoke questions."

"I look forward to your visiting them as you did me. It will be soon, I trust. I expect they are also close by."

"Not at all close by. They are inconveniently scattered all over the country. Shrewsbury. Devon, I think. Manchester." He speared her with a sharper gaze. "Why would you look forward to my visits to them? Are they acquaintances of yours?"

"I am only praying that they provide you with new distractions. I find the inquisitiveness that you aim in my direction excessive."

"So do I." He laughed lightly at himself. "It happens sometimes. There is really no predicting or explaining it. I am confident this little bout of curiosity will pass soon, however. In a week, perhaps, or a fortnight. Three weeks at most."

She did not want him inquiring about her at all. "Would it not be more useful if you turned your curiosity to the mysteries of the natural world? To questions of philosophy? You waste your abilities on a matter of insignificance."

He reacted as if she had scolded again. Which she had, she supposed.

"Mrs. Joyes, be assured that my abilities are devoted to matters of consequence most of the time, and the small puzzle you present does not interfere. Among other important vocations, I am writing a book that will be a great boon to mankind. It was that which you interrupted when you arrived."

She felt her face warming as he dismissed her importance. How vain and stupid she must appear to him. He merely toyed with her as a momentary diversion, and she had taken to attributing sly and lengthy plotting to him, without true cause.

She looked at the writing desk and even took a few steps in that direction. All those papers. He had appeared most intent too and had bluntly told her he did not write letters.

He had not been whoring and drinking all night but engaged in this literary endeavor, and so absorbed that he did not even sleep. In light of such ambitions, it was a small wonder he had not even dressed for their meeting.

She had forgotten whom she really dealt with here. Her little property would barely signify to such a man. Neither would the person who lived on it. His game with her only occupied the dregs of his time, and he even resented his inclination to play it.

"I must apologize, Your Grace. I have allowed the prejudice of the scandal sheets and the gossips to influence me too much. I have been shamefully quick to assume you are the notorious, profligate scoundrel they describe." She gestured to the papers and tried to make amends by showing some interest. "Have you been at it long?"

He went over and lifted a few of the sheets. He peered at them critically. "Some months now. There are parts that bedevil me and are taking too long to get right. I hope with experience it becomes easier. I never thought writing a book could be so difficult but also so engrossing."

He had turned his mind to an important task and was

finding it a challenge. She could not imagine he admitted that often, about anything.

"May I ask the topic? If it is a secret, forgive me for prying."

"It is not a secret. I have already confided my intentions to a few friends. I would not want to bore you, however."

"I would not find it boring."

He gazed down at his words and appeared charmingly proud of whatever it was that he read. "It is a guidebook. To London. For the average citizen. Advice on where to go to find diversions."

That was not nearly as elevated and scholarly as she had assumed, but it was still worthwhile. "How helpful. Visitors will be happy to have advice from a man of your taste and station on the theaters and races and such."

"Mmmmm. Well, that has been done before, though, hasn't it?" He muttered, distracted now by the prose on the sheet of paper. "This book will not plow previously tilled fields but break new ground. It involves very special diversions, in which few other men have my level of connoisseurship."

She looked at him, then at the papers, then at him again. She caught him smiling over some passage he read.

"What sort of diversions, Your Grace?"

He did not hear her, he was so absorbed. He frowned. "Have you ever noticed that there are whole areas of experience for which the English language is inadequate? I had never acknowledged the deficiencies before I began this exercise."

She could think of one area of experience where that might be true. Just as she could think of only one kind of diversion in which Castleford was said to have a rare level of connoisseurship.

He was writing a London guide to sinning.

"I surmise that this will be a book for men, Your Grace."

He sighed while he shuffled the pages and put them down. "Unfortunately, I expect so. I have no experience with which to write chapters for women. I could ask some ladies whom I believe to be knowledgeable for their advice, but I doubt they would admit enough to be helpful. Women tend to be very secretive about enjoying diversions such as this. It isn't as if the world is fooled. Everyone knows there are some very fine establishments that cater to females. They could hardly thrive in their trade if no females made use of them, now could they?"

She blinked hard. It was worse than she thought. He was not penning a tome about gambling hells and cockfights and such, but about *brothels*.

"I can see why you find this book so engrossing to write."

"In truth, the research became burdensome, but on those thankfully rare occasions when I put my mind to something, I normally feel compelled to see it through. Fortunately, that part is well completed."

Really!

"I will take my leave now, Your Grace, so I no longer inconvenience your day and so you can return to preparing your great gift to the men of England."

For some reason that caught his attention. Perhaps it was her tone or maybe the way she executed a stiff, quick curtsy.

Suddenly the devil was watching her, and amused at what he saw.

"Are you jealous, Mrs. Joyes? Or scandalized? I cannot tell which emotion accounts for your blush."

Jealous! "Neither. If there is color, it only comes from struggling to swallow another well-deserved scold."

"You must hold it in. Summon all your strength. In fact, allow me to help you conquer the impulse." He pulled her to him so quickly that she gasped. Suddenly his hand was pressing her nape and his mouth was pressing her lips.

She could not find the presence of mind to react at first. During that brief lull—she was very sure it was extremely brief—while she was taken aback, that kiss deepened to something other than a joke. First tender, then wicked, the kiss began to claim her, as if the notion to do so dawned on him even as pleasure dawned in her.

The mood changed quickly. He loosed his sensual power, and she felt it like a tangible wind. He began to embrace her. She placed her hand on his chest—to resist him, she was sure—and the clear feel of the naked body beneath that blue morning coat jolted her out of her shock.

Aghast at herself, she broke free, jumped out of reach, and glared at him.

"Come back here now," he said in a quiet, soothing, alluring voice. His gaze, sardonic, amused, and knowing, insisted she not look away. "You know that you want to."

She gaped at his outrageous conceit. "I certainly do not!"

His eyes darkened. "Perhaps that is true. Perhaps you do not know yet."

He strolled to the table and poured himself more coffee.

"What a stroke of inspiration that was," he said, raising the cup. "I think that whenever you subject me to a scold or get that look in your eyes that says one is coming, I will have to subject you to a ravishing kiss. You get the better half of the bargain to my mind, but at least I will know some compensation."

Disgracefully pleased with himself, he called for a servant to see her out.

She was already at the door by the time one of the footmen pushed it open.

Chapter Eight

Castleford wondered about Daphne Joyes while he rode his horse east through London. He was doing too much such wondering these days. That would surely end once he seduced her.

But in the meantime, he was wondering what she really thought of him. From her astonishment at learning he was writing a book, he suspected she might have concluded he was not very smart.

People did that sometimes. His good nature was to blame. The world considered scowling, brooding fellows intelligent, and pleasant, contented ones dim. Since he was only the former on Tuesdays, he was often underestimated. The misunderstanding put those in error at a disadvantage, so he normally did not care.

She also thought him a drunkard. She had made that

clear enough. There was no point in trying to disabuse her of the notion either.

Then, of course, there was his reputation regarding women. She had heard about that. The whole world had heard about that. And if Hawkeswell and Summerhays had been indiscreet with their wives about his whores, Daphne Joyes undoubtedly knew he did not indulge himself thus only for the purposes of research.

Not that he had indulged recently, he noted with annoyance. He never did when his eye settled on one specific woman. He had learned long ago that, for him at least, desire for one woman made pleasure with other women no fun. A relief still, much like farting out a bad gas, but joyless.

Abstinence, unfortunately, only made the desire increase. It could be a hellish cycle, and reason enough to avoid allowing his eye to settle at all.

Dwelling on his current sexual situation made him surly, so he returned to wondering about Daphne. She probably did not think the duels spoke well of him either, now that he considered the matter. Women never liked duels. So that was one more likely objection she might have to his character.

The list of those objections became quite long by the time he swung off his horse in front of the collection of old, attached buildings that made up the War Office. So long that he wondered why he had been fool enough to begin wondering in that direction in the first place.

It probably had to do with his sobriety today, donned in part for the task at hand. He trusted the next hour would divert him from lists of reasons the cool, incomparable Mrs. Joyes might not admire him.

He entered the center building and made his way to its stairs, greeting stunned and cautious aides and clerks along the way. Two ran off as soon as they bowed, probably to inform their superiors that a certain duke had decided to grace the premises with his presence again.

Castleford did not go up the stairs to meet those superiors, but down. He found his way to a chamber in the bowels of the building. Light from high windows kept it from being a true dungeon. Golden beams sliced through the heavy shadows, illuminating the two men whose desks had been placed to take advantage of them, much like characters in a Caravaggio painting.

The older man's smile of welcome dropped when that light fell on their visitor too. He stood and bowed and nervously fixed his spectacles on his nose more securely.

"Your Grace. We are honored. It has been some time. However, if you require records again, I must tell you that after the last time the minister strictly corrected us to always obtain his approval. He said he would explain this to you, sir, and—"

"I have all the approval necessary, Mr. Trilling."

Mr. Trilling's clerk watched, wide-eyed. Something about his expression piqued Castleford's memory, but he could not place why.

Trilling fussed and flustered. Castleford subjected him to a level gaze that normally reduced government functionaries to cowering obedience.

Not this time, unfortunately.

"I think I should speak with the minister, sir. Just to ensure there is no misunderstanding," Trilling said. "I hope you will not mind that, Your Grace."

"By all means, go speak with Bathurst, if he is here. I will wait." He dropped onto one of the uncomfortable wooden chairs, stretched out his legs, and smiled up at the old man.

Trilling shuffled away. Castleford took out his snuffbox, took a pinch, then held it toward the young clerk. "Join me while you can. I am sure Mr. Trilling allows no such indulgences."

"You can be sure he never does, sir." With a conspiratorial smile, the young clerk came over. He accepted the box and helped himself.

"What is your name?" Castleford asked.

He flushed and bowed. "My apologies, Your Grace. I am Harry Sykes, first clerk to the director of records, sir."

"You look familiar to me," Castleford said. "I am sure we have met."

"Met? I am sure not, Your Grace. Why, when could that have been? I have only been employed by Mr. Trilling since June." He beamed with pleasure at the notion that a duke thought there had been a meeting, though.

"I am sure all the same. Perhaps it was not here but elsewhere." He pondered it. "Do you gamble?"

Mr. Sykes's expression turned guarded. "A bit, sir. Not overmuch."

"Ah, now I remember. It was at Damian's, not three weeks ago. I am sure of it. You were with two junior army officers at the wheel. You were much distracted by the play."

Mostly Sykes had been distracted by his large losses in that gaming hell. His panic had been visible and palpable, which was why Castleford had noticed him. When desperate, Sykes appeared much as he had when awed by a duke's entrance into his dungeon.

"I have been there on occasion, I think. Your memory is excellent, sir, if you noticed such as me."

"My memory surprises even me sometimes. There is no accounting for what sticks in it."

Mr. Sykes nervously opened and closed the snuffbox and, after admiring it a moment, handed it back with his thanks.

"Keep it, Mr. Sykes. Be sure to pawn it well, however. The top is gold and the bottom silver, and those are real sapphires as the lion's eyes. Oh, and while you contemplate how far it will go to settling your gentleman's debts, would you be good enough to bring me the books that have the war deaths?"

Mr. Sykes looked at him. Then at the snuffbox. Then at the door.

"Mr. Trilling will be some time returning, I promise you. Bathurst is in a meeting this morning, so there will be a delay for any other conversations. Mr. Trilling cannot return until he can let me stay or kick me out on the minister's authority," Castleford said. "If it makes you feel better, after you bring me the list, you can keep watch at the door."

Mr. Sykes thought it over for a long moment. Then he went to the bookcases that held the records, climbed two rungs on the ladder propped there, and pulled out a large, bound volume.

Daphne set aside the letter she had received from Katherine, in which Katherine described how everything at The Rarest Blooms progressed. Katherine gave repeated reassurance that Daphne's presence had thus far not been missed. Her pride in managing everything on her own could be sensed through her words.

Daphne rather wished Katherine were not proving so

competent. She should not go home until all was settled with Castleford, she knew, but if she had no choice, due to some disaster . . .

Her reaction was cowardly and uncalled-for. All she had to do was wait him out and make sure he never touched or kissed her again. He would lose interest quickly and most likely give her the property outright just to be rid of her.

She penned a quick response to Katherine, one full of praise. After she sealed that letter, she dipped her pen again and faced a blank sheet of paper.

It was time to write to her friend Margaret. Not only did she owe Margaret a letter, she also wanted to learn how things really fared in the north, where Margaret lived.

The reports read in London made the situation sound very dangerous, and she needed to know if the danger only existed in big towns like Manchester or elsewhere as well. Certain lords with property up there seemed to believe that rebellion might break out and that bloody unrest would spread like a fire. She prayed that they exaggerated. It would be good to get a sensible woman's view of the common people's mood, however.

Margaret would answer honestly, because she was an old friend. Older than Verity or Celia. She had never lived at The Rarest Blooms or taken refuge with Daphne, however. Rather, the opposite had happened. For a while, before Daphne obtained aid from Becksbridge and established her household near Cumberworth, Margaret had been the one to offer help and sanctuary in her small home outside of Manchester.

Daphne wrote the letter easily until she had almost finished it. The impulse to write in the first place had not entirely been due to the unrest up north. Now that she tried to form the words to pose her questions on another matter, her confidence faltered.

What would Margaret think, to open a letter and read such queries? She might be insulted or even afraid. Daphne realized that she, who lived by a rule that said one did not pry, was about to pry disgracefully into a good woman's privacy.

A letter would never do. If she wanted to ask such things, if she wanted Margaret to confide, she would have to do it face-to-face.

She put her other questions aside. Instead she penned a few final sentences that expressed a desire to visit. It was perhaps time, she wrote, to talk honestly about the past.

Castleford thumped the lion's head door knocker on a house near Bedford Square. While he waited for a response, he looked up and down the street to see what attention he might be garnering.

The last time he had come here, some months ago, he had been in his state coach. A mistake, that. He had drawn a crowd within minutes. Today he had more sensibly ridden his horse and had escaped attention.

The door opened and a handsome, buxom, red-haired woman faced him. She took his card and gave him a hard, stony gaze before standing aside to let him enter. He looked hard at her as he did so.

She appeared familiar to him. Damned if he knew why. First Sykes this morning, and now this servant. It was annoying to have faces poke at your mind like this.

She led him to a front sitting room. His continued

scrutiny of her seemed to annoy her. She left in a manner almost rude.

Soon boot steps sounded on nearby floorboards. Jonathan Albrighton entered, dressed informally, his angular face wearing the vaguest of smiles and his dark eyes showing their inscrutable depths.

"Castleford," he said in greeting. "What a stunning surprise."

"I was in the City, and thought I would call as I passed by on my way home." He made a show of glancing around with appreciation. It was a modest home, of the sort he rarely entered. Albrighton could afford better now. Presumably he stayed here because it was away from society's eyes. Albrighton had perhaps become too used to obscurity to be comfortable with anything else.

"We are honored. Celia would receive you too, but she insists she is not dressed well enough. I said you would not mind, but you know how women can be." Albrighton gestured to a chair, by way of invitation. "May I offer you some brandy? Whiskey?"

"I think not, although I probably should. I have been busy of late, and more sober than is healthy, I think."

Albrighton laughed in that almost silent style he had.

"It was not a jest, Albrighton. Sobriety is playing games with my mind. That servant here, with the red hair, for example. I wonder if I know her, but have no idea why I think I do. It is like a damned itch that can't be reached."

Albrighton thought before speaking. He always did that. It usually left Castleford wondering what was not being said. "It is possible you have met her before."

"That is unlikely. I have not 'met' more than a dozen servants in my entire life."

"She was not always a servant. She used to live in Covent Garden." Albrighton looked over placidly. Meaningfully.

"*Ah.*"

"She fears you recognized her. She is being comforted by Celia, who has assured her you are too drunk ever to remember anything when you go whoring."

"That is not true. I remember almost everything."

Albrighton just looked at him.

"But not this time. Just her face, vaguely. Nothing specific otherwise."

"Good."

"Although it does occur to me that she may have been the one with—" He noticed Albrighton's eyelids lower. "No, surely not. Try as I might, the details are completely lost. Most likely she was just a friend of some woman I knew much better."

Albrighton acknowledged the effort with his damned vague smile, then turned the topic neatly. "As I said, you honor us with this call. Is there a reason for it?"

"Does there have to be a reason?"

"For most friends, no. However, you are not known to make calls even on the best people, let alone go out of your way like this." He said nothing more. He just waited.

That was the problem with Albrighton. He made one show one's hand in order to get anything out of him. His years employed by the Home Office, his role to ferret out information, no doubt accounted for that. "I merely found myself passing by. However, your mention of your wife does bring to mind my recent acquaintance of Mrs. Joyes. If I remember correctly, your wife lived with her for some time."

"For five years, until she inherited this house upon her mother's death."

Castleford waited for Albrighton to offer something more. Anything. However, unlike with Hawkeswell, conversation, let alone gossip, did not flow freely with this man.

"She mentioned in passing that she sends flowers and plants to a friend in London to distribute. I immediately thought that friend must be Mrs. Albrighton. I don't know why the notion came to me."

"It was a logical deduction, I suppose. It was unlikely Mrs. Joyes had Lady Sebastian or Lady Hawkeswell as a partner. That is why Celia is not running above to dress better, to receive you. She expects that wagon from The Rarest Blooms today."

"Soon? I hope that I have not intruded at an inconvenient time."

"Not too soon." Albrighton cocked his head, as if listening for sounds from the back of the house. "Let us take a turn in the park, however, so we are not a nuisance when it comes."

Castleford agreed that was a fine idea. Albrighton looked like a man who wanted a private word, for one thing. For another, with any luck that wagon would have come by the time their walk was completed.

They walked all the way to Bedford Square before Albrighton spoke again. "I thought perhaps you had sought me out for a different reason besides your curiosity regarding Mrs. Joyes."

"I am not curious. It was merely small talk. Everyone

in the world except you engages in it. If you are going to
have any chance in society, you must learn to bore people with insignificant chatter too."

Humor showed in Albrighton's eyes, but it dimmed fast.
"I thought you had come about Latham. He is in town. He
came up from his county seat two days ago."

Their gazes connected directly for a five count. For that
brief spell they were not in Bedford Park or even England.
They were in France on a damp night a little over two
years ago, and acknowledging without words that Castleford was betraying his current lover and probably sending
her to her death for the good of England.

They had never spoken of that business. If Latham had
not returned to England, perhaps they never would have.

That night was in the past, and Castleford did not
dwell on it. He had decided not to blame Albrighton for
doing his duty as he saw it, just as Castleford had done
his own in revealing what he had discovered to a man he
knew to be an agent for the government. A man who was
also a distant, old friend and who would know better
than to congratulate His Grace for being so damned
selfless and honorable.

"Latham can go to hell for all I care," Castleford said.
Mostly he did not want to care, because thoughts of the
new Duke of Becksbridge conjured up a complicated
emotion that strongly resembled guilt. About that night
and about other things.

"It appears he has gone to court instead. And to visit
the Earl Bathurst and Lord Liverpool."

Albrighton clearly had something to say. Since the
man rarely spoke plainly, when he did so it was usually
worth hearing.

"I expect they sat and drank port and decried the disgraceful state of the realm," Castleford said.

"I think it more likely they discussed the need to prepare for insurrection. If you made more calls on the best kind of people, you would appreciate just how worried your fellow peers are."

"I do not have to endure calls to know. Talk of it is everywhere. I tire of hearing it. It bores me to death."

"It is not the talking that might lead to deaths."

Now, that was regrettably interesting. "Have you heard something that goes beyond talk? Do not get dodgy on me, Albrighton."

"I only pick up pieces now, since I am officially severed from service to the government. Word of meetings drifts to me, though, from others who still know things." He looked over and caught Castleford's gaze again with his own. "There is talk of sending the army to Manchester for that demonstration planned next month."

That was enough to make Castleford stop walking.

Hell and damnation. He had little interest in parliamentary sessions where peers droned on and on, but he prided himself on being aware of the real decisions, the ones made in private chambers. Mrs. Joyes had been distracting him too much if he had missed this. Quite likely he had been poking into her past in the War Office cellar today while ministers plotted something insane right above him.

One would think none of England's government leaders were educated, from the way they turned stupid when they got together. Both common sense and experience said the presence of the army would not maintain order if a large demonstration in support of radical government reform took place but would only incite trouble.

"I thank you for sharing the gossip, Albrighton."

They strolled on. Castleford pictured Latham at those meetings, basking in the attention. He saw Latham using his eloquence to make the oppression of free men's rights sound reasonable and necessary.

"Have you seen Latham?" he asked.

"In passing. He did not recognize me," Albrighton said.

"I doubt he will. You were only the man who handed his slave over to face the guillotine, after all. I am the one who told him to his face that I knew he had pulled the strings and had been treasonous for no more reason than his own amusement and a few francs."

He was sure his voice did not falter as he spoke. Yet putting it into words, what had happened and its horrible conclusion, stuck in his throat as it emerged.

There had been no choice, of course. He often told himself that. But if ever his curiosity had led to unexpected results, that was the time. He had suspected soon enough that Marie was fleecing wealthy Englishmen as she sold shares of her estate to them. He had not expected to discover that the money was going to Napoleon loyalists desperate to raise yet another army in his name.

Now he walked beside Albrighton, much as they had walked on either side of Marie as they handed her over to the French and her fate. He'd had to know, of course, if his last suspicion about the intrigue surrounding her was true.

You were Latham's lover too, weren't you? Did he

*point you at me, so I would be complicit even as I was
unaware?*

He had seen her face in the twilight as she gazed at
the last of the setting sun, looking so young and frightened that his heart broke for her.

*He discovered early where the money that I accumu-
lated was going. He explained that the price of my freedom was my body and half of all I raised.*

*I do not hate you for this, Castleford—I know you
only do your duty, and even if you had loved me it would
be the same. But him—unlike you, he has no honor and
no loyalty to anything. Kill him, if you ever get the
chance, Tristan.*

"You are lost in your thoughts, Castleford. If I have
called forth unpleasant ones, I apologize," Albrighton
said as their steps took them out of the park and toward
the house.

"Unpleasant enough, and sobriety has made them too
vivid. Thank you for ruining my day. I will return the favor sometime." It had been inevitable, however, sober or
not. Sooner or later, he would be dealing with Latham's
reemergence in his life. He had known that since he received word of the old duke's death.

Albrighton actually made an attempt at small talk then,
to distract him. The effort was valiant but the results
awkward. All the same, the last of the memories had faded
by the time they approached the house.

"The wagon is here. You should make your escape
while you can," Albrighton said.

Another set of wheels rested behind the wagon's.
Castleford recognized the carriage as one of Summerhays's.

A few queries by his steward to households that

contracted with The Rarest Blooms had told him the wagon would probably come today. He was delighted that his guess regarding Mrs. Joyes coming as well had been correct.

"I would not think of leaving without paying my respects to your wife, no matter how she is dressed. That would be rude."

Chapter Nine

"**Y**ou could just enjoy town while you are visiting," Celia said. "You do not have to spend the days on trade."

Daphne did not think Celia's dismissal of her plan a good sign. They were partners in The Rarest Blooms now. Celia should be more interested in seeing it prosper.

Of course Celia no longer needed the partnership to put food on the table, now that she was married to Jonathan. Her condition, now apparent in the gentle bulge below her garment's high waist, no doubt accounted for her lack of enthusiasm too.

"I have been enjoying myself. I have already been to Bullock's Museum and done some shopping on Ludgate Hill. However, I am unable to fill my days with outings completely, Celia. Calling on the steward or butler of one house each day is concluding discussions more quickly than writing back and forth."

Celia shrugged. "If it gives you pleasure to do so, then I am not going to object. However, it will be some months before they want those flowers or plants, so writing back and forth is hardly a significant delay."

They sat in her back sitting room, the one where Celia had built shelves near the big window to hold the plants that arrived from Cumberworth. Even as they spoke, the last of them were carried in and handed to Daphne, who placed them where they would not get too much summer sun.

Daphne noticed that a good deal of dirt had found its way onto Celia's floor. "Where is Miriam? We need a broom."

"She went above. I do not think she will be down for a while." Celia smiled impishly. "She is hiding."

"Not from me, I hope."

"Of course not. She is hiding from the owner of that horse tied up outside. She recognized him from her past."

"I expect that was startling. Although she is safe enough if she remains indoors."

"Not really, since he came indoors too, and she came face-to-face with him. He was not a patron, but she is convinced he saw her in her glory, as it were. I told her it was unlikely he remembers, but up she ran. She took Bella with her, because she does not want Bella to come to the attention of such men."

Daphne looked out the window, perplexed. "Is he in the garden? I saw no one in the library or front sitting room."

"He is with Jonathan. They went to the park for a private talk."

Just then the sounds of a door opening reached Daphne's ears. The boots that entered the house did not stop at the front chambers but continued toward the back of the house.

Celia's blue eyes widened in alarm. She glanced down at her soiled apron, quickly untied it, and threw it behind the settee. Her cap followed it. Celia dressed her golden hair so artfully that it made her appear ready for a dinner party no matter how simple her dress might be.

Daphne watched the hurried preparations. She hoped this visitor did not expect her to do the same. Her lilac muslin would have to be good enough.

The steps closed on them. Jonathan appeared in the doorway. Celia gave him a good glare, then quickly masked her face with a broad smile just in time for the visitor's entry.

Daphne almost dropped the pot she held when she saw the man with Jonathan. Celia might have warned her!

Celia curtsied and Castleford bowed while they exchanged greetings. He turned to Daphne. She remembered to curtsy too.

Celia hid any fluster beneath well-trained poise. "Your Grace, my apologies for not greeting you when you arrived." She gestured helplessly around the chamber at the plants and dirt. "You can see that I had reason to be less than appropriately dressed for visitors."

"My dear Mrs. Albrighton, you can never be other than lovely to a visitor's eye."

"I hear it said that Lord Castleford is not a stickler about such things, Celia," Daphne said. "Indeed, he is very open-minded on the entire question of appropriate dress, even when entertaining, I am told. Is that true, Your Grace?"

"It depends entirely on the visitor I entertain, Mrs. Joyes, as well as the form of the entertainment."

Jonathan smiled and Celia giggled at the bawdy allusions. No wonder Castleford was incorrigible, Daphne thought. Everyone indulged him and only encouraged him to preen in his delight in his own badness.

He had effectively silenced her, however. She could not think of a clever comeback, try as she might.

"The afternoon is warm, Your Grace. May I offer some refreshment?" Celia asked. "Some lemon and honey punch, perhaps? We can all enjoy the garden."

Daphne all but rolled her eyes. Celia did not know Castleford well if she thought this duke would want to sit in a garden drinking punch. Fortunately, the offer would get rid of him fast.

"That sounds splendid, Mrs. Albrighton. You are too kind." He turned ever so graciously to Daphne. "I trust you will join us, Mrs. Joyes. I would not want to think that my visit caused you to shorten your own."

"Of course she will join us," Celia said. "She is the last woman to run away from anything, even you, Your Grace."

Celia thought herself very humorous, from the sparks in her eyes. Jonathan's smile turned a little sardonic.

Trapped before she had time to plan an escape, Daphne of course agreed to join them.

The gentlemen went out to the garden. Celia pulled Daphne aside. "Oh, dear. I just realized that the punch is down below and Miriam—"

"Go out to your esteemed guest, Celia. I will bring the punch."

*   *   *

"Mrs. Joyes will join us soon," Mrs. Albrighton said as she settled on the chair her husband held for her. "My woman has taken ill, and, fortunately, Mrs. Joyes is not only capable in every way but also not too proud to help a friend in need."

Castleford muttered words of admiration for a woman not too proud. Mrs. Joyes had looked none too pleased to see him walk in that sitting room. She might take a good while to arrive with the punch.

In the meantime, here he was, hellishly sober on a sunny afternoon, about to spend a good deal of time talking about nothing of importance.

What in hell was happening to him?

He decided to pass the time doing a bit of prying. Mrs. Albrighton had lived at The Rarest Blooms a long time. She probably knew Mrs. Joyes as well as anyone did.

He doubted that she knew Mrs. Joyes's secrets, however. Mrs. Albrighton would not know about Becksbridge or how Mrs. Joyes came by that property. She also probably did not know what he had discovered this morning in the War Office cellar—that Mrs. Joyes had been living a long lie about her past.

"Your friend is a lovely woman," he said to Mrs. Albrighton. "And very considerate, I see. I trust that she is enjoying her visit to London?"

Mrs. Albrighton pursed her lips. "She has found ways to make it other than a sojourn of pleasure. I am not surprised. She has a tendency to seriousness that requires her to be industrious in some way or another."

"Perhaps travel is a common experience for her. If so, a visit to London might be too ordinary to require diversions."

"She traveled when she was married, of course. When

she followed the drum. Since moving to Cumberworth, however, she rarely missed a night there." Mrs. Albrighton paused thoughtfully. "There were a few occasions when she removed herself for several days. And once for a longer spell. A fortnight, I believe, although I do not remember well since it was many years ago."

"Perhaps she prefers friends to visit her in the country."

"No, not that I recall. Well, Audrianna and Audrianna's mother, but otherwise we had no visitors from London, for example."

So, even if the affair with the old duke had continued while Mrs. Joyes used that property, it had not been during the five years that Mrs. Albrighton lived with her. Castleford had wondered about that.

"She holds her own counsel, but I surmise that her life has not been an easy one," he said.

Mrs. Albrighton glanced over her shoulder, checking to make sure the subject of their conversation was not visible. "Not at all easy. When her father died, her family's property went to a second cousin who felt no obligation to her. Nor did her other relatives. Audrianna— Lady Sebastian Summerhays—is her cousin, you may know, and Audrianna has told me how humiliated she was that her parents concluded they could ill afford to take Daphne in. When Audrianna herself needed a home, however, Daphne did not hesitate. There were other relatives who were no more helpful, so Daphne had to go into service as a governess."

"You must encourage her to make the most of this week, Mrs. Albrighton," Castleford said. "A life with no fun is sad, no matter how admirably virtuous it may be."

Albrighton raised one eyebrow at that. He said nothing, however, good man that he was. If Hawkeswell were here, he would immediately remark upon the peculiarity of the words "admirably virtuous" coming from a man who never admired virtue.

"I agree," Mrs. Albrighton said. "Lady Hawkeswell does as well. She and I have been plotting what to arrange. I proposed Vauxhall Gardens. I do not think Daphne has ever been there."

"Everyone should see it at least once."

"Some people think that once is more than enough," Jonathan said dryly.

"Why not invite Mrs. Joyes to go tomorrow night, if the weather is fair? You will not mind accompanying the ladies, will you, Albrighton?"

Albrighton cast Castleford a glare.

"Why not indeed? I will send a message to Verity this evening," Mrs. Albrighton said, pleased with the idea.

"I will encourage Hawkeswell to be agreeable," Castleford said. "In fact, why not make a party of it? If you would not mind my presence, and would honor me by being my guests, we can all take my barge there and have a decent meal on board, instead of pretending to enjoy their ham."

Mrs. Albrighton appeared surprised at his offer, but pleasantly so, even flattered. Her husband's gaze darkened with curiosity.

Mrs. Joyes emerged from the house then, carrying a tray laden with that lemon and honey punch. Albrighton rose to help her. Mrs. Albrighton passed around the glasses.

Castleford sipped. It was very good. Nicely tart and sweet at the same time. A bit of brandy would improve it considerably, though.

"Daphne, you will not believe what His Grace has offered," Mrs. Albrighton said. "We are all invited to use his barge tomorrow evening for a dinner party, then to visit Vauxhall Gardens as his guests."

The exquisite Mrs. Joyes smiled at her friend very sweetly. She said all the right things to thank him for his condescension. The slight tint on her cheeks, however, suggested she was extremely surprised to find herself cornered again.

A letter awaited Castleford when he returned home. It came from Mr. Edwards. He reported that the engineers and surveyors had arrived and taken over the inn at Cumberworth. He had been most firm with all of them that the women on the property in question were to be avoided and in no way importuned.

He had visited The Rarest Blooms to reassure Miss Johnson and Mrs. Hill. He estimated that work would begin immediately in the morning and promised to oversee all matters with great care. He concluded by mentioning his suspicion that the inn, in which he had slept last night, was infested top to bottom with bedbugs.

With no secretary readily available, Castleford was forced to pen his own response. He instructed Mr. Edwards to make sure the examination of the property was very thorough. The men were not to rush it in any way. Indeed, if they completed their labors in less than a fortnight, he would be forced to conclude the report could not be trusted.

He poured himself some brandy and gave orders regarding the barge and tomorrow's dinner to his steward. He then went to his chamber to work on his book.

The manuscript could not hold his attention. That was another problem with his relative sobriety these days. It was much more fun writing a guide to London brothels when one was drunk.

His mind wandered to the lovely Mrs. Joyes. He considered what he had learned of her character today and whether the revelations were of any significance.

She was a fraud, it appeared. A liar, to be blunt about it. No Captain Joyes had died in the war. That had been clear after the hour he spent in the War Office cellar with the documents Sykes had handed him. He had read the lists of dead and wounded twice to make sure he had not missed the name.

He now doubted there had ever been a Captain Joyes at all, although it was possible there was one somewhere still, alive and well. He would have to find out.

However, if he were correct, she was not a widow and perhaps had never been married.

There were reasons to lie about that, he supposed. Widowhood gave a certain protection to an independent woman. She may have also wanted an excuse to be known under another name. With family in London and about in the country, she would need a reason to give them for a different name, and marriage was the only one that worked. But why change her name at all?

It was also a way to hide one's identity and to make it hard to be found. Except she hadn't been hiding these last years. She had family in London, and she had lived in its environs.

If she wanted to hide, she would have taken herself off to someplace far away, where she might never be found. Furthermore, while she lived in Middlesex, she walked about London frequently. Finally, people chose to hide because they had done something wrong, and if she were a criminal he would lose all faith in his judgment of people.

His ruminations soon brought him to the most logical and simplest explanation. Old Becksbridge had probably insisted she adopt that name and a widow's identity. Her maiden name might raise questions if members of his family knew she lived on Becksbridge's land and enjoyed Becksbridge's patronage.

They might recognize the name of a girl who had been a governess in that household. No one would know anything about a Mrs. Joyes.

He had assumed an affair from the beginning, and this would seem to confirm it. A new annoyance with Becksbridge accompanied his conclusions. Daphne had been dependent on the duke back then. She had probably entered his service as an innocent. Her father had been the duke's friend.

Her father had also been known in the same county as Becksbridge's main estate, and there would be a scandal if the other landowners came to know of the duke's misuse of her.

Small wonder the paragon's conscience had led him to have a "committed interest" in his prey's welfare after the affair ended.

Chapter Ten

"You are early, Hawkeswell. We do not embark for half an hour," Castleford said when he noticed his first guest striding down the dock.

"It was my goal to be here when you arrived so we might have a private word. Several of them." Hawkeswell stepped off the pier and onto the barge.

Castleford continued watching the servants set up the little tents that would serve as pavilions on the far lower deck. This was not his yacht, which he kept down near the Tower and which could easily sail the open seas. Rather this large shallop served only as a pleasure craft, designed for the river, with plenty of space for the table, chairs, and settees up here above the roof of the wooden tilt, under which passengers might find shelter from the sun or rain. Only the sky would form a canopy to the dinner party up here.

Servants and crew moved about, seeing to the preparations. Several men rolled back the large canopy sometimes used up here for additional protection. Others lit the lanterns hanging around the table. This shallop had been built with a galley down below for the oarsmen and food preparation, and feet thudded on steps up and down. The crew's and servants' glances said they thought it odd His Grace was present. Normally he came late, if he came at all.

"Speak your private words, if you must," Castleford said to Hawkeswell. "I assume that you want to complain that my plans are forcing you to go to the gardens tonight. I promise to feed you well, at least."

Hawkeswell leaned against the railing and gazed at the elaborate dinner table. "It is bad enough I know what you are up to with Daphne Joyes. Making me complicit is going too far."

"It is not possible for you to be complicit in a seduction. Only two people are involved. The seducer and she whom he seduces."

Hawkeswell pointed at the table. "You are making us all complicit."

"I am not going to take her between the fish and fowl courses and expect all of you to watch, Hawkeswell. Actually, I doubt I will be so lucky as to seduce her at all tonight." He shrugged. "Unless the barge capsizes and she and I sink to the bottom of the river, where we find a secret, dry cave that we cannot leave until the tide turns." He went to the table and fractionally adjusted the position of a vase of flowers.

"What an active imagination you have. I had no idea your pickled mind came up with such vivid imagery and devices."

"If my mind were sufficiently pickled today, I would find your tone's resemblance to that of my old tutor more bearable. As it is, I can only implore you not to be insufferable all night."

Hawkeswell gave him a good, hard look. "You are sober, aren't you? I'll be damned. Have you stopped drinking for this woman?"

"You *would* put it that way. No, I have not. That glass of wine over there is mine, for example. However, if you must know, I have chosen to make sure that I enjoy her favors to the fullest when they are inevitably mine, not to be foxed senseless when I see her."

Hawkeswell appeared astonished. Impressed. Befuddled as hell. Then his eyes narrowed. "She told you she would never have you drunk, didn't she?"

"She said nothing of the kind."

"That is fine. Say no more. It is not as if you would admit it, if it were true." Hawkeswell scrutinized him like an old aunt judging an errant nephew. "So, how is it, seeing the world most days without a haze in your head? I found it an improvement, myself, after the initial shock."

"I, on the other hand, have only rediscovered how boring the world can be." It was a lie, spoken in pique at Hawkeswell's damned perspicacity. "It is livable."

Hawkeswell grinned. "Woe unto the world if you decide it is not only livable but preferable."

Castleford had no idea what that was supposed to mean. Fortunately, the conversation abruptly ended because the carriage with the ladies was arriving, with Albrighton up beside the driver.

* * *

"I heard a rumor about you this afternoon, Castleford."

Hawkeswell shared the news with a mysterious wiggling of his eyebrows.

"What rumor? I hope it was a good one."

Happy peals of laughter greeted that, as if he had displayed great wit. Daphne joined in simply because laughing felt good.

Everyone had been enjoying dinner under the stars while the boat slowly steered from one riverbank to the other and back again, in a slow meander upriver. A good deal of wine had been had, and even commonplace comments had begun to strike them as droll some time ago. Daphne admitted her own sense of humor had improved considerably in the last hour due to the warm glow induced by the unbelievably rich liquid.

She looked at Castleford, who waited for a response to his query. He appeared surprisingly unaffected by that which lubricated their revelry, but then he had more practice than most with such things.

Except, now that she thought about it, perhaps he had poured more into her glass than his own since they sat down. He had imbibed to be sure, but if she put her mind to it, she suspected he had consumed fewer glasses than his guests. Including her.

"Let me see if I can remember all of it." Hawkeswell frowned over the effort.

"I remind you that there are ladies present," Albrighton said. "Perhaps all of it is not wise?"

The ladies thought that was very funny. Verity and Celia could not contain their giggles.

"I heard that you have sent a crew of engineers and

whatnot out to some property you own somewhere, looking for gold or something," Hawkeswell rambled out.

Daphne's mirth caught in her throat. She glanced askance at Castleford. He made a dismissive gesture, deciding the gossip was not important after all.

"I have some men checking some farmland. I was advised to consider it due to discoveries nearby."

"I trust that if anything is found of value, and you form a syndicate to mine some treasure, that you will inform your friends first," Hawkeswell said.

"I do not expect anything to come of it. The enterprise is so minor that I am surprised it is grist for the rumor mill. Where did you hear about it?"

"At Brooks's. To be fair, I overheard it, but the two fellows were whispering so loudly I could not avoid it."

"Which fellows?"

"Their chairs were turned away. I could hardly go peer around to see who they were."

"You are known to have a Midas touch, Castleford. It is inevitable that your activities will attract interest, if men think money is going to be made," Albrighton said.

Castleford did not demur regarding that praise. Instead he sighed, as if this were just one more burden he carried on his privileged shoulders. "They waste their time, but it is theirs to waste. Still, it is a nuisance if my every move is noted."

Albrighton looked at him in a way that implied he saw much more than the duke ever thought he revealed. "I expect one of those engineers or whatnots spoke indiscreetly, and it got out."

Hawkeswell lost interest in the gossip as quickly as he had thought of it. He stood and offered his hand to

Verity. "If you do not mind, Castleford, I think that I will take a turn around the deck with my wife and enjoy the night sky before we arrive at the gardens and face the noisy crowds."

The two of them wandered off and soon became a single silhouette fading away. Celia looked at Jonathan. A slow smile on his face responded to a teasing one on hers, then they were gone without even taking their leave.

Daphne craned her neck this way and that to see either couple. She was dismayed that her friends had abandoned her, sitting on an upholstered settee next to Castleford, whom they knew could never be trusted.

"You will not see them," he said. "They have strolled toward the stern. There are little pavilions there, done up like Arabic tents."

"I think that perhaps I will take a turn as well and see these pavilions too."

"I do not advise it, unless you want to witness true marital bliss."

She was half standing before she comprehended his implications. She froze and looked at him. "I am sure that they are not . . ."

"I would lay odds they are. I know Hawkeswell from well before he reformed, and one of the joys of marriage is that one can be bad again. As for Albrighton, he ignores rules that are inconvenient to his goals."

She was about to argue when she remembered the gaze Jonathan and Celia had exchanged and Celia's private smile. The notion that her friends were in the dark back there, engaging in "marital bliss," dismayed her.

She sat again and eyed Castleford suspiciously. "Is that why the lanterns are only on this end of the barge? You are a very thoughtful host."

"I was thinking only of myself. I hoped that deep shadows beneath a starlit summer sky would lure them away from us. Lo and behold, they have."

She set her gaze at the remnants of wine in her glass. If she had not had more than was wise, perhaps she would be indignant and outraged and would pointedly discourage him from any seductive intentions.

Unfortunately, the warmth provoked by the wine and the happy laughter of the night only made her weak to the inexplicable appeal of this man. Even the knowledge that he was dangerous to women and represented potentially serious trouble for her in particular only managed to titillate her right now.

She turned her attention to the front of the barge. In the distance, beyond the bend of the river, she was sure she could see some of the lanterns of Vauxhall Gardens twinkling like tiny stars.

"We should probably head upriver now," she suggested. "We will never get there if we keep going back and forth like this."

"We will arrive soon enough. I do not want to rush our mutual friends. Do you?"

She was trying hard not to imagine what their friends were doing, let alone estimate how long it would take. Scandalous images wanted to enter her mind of how they were doing it too. Were there even beds back there?

She felt herself flushing. Out of the corner of her eye she could see Castleford turned toward her slightly on the rather small settee, his head propped on his hand and his elbow propped on the table.

He watched her ever so calmly—almost, it seemed, with consideration—and she would be hard-pressed to identify anything particularly threatening about him. He appeared quite sane and not even especially seductive. His attention might be that of any host to a guest left to her own devices by friends who forgot their duty to her.

All the same, her instincts screamed that she would be wise to run away—if only there were someplace to run to. She felt him there, felt his proximity and gaze, and she noted with alarm the sensations sparkling inside her.

"I have something for you," he said. "A small gift."

She turned to him, surprised. "I do not think—"

"Hush." He took her hand and held it palm side up. He dropped something small and hard in it. The candlelight caught the item, and a new star was born in the night.

He had just dropped a diamond in her hand. A good-size one.

"Of the finest clarity, as you demanded," he said.

"I did not demand any—" She lost the path of her thought. She had to pick up the stone and hold it to the light. The clarity astonished her. But for all its brilliance, the human warmth of his hand on hers distracted her more.

His touch felt so good, so intimate and human. She should withdraw her hand, but she did not. The careful, firm support seemed protective. What would it feel like to turn her hand, so it was palm on palm?

She placed the diamond on the table. The dancing candle flame made its surface flash. "I cannot accept it. You know that I cannot."

His other hand reached toward the stone. The move angled his body closer to her. His long fingers turned the diamond, almost absently, while he looked at it. She gazed at it too, keeping her eyes averted from that face and that dangerous appeal.

"What are you afraid of, Mrs. Joyes? If I thought to buy you, I could do better than this."

Tonight the implied proposition charmed her more than irritated her. No doubt that was the wine again.

He angled closer yet. "Is it scandal that you fear? I think not. You are too self-possessed to worry overmuch about it, and you are unlikely to be indiscreet enough to be a victim of it."

"I do not fear scandal so much anymore. When I was young it terrified me. Ruled me. However, maturity brings a new perspective to such matters."

"Then what is it that you fear?"

"Do not pretend that you do not know."

"A week ago I would have said you were afraid of me, but now I am wondering if perhaps you fear yourself instead."

She dared not turn her head, because he would see her surprise at his insight. He was also too close now, so close that his breath feathered her ear. He turned her hand on his own and stretched his fingers between hers so he held her fast.

Her own breath jumped around inside her, not knowing where to go. She wanted to close her eyes and relish the lovely stirrings in her body.

"I am not afraid of you." Not truly. Not in the sense that he might physically harm her.

Right now, tonight, with the stars above and the breeze teasing her, with the wine making her lighthearted and with romance in the air, the many reasons for resisting his temptation seemed part of a different, distant world.

"Perhaps it is pleasure itself that you fear and the loss of your careful composure." The words whispered in her ear, so low they might be her own thoughts. His breath, so close, became an irresistible tease.

And still the barge floated back and forth. It would continue doing so until he signaled otherwise, she knew. Her friends would not return either until that happened. They would continue indulging in marital bliss, moved by the wine and the night and the stars and their love, until the barge clearly turned to go upriver.

The deep, sensual purr inside her overwhelmed attempts to scold herself. A subversive notion entered her thoughts instead—that he would lose interest once he won his game, and therefore surrender might not be so foolish. That her resistance only intensified his pursuit. But more than anything, a poignant ache made her weak and unable to remember why she had to deny herself.

A kiss most discreet, on her hand. A small thing, yet it shook her to her essence. Another, on her shoulder, and a hand sliding her shawl down before one more scorched the skin there. He embraced her shoulders and kissed again, this time the crook of her neck.

Heaven help her, she savored every sensation. She closed her eyes so she could revel totally. Further kisses on her neck, on her skin and hair, did glorious things to her, unbearably wonderful things. The wine had demolished her best defenses, and these small lures too easily breached what was left.

She did not resist when his embrace lowered and drew her closer nor when his kisses claimed her mouth. She was glad the pleasure did not sweep her away to some unearthly realm, because she ached to feel everything. She dwelled on the warm, dry pressure of his lips and relished how inner shudders flowed down her body.

Misgivings could not survive such a sensual onslaught.

They sank beneath a euphoria born of intimacy and delight and pleasure. Astonishing pleasure. With each sensation more powerful than the last, pleasure stole her breath and made her hunger for more.

Her lover knew what he was about. That small thought entered her mind as she submitted to the art of those kisses, to the way he used his mouth and tongue and even his teeth. It intruded once more when he began to caress her. His hands knew just what to do, just how to move. She waited for the masculine press against her body, and her wanton desire impatiently urged more scandalous touches.

His caress moved up her side, skimming the outer swell of her breast. A jolt of excitement drenched with anticipation shot through her, then lowered and pooled in shocking places. The caress smoothed over until he cupped her breast, and delirium descended. He withheld what she wanted for a torturous minute, so long that she wanted to weep or curse him. Finally, finally, the caress she craved sent shimmers through her body.

She luxuriated in the thrills and the ruthless way he drove her mad. The pleasure grew more intense with each touch. She sensed all control slipping from her grasp as her awareness constricted to her body and his aura and the abandon crying for completion.

Dazed now, existing in a sensual stupor, she could only follow when he stood and guided her by the hand away from the table and settee and down some stairs. In the dark, on the side deck, the lanterns barely illuminated the spot where he stopped beside a pier of the tilt house. The silhouette of one pavilion could be seen near the stern.

You must stop him now, because he will not stop

later. The warning barely whispered in her mind. Tonight it sounded like a lesson memorized to no purpose,
not some hard-won truth. He pressed her against the pier
and passionately kissed her neck and demolished the
small foothold her common sense had managed to find.

He set her arms to her sides and took her two breasts
in his hands. Despite her garments, his touch found the
tips and teased until she would not have stood but for the
wall at her back. She could not believe what it did to her,
the way desire taunted her to distraction.

She opened her eyes so she might not go insane from
it. The light from the nearest lantern made him barely
visible to her, but she saw his face, taut and hard, while
he watched her.

Firmly, he turned her so she hugged the wall. He covered her with his body, and his arm circled her shoulder.
His hand slid below her dress's edge so he touched her
naked breast.

She had thought it could not be worse, but now she
truly suffered from pleasure. Her body silently cried and
begged and screamed. He caressed her freely, shockingly, everywhere, her hips and bottom and thighs, while
his body pressed hers and his hardness taunted her even
more.

A new coolness flowed on her legs. She realized her
skirt was rising. Higher now. The shock gave her a jolt
of sobriety. She looked over her shoulder, alarmed.

"No," he said quietly. "Not here, although later tonight
I will be cursing my deference to your need for discretion
and privacy."

"Perhaps I will be too," she muttered. The bottom of
her dress was at her thighs now. The wickedness of that

rising hem made her shiver with anticipation, even with his reassurance that this would not go too far.

Suddenly his hand was on her down there again, beneath all her garments, skin on skin, stroking her thigh, and higher.

"You will be cursing no one, I promise. If anyone suffers for this inopportune passion, it will be me. Again."

His hand firmly followed the curve of her bottom, startling her. The anticipation became a yearning throb. She was in much deeper than she expected, and her vulnerability alarmed her.

Castleford stepped closer, so he pressed her to the wall, his one hand tantalizing her breast and the other caressing her bottom in the narrow space between them. "You will do as I say now. You will move one foot to the side a bit. Then you will let pleasure have its way with you and not deny yourself or me the experience of that wildness."

He touched her then, before she even absorbed what he said. Touched her so intimately that she gasped. She moved her leg as he had commanded, allowing a new exposure. Then he stroked her so effectively that she barely swallowed a moan.

She surrendered completely. She had no choice, no will, no desire to stop any of it. His odd embrace kept her standing or else she would have collapsed, she was sure. She could not feel her legs or anything except the excruciating tease at her breasts and the exquisitely carnal demand that intensified until she wanted to beg for mercy.

Something broke in her, split and burst. Deep where he touched a painful barrier fell, and a new pleasure crashed through her. The shock made her essence scream, first with shock, then with relief. The waters of that flood were so beautiful that she had the urge to weep. They filled her so completely that for a timeless spell nothing else existed.

She could not speak afterwards. She had no strength. He turned her into his embrace and held her, and she huddled against him while her heartbeat gradually slowed.

His head turned, and she looked where he did. A thick shadow moved toward them, and she heard Verity's quiet conversation with Hawkeswell on the breeze.

Castleford led her through the dark, back up to the table and the lanterns, all but carrying her as if she was too infirm to manage her own limbs. He sat her down on the settee.

She heard steps coming closer and collected herself. She looked to her dress and readjusted the skewed bodice. She looked at him anxiously. "How do I appear? Normal?"

He laughed quietly. "I fear you look like a beautiful woman who has just been overwhelmed by pleasure."

That would never do. She closed her eyes and, before Verity arrived back at the table, she found something of herself, of the Daphne she knew, even though the other one she had met tonight was much more exciting.

Chapter Eleven

Castleford could not believe that once again he had been thwarted, only this time by his own unaccountable impulse to spare a woman's sense of delicacy.

He took some solace in having driven Daphne Joyes to ecstasy. However, his failure to achieve the same bliss suggested he would soon dislike Vauxhall Gardens as much as he currently did not favor flowers. It did not help that Hawkeswell and Albrighton appeared smugly contented when they strolled back from the stern of the barge.

By the time the shallop pulled over and they all walked up the steps, Castleford had recovered physically, but an irritable humor had settled on him. Fortunately, the ladies occupied themselves in exclaiming over the sights and musicians and the fireworks that soon commenced. He therefore did not have to converse much with anyone.

"You seem out of sorts," Hawkeswell said an hour later while they trailed Albrighton and the ladies.

"It is nothing that two fingers of brandy will not fix."

"Ah. I understand. I remember that happening, now that you mention it. When I stopped getting raving drunk three times a week, I would sometimes find myself suddenly in a bad humor too."

"I must have a stronger constitution. I find it hardly affects me and does not account for my moods at all." That was not entirely true, but it was now. "If I am in a bad humor, it is not because of lack of drink. I merely said drink would cure it."

Hawkeswell paced on. "I believe, then, that apologies are perhaps due for spiriting off my wife like that. Did you and Mrs. Joyes have a row while we were gone?"

Castleford took a deep breath to rein in his impatience. "Do not apologize for going off. The pavilions were put there for that purpose. My only regret is that I did not have three set up."

"You mean Albrighton . . ."

"Yes."

Hawkeswell thought about that. "I fear that we denied you your cave below the river. However, with all of us gone, you had the rest of the barge to yourself. The lack of a pavilion on one of your floating dens of pleasure has never stopped you before."

"Hell, she isn't a whore, you ass. I am hardly going to bend her over the railing."

Hawkeswell did not like being insulted and had a quick temper that now prickled. "You have never worried about such niceties before. Can you swear that no woman of gentle breeding has ever found herself stripped naked under that barge's canopy in full daylight, let alone in the dark of night?"

Castleford marched on, thinking that a good bout of fisticuffs was just what his mood wanted, and that Hawkeswell's nose was asking for a punch.

"No answer, I see," Hawkeswell taunted. "You had better be careful, Castleford. Mrs. Joyes may be making you *boring.*"

"Not so boring that I won't thrash someone senseless in the middle of Vauxhall Gardens."

"Hell, you have never been able to thrash me senseless, even when your dissolution had not yet sapped your better strength. But if it will make you feel better about your intended conquest bringing you to your knees, take your chance."

"Thrashing? Gentlemen, gentlemen—that will never do."

Hawkeswell stopped in his tracks and turned to look at the man that had just chided them. Castleford stopped too, but he did not bother to look. He recognized the voice.

Fate was conspiring against him tonight. That it should do so on a day when he had shown uncharacteristic consideration toward a woman, much to his own inconvenience, seemed very unfair.

"Hell, Latham, did the French teach you to eavesdrop?" Hawkeswell snapped.

"One does not have to eavesdrop to hear two men having a loud argument."

Castleford sighed and turned around. The Earl of Latham, now the Duke of Becksbridge, beamed a bright smile. His expression said *Here I am. I know that every-*

one wants to welcome me back. Isn't it wonderful to see me again?

The exaggerated bonhomie did not become him. Latham's face had always been a bit soft and given to ruddiness, and living in Paris had taken its toll. So his bright blue eyes, which tended toward glassiness even when sober, peered out like two shallow pools sunk in a rosy sand landscape. His tawny, sedately dressed hair formed some surrounding brush.

"Latham," Castleford said. "I had no idea that paragons of virtue visited Vauxhall Gardens. Isn't it a sin to enjoy yourself?"

Latham laughed, as if it had been a joke. "I came to witness people of all classes mixing freely, enjoying their commonalities. As for paragons of virtue, I cannot claim to be one, but my uncle the bishop is here with me, along with his wife, so I trust there is no sin in it."

"Only one of your family's bishops is here?" Hawkeswell said. "Makes one wonder what the other one is doing."

"Perhaps he is enjoying a quiet evening of marital bliss," Castleford said.

Hawkeswell craned his neck to look over the crowd. "We should find the ladies and relieve Albrighton."

"You go. I will join you soon."

Latham's smile grew sardonic with Hawkeswell's departure. "I have a supper box. Come join me for some wine."

The boxes were not far away, and Latham's was near the end of the row. The bishop and his wife had left, so they had the box to themselves.

Castleford stretched his length on the chair and looked out at the passing crowd that in turn looked in at him.

Latham poured some wine. It tasted off. The man had no taste, among other deficiencies. Castleford set the glass on the table.

"What are you really doing here, Latham? Looking for a servant to grab and rape on a dark path?"

Latham's lids lowered. "Are you still fussing like an old lady about that, after all these years? I told you long ago that you misunderstood what you saw."

"I misunderstood nothing, or the way that girl ran for her life when I pulled you off her."

"She was embarrassed, that is all. She wanted it. You know how it goes. She came back for more later, after all."

Castleford did not need to hear that. He did not want to know that his silence on what he saw had left that girl vulnerable to more of the same.

"I hear that you did not attend my father's funeral," Latham said.

"Nor did you. Too busy settling your affairs in Paris?"

"An unavoidable matter delayed me a few days, and it is best to bury quickly in summer. I was at the reading of the will, of course."

"Of course."

"And so, also of course, I am aware that my father left you a bequest." He cocked his head. "How odd."

Castleford shrugged. "I took it as a very small token of his very small affection."

Latham laughed. "Rather like damning with faint praise, eh? *I have remembered you in my will, and this is what I remember your being worth.*"

"Of course, he could not do the same with you. He could not keep you from the bulk of it, no matter what he thought you were worth." Castleford gathered his limbs and sat forward. He gave Latham a good look. "Did you get anything that was not yours by entailment? Or did he make sure it went elsewhere, with these small bequests?"

Latham's face flushed. His eyes glinted. "Of course he left me more. Among other things, he left me his power."

Castleford laughed heartily. "Damn, you sound like the villain in a bad comic opera, Latham. *His power*. The only power you will have is what your birth always gave you, and the only people who will tremble in awe are the servants you treat like slaves."

"Perhaps you are right. I have discovered the might of the pen, however. Words are so much more efficient in their influence when published. It is astonishing, really, how easily people can be led by prose that appeals to their sense of their own righteousness."

Latham spoke bluntly, the way they had always spoken with each other. He admitted his hypocrisy with impunity to the only person with whom he had ever truly revealed himself.

Castleford sensed an effort here to re-form those old bonds. Maybe Latham found it lonely to have to play a role with the world and wanted a fellow sinner available again, so he might be offstage on occasion.

"So you pander to what people want to hear and read and call it moral philosophy," Castleford said.

"I do not call it that. If others do, I cannot stop them."

"What do you call it?"

"Fun. A wonderful joke. A game to see how many sheep will follow and just how far they will go with me. I have entertained myself to no end the last few years, Tristan. While I wield my pen, I often think of you and how you will howl with laughter when you read the treatise."

Unfortunately, he was the only one laughing. Others took this fool seriously.

Castleford had already accepted that he was going to have to exercise his own power more regularly now, just to make sure that Latham did not accumulate too much influence in the government. What a bloody bore that would be. The reemergence of this man promised to be a tedious nuisance all around.

"I saw you walking by with Hawkeswell and that other man. The three ladies with you were notably beautiful," Latham said. "I think that I recognized two of them."

Castleford waited and said nothing. Latham had seen them walk by, and these two women were the reason why he followed, apparently. How ordinary.

"The golden haired one, the shorter blonde—isn't she that Northrope whore's daughter?" Latham asked.

"She is married now."

"Pity. I offered for her, back when her mother was hawking her like a prize calf. The bitch of a whore would not hear me, because she had some fool of a boy in mind."

More likely Mrs. Northrope sensed the character of the Earl of Latham. "She never entered her mother's trade, and her husband would not hesitate to kill you if you insulted her. I am not joking, Latham."

Latham seemed to accept the wisdom of not pursuing Mrs. Albrighton. "The other one—the tall fair woman. I am sure I know her too."

Castleford ignored the prompt. He'd be damned before he encouraged this turn in the conversation.

"People change with the years, and she has matured, but I think that is Miss Avonleah. She was a governess for my father's young girls after I had left the household."

"I know her only as Mrs. Joyes."

"I am sure that it is the same woman, although I have not seen her in—well, it must be eight or nine years now." Latham speared him with a quizzical stare. "Is she your mistress? Or was she the intended conquest Hawkeswell spoke of?"

"She is a friend of Lady Hawkeswell and not my mistress. As for a conquest, she is too refined and reserved for me."

Latham laughed lewdly. "That is right, I forgot. You like them vulgar, fast, cheap, and willing, Tristan." He sipped more wine. "Unless they are vulnerable, sweet, and criminal instead."

"I am in no mood for your poor attempts at being sly, Latham. Nor for this odd pretense that we still have a friendship and that I will not mind your addressing me by my Christian name the way you did when we were boys. You are bold to make even that oblique reference to Marie. You are even bolder to return to England with that on your head."

"I had to return, but that business would not have stopped me anyway. I stole from a thief, at worst, if you insist on being meticulous. As it turned out, I also sold her a few extra months of life."

"You remained silent when you knew where the money was going."

"Hell, you have always made too much of that too. Her friends were never going to succeed in funding an army. She was on a fool's errand, and at worst I fleeced a spy." He smiled his old smile and tried to look appeasing. "Let us not talk of it. I would much rather learn about the lovely Miss Avonleah—your Mrs. Joyes. I vaguely remember her as a pretty girl, but she is a stunning woman.

Rarely does maturity suit a female so well. I am relieved for my own sake that you have not put your brand or set your sights on her."

The night's collective annoyances crystallized in that instant. Castleford came very close to breaking the wine bottle over Latham's head. While he restrained himself, the notion entered his head that if Latham did pursue Daphne Joyes, a good reason would inevitably be found to call him out one day. God knew the world would be better for it.

If you ever get the chance, kill him, Tristan.

"Try for her if you dare," he said lazily. "She is known as a very proud woman, however. Formidable, she is called. Not your sort, really. Not at all helpless."

Latham thought that was very funny. He grinned into his wine while he drank.

Castleford decided he had suffered the man's company too long. That he had been subjected to this tête-à-tête only because Daphne had caught the blackguard's eye did nothing for his mood.

Just as he was about to take his leave, the lovely woman in question strolled by with the rest of his party. Latham noticed. He hailed Hawkeswell, who did not know better and came over. Introductions ensued.

Latham paused a five count on meeting Jonathan Albrighton. His attempt to place the face if not the name produced a frown but ultimately failed. Latham then turned his charm and eloquence on the ladies one by one, and finally on the object of his interest.

Daphne Joyes did not react much at all to the new duke's recollection of her service in his father's house. She did nothing to reveal her dislike of the man, either. Instead Castleford watched her smile in that cool, distant,

utterly composed manner she could assume, while her
gray eyes looked through Latham as if he were made of
glass.

Seeing Latham was, Daphne decided, a hideous ending to a glorious night.

Punishment, that's what it was.

She had barely experienced Vauxhall Gardens due to
her sensual daze. Even as she talked with her friends and
listened to the music, even while she strolled the grounds
and watched the crowds, the entire place appeared like a
magical world just out of reach, not quite real.

It was all pleasure's fault. Shocking, extreme pleasure. Long after the physical effects had faded—and it
took a good while for that to happen—the mist on her
senses had not lifted.

That all shattered when she heard the voice calling
Hawkeswell. She looked toward the call, and reality
slammed into her hard. There, in one of the dining boxes,
sat Latham. And beside him, sprawled on a chair that
was not inclined to accommodate such relaxation, was
Castleford.

They had been drinking wine together, she noticed
when Hawkeswell dragged them all over there. Castleford
did not appear especially pleased by whatever Latham
had been saying, but then, now that she had the clarity to
think about it, he had not appeared in good humor ever
since they left the barge.

She tried not to see Latham during the introductions.
She pretended he was not really there even while she responded to his recollections about meeting before. She

sought sanctuary in her poise, because she would be damned before she let the man glimpse evidence of the visceral reaction churning inside her.

"Do you live in town now, Mrs. Joyes?" Latham asked. "I vaguely remember your moving north when you left the girls."

"My husband's regiment was in the north."

"Mrs. Joyes is only visiting London," Castleford said. "She lives in the country. Kent, I believe, Mrs. Joyes?"

A few of their party exchanged curious glances at that, but none corrected him. Daphne only tipped her head in what might be seen as a gesture of assent.

Verity made reference to completing their promenade. Castleford left the box to join them. No one invited Latham.

Daphne turned, grateful to escape. It was not to be, unfortunately.

"Mrs. Joyes," Latham said, claiming her attention as they began walking away.

She turned back. She felt her party drifting away. All except Castleford, who remained near.

"Mrs. Joyes, I look forward to seeing you again before your visit in town ends," Latham said.

"How generous of you, sir."

He smiled. His shallow blue eyes sparkled with flirtatious appreciation. He bowed. And looked at her in a way that made her heart sink.

It was all there in his gaze, the memories from years ago and the interest now. The awareness that she knew more than he cared anyone to know. The rapaciousness that had no honor and accepted no laws.

She refused to join in this darker recognition. She left

him as if he were a stranger. She turned on her heel and marched away, passing Castleford without ceremony, putting distance between herself and that supper box.

A hand on her arm urged her to slow down. Castleford fell into step beside her. She continued to look straight ahead.

"You know about him, don't you?" he said.

"I don't know what you mean."

"I think that you do. More than dislike is written on your face right now. You are in high color in the worst way, for the worst reason."

She did not doubt it. She was truly distressed. Embarrassed and furious at the same time. Each step made it worse, not better.

"A month before I left Becksbridge's house, a girl, a servant, confided in me. She worked in the kitchen," she said. "A pretty, young, innocent girl. She had been full of joy. Then, suddenly, she became so melancholy that we feared for her health."

She stopped and looked Castleford in the eyes. "He had forced her. She showed me bruises that even days later had not faded. I had been suspicious of him, but I knew then for certain. So, yes, I know about him. And I do not understand how you, or anyone else, could ever call such a rogue a friend."

She strode on. Once more that hand took her arm. This time he guided her out of the crowd's flow. He escorted her this way and that, until they were in the paths known to hide lovers and clandestine meetings. Few lanterns lit this wooded area, and long shadows kept one's identity obscure.

He stopped her in one of those shadows and took her face in both his hands. A kiss, hard at first, almost cruel.

Then softer, and sweet with care. Memories from the barge poured into her. They left little room for her anger about Latham to remain.

He turned her in his arm, and they strolled in the dark.

"Imagine for me, if you can, that you were born the first son of a duke," he said.

"I dare not. I would be spoiled just picturing the indulgence I would have to suffer."

"Indulgence enough. But also, as soon as you could speak, lessons and preparation. Not for a minute are you allowed to forget the station waiting. Everyone treats you differently. Even your tutor defers to you. Then you go off to school, and it is worse with the dons and the beadles and with the other boys. Even sons of earls curry your favor and friendship because of who you will be one day."

"Not Hawkeswell, surely. Not Lord Sebastian."

"It took me a good long while to accept neither had ulterior motives. Years. It was not anything I blamed people for. It simply was the way it was. I expected it. Even now I do."

She wondered what that was like, to always assume gestures of friendship were the giving that anticipated a larger taking.

"Latham, however, was just like me," he said. "Is it any wonder we became friends as boys? Our alliance was of no special benefit to either one of us. We would never have cause to seek each other's patronage. Since we would both be dukes, we did not have to play the future duke with each other either."

She did not want to accept what he said. She preferred to believe that Latham's character would be obvious even so. Except she knew it would not be. Almost the whole world still did not comprehend what he was. It had even taken her a long time to see the truth.

"When did you know the friendship would not last?"

He shrugged. "I sensed it by the time I reached my majority. We had wallowed together in hell by then. He insisted on labored discretion, because of his father he said, and those bishop uncles. But that gave him a freedom that he used ignobly. I found some of his actions increasingly distasteful. He took pleasure in the worst kinds of badness." He paused, then spoke more thoughtfully. "He took pleasure in being cruel. To horses, to people. He showed no conscience about it."

"And now he is a duke, and he can be cruel and no one will gainsay him. Small wonder he appeared so happy tonight."

They reached the end of the path. Lanterns beckoned ahead and the noise of the gardens flowed in a low din.

"He seemed much taken by you," he said. "He sought me out to learn who you were for certain."

"I wish he had not seen me or learned my name now." She fought to keep fear from her tone, but the idea that Latham now knew her name terrified her. "I do not think he was much taken at all. He guesses I know the truth about him. He does not like the fact that I am friends with people whose opinions may matter."

"Perhaps that is all it is. Perhaps not. If he pursues you, you must tell me."

She laughed. "There are men who might be rivals for you, Castleford, but he is not one of them."

"All the same, you must tell me."

They sought out the rest of their party and headed back

to the stairs. Castleford hailed the barge, which waited down the riverbank.

Celia gave Daphne a knowing look as they stepped onto the deck. "You do know he is nothing but trouble," she said privately.

Daphne thought she meant Latham, and was about to agree. Then she realized her friend had drawn conclusions about her time alone tonight with Castleford.

Celia tipped her head closely. "Although, it is said, he gives his lovers magnificent gifts, so if one is of a mind to be foolish—well, my mother always said one can court scandal with a rich man as well as a poor one."

The mention of gifts made Daphne's gaze dart to the table. She went up to the dinner table and peered down. No sparkles flashed near where she had sat. She wondered if the diamond had rolled onto the floor, or if one of the servants or crew had taken it.

"I have it." Castleford stood at her shoulder. "I took it back, to have it set. Ear bobs, I have decided. That means it needs a mate."

"I do not need diamond ear bobs. I do not want you to do this."

"I know. But you will have them anyway, so I can see you in them—and nothing else, I might add. You can sell them afterwards, if you want."

Afterwards.

Never let it be said that the Duke of Castleford did not make his intentions clear. All of them.

Chapter Twelve

The weather turned hot the next day. So hot that Castleford, while he lay abed the next morning, actually entertained the notion of going down to the country.

That was peculiar. He loathed the country.

Only this time, if he went, he would take Daphne. They could make love in the lake. He had never found that notion appealing before, but imagining her naked and slicked with water was changing his thinking on it.

His mind was full of such images when the mail came up with his coffee. He flipped through the letters, stacking them against his naked chest while he sipped. He decided they could all wait for Mr. Edwards's return. At the bottom of the pile, however, he found a fat letter from Mr. Edwards himself.

It would hardly do to hand the man his own letter to answer, so he tore it open. Four pages unfolded.

After beginning with aggrieved complaints about bed-bugs, Edwards moved on to a lengthy, boring, exacting description of the engineers' progress.

At the bottom of the third page, the tone and penman-ship changed. Mr. Edwards broke off his report abruptly, then scrawled with visible agitation that a stranger had just been seen on the property, spying on the house. He had given chase to no avail—his words managed to con-vey his breathlessness from the run—but he worried now about the ladies, if this enterprise had attracted attention to the point where strangers trespassed.

He begged His Grace to advise him on what to do with this dangerous complication that jeopardized both the privacy of His Grace's business and the safety of the women he had been commanded to protect.

He closed by saying he was writing from the ladies' house, where he had taken position in the front chamber, pistol at the ready, and asked whether he should write and inform Mrs. Joyes of this development.

The last words made Castleford sit up straight and curse.

He set aside the coffee tray and threw back the sheet. He went to his writing desk and penned a reply without bothering to don a robe.

He exhorted Mr. Edwards to of course do what was necessary to protect the ladies but to also exercise good sense. He suggested that Mr. Edwards remain at the house in the future and allow the men to report on their progress there. He explained that this stranger probably represented no real danger. He assured his secretary that he had every faith in his judgment and courage but that it would probably be best not to shoot anyone if it could be avoided.

He closed by writing that under no circumstance was Mrs. Joyes to be worried about this matter, lest she feel obliged to return home to brandish a pistol as well.

Trusting that he had averted the two disasters of Mr. Edwards being tried for murder and Mrs. Joyes departing London, Castleford then penned a letter to the lady herself.

He forced himself to add enough words to make it look gracious and not too brief. Then he informed her that he required her presence at another meeting regarding her property. Would she be good enough to indulge him and attend one tomorrow at five o'clock?

He sealed both letters and gave them to one of his valets. Content that his day's work was done, he went back to bed.

A hot August day has a way of burning through illusions. So it was that while Daphne woke the next morning still in a daze—due to shockingly explicit dreams involving her, Castleford, and a bed made out of a huge diamond—she felt very much her old self by the time she finished her breakfast. Decidedly so. Somewhat sadly so.

Sitting in the late morning light pouring through her chamber window, she assessed what had happened the night before and spared herself not at all.

She had imbibed too much wine. She would like to claim Castleford had pressed it on her as part of his plot, but nevertheless, she had, of her own free will, drunk sufficiently to abandon all good sense.

True, a different man might have refused to take advantage of her condition, but this was Castleford, for heaven's sake. It was a miracle he had not ravished her while she stood against that wall.

She could not ignore that, while he had unaccountably not ravished her, what he had done had convinced him that she was his to ravish in the future. That business about wearing diamond bobs and nothing else—it was not so much that he had said it but rather how he had said it. Calmly, frankly, as if it were inevitable. As if he had a right to her now.

When the mail arrived, she eagerly looked through it, hoping for a return letter from Margaret. Her spirits sagged when there was nothing from the north.

Perhaps she should just make that journey uninvited and hope for the best. She might have given Margaret pause by mentioning the past. This visit had become more of a necessity with each passing day to make sure that people dear to her were protected. The way emotions kept running higher about the trouble up there only increased her worry.

She flipped past two letters from writers she did not recognize. They appeared to be invitations. She wondered who would be inviting her to anything.

Then she found the letter from Castleford himself.

Very gracious, very polite, and containing only the barest allusion to last night's intimacy (he had delighted in seeing her "freely enjoy her own high spirits" during the party), he finally mentioned that, by the by, they needed to meet tomorrow about her property.

She set the letter down and wondered how long it took a jeweler to make diamond ear bobs.

*   *   *

D aphne went out later that morning to meet with one of the stewards who had written about contracting for plants. She did not return until one o'clock. Having concluded that she could not avoid the meeting with Castleford, she penned a response and told him she would attend. She politely declined the two invitations from hostesses whom she had never met. Then she wrote another note to Celia and sent it off too.

She was just sealing Celia's letter when a footman arrived to announce that a caller waited below. No card had been sent up. Instead the footman bore a nosegay of yellow roses and a letter.

Ten minutes, no more, I promise, was all the letter said. It was signed *Latham*.

She set the flowers aside to wilt and contemplated this request for a visit. After debating it every which way, she decided she should discover what the man had on his mind. Not a pursuit, the way Castleford expected. She was almost certain of that. Even Latham could not be that conceited.

She found him below in the drawing room. During their greetings, she gave him a better examination than she had last night.

Nine years changed any person, but it particularly affected men if it spanned the end of their youth and the beginning of maturity. She noted that the slight softness in Latham's face had ceased being the remnants of his boyhood and become instead the evidence of a man who indulged his appetites. Still, most women would find him attractive, even handsome, she admitted. They would also find his sedate dress and hair and his easy, amiable charm reassuring and comforting. Thus did wolves hide in sheep's clothing.

"Miss Avonleah—excuse me, Mrs. Joyes now—I had to call."

"How did you know where I was staying?"

"I had but to ask around. Society is aware of your visit in this house. I hope that you do not mind that I did ask and sought you out."

"I am not pleased. Last night was unavoidable for me. This was not."

He smiled politely, but merriment at her formality showed in his eyes. "Seeing you astonished me. I never thought I would again. Also, I confess it made me nostalgic for those years when I was much younger, and my father's household was my second home still."

Did he think that was humorous? Or, heaven forbid, that seeing him had made her nostalgic too? "It is your home completely now, so you can indulge your nostalgia daily. Will you be going down to the country again for that purpose?"

"I do not think so, not soon at least. I have been asked to stay in town. Liverpool thinks I may be needed."

Already he had insinuated himself into the highest ranks of influence. She found that dismaying. Of course, he was a duke now. Probably all of them were needed in times of trouble, if they were of a mind to heed England's call.

"I assume that Lord Liverpool has read your essays, if he favors you now."

"He has read them. Have you? Did you find them at all inspiring or useful?"

"I found them humorous, coming from you. Let us not pretend that you do not know why."

He acknowledged that he did know why with a vague bow of his head and a boyish smile that feigned a degree

of chagrin. He probably thought that little gesture of embarrassment apology enough for his youthful sins.

She suspected he had practiced the expression in the
looking glass for just those occasions when someone mentioned they knew a great deal more about him than he
wanted remembered.

He did not appear inclined to say only a few words
and then quickly leave. She in turn felt obligated to sit,
so he could make it a proper call. Ten minutes the note
had said. He would not get eleven.

"I was not aware that you had married, Daphne."

She marked his change of tone. And the way he used
her Christian name. And the way he looked at her. His
attempt at intimacy was bold and insulting, but perhaps
she should have expected it.

She remembered how he used to slyly flirt with her
when he visited his father's house. Being young and lonely,
she had actually found that charming, even flattering. She
later blamed herself for the kisses and intimacy that followed, but after years of doing so she had come to realize
how dishonorably he had behaved. No one, not even she,
would claim it had been like that poor scullery maid, of
course. Her gentle birth had spared her that.

"It was commonly known in your father's household
that I married. Probably no one thought it worth mentioning to you."

"I would have expected my father to do so."

"Servants come and go, and their lives are not fodder
for drawing room discussions."

"You were not just a servant."

"Actually, that was all I ever was. Your father and his
wife indulged my pride in small ways, but in the end I
was no better than a scullery maid to your family and

would have received similar consideration in all things, if not for my connections to the county where you have your country estate."

His smile fell at the comparison she used. His pale eyes lost more color. He speared her with a curious, almost cautious gaze.

"Do you still visit the county?" he asked. "I have not been back long enough to call on any of the old families."

"I correspond with a few of them." She told him some of the events in those lives from the last few years. She made sure he understood that the daughter of one of that county's gentlemen would still be heard and received by some of Becksbridge's neighbors.

He listened as if she made small talk, but she trusted she had made her point. When she was done, he smiled in a too-familiar way, as if he had not understood her meaning at all.

"You are so formal now," he said. "Not the happy girl I remember. I confess that I was hoping last night's coolness was only surprise at work. And discretion."

His boldness astonished her. "I am happy enough, but no longer a girl. No longer ignorant of the world. No longer innocent and not nearly so trusting."

"That is perhaps for the best. And as a widow, you understand what men are about now, don't you?"

She could hardly believe her ears. She worried that he was going to fulfill Castleford's prediction and say something stupid now, and that this inappropriate turn in the conversation might be the prelude to a proposition. Surely he could not be that much a rogue.

"Yes, whether they are honorable or not, I know what men are about. Just as I know about the protection that privilege gives some men, if they are such scoundrels as to exploit their stations."

He looked at her, not pleased and, she hoped, at least a bit concerned. She looked right back. She wanted him to know that she now understood what *he* was about. She wanted him to worry that she might share it with others.

"Will you be in town long?" he asked.

"A week or so, no more."

"Then you will return to . . ." It became a question.

She chose to let his words dangle there.

Silence ensued. He finally gathered his gloves and hat and took his leave.

"I am sure that I will see you again before you go down to the country," he said on departing. "You may not believe this, but I have thought of you often over the years."

She watched the drawing room door close behind him, then released in a long exhale the emotions she had been holding inside her. What a horrible man, not to have the decency to stay away from her.

"You are creating a spectacle," Hawkeswell said. "It will be the talk of the clubs and coffee shops all day."

"I assumed they were all staring at you," Castleford replied.

Actually, he assumed nothing of the kind. The reactions as they rode their horses down Bond Street beneath the late morning sun could not be missed, and it was obvious which gentleman was causing the surprise.

People he knew well and others he barely recognized actually stopped their horses and feet to watch him. A few women in a passing carriage were so rude as to point out the window in his direction while they exclaimed over his presence. One would think the prince regent was riding by stark naked, from the attention sent his way.

"They can all go to hell," he said. "If I want to be up and about town at this hour, that is my business. This gawking only proves my long-held opinion that most people are small-minded fools."

It also proved that Daphne Joyes was ruining him, and he had better put an end to it. After all, he was riding about town at this hour because he had discovered that being in bed got boring if one was awake and alone at the same time.

Since he did not spend the nights now taking his pleasure with a woman, he tended to fall asleep the way most people did. That left the days for doing other things. He was having some trouble recalling just what those things might be.

"What is this business that you are about, that is important enough to draw you out of your luxurious cave?" Hawkeswell asked. "I only fell in with you because I wanted to witness the show. It is even better than I thought. We may have a crowd following us soon." While he talked, he played to the onlookers like a circus master, smiling and nodding left and right, approving their bad behavior. *Amazing, isn't it? Your eyes are not deceiving you, it is truly he!*

"You can leave at any time now, Hawkeswell. I did not invite your company."

"And miss this? Although if this business you are about is lengthy, I may have to depart before the final act. I have a meeting at the White Swan this afternoon."

"If you must know, I have several errands to attend

to, and they will undoubtedly bore you as much as I expect them to bore me."

Hawkeswell said nothing. His silence became so resonant that Castleford looked over at him. Hawkeswell was watching him with a confused expression.

"Errands?" Hawkeswell finally said.

"Appointments with tailors and such."

"You never have appointments at tailors' shops. Tailors have appointments in your dressing room. You have three valets when one is plenty for most men, just so you do not have to be bothered with anything resembling an *errand*."

All that was true, but he had to do something with all this time burdening him.

"I think the only appointment you should have today is with a physician," Hawkeswell said. "Or one of your soiled doves, so some regularity returns to your habits and you relinquish this farce of temporary reform."

"It is a hell of a thing if a man cannot ride his horse before noon without having a friend insult him by assigning virtue to his character when none exists."

"I accused you of no virtue. I said it was a farce of feigned virtue. Do you deny that your unusual behavior is directly the result of being unable to conquer Mrs. Joyes without such excess? That once you do conquer her, you will return to your whoring and drinking?" Hawkeswell scolded. "Why not just give up, admit there is one woman in the world who finds you beyond the pale instead of intriguing, and go back to enjoying your life?"

Why not indeed? Castleford chose to ignore the questions, but it was not as if he had not asked them of himself.

He had no intention of giving Hawkeswell any reason

to gloat about the lack of progress with Mrs. Joyes. Quite the opposite. So he made his first stop Phillip's jewelry shop.

Hawkeswell trailed him inside, which meant Hawkeswell had the fun of seeing the proprietor fluster, flush, and almost faint at the sight of one of his most august patrons crossing his shop's threshold for the first time in the history of his patronage.

Hawkeswell hovered at his shoulder while the ear bobs were unveiled. They impressed Hawkeswell, which meant they were sure to impress Mrs. Joyes.

"Perfect," Castleford said. "Be sure to add an appropriate amount for the speed with which you completed setting them."

Phillip began to wrap the handsome box. Castleford lounged in his chair. Hawkeswell gazed over with a scowl.

"Are those for Mrs. Joyes? They must be worth a small fortune."

"A goodly size fortune, actually."

"She may be insulted. She may think you are trying to buy her."

"Women are never completely insulted by diamonds. A little, perhaps, if it is a woman such as Mrs. Joyes, but my experience is that they overcome their suspicious interpretations with unseemly speed." He accepted the little package from Phillip. "Besides, she has already accepted them, so she cannot be insulted now."

That impressed Hawkeswell even more. So much that when they left the shop, Hawkeswell did not go his own separate way.

"Do you plan to follow me to the tailor too?" Castleford said.

"Weston may have apoplexy when you walk in, and need assistance. Do you even know where to find him?"

Of course he did. His head valet had provided the address, after all.

C astleford completed his errands by two o'clock. The show over, Hawkeswell finally departed to go to his meeting at the White Swan. Castleford was left to wonder what the hell he was going to do between now and five o'clock, when he would meet with Daphne.

He could go to one of his clubs, but of late everyone was in high temper about the inevitability of insurrection in the north by month's end. He doubted he could listen to that nonsense for long without telling them all that they were idiots. That would probably start an argument, which could lead to insults, which might result in a challenge.

The way life was going these days, he would probably lose a duel for the first time in his life and be shot in the balls no less, thus making all these disruptions to his habits in the interests of seducing Mrs. Joyes a tragic waste.

Instead of visiting a club, he could return home and work on his manuscript, he supposed. Except she was ruining that too, wasn't she?

Recently, when he wrote, he found himself resorting to the kinds of euphemisms and poetic allusions in his prose that might not embarrass a woman like Mrs. Joyes too badly, if she picked up the guide by accident and read it.

The results, evident once he took an objective, critical look at the chapter in progress, had been boring, ambiguous, and horribly fourth-rate, when the whole goal was to be daring, frank, and refreshingly clever.

It now read as if the real author—the fun, bad one, who knew well of what he wrote—had died halfway through composing the guide, and his virginal vicar of a cousin had taken up the pen in his stead after the burial, in the hopes of bluffing through to the end and making a few pounds.

He finally decided that following Hawkeswell to the White Swan was the least boring of the boring choices he had, which alone reminded him why he did not live like normal men most times. However, if Hawkeswell could interfere in his morning, he could interfere in Hawkeswell's afternoon.

Along the way, he plotted the final chapter in a book titled "The Seduction of Daphne Joyes by the Decadent Duke of Castleford (A History of London Life, complete with appendices, glossary, and maps chosen to enhance the reader's edification)." He fully expected to bring the story to its conclusion this evening.

Entering the White Swan, he spied Hawkeswell sitting alone. Hawkeswell laughed when he walked over.

"What in hell are you doing here, Castleford?"

"Planning to drink some ale. What are you doing here alone? I thought you had a meeting."

"Latham should be arriving soon enough. There is a matched pair in the stable here that he is thinking to buy, magnificent cattle from the talk, and he asked my opinion on them and—"

"Damnation. Are you good friends with Latham now? He is an unbearable ass. Have you no pride at all?"

Hawkeswell looked taken aback. "We stumbled upon each other yesterday. In talking he mentioned the horses and remembered I have an excellent eye for them, so I agreed to give my opinion." His astonishment gave way to annoyance. "Why am I explaining myself? Hell, I am friends with you, aren't I? That is proof that I am not too particular. One ass is as good as another, it seems to me."

This talk of horses piqued Castleford's curiosity. He ignored Hawkeswell's bluster and got to his feet. "This pair is in the stable?" Without waiting for an answer, he headed toward the door.

He might have found something fun to do this afternoon.

"Damnation, here he comes," Hawkeswell muttered. Castleford looked into the tavern's yard, where Latham was dismounting from his horse. Then he turned away and stroked the nose of one of the huge white geldings that he had just bought. They really were magnificent and worth every pound of their considerable price.

"If you actually care a farthing for your friendship with that scoundrel, and I don't know why you would, tell him you have been threatening me with bodily harm if I did it, but I would not listen. I will not gainsay you."

Hawkeswell sighed deeply. "I realize that the two of you have nothing in common anymore and are no longer friends, but to deliberately anger him—Latham, there you are! I fear we are too late."

Latham came over. Castleford barely acknowledged him. Latham saw the horses and his face reddened. He glared at Hawkeswell accusingly.

"Hawkeswell chanced upon me here, just as I was striking the deal," Castleford said. "I read the *Times* ad-

vertisements too, Latham. You had to know you would
have competition for horses like these."

Latham gave the horses a good look. Standing aside,
Hawkeswell did not see what Castleford did. Latham's
expression momentarily turned its most dangerous, and
with a glancing sneer he sent true hatred in Castleford's
direction.

In the next moment, he appeared calm and amiable
again. He smiled at Hawkeswell. "I should have moved
on them faster, I can see. But if any man were to beat me
to them, just as well it is Tristan here."

What an accursed thing to say. It took some of the fun
out of the victory. Not all of it, but some.

"Let us all have some ale," Latham offered. "It is hot
enough for at least a pint, I'd say."

A glare from Hawkeswell induced Castleford to reluctantly join them as they set off in the direction of the
tavern.

Thinking the hour had not turned out nearly as well
as he had planned, Castleford sat in the tavern in a
daze of languor.

To say that small talk filled the next ten minutes was
to give the conversation too much credit.

It took a moment, then, to gather his faculties when
Latham turned that false affability in his direction. "You
are being much discussed these days, Tristan."

"Latham, I told you not to call me by my Christian
name. No one does anymore, not even Hawkeswell here,
unless we are both thoroughly foxed."

"Or thoroughly furious," Hawkeswell offered with a

laugh. "Have you heard good gossip, Latham? I often miss the best bits because I am his friend."

"It is said he has found iron in the south, to add to his mines in the north." Latham watched him carefully, looking for a reaction.

"Oh, that old rumor," Hawkeswell said, disappointed. "Iron now, is it?"

"I have found nothing. No iron or anything else."

"It is said this is very recent. On land you recently came by."

"You know how old women talk, Latham. It has been established by experts that there are no iron reserves in the south." Castleford let his voice communicate his boredom with the topic.

After a bit more small talk, Hawkeswell excused himself and left. Castleford rose to follow him.

"Is it my father's land?" Latham demanded, spearing him with a look of suspicion. "This discovery of yours, is it on that gift he left you? I can't think of any other property that you recently acquired."

"You have no idea what I acquire and when. You must stop listening to every whisper passed in the clubs, Latham."

Latham's eyes narrowed. "You are looking very smug, *Tristan*. I have it right, don't I, damn it."

"That is not smugness you see. It is ennui claiming me, *Gerome*. I have always found paragons of virtue tedious, especially when they are actually treasonous rapists."

"Damnation, you are the one who is tedious. You only hammer on that business in France because you are jealous now. No one has asked to consult with *you* about the state of the realm."

"They already know my advice. Be sure the people do not go hungry, and all will be well. It is such a simple, sure idea that even primitive people see the logic of it. Yet we have once again made sure that men will watch their children starve, then expect them to be happy and peaceable while they do. If you have any influence at all, address that immorality, and I may not think you a total scoundrel."

"I am thinking that I would rather address the immorality of the notorious Duke of Castleford. Perhaps just for fun I will make you a public symbol of depravity in my next essay."

"Please do. It will be the finest jewel in my crown."

"You joke, but you like power as much as any man. You will not be such a wit about it if I paint you to be so sordid that you are pushed to the edges of all that matters." Latham warmed to the threat, finding it more amusing with each word.

Castleford placed his palms on the table. He leaned forward so this fool would know there was no wit at all in what followed. "Do your worst. But before you wage war with *me*, do not forget that towers of rectitude that are made of straw can be easily burned to the ground."

He went off to arrange to have the new pair of horses brought to his stable. Latham tailed him out to the yard.

"Oh, I forgot to mention that I saw the lovely Mrs. Joyes yesterday," Latham said from his saddle once he had mounted. "I called on her, and we reminisced about old times. I reminded her how she was a little flirt back then. Hard to believe, isn't it? She has learned to hide that side of her character well."

Castleford walked on, giving the ass no response. He

would not let the man see his anger at that parting shot and at learning that Latham had boldly called on Daphne. And that she had received him.

Someone needed to shoot down Latham's ascendant balloon, he decided. As it happened, the Duke of Castleford found himself of late with endless free hours available, and he needed a good diversion.

Chapter Thirteen

"I won't do it," Celia said. She slid another spoonful of ice into her mouth.

Daphne's own spoon halted halfway to its destination. Surely she had heard wrong. "It will only take a short while. A half hour at most."

Celia kept her attention on the ice. She luxuriated in the taste of it, moaning from the pleasure. Daphne ate her own, but kept her eyes on her friend.

Finally they were done. They passed their little cups out to one of the servants from Gunter's who tended to the carriages surrounding Berkley Square. All of them held ladies indulging as they did. Celia dabbed at her mouth with a handkerchief.

"I was not invited," Celia said. "If you needed a chaperone, you should not have accepted without arranging to bring a companion. For me to now accompany you is pointless anyway. If it is Castleford's intention to get you alone for seductive purposes, he will manage it whether I walk in the door with you or not."

"I did not say I feared he had seductive—"

"Oh, *please*, Daphne." Celia looked to heaven in exasperation. "It is very clear he is pursuing you. Everyone has noticed. This is *Castleford*. If he pursues a woman, it is for no other purpose except seduction."

Everyone had noticed? Daphne hoped Celia only meant their friends. Her and Verity and, at worst, their husbands.

Of course, there had been those two invitations . . .

"You appear very concerned, Daphne. Tell the man that you will not have him, if you are not interested in his intentions."

If?

"I have told him. I have even been rude about it. He does not hear me."

"Perhaps he sees something in your reactions to him that have convinced him otherwise?"

Daphne felt her face warming. Celia's blue eyes widened.

"Are you blushing? You *never* blush. Oh, my." She giggled behind her hand. "Mrs. Joyes, have you been naughty?"

"If I have not remained strictly proper, I can be forgiven, I think." *Not strictly proper* was hardly adequate. "He is just so overwhelming. Relentless. I never appreciated all those references to women having their walls breached, like such things are battles or sieges, but I tell you, Celia, this man has managed to exhaust my defenses."

"Well, he is not without appeal. I expect you find him exciting?"

"Yes, I do. There, I have said it. For many reasons I dare not be so rash as to succumb to his appeal, but—I am losing the ability to explain why, even to myself, when he plays his games." She looked down miserably. "He can be very persuasive in the worst ways, I am embarrassed to admit."

"Do you need an excuse to put him off until you buttress your defenses? Is that the problem?"

"Yes. Exactly. He will lose interest soon, I am sure. I only need to discourage him until he does." Or until she journeyed north. She would do so very soon, she had decided. To see Margaret and ask those private questions and to reassure herself about matters up there.

Celia assumed the very worldly expression that she could at times. Five years ago, when Celia joined The Rarest Blooms, Daphne had found that expression disconcerting. Sometimes she still did.

"Putting him off is easy enough to effect," Celia said.

"It is?"

"What I have in mind will not work forever, but it should at least delay a determined assault. Instruct your man to take me home. While we ride, I will tell you what to say to Castleford today."

D aphne presented herself at Castleford's door a little after five o'clock. The captain of the guard handed her over to a minion at once, and the footman escorted her through the house's first level.

They emerged at the other side on a low terrace that

overlooked the gardens. There, in the middle of the flowers and plantings, on a circle of lawn, stood a large tent.
It bore a striking resemblance to the pavilions that Castleford had erected on his river barge. The ones in which
their friends had enjoyed marital bliss.

The man was not being subtle. Daphne tried hard to
fortify her defenses as she walked the meandering path
that took her to that tent.

A flap had been fastened open. She peered inside and
let her eyes adjust to the dim light. She noticed the thick
netting that circled the top of the tent walls, allowing in
air. She could not miss the table and chairs, or, up against
the tent's billowing walls, the wide chaise longue decorated with many pillows and looking like a sultan's bed in
this setting.

Castleford came forward to greet her.

"I thought the day should not be spent in a study," he
explained. "It is far cooler out here, and since we are not
alone inside, proprieties are being maintained in the strict-
est sort of way."

She laughed. They were not being maintained even in
the loosest way, and he knew it.

He was in dishabille again. Not as bad as when he received her in a morning coat, but there was nothing formal
in his attire. No frock coat covered his shirt and waistcoat,
and his cravat had been tied into the most casual, loose
knot. He appeared every inch the dangerous rogue he was.
She decided that he had planned that, to put her at a disadvantage again.

Wine and lemonade waited on the table. She chose
some of the latter and accepted a comfortable chair with
its back to that sultan's bed.

"You are shameless," she said. "Really, you are."

"See how well you have come to understand me? It has been years, I believe, since any woman has known so well what she has in me."

"Oh, I know what I have in you. If you have some notion that I am going to play a role today in some fantasy about a seraglio, please disabuse yourself of that idea."

His eyes narrowed thoughtfully. Mischievously. "Is that a scold?"

"No!" She veered back in alarm, lest he conclude he had leave to grab her now.

He did not laugh at her reaction, but it amused him.

"Are you sure you would not like some wine?"

"I am very sure that I would not like some wine. This is not a social call. You wrote about needing to talk about the property, so I am here. A business meeting was needed, you indicated in your letter."

"Did I? Yes, quite right." He folded his arms and stretched out his legs. She wondered if he took that pose when meeting with the prime minister or prince regent. Probably.

"Let me see. . . . Mr. Edwards writes that the examination of the property continues at a pace, and thus far nothing of note has been found. He says it should not take more than another fortnight or so."

"Another fortnight or so? I think these men you sent are enjoying too much country air at your expense, if it takes that long."

"It must be done methodically and carefully, or it will have to be done over. That would leave you here in London for months. We don't want that, do we?"

"I am beginning to think this would all have been decided faster if I never came up to town. It is now sounding as if it will be months before I know my fate."

He studied her. He looked at her so specifically that
she stirred, even though there was nothing seductive in
his gaze.

"Allow me to remove your fears about your fate, Mrs.
Joyes. Should I conclude that you can no longer use that
property, I will move you to another that is at least as
good, and even construct another greenhouse for your
use."

She had not expected that. He managed to astonish
her still, sometimes. She gazed down at her hands in her
lap while she accommodated what this abrupt generosity
did to her.

The weight of worrying about The Rarest Blooms
drained away, leaving her almost empty with its passing,
since it had preoccupied her so much. The breeze sifting
through the tent seemed to enter her heart with its cool,
light flow.

This promise was not a small thing. True, she would
have to reestablish the gardens, so it was not as perfect a
solution as staying where she was. However, suddenly
the future stretched securely and sure, not like a path lost
in the near distance in a dank mist.

All of her plans resurrected, now that they could, exciting her. Moving her. Her immediate plans, and even the
special ones for the future that had been little more than
dreams for years. He had no idea what he had just given
her, of course. A man with his privilege and wealth would
never understand how just knowing one had a permanent
home could affect everything in one's life.

His boots moved back. He leaned toward her. His hand
appeared on the table near her, then left. A small box now
rested in front of her, opened. Inside it, two stunning dia-

mond ear bobs rested on a bed of velvet. They flashed in the low light.

"You are too generous," she said, carefully. "You have already given me a great gift with your reassurance. To add these is too much."

"These are old gifts, not from today. They are only being delivered today."

"I cannot accept them. Please do not be insulted." She truly did not want to offend him right now, and not only because he had taken this weight from her soul.

"I am not insulted, but you have already accepted them. Remember? You certainly did not refuse them."

"I understand how you may have misunderstood my silence when you mentioned them. However, I am not befuddled by wine this evening."

"You were not befuddled on the barge."

"I was thoroughly befuddled. Foxed. I would have never, *ever* been so . . . wicked, otherwise."

"Nonsense. You loved being wicked. I know of what I speak, so do not try to be a fraud with me. I am a connoisseur of inebriation and wickedness, and you were not too much the first to be ignorant of embracing the latter. You were pleasantly relaxed but not thoroughly foxed."

She felt her face warming. "A gentleman would allow a lady her excuses, it seems to me."

"Fine. If you require wine to have an excuse, I will pour you some."

"No!"

He just waited for more. He watched her in that seductive way he could call up at will, where nothing ostensibly changed, but it was just there, in the air, the appeal that led a woman to think of him in sensual terms. There should be a law against a man being able to do that. She felt her armor falling off, item by item, under that gaze.

She would try honesty first. He had been sympathetic today, so far. He might be still.

"I believe that you have misunderstood, due to the wine and my bad behavior, and that you now think . . . well, you assume that with these diamonds that . . ."

He just looked at her. He did not show any inclination to help her by showing he understood the rest. He just let her twist in the wind at the end of her words.

"It would be most unwise for me to be befuddled again, whether by wine or diamonds. I do not choose to be wicked with you anymore."

No insult showed in his expression. Rather, she saw curiosity claim him. That could be more dangerous, she knew.

He dropped his elbow on the table, propped his chin on his hand, and considered her. "What an interesting woman you are. It is not shyness that makes you refuse me on all counts, I do not think. Or lack of desire. Do not protest that point, please. I will go to France and enter a monastery if I cannot recognize desire in a woman by now. As for your ability to respond to pleasure, well, we settled that question on the barge. So, what is your objection when it is very obvious that we want each other? Considering how I have suffered, I claim a right to know."

When she had thought of honesty being a good idea, she had not expected quite this much to be required of her. What would he think if she answered with the whole truth? If she satisfied all his curiosity?

She had never explained herself to anyone before, of course. Perhaps, if Latham had not returned to London, she might have considered it now. Only she did not trust Castleford, or anyone, to know the truth and keep it private.

She picked over his little speech, to find something to say. "I do not think it is very obvious that we want—"

His dramatic sigh cut her off. He just looked at her, expecting an answer.

Rather suddenly she found herself at that point where she was hard-pressed to come up with a reason that made sense, that he would not demolish with ease, and that she wanted to share. Bereft of an excuse, she used Celia's advice for delaying this pursuit.

"You are known to frequent brothels, sir. For my health alone, it would be most unwise to succumb to your blandishments."

She stunned him. At least she hoped that was the explanation for the way his face froze. Not only stunned but dumbfounded, apparently. He stood up and looked down on her, speechless. Then he walked away.

She felt obliged to stand too. She saw him near the open flap, appearing very thoughtful and, she regretfully noted, angry. Celia had warned he would not take it well. That was an understatement.

His attention settled on her again. A bemused half smile broke, but danger lurked in those eyes. "Mrs. Joyes, did I hear correctly? Are you accusing me of being diseased?"

"The possibility is there. That is all I am saying. One cannot be too careful."

"I agree. Which is why I am most careful. I assure you that I am not a danger to you."

She swallowed hard. "One never knows."

His gaze sharpened. "One most certainly knows."

"The results of recent debauches may not be apparent

yet to you." She had no idea if that was even true. She just trusted that Celia's reference to at least a reprieve referred to something having to do with that.

He sighed audibly. Not in exasperation, the way he normally did. This deep exhale sounded too much like a man seeking to keep his temper in check.

"Mrs. Joyes," he said with strained calm. "There are certain establishments known to be fastidious regarding the health of the women who work there. This is why I am writing my book—so men coming to town can be directed to such places and not find themselves lured into others. I limit myself to such establishments, as do all men of good sense." He sighed again. His jaw twitched. "Furthermore, there are steps to protect oneself from such disease, which I am known to take." He sighed once more, then scowled. "Damnation, I cannot believe I am explaining this as if you have a right to hear it."

"Book or no, steps or no, I dare not consider a liaison under the circumstances."

His eyes narrowed on her. His expression hardened. He advanced toward her, and she instinctively backed up. If she ever saw Castleford this angry again, she hoped it was from far away.

He subjected her eyes to a deep scrutiny. "So you have been dodging me because of this. I suppose, with the stories you have heard, there is some sense in denying us both out of fear of the worst."

"I am relieved that you understand. I think that, under the circumstances, it would be better if I took my leave now and—"

"Will a physician's letter attesting to my health satisfy you?"

She had to firm her jaw to resist gaping at him.

"It would be presumptuous of me to expect you to procure one. Better if we just agreed that you will keep the diamonds, and I will keep my . . . privacy."

"I do not mind procuring one. In fact, I insist on doing so. I will also get letters from the physicians who examine the inhabitants of the establishments that I have visited the last year."

"How . . . thorough of you."

"Answer my question. Will this satisfy your concerns?"

"I expect it would take a good while to obtain all that documentation. By then you will have set your sights elsewhere, anyway, so it is rather silly for us to agree that—"

"Damn it, Daphne, will it satisfy you or not? Is this a true objection?"

"Yes." It had become one. How reckless not to have thought of such a thing before. She felt very fortunate that one of her best friends was the daughter of a courtesan.

"I will concede that while I know this is unnecessary, you have no way to be sure," he said. "Therefore, I will see to it, and I will not attempt to thoroughly seduce you until I can reassure you."

"Thank you. That is very thoughtful." Assuming that she had just ended their conversation and most likely his pursuit, she turned to leave.

"Where are you going?"

"I would say our business is finished, Your Grace. All of it, for some time. At least a week, I would guess. Or perhaps ten days." Or forever.

"The hell it is."

He grabbed her arm and pulled her toward him. She almost sailed through the air. She landed on top of him, on his lap, where he had sat in a chair.

He began to kiss her. Startled, she pressed against his chest and angled her head away.

"What—we just agreed you would not—"

"Not thoroughly seduce you. I did not say I would not seduce you less than thoroughly. Surely you and Captain Joyes enjoyed each other on occasion without intercourse."

She looked at him.

"No? Ah. Well, you already know that you can know the heights of pleasure that way. We only need to make it mutual this time. Besides, you promised me that I would see you in these diamonds, and nothing else." He handed the box to her while holding her firmly in place with his other arm. "Put them on."

She refused to take it. "*I* did not promise that. *You* promised that."

"And I am always good to my word. Put them on."

She had no intention of being seen in diamonds and nothing else. She squirmed to get loose.

"If you think I am so stupid as to believe I could take off my clothes and you would respect my preference not to—well, not to, then you are a madman." She pried at his embracing arm. "You think far too highly of yourself and could use a few lessons on being a gentleman."

"I just heard a scold. How convenient your behavior can be." He set aside the box and proved what he meant by kissing her.

She managed a few more squirms of resistance after that, but it was very hard to truly fight something that your weaker self remembered as a wonderful thrill. Her mind kept scolding him and herself, but her body abandoned the battle in a disgraceful mutiny.

The pleasure was just too luscious. That was the last

clear thought she had, and it was more an excuse than it was an argument for restraint. The thrills distracted her fast. It was as if her experience on the barge had only made her more sensitive and less able to deny herself.

Everything happened more rapidly. The heat escalated fast. His hands were on her from the start, caressing her body, encouraging the arousal that left her weak.

The little resistance that remained flowed away as the warmth and excitement flowed down. She hooked one tether of consciousness to their conversation and his promise of restraint and let herself drift on the currents of sensation, floating at the glorious freedom.

Yes, she whispered to herself as his mouth scorched her neck and chest. *Yes*, as his fine hand raised shudders in her while it smoothed over her thighs and waist and finally over her breasts.

His fingers rubbed her through her garments, and sensuality's daze descended on her. That special tension filled her body and tightened more with each wicked tease on her breasts. Soon she inched toward desperation. And so it took her a while to realize the kisses had stopped.

She blinked her eyes open when she did, to find Castleford watching her. Not with triumph or his own desperation but rather with curiosity. She had a moment of lucidity in which she remembered how dangerous his curiosity could be and that she had come here today determined to discourage it.

He nuzzled her neck. "He did not teach you much, did he?"

It took a heroic effort to push aside the haze enough to comprehend what he said. Since he did not stop caressing her, it took even longer to consider why he might have said it, and at such a moment.

He kissed her and did something with his tongue and mouth that seemed an invitation. She understood then. Feeling incredibly wanton and relieved that his probing gaze had been about something so simple, she tried to kiss him the way he had kissed her.

No, she had not been taught much, but in the minutes that followed she had her first lesson in expressing her passion more mutually. She became an active agent in stoking this risky fire, but it made her heady with power and impressed by her own audacity. She even ventured a kiss to his neck and tentatively slid her hand beneath his waistcoat.

Moving now, in a flowing weightlessness, as he carried her to that sultan's bed and laid her among the silk pillows. He looked down while he stripped off his cravat, then his waistcoat and shirt. She closed her eyes because he frightened her a little, the way he looked at her.

You are a fool to trust him. You know he will not stop. Better men would not, and he is proud of his sins.

Whatever power that inner voice had was defeated in the next moment. He joined her on that chaise longue and took control of her with one masterful kiss and one devastating caress.

With the way he embraced her, there was nothing to do but embrace him back. His warmth surrounded her, encompassed her, and the sensation of his skin, of the hard shoulders and back beneath her hands, entranced her. She caressed as if by instinct, and it increased the intensity and heat like her kisses had.

He released her. Turned her. Her dress loosened. Then the stays she had sensibly worn. Fabric slid off her shoulders and down her body until her breasts were naked.

He turned her again, and she tried to cover herself

with her arms. He moved her shields away so nothing protected her from his gaze. While he looked, the fabric slid lower yet, making her gasp from shock and arousal and the feel of the breeze. Then she gasped again, as his hand moved down her nakedness and removed her dress and chemise entirely.

She dared not look at herself or him. She could barely contain what this did to her, this exposure and vulnerability. Real fear moved in her, but so did powerful desire that made her shake.

Then he no longer touched her at all. He moved, and she opened her eyes to see him stretched out next to her, his head resting on his hand while he looked at her. His other hand placed the small box with the ear bobs between her naked breasts.

"Put them on for me."

She knelt so she could fasten them correctly, sensing as she did that she had just ceded some vital ground, even though she did not know what it was.

The ear bobs were not heavy or overlong. She screwed the backs until they held. Castleford rose up on his arm to get a better view of them. And her.

His hand touched one of her ears, then moved down. He fondled her breast. Torturous pleasure poured down low in her, tantalizing her in the worst way.

"They are the only jewels for you," he said. "You are perfect in diamonds. Exquisite. Beguiling." He kissed her ear, then her chest, then bent and kissed her breast. His tongue flicked on its tip, and a shock shot through her. "Now do as I do, so we both know some relief this day."

He knelt tall and worked the fastenings on his lower garments. Astonished anew, but too far gone to care, she fell back on the cushion while he removed them entirely.

He knelt there, looking down, those golden flecks in his eyes so dangerous now. They mesmerized her, and she knew, just knew, what he wanted her to do. She wanted it too, so she did not even feel shy when she stretched out her arm and touched his naked chest. She allowed herself the pleasure of watching her hand move over him, over the hard ridges of his muscles and the soft smoothness of his skin, over his taut stomach and around the tight swell of his rear hip.

His expression and body hardened with her caress, and his arousal did too, growing more as if demanding attention. Shyer now, but not too much, to her own amazement, she caressed around his hip and touched him with her fingers.

His eyes closed briefly. When they opened again the devilish fires burned in them. He leaned forward until he hovered over her on hands and knees.

"Do not stop." His head dipped, and his tongue and teeth and mouth began devastating her with erotic teases on her breasts, with licks and nips and finally more determined arousals that had her mind dimming to everything except pure sensuality.

She did not stop but sought to madden him in turn so she would not be so vulnerable. She stroked his shaft and the tip and circled him with her hand. When the pleasure began crying in her, she ceased knowing much what she did. When he lay beside her again she could no longer reach.

She parted her legs too gratefully when his hand began to stroke her down there. She lifted her hips to his touch, too eager, shameless in her need, indifferent to her pride. She almost begged him for more, for faster devastation, for him to forget what had been said and to thoroughly take her. She clung to him and reached for that wonderful release she had known on the barge.

She came close, painfully close, but he surprised her again. He moved below her, between her legs, then left the bed. Kneeling there, he pulled her toward him. He spread her legs wide and lowered his head.

Her body convulsed from the shock of that kiss. She lost awareness, because the pleasure became so intense. She thought she might be begging now, or crying, because she was doing both in her head, in a chant of urging and fear.

It happened, finally, that burst of white heat that relieved the tight coil of pleasure. The perfect sensation spread like a warm river all through her, making her lose sense of her own physicality.

He moved up and covered her, totally, as she drifted in that momentary heaven. His forearms flanked her, and his hips rested between her thighs. It entered her mind that he would take her now. Enter her. Alarm managed to rise through her stupor.

Then she felt the evidence that sometime in this passion he had also found relief. Her vulnerability being beneath him did not frighten her after that.

He angled his head and kissed her ear. Then his finger toyed at the ear bob as he watched it move. The sensation of that little weight against her jaw made the daze lift a little. Enough for her to consider the truth that she was naked with this man on top of her, after she had come here determined that nothing like this would happen.

She claimed most of herself, but she could not shake off the intimacy. It altered her senses and her mind and even what she saw as she looked up at him.

Still Castleford. Still dangerous. But less of a devil right now, it seemed, and more of a man. Not so cool and indifferent or viewing all of life as a good joke.

That was the pleasure affecting her, no doubt. It softened her perceptions and tempted her to think better of this than it had really been.

She closed her eyes because it affected her too much, looking at him. It was as if she lost another little piece of her soul and will with each passing moment.

"Thank you. For being good to your word," she said.

"You must now give *your* word that you will never tell anyone that I had you here in bed, naked, and was so stupidly decent. Such gossip would ruin me, utterly."

She laughed, grateful that he sounded once again like the Castleford she knew. "I promise to keep your secret that you can be honorable, even when inclined not to be."

He eased off her and lay beside her. His fingertips absently traced her body, its curves and swells, like a brush outlining her in paint.

"You do not really fear I am diseased, I think."

"Are you convincing yourself that I am taking joy in frustrating you?"

"I believe your hesitation is real, but this new reason is an excuse conjured up to explain it. You are afraid of something. I sense it, when you are at your most vulnerable. Not disease, I think. Not even me."

An urge to confide swelled inside her. It came on quickly, unexpectedly, provoked by the intimacy, she was sure, and not by any rational considerations. The words were nearly on her lips before she checked herself. She forced the impulse down.

"You misunderstand what is only a woman's natural

caution, and my worry about putting faith in the word of a man who is not known for denying himself."

"I see."

That was hardly agreement, but she was glad to let the query die with that.

"I heard that Latham visited you," he said.

"Who told you that?"

"He did. He said that you received him. You add insult to insult in doing so, since you do not receive *me*."

"I agreed to receive him in order to see what he wanted. And to see if I might learn something that would enable me to bring him down."

"You are not to attempt that. I forbid it."

"Where did you get the notion it was your place to forbid anything?"

He rose up and looked at her. His expression said it all. That in giving her favors, incompletely though it had been, he would assume it was his place as long as he wished.

"You are not a person equipped to battle such as he."

"Well, *someone* has to do it."

"Why? He is not the first peer to be of poor character. Hell, look at me."

"It is not the same."

"Close enough. Do not entertain this foolhardy notion, Daphne. Do not entertain *him* either, damn it."

The little argument provoked her. He played with the ear bobs again, causing them to tap against her skin.

"I know that you have been living a fraudulent history, Daphne."

Her breath caught. The world seemed to freeze, and a chill slid down her back.

She looked at him, searching to see what he knew and what he might not.

"The records show no Captain Joyes dying in the war," he said almost gently. "Did he even exist? Were you even married?"

She silently cursed his curiosity and her naïveté in thinking that dodging him would discourage him.

Now what? Would today only make that worse or dull his fascination?

"You do not speak," he said. "I think I will choose to be flattered that you do not want to lie to me more."

"You should not have pried." Fury burned in her, and she wanted to hit him. "It was nothing more than a way to pass the time for you."

"I always pry if I am inclined to. I think I know what happened. I only do not know if there ever was a Captain Joyes and if you were ever married or are married still."

He thought he knew it all, but he would be saying more now if he did. That relieved her trepidation, and she forced her anger into control.

"Never," she said. "I was never married."

It was what he expected, she could tell.

"Latham knew, didn't he?" he said. "He knew about you and his father. He thinks to take his father's place in more than the House of Lords. Do not demur. I know of what I speak. This is why you are not to receive him again. Doing so will tempt me to call him out, and it would be best if I don't kill him over you."

"I doubt either of you would be moved to such drama over me, let alone to contest who receives my favors."

"I would not know yet, since I have not had all your favors. In a few days' time, however, I may take it very badly if another man, let alone Latham, tried to displace me."

A few days' time. He did not sound like he expected those physician's letters to take even a week to procure.

Worse, he spoke of a fascination that did not die with victory, but increased.

She had lived almost invisibly for years, and now this man's interest threatened to rend her privacy to pieces.

She closed her eyes when he began touching her again. She wallowed in the intimacy and warmth of this sultan's bed. She made herself feel each pleasure as much as possible while he caressed and kissed her, and as abandon made her free.

Sadness gathered around the edges of her emotions, however, even when she cried from the intense release that shattered her need. She succumbed more than she ever had, because she dared never do so again.

She left as dusk fell. She rode back to Park Lane in Summerhays's carriage, not yet ready to consider how big a mistake the evening had been. Castleford's commands about Latham played in her mind instead.

For all of his statements of concern for her, he was protecting Latham as well. They may not be friends now, but the past—those boyhood games and the sins they shared as young men—stood for something. And dukes probably all hung together in any case. An assault on one diminished all of their power.

The peerage had a vested interest in taking care of each other. Latham being a relative would only reinforce that inclination with Castleford.

As badly as he thought of Latham, he would never side against him. No matter what the insult, there would never be a challenge either, least of all over her.

Which meant that if she ever found the courage to make Latham pay for the past, it would be best not to inform Castleford about her plans.

Back in her chamber, she undressed on her own, not calling for the maid. She wanted no company. She sat at her dressing table to unpin her hair.

Two stars glittered in the looking glass, one on each side of her face, reflecting the light from the candles. She still wore the diamonds. She had forgotten to remove them and leave them in their box in the tent.

Chapter Fourteen

"Now," Castleford said.

"I should return to my chambers and compose this letter, Your Grace. It requires some thought, due to the delicacy of the subject."

"*Now*." Castleford pointed to the writing table in his bedchamber.

Dr. Neverton flushed and appeared distraught and annoyed.

Their meeting had not gone well. Upon receiving the message to come with all haste, Dr. Neverton had hurried over, a valise full of tonics and metal implements in hand. He had run up the stairs and burst into the apartment, issuing a rush of questions to the valets in the dressing room.

"What is it? A bullet wound from a duel? A fever brought on by his profligate living? Has the drinking finally done in one of his major organs?"

Castleford had heard it all from his bedchamber, where he had been thinking dark thoughts. He was in no mood for what was coming with Dr. Neverton. The woman had really gone too far in making such a thing a condition of receiving her favors. Daughters and wives of peers had not been this bold.

Dr. Neverton had entered the bedchamber resentfully, having learned that no bullet wound or illness had summoned him on this dire emergency. He had been stunned to learn of the examination required instead.

Now, the annoying business finished, Castleford was not going to let the man go free until he had that damned letter in hand.

"Sit. If words fail you, I will help," he ordered.

Dr. Neverton sat. He glanced at the papers spread on the surface in front of him, then peered more closely. "Are you writing your memoirs, Your Grace?"

Castleford cleared the table of the papers and stacked them roughly on one side. "Not at all. Why do you ask?"

"Forgive me, but I could not help but notice that the top page extolled the charms of a certain damsel of the night named Katy. A little blonde, it said." He glanced up roguishly. "I think I know her."

"Do you now?"

"Oh, yes, if it is the same Katy. The one I know has a mole, right—here." Neverton pointed to the side of his chest.

They exchanged details, far more than necessary, to ensure it was the same woman.

"Your experience with Katy and others may prove useful," Castleford said. "Now, I want you to write the letter, no salutation, regarding my health. Especially the health that you examined today, if you understand what I mean."

"You want me to explain that you are in fine health, I assume. May I ask, sir, are you planning to marry? I have only been asked to write such a document once before, when another gentleman with extensive, um, experiences planned to wed. It was required by the intended's father."

"No, you may not ask such an impertinent question. Here is how I think you should start the letter. I will dictate. Are you ready?"

Dr. Neverton sighed and dipped the pen.

"'The patient who bears my letter of testimony to you'—do not use my name, Neverton. I do not want anyone to know I did this should the letter fall into the wrong hands—'is in remarkably good health. Indeed, it is unusual to find a man of his age so youthfully strong and vigorous. One might think time stopped when he left university. It is my professional opinion that the rumors regarding his habits must be in error'—don't give me that look, Neverton. Just write, damn it—'for if even half of those stories were true, a physician would expect to see some effects on his person or mind, when in fact none exist.'"

"Your Grace, really, I do not think I should allow you to dictate this—"

"'Regarding any passing experiences this patient may have had of a carnal nature—'"

"That sounds as if they have been few and far between, when you admitted just a quarter hour ago that—"

"'—it is my medical opinion, which is sought even by members of the royal family, that he is totally free of any of the diseases that are associated with such activities.'"

Neverton put down his foot. Or rather, his pen. "I cannot say you are totally free. I cannot. You appear to be, yes. I believe you to be, yes. Your precautions, if you did use condoms as you say, support that you are. But I cannot be certain, one hundred percent. I am unable to vouch in that manner about any person who has had sexual congress with another human being."

"Then say all that, much as you said it to me. Only leave out the part where you impugned my honor with the 'as you say,' which I will generously overlook if you write this letter very, very well. I have dueled over lesser insults, as you know, since you have attended on the field along with the surgeon."

Dr. Neverton blanched and looked up with caution in his eyes.

"And, Neverton, I have decided it would indeed add a nice touch if you wrote that you yourself have indulged at the establishment that I favored when I had such passing activities, and that if you did not know that the house was clean, you would not use it yourself."

"Your Grace! You cannot expect me to incriminate myself for your benefit, and in writing no less!"

"Then be available to say it in person, should I need your testimony. The choice is yours."

Mouth folded tightly, Dr. Neverton penned the letter, signed and dated it, and handed it over. Castleford made sure it covered all the points expected, as emphatically as required.

He then released the physician. Not happy at all, but very well compensated, Dr. Neverton took his leave.

Castleford folded the letter and placed it in a drawer. Now he had to track down the physicians who attended to the women in Katy's establishment and the other brothels he had used in the last year. It should not take more than a few days at most.

He went to his dressing room and gave his valets orders to prepare him for the day. While he submitted to their attendance, a letter was brought up that had arrived in the midday mail.

Mr. Edwards had deigned to write. It was the first letter to come since that frantic one about the trespasser. Castleford read it while one valet shaved him and another pared his other hand's nails.

Compared to the last massive missive, this time Mr. Edwards proved remarkably brief. In a few short lines he said the examination of the property progressed well, that all remained quiet on the property, and that he anticipated completion by week's end. He did not even complain about the bedbugs.

One week. It only served as a reminder that matters had been dragging on with Daphne Joyes longer than they should have.

Castleford stood while the valets dressed him, and he calculated the battles won or lost thus far in that little siege. Memories from their evening in the garden tent had him smiling, then cursing himself for sentimentality in the next moment.

It had hardly been a victory. She had walked away with diamonds worth a nice-size fortune and a guaranteed home for life at his expense. There were mistresses of wealthy men who did not accumulate that much after a year of extending favors, rather than withholding them.

And he had walked away with temporary relief of an adolescent nature and a familiarity with her body that kept him awake at nights now.

No doubt his recent abstinence accounted for how vivid the memories of her passion and body were. Even now, if he did not consciously block the thoughts, he could hear her begging cries like her mouth was beside his ear. Just as he could feel her hand on him in her awkward, tentative caress. She might have been used by old Becksbridge, but she had not participated much if she showed so little skill. He liked knowing that more than he knew he should.

And yet there had been that moment afterwards, when he settled atop her, when he had sensed a stillness, as if her whole body held its breath and her soul calculated her danger. It was much like what he sensed when she looked back at him on the barge. And it was, he decided now, a milder form of the way she turned to stone in the greenhouse.

It had passed once she realized he was in no condition to ravish her. Yet it had been there, clearly, like a break or pause in her bliss, strong enough to interfere even with the aftermath of her violent sexual climax.

Perhaps now that she knew that he knew the truth about her history, it would disappear. She had not been pleased that he had pried. People never were, even if the outcome benefited them. As long as he knew what he knew, he had decided it was best to let her know he knew too.

It was possible that her sense of danger would always be there, however, unless she were totally agreeable in advance to be thoroughly seduced. So he would do what she wanted to make her so.

He would obtain the damned letters he had promised her, and he would finally have her.

Then—what? Loss of interest, most likely. A return to his habits and his whores, no doubt. The renewed onset of endless ennui, probably.

On the other hand, since Daphne Joyes had already

been gifted as well as a mistress kept for a year, he might decide to enjoy the year that he was due.

D aphne eyed the garments spread out on her bed. Simple and practical, she reminded herself. She lifted a white muslin dress and set it aside.

She began folding the clothing and placing it into the waiting valise. She tucked ten pounds deep inside one of the shoes too. Her hands shook while she worked, a result of the excitement that had claimed her once she made her decision to take this journey.

She unfolded Margaret's letter and read it again.

I have been thinking of you often, Daphne, for reasons that I think you have guessed. Yes, come, quickly if you can. My situation will be changing for the worse, I fear, and I may not stay here much longer. I am afraid that the past threatens to catch us both soon. Currently all is calm in the towns, but there is anger in the air, and I am sorry to say that it extends to the whole region. Take care if you make this journey, and be sure to avoid the coaches that might take you into the city.

Did she imagine the urgency of the letter? The plea, and worse, the warning. She dared not assume so. Nor could she hope that all would remain calm up there. Certainly the newspapers printed nothing to support such a view.

Margaret's letter worried her. An emotion akin to terror threaded all through the excitement with which she prepared, making it unpleasant and colored with the worst kind of foreboding.

It was time to leave London anyway. Dodging Castleford had done no good. Nor had succumbing far more than was wise. Perhaps her absence would finally turn his curiosity elsewhere or dull it enough.

She should experience relief at the notion of ending that game. Instead it saddened her. Life had certainly been more interesting the last weeks. And the duke—he had been more compelling than she had expected. Beneath that insouciance, that bored indifference, there dwelled a man much better and more complex than his public face suggested.

She called for a footman. He arrived while she cleared her dressing table of its brushes. She pulled her composure together and tried to sound authoritative.

"I will be making a short journey of several days. Please have the carriage prepared and brought round."

The footman's gaze rose from its discreet focus on the floor. She had surprised him. She hoped he would not ask for any proof that she had Lord Sebastian's permission to use the carriage thus, because she did not. If Sebastian and Audrianna knew what was at stake, she was sure that they would not stand in her way, however.

"May I ask how many days, Mrs. Joyes? The coachman will want to know."

"A week perhaps."

His eyebrows rose slightly. "Will you be requiring an escort?"

She could probably use one, although it might only be awkward. "The coachman's services will suffice."

"I will ask the under butler, Mrs. Joyes."

He left, and she returned to packing. If she were refused the carriage, she would just have to take the stage-coach.

She opened the dressing table's drawer and paused when her gaze fell on the earrings that Castleford had given her.

She held them to her ears and bent to see them in the looking glass. What had he really thought as he looked at her wearing them, and nothing else? That she was the most expensive mistress he had never had? That she teased him because she was cruel or to obtain such gifts? That she had been a fool to give herself to Becksbridge for anything less?

He had not treated her as if he thought any of those things. Oh, he had a game of seduction afoot, that was undeniable, but twice now he had shown uncommon decency in how he played it.

His questions about her marriage echoed in her head. She was not convinced he would let it rest there, even if he thoroughly seduced her now. Not unless she was out of sight and, eventually, out of his mind. He was not known for any constancy, and a week should discourage him.

She went to her little writing table and dipped the pen. She did not write to Castleford. Instead she penned a note to Lord Sebastian and Audrianna, to leave in the drawer, asking them to put the ear bobs in safekeeping, should they return and chance upon them. Once she finished her journey, she would hand them back to their rightful owner.

Chapter Fifteen

Two days later, Castleford took pains in replotting the final chapter in "The Seduction of Daphne Joyes," well aware that by now the story should be in its epilogue, at least.

He even went about town himself to do it.

He called at the jewelers again. Phillip all but kissed his feet as he left with another little box in his hands.

He stopped at a flower shop and personally chose the blooms to be delivered to his house.

He kept an appointment with a famed musician, bought him very expensive wine, and after some small talk offered him a ridiculous sum to play his violin that evening on the garden terrace.

Prior to going to Park Lane to call on Daphne and lure her away, he rode to Brooks's. He needed to make quick use of their library to jot a note.

No sooner had he entered than three men sitting together near the window hailed him and called him over like old friends too long parted.

He recognized them as Sir Marcus Valmare, his son Cato Valmare, and Mr. Jeoffrey Drumblewhite. The last was a gentleman from Hampshire known to dabble in more trade than was truly acceptable. Commercial interests were a late development in his life, and there had been talk of severing his membership in the club because of it.

"Castleford, you look well." Sir Marcus effused so loudly that he might be speaking to an old, deaf relative. A beefy, tall bear of a fellow, he owned a florid face and a good head of white hair that he kept long and wavy, as if to rub it in the noses of his balding contemporaries. "Doesn't he look well, Drumblewhite?"

"Most well. Most well." Drumblewhite was one of the balding ones, with a slight build and squinting eyes. He sounded like he spoke through his nose.

"Sit, sit," Sir Marcus insisted. "It has been too long."

It had been forever, but Castleford was in too good a mood to make a fine point of it. "I have something I must do. Perhaps another time."

"Ohhh, *siiittt*, Your Grace. Pass a few minutes with an old friend," Sir Marcus cajoled with a big smile. He pulled a chair out and all but pushed Castleford's ass into it.

He sat. Cato Valmare, who thought himself very clever—he actually went around calling himself that, lest the descriptive not stick merely on account of others' impressions—watched with lids at half-mast. Castleford gazed back just as lazily. They began a contest to see who could appear more indifferent.

"I say, Castleford," Sir Marcus said casually. "Quite a

find you have had on that land. Whoever expected such a thing?"

"Everyone except me, it appears," Castleford said.

"Of course, finding minerals and extracting them are two different things," Cato said with a superior tone.

"I cannot disagree with that view, Valmare. No matter how one cuts it, they are two different things," Castleford said.

"It takes considerable investment to mine land properly," Mr. Drumblewhite said in a nasal voice, as if he taught a lesson to a child. "It is always a big gamble, since the deposits may not be what are expected."

"I am told that it is wise to watch the managers every hour too," Sir Marcus said, leaning forward in confidence.

"How boring," Castleford drawled.

Sir Marcus slapped his knee. "Exactly. I was just telling Drumblewhite here that you are not a man who likes to be bored. You have better ways to spend your time, eh?" His eyebrows rose with insinuation. "Better if he sold out, then, Drumblewhite said. Did you not say that, sir?"

"Indeed I did, Sir Marcus. While you are reputed to have great luck in the financial area, Your Grace, no doubt you prefer other activities, as suits one as esteemed as yourself. The natural order is to let other men get their hands dirty; those born to it."

Castleford folded his arms and extended his legs. "Alas, one cannot escape such matters entirely. And I have a rule against ever selling land. It is a family tradition."

Sir Marcus glanced at Drumblewhite, then at Cato. "How unfortunate for you. But, perhaps not entirely so. With the right partners much of the nuisance can still be relieved. Why, Drumblewhite here, for example, has a way with such affairs, inherited no doubt from that merchant hidden among his mother's ancestors. You understand that I mean no offense by mentioning that, Drumblewhite. I merely point out that your talent comes with your blood and is a natural inclination that cannot be resisted."

Drumblewhite bowed his head, whether in modesty regarding this talent or in shame, Castleford could not tell. "I would, of course, be happy to help Your Grace in any way, should you have need of me."

"Why, we all would, would we not? Eh, Cato? It is what friends are for," Sir Marcus exclaimed.

Cato finally chimed in. "I wonder if a partnership is the best way to handle such help, however. Drumblewhite, when you manage another's business, what is the fee?"

"Fee? I am a gentleman, sir. I take no fees."

"No fee?" Castleford said. "You would do this as a kindness? I am touched, Mr. Drumblewhite."

"I only ask a consideration for my expertise. Another esteemed gentleman in a similar situation generously gave me one quarter of the ownership in his canal, for example. He is freed of all concerns as a result."

Three pairs of eyes settled on Castleford. He gazed back placidly. Silence ticked by.

"Of course," Sir Marcus said. "That canal needed building. Managing the extraction of minerals from the ground, while serious business, would not necessarily require that size consideration. Fifteen percent might be considered fair."

Castleford just looked at them.

"I would do it for ten," Cato said.

His father turned to him in surprise, but Cato forged

on. "It would be a step down, of course. I would only do so to break the ennui, which I suffer from as much as Your Grace."

Drumblewhite could hardly contain his rage that the young pup had tried to cut him out. "More experience is required than you have, Mr. Valmare."

Sir Marcus reddened at his friend's condescending tone. "We could do as well as you, sir, I am sure."

Castleford gathered his legs and stood. "I have no need of anyone's services, because I have found no minerals."

Sir Marcus smiled knowingly. He glanced around the chamber, then winked. "Then forgive us our presumptions and assumptions. However, should you decide to exploit these unfound minerals and require either partners or investors in a syndicate, I trust that you will remember our old friendship."

Castleford nodded his head in what might be seen as assent. Sir Marcus seemed to have forgotten that their old friendship involved the man's female cousin, a summer night seven years ago, and passion amid the trees of Hyde Park. Or was it St. James Park? Other than the blustering threats Sir Marcus had flung the next morning, the two had not spoken much before or after that until today.

He made good his escape and aimed toward the writing table. Along the way three more men waylaid him. Each one privately apologized for having overheard Sir Marcus and confided that he had a brother or cousin who could do far better than Drumblewhite or Cato. And, oh, if a syndicate were formed, he hoped His Grace would please keep the speaker in mind.

To each one he explained that any talk of new discoveries of minerals on any of his land was an unfounded rumor and nothing more.

Finally breaking free to complete his task, Castleford sat at the writing table. He took one of his calling cards from his case. On the back of it he wrote, "I am cold sober, so I expect to be received this time."

He was blotting the card when a shadow fell over the table. He turned to find Latham trying to peer over his shoulder.

He slipped the card in his pocket. "You learned some bad habits in France, Latham. Your social behavior has become inexcusably rude."

"I merely waited for you to complete your note before seeking some conversation with you."

Castleford turned in the chair. "I can't imagine why you would bother, since we have nothing to talk about."

Latham put on his false face, the jovial one that inspired so much confidence among the easily duped sheep. He moved another chair closer and sat in it.

"We parted last time on a discordant note, Castleford. It will not do."

Castleford thought it would do just fine.

"We need to talk about my father's will and the oddity of those bequests to you," Latham said.

"Should you not speak with a solicitor if you have questions? I never even read the will."

"Do not pretend that you do not know the concern I have."

"I never pretend. I would truly be befuddled if I were not too bored to be befuddled."

Latham eyed him skeptically. "I think he made a mistake in giving those holdings to you. He was not well toward the end, I am told, and often confused."

"So you think he mistook me for you? Wrote *Tristan, the Duke of Castleford* when he really meant to write *my heir*? By Zeus, that *is* confused."

Latham ignored the sarcasm. "I obviously would like to keep the estate intact."

"Would that your father had wanted to as well. I might be spared this conversation."

Latham leaned forward and whispered in a sharp staccato of anger, "See here. I want to buy it back. The land. I will pay the going rate for good farmland, so you are not out anything except tiny estates too troublesome to matter."

Castleford stood. "How generous of you. But I think not."

He walked out of the club. Latham was on his heels the whole way.

"You did find something. I knew it. Damnation, he never intended for you to get richer off those bequests. If he had only known—"

"Ah, *if he had only known*. Those are among the saddest words in our language, don't you think?" Castleford pulled on his gloves and gestured for the groom to bring his horse. "Calm yourself, Latham. Your face is turning that shade of red that speaks of a man tempting the limits of his health."

Latham stuck that red face close to Castleford's own. "I'll see that you reap no profit from what is in that ground. I'll contest those bequests and tie them all up in the courts so long that you will be dead before it is over."

Castleford swung up on his mount. He looked down. "There is nothing in that land to provoke your avarice."

"Those others in there offered you more, didn't they?"

"I treated their strange certainty of discovered riches the same way that I have treated yours." He pointed his horse west, to where paradise waited. "Really, this nonsense is all too tedious."

Chapter Sixteen

Park Lane appeared unusually busy for a street flanked by a park on its west and noble houses on its east. Castleford rode his horse past three of those great homes before realizing all the activity was in front of the one he sought.

Wagons lined the walk, and servants buzzed about. He handed his horse's reins to one, went to the open door, and peered in.

A footman hurried over. Not young, green Perthy, but a hearty fellow of more exacting demeanor. Castleford handed over his card, and asked to speak with Mrs. Joyes.

The fellow's eyebrows did not even register vague surprise. Impeccably proper and deferential in every way, he escorted Castleford up to the drawing room.

It did not take long for the servant's steps to sound outside the chamber again. Just male footfalls approached, however. None others.

Castleford's temper spiked. Damnation, the woman was going to refuse to receive him again. Well, if she wanted it that way, so be it. No more patience. No more gentility. He would just go up there again and lock that door and have her right there in that pale chamber. He would be damned before he allowed her to lead him in this dance one day longer. It was damned well past time to—

"Summerhays," he said with surprise, the angry monologue dropping from his mind.

The door had opened while he fumed, but the footman had not returned. Instead, Sebastian Summerhays stood there. The same Sebastian Summerhays who was supposed to be on the coast with his wife.

"What a surprise to see you, Castleford. Has word spread so fast that we are back?" Summerhays greeted him warmly, with one of the charming smiles that turned women into fools.

"You know how it is in town in summer. Any bit of talk spreads fast, there is so little to discuss," he replied. It sounded like something Albrighton would say, all dodgy and indirect. "Why have you returned? Did the prime minister call for you?"

Summerhays scowled at the reference. "They are asking no counsel from *me*, which only makes me fear whose counsel they are getting instead. Yours?"

"We should be so fortunate. If you are not returned for that, then why? It is an odd time to leave the coast, with your wife close to being brought to bed."

"It appears that will happen here. She insisted on

coming with me. It took four days, because I dared not let the horses do more than a moderate pace." Summerhays sat and gestured for his guest to as well. "We came back because I expect my brother's return from the Continent. I received the letter a week ago. His ship should arrive any day now, I expect."

Summerhays's brother, the Marquess of Wittonbury, had left England a little over a year before, for his health and for other reasons having to do with honor. An acknowledgment of the history of the marquess's departure passed between him and Summerhays in the look they exchanged.

"So that explains why I am here," Summerhays said. "And why Audrianna accompanied me. She has a special bond with him. Now all that remains is an explanation of why you are here." As he said the last part, he reached into a pocket and removed the calling card just sent up with the footman. He made a display of reading the note on the back. "Sober, no less. I am impressed."

Damnation.

Summerhays looked over with a merry twinkle in his eyes. Castleford acted bored and indifferent.

He doubted Summerhays believed the act. Of all their circle, Summerhays had the best cause to assume the worst. Prior to Summerhays assuming the mantle of respectability in order to stand in for his brother, the two of them had joined together in sprees of wonderfully disgraceful rakish hedonism.

A few memories of those glory days drifted through his mind, and Castleford sighed inwardly. He truly missed the old Sebastian sometimes.

"I have some business with Mrs. Joyes."

Summerhays laughed. "Is that what you call it now?"

"I do not use that word euphemistically, Summerhays. There is really business between us, of a nature I am not at liberty to describe."

Summerhays grinned. "I am sure there is."

"Stop smirking like a lewd old man and send up for her, if you do not mind."

Summerhays fingered the card. "I would, and I would even leave you alone with her to discuss this *business* in privacy, only the lady is not here. She left the house two days ago."

Castleford made sure he did not react in any visible way, but a scathing anger flared in his head again. If she had left this house, she had left London. She knew that he would be coming for her after he procured those damned letters, and s*he had run away*.

The coward. The *bitch*.

This was not to be borne. To allow this would mean admitting she had played him for the worst fool in a long game, with nothing more than his humiliation as the goal.

Summerhays watched him. Castleford sprawled, crossed his arms, and pretended to swallow a yawn. "Left, did she? That is good to know. I will have to write to her at Cumberworth instead, and settle the matter by mail."

"I do not think she is in Cumberworth. She took one of our carriages, and one of our coachmen, and neither has returned yet."

Fury gave up some ground to a surge of profound curiosity. "That is odd."

"Yes, isn't it?"

"Do the servants know where she went?"

"They only report that she took a valise but not all of her things, and that she told the coachman that they would first go west, then north."

North? She had once said that Captain Joyes's regiment had been in the north when she married him. Only there had never been a Captain Joyes.

"I don't suppose Lady Sebastian can guess where she went?"

Summerhays set the card down on the table near him. "She assumes that Mrs. Joyes went to The Rarest Blooms first, then perhaps to visit her husband's family, whom she recalls perhaps living in the north. It had been some time since Mrs. Joyes was home. If she intended a journey of any length, she would want to make sure all was in order at The Rarest Blooms first. Other than that, Audrianna has no idea. This uncharacteristic behavior on the part of Mrs. Joyes has distressed her, however. I fear that she will worry."

West first, then north. It was possible that Daphne had not left The Rarest Blooms yet. He could write to Edwards, he supposed, and find out, and also ask where she had gone after if she had already left.

He stood. "I will leave so you can settle your household back in here. Give my warmest regards to your wife, Summerhays, and to your brother, when he arrives.

D ark had enshrouded the property when Castleford rode up the lane of The Rarest Blooms. Light glowed behind the windowpanes of the first floor, however.

He tied his horse and used the door knocker. It seemed as if the house's stones held their breath at the sound he made. After a protracted pause, the door opened a crack. Spectacles peered out. Castleford peered back.

What in hell—

"Sir!"

"Open the damned door, Edwards."

It flew wide. "Your Grace, this is so unexpected."

"It certainly is. What do you have there? A pistol? Hell, point it elsewhere, you fool."

Edwards remembered the gun in his hand and let his arm fall so it aimed at the floor.

"What are you doing here, sir?"

"What are *you* doing here?"

"Protecting the women, sir. The way you commanded me."

"Do you stay on guard all night? You took my words most literally. No wonder your last letter did not complain of bedbugs."

He pushed past Edwards and strode into the house. He paced to the back sitting room and peered through the panes to the greenhouse to see if anyone was in there. Especially anyone with very fair hair, maybe wearing extremely expensive diamonds.

Curiosity and anger had battled all the way down here. As he approached, anger had won out again.

A small noise to his right made him pivot. The sound had been a woman's step on the floorboards, he was sure.

"Come out now. There will be no running away any longer," he said. "I'll be damned before I allow this farce to continue one more day."

A little gasp sounded. A feminine foot appeared. She stepped into view at the doorway to the dining room.

It was not Daphne, but Miss Johnson.

"Where is Mrs. Joyes?" he demanded.

She shrank away, terrified. Mr. Edwards hurried over to reassure her with some whispered words.

"It would help if you did not yell like that, sir. She has a very delicate constitution," Mr. Edwards had the temerity to say.

"I may do more than yell if she does not answer me. I have reason to think Mrs. Joyes is here, or was recently."

"She was here, that is true," Edwards said, yelling a bit himself. In fact, he dared to act piqued. "I saw her. She stayed one night, then left in the morning. She did not say where she was going."

Castleford kept his attention on Miss Johnson. "She did not give her destination to you, Edwards, but I think she did to her dear friend here. Miss Johnson would need to know where to write to Mrs. Joyes, in the event there were a problem with the business."

Edwards frowned over that. He turned to Miss Johnson. "Did she leave such information, Katherine?"

Katherine?

Castleford suddenly noticed the gentle way Edwards spoke to Miss Johnson. He finally became aware of the nice dress Miss Johnson wore. He assessed the total absence of Mrs. Hill from these chambers.

Miss Johnson appeared distraught. She turned those dark, limpid eyes on Edwards. "She said she was going north, to her first sister."

Edwards turned to Castleford. "There you have it, Your Grace. She went to visit her sister," he said defensively.

"A lot of good that does me, since she *has no sister*. An address, Miss Johnson. I will have it now, please."

"She only said I could write if I had to, to the town of Failsworth, in Lancashire. She would get the letter."

Failsworth. She was not just going north, but far north. The woman was traveling right into the heart of the danger up there.

Castleford turned on his heel. "Come with me, Mr. Edwards. That front sitting room will do, I think."

Once they got there, Castleford made himself comfortable on a chair. He did not invite Edwards to do the same. He gave his secretary a good examination.

Country air suited Edwards. He did not appear so pale now. He even held himself differently, as if he found his body more comfortable than before.

"Enjoying your sojourn amid the blooms, are you, Edwards?"

Edwards gazed straight ahead at nothing in particular. "I do not mind the country as much as you do, if that is what you mean, Your Grace."

"I was very surprised to find you here and not at the inn."

"You told me to stay here, sir. In your last letter. You said it would be best if I stayed with the ladies."

"I did not mean at night, Edwards."

"Then perhaps you should have been explicit, sir. I always do as you order, and your letter ordered me to—"

"Have there been any more trespassers?"

"Several. Two near the men examining the land, that they reported to me. One on the property next to this, peering over the garden wall. I pursued the last, but he lost me in the woods." He looked at Castleford. "I do not think he was with the others. I think the one who is so bold regarding this house is less interested in your affairs than in the house itself."

"Why do you think this?"

"We would not be mining for minerals in the garden, would we? I am fairly sure he was the same one as the first time too, not that I saw clearly enough either time to be certain."

Castleford stored away that observation. He would have many hours in his saddle to contemplate it later.

He gave Edwards another good look. The secretary's gaze settled elsewhere again.

"Mr. Edwards."

"Your Grace?"

"I trust that you are being a gentleman with Miss Johnson."

Edwards swallowed hard.

"Because, Edwards, I gave instructions that you were to protect the women here and see they were not bothered. I do not remember giving you permission to seduce her."

"I have not seduced her."

There had been a peculiar emphasis on the word *seduced*. "You wouldn't be parsing words with me, would you, Edwards?"

Edwards ignored that. "If I had seduced her, which I have not, is it common to request permission first, the way you imply? I mean, do you? Request permission of anyone, that is?"

"Your time in the country has emboldened you. It must be all that pistol wielding you are doing."

Edwards flushed. "Perhaps so, sir."

"On a different day I might find it amusing. Today I do not. As to your impertinent question, no, I do not ask permission first. But then I have never seduced a woman I was charged with protecting either. It does matter, you know."

Edwards nodded. "I see, sir. It is a fine line, of course."

"Not too fine to miss, I hope."

"No, Your Grace."

"Good. Then do not cross it while you are here. Other

than that, are you comfortable? Do you require the servants to send you anything?"

"I am very comfortable. I am in a chamber full of blue and yellow flowers. It is much like the garden coming indoors. I found it silly and feminine at first, but I have grown somewhat fond of it."

Castleford knew that chamber too well. He hated it.

He studied Edwards one more time to see if there were any smugness or hiding merriment that indicated he was indeed enjoying this sojourn more than he ought. When he caught up with Daphne, he did not want any guilt about Miss Johnson interfering with his righteous annoyance with her.

He rose to his feet. "I will leave now. Go to the village every day to see if I send any letters." He paused after a few strides. "When Mrs. Joyes left here, do you know if she took her pistol?"

"I believe Katherine mentioned that she did, sir."

Castleford was untying his horse when he realized Edwards had called Miss Johnson by her given name again. He looked at the house. No wonder Edwards had grown fond of that flowered chamber.

He shook his head in exasperation. If Daphne Joyes found out about the bliss being enjoyed in that house, Edwards would be lucky to survive with his manhood intact.

Chapter Seventeen

•

Castleford was almost in Lancashire before he took more than an hour's rest. He stopped at a staging inn, handed his mount over to the grooms to rub down and feed, then went to find food for himself.

The inn proved crowded. A glance at the women and children identified them as gentry or better. Servants attended them, and the coaches outside were burdened with boxes and portmanteaus. It appeared a scene from a war, when refugees flee the city before the enemy takes it.

With the threatened demonstration tomorrow, that was probably what it was too. Alarmed, the better people, the ones who thought themselves at risk, were streaming away. He suspected that those who stayed had fortified their properties.

While he ate the watery stew at a private table procured by his title, the inn instantly became more crowded yet. Redcoats streamed in the door, looking for spots to sit and calling for beer. The public room could not hold them all, and the proprietor waved them to another chamber in the back.

The officers entered last. Castleford spoke to the inn's owner and sent an invitation for the officers to join him.

They did so gladly, perhaps grateful that at least the bad stew would not hurt their purses.

Colonel Markins, a man of suitable military bearing and a serious, stony face, accepted the hospitality with reserved politeness. As the ranking officer, he also felt obligated to make conversation that his younger officers seemed too hungry to engage in just yet.

"Are you aiming south with the others, Your Grace?"

"No, north. And you?"

"I'm not to say, but considering it will be no news to yourself—" He leaned across the table confidentially. "We've been sent to Manchester. To keep the peace. Requested by the magistrates up there, we were."

So it had been done. Albrighton's information that day in Bedford Square had not been corroborated by anyone else, and Castleford had hoped Liverpool and the other ministers had thought better of involving the army.

"I trust you will not parade the colors in front of the speakers," he said.

"Remains to be seen what will be required."

"Are you in command?"

"Of these men here, yes. But I'm to heed the demands from magistrates. Order must be maintained and property protected—those were the instructions I received."

"There's word already of thousands on the move," one of his junior officers interjected. "Maybe tens of thousands, from all over the county and region."

"There may not be enough of us, then," another man said.

"Order will be maintained, one way or another," Colonel Markins said.

The conversation moved on to more pleasant subjects. One officer asked if Castleford had attended the Ascot races this year. A major, whose father was a baron, found the opportunity to allude to the new syndicate Castleford was said to be forming, to mine gold from some land in Kent.

The soldiers did not rest long. A half hour later their red coats filed down the road. Castleford claimed his own horse an hour after that. He decided to ride on for a while before he bought a bed for the night.

He fished in the saddlebag for his map and found the village of Failsworth, to plot the fastest route through Lancashire. He cursed when he saw that Failsworth was at most five miles from the outskirts of Manchester and north of the city.

What was Daphne thinking, going there at such a time? Not running away from him, he guessed. She could go anywhere for that.

He would be the one to scold this time, about her recklessness.

Ill ease replaced his anger. His heart might have thickened, the sensation became so physical. He was not accustomed to worrying about people, and he did not know how to accommodate his growing concern. He took some comfort in knowing that at least she had Summerhays's coachman with her.

He stuffed the map back in his bag and mounted. Then he paused and pictured that map again. There had been something familiar to it. He now realized what it had been.

He reached into the bag once more, fished down, and withdrew some loose papers. They were four pages from a pocket map, torn out for reference. Mr. Edwards had handed them over some weeks ago.

Each one had a neat circle penned on it, and some notations and directions. One showed how to reach a property near Cumberworth in Middlesex.

Another showed the region around Manchester, with the village of Failsworth circled.

He cursed himself for not realizing the connection sooner. Of course he had been foxed when Edwards gave him these map pages, so it was a wonder he remembered them at all.

That circle indicated the location of another spot he had just inherited. One where another tenant lived, in whose welfare Becksbridge had committed interest.

Daphne had gone north to visit one of Becksbridge's other mistresses.

Chapter Eighteen

Daphne sipped some tea while the low fire toasted her feet. Another pair of slippers poked the air beside her own. Margaret's arm kept moving up and down in a slow movement, while she brushed her long red hair.

"Are you less worried, Daphne? Now that you visited Mrs. Forester, and have seen that the village of Eccles is calm?"

"Much less worried." It was a lie, but there would be little point in making Margaret know the sickness in her heart. Oh, visiting the Foresters had been wonderful. Those two hours had been sweet and joyful and full of nostalgia. The nearby village had indeed been calm, and she thanked God for that.

The problem was that after two days, Daphne understood too well what Margaret had meant about there being anger in the air.

One could sense it. Smell it. It marked the faces of men one passed. It changed behaviors too.

Summerhays's expensive carriage had attracted enough angry glares that she had told the coachman to stay at the inn in Failsworth, and she no longer made use of the conveyance. Today, when she and Margaret traveled the few miles to Eccles, they had taken Margaret's little gig.

"I hope we made the correct choice, not bringing them back with us," she said about the Foresters.

"This house is right on the road to Manchester. They are out of the way, and much safer there," Margaret reassured. "If the inn at Eccles had room, I would have gladly left you there."

Unfortunately the inn had been full. So now they would just go back tomorrow and make sure all was well. It should be, Daphne told herself. That did not help her nerves, though.

"Thank you for the tea," Margaret said. She put aside her brush and picked up her cup to sip.

Daphne had purchased the tea on the way here, not sure what she would find. Fortunately, it appeared that Margaret lived comfortably and might well afford her own tea.

The house was not nearly as big as The Rarest Blooms. It did not have as much land attached to it. Nor did Margaret have a business, from what Daphne could tell.

"I also thank you for giving me hope about the property," Margaret said. "When Becksbridge died, I thought for sure that his son would inherit and, of course, put me out. In the least I expected the rent to increase and my allowance to end. That will probably still happen, no matter if this other relative has received the property instead and lets me stay."

"I do not believe that Castleford will leave you destitute." She had no right to reassure Margaret. She did not even know for certain that this land had been part of Castleford's inheritance. Yet with Margaret's recent admission that she lived here due to Becksbridge's benevolence, it made sense. Becksbridge must have sensed that Castleford would be more sympathetic than Latham ever would be.

"Perhaps, as a duke, he is so rich that he will not even bother with me," Margaret said. "He may just forget about such a small inheritance."

"Maybe so." Daphne doubted that. Eventually the Tuesday would come when Castleford turned his mind to it all. It might be best for her to talk to him about Margaret and the others on the two remaining spots of land. She would not have to explain anything, since he had indicated he already had drawn conclusions about the four of them.

Margaret rose and walked to a window. She opened the casements to the night air. The middle of August brought chill with it in the evening, and the breeze wafting in made Margaret pull the knitted shawl that she wore tighter.

"It is so quiet," she muttered. "Too quiet. I should not have encouraged you to come now. It could have waited, I suppose."

"I wanted to come. To see you. I needed to know if my long suspicions that we shared a common history were correct. I should have guessed that your kindness to me was not an accident, but I confess it took me years to even wonder." She paused. "And I needed to see that you were safe and the neighbors I came to love were too. And the Foresters. I needed to visit them and reassure myself that their village would not be burned to the ground or something, if trouble started."

"They are all sworn to be peaceable, Daphne. I know these people. They are not only my neighbors, but some are my relatives and some are my dearest friends. All should be well at the demonstration tomorrow."

Yes, all should be well. Yet the anger was in the air, and in men's bodies and faces. Women too would march to Manchester. Margaret had described how some women had become very active among the workers and formed their own societies to hold meetings. One woman would even speak to the crowd tomorrow.

Margaret pulled her shawl tighter yet and looked out to the night. "It is so quiet," she muttered again.

Very quiet. Like the whole world waited for something, while holding its breath.

Castleford's concern only grew as he rode toward Manchester the next morning. He passed people on the road, most on foot and others in wagons. Far too many used the road to be explained by any normal event or routine. They all headed north, toward the city, and their expressions spoke their serious purpose. They wore their best clothes, as if they were to attend a church service.

His instincts responded anyway. He found himself too alert, too observing, as if his soul sensed peril. His appearance attracted gazes that were not friendly, that was certain, but nothing was said or done to challenge him.

It was not these people that had him tense like an animal in a foreign forest. Rather a mood hung over the world and seeped into him that spoke of risk and hard decisions and of men being required to do unpleasant things because there was no other choice.

It reminded him of that night in France too much. Of

being caught up in events that had taken a turn not expected, and which demanded actions more serious than
ever anticipated. *Do not challenge me*, he silently said to
two burly fellows who paid him too much attention as he
trotted past them. *Do not make me hurt you in order to
protect myself.*

He circled wide around Manchester, to the north, and
joined yet more marchers heading south. When he entered
the village of Failsworth, he realized he had been passing
the stragglers, not the main column of workers. The greater
number must have passed hours before. A few more stragglers moved through the village itself, their faces firm with
resolve. The village's few shops had been closed, and other
than the low muffle of those shoes and boots on the lanes,
all was deathly still.

One door remained open, that of the tavern. He dis-
mounted and entered, glad that one person had decided to
sell drink and food to the demonstrators passing, rather
than march himself.

The tavern was not crowded, since the day was passing
and those still en route to the city still had a few miles to
walk. However, enough eyes turned to scrutinize him that
his senses sharpened in caution yet again.

He ignored their interest and peered around for the
owner. His gaze was arrested on the figure of a man in a
corner. Seemingly oblivious to the oddness of the village
today, the fellow read a book by a window's light while
he sipped at a pint that had probably lasted hours already.

The man did not look like he worked in a mill. Castleford walked over, convinced he had seen the fellow
before in London.

The man looked up blankly. Then he sat a little
straighter. "Your Grace!" He began scrambling to stand.

Castleford subtly cut the air with his hand to indicate the man should remain seated and also that he not speak so loudly. "I have seen you at the ribbons of Summer-hays's coach, have I not?"

The man nodded. He glanced askance at the nearest table, from where eyes watched.

Castleford sat with the coachman. "Where is she? Mrs. Joyes? Is she in this village?"

"No, Your Grace. She is at a cottage a bit up the road. I have been staying here, up above, and the carriage and horses are at a stable."

"Have you seen her since you brought her to that cottage?"

The coachman shook his head. "She told me she would come for me or send word if she needed me. Just gave me the coin to buy a bed and food, and that has been the whole of it the last two days." His gaze slid sideways again. "I am trusting the lady is of sound sense and is not planning to walk with them, like the wives and children seem to be doing? Some ladies get these reforming notions sometimes and can do foolish things."

"I do not think that is her intention, but perhaps not for lack of sympathy." Daphne had not come here to march with workers, but she may have come here because workers would be marching. "I have a map with directions, but perhaps you would just describe this house and how to find it."

The coachman explained how to find the little lane that led to a cottage with a blue door.

The proprietor walked by to serve some beer at the neighboring table and overheard while he did. He paused and gave Castleford a good look. "You be looking for Mrs. Rolland, are you? Have you business with her?"

Castleford called him over, then placed a guinea on the table to calm any suspicions. "Is that who lives up the road at the cottage?"

"That be the tenant there. She has lived here, oh, some ten years now. No, eleven. She came the year my son was born."

"I am not looking for her as such. I am here to meet with her visitor. Perhaps you have seen this friend of hers. A tall woman, very lovely and very pale."

The proprietor's smile showed two broken teeth. "That would be Mrs. Joyes. Lovely ain't the half of it, now is it? She is back for sure. She was seen yesterday in Mrs. Rolland's gig, on the road to Eccles."

"You know her then. Mrs. Joyes. Has she visited here often, then?"

The man laughed. "Doesn't visit so often, but she lived in these parts, didn't she? 'Bout for two years, on and off, some time ago. She stayed with Mrs. Rolland a while back then." He wandered off to take care of his other patrons.

The tavern owner's familiarity with Daphne did not surprise Castleford too much. If she had not followed the drum with Captain Joyes, she had to have lived somewhere those two years.

He stood. "You stay here," he told the coachman. "Be ready to have that carriage ready fast if I send word."

He went outside and mounted his horse again. He pointed its nose south, in the same direction those workers' boots had trod.

Very few trod now. An unnatural silence had fallen on the village.

He found the cottage with no trouble. In easy walking distance to Failsworth, it was visible from the road. The little lane that the coachman had described was really a path through a deep front garden.

It occurred to him, as he swung off his horse, that he should have something to say, to explain his intrusion. *You are not supposed to be risking your neck with this foolhardy journey right now, Mrs. Joyes. You are supposed to be spending the week in my bed.*

That no longer seemed an adequate explanation for his presence, or even accurate. He had spent too many hours in the saddle convincing himself she would not be in danger to deny now that the chance for danger was what had put him in the saddle to begin with.

If you were worried for friends up here, why did you not ask for my help? He knew why she had not. He had hardly presented himself as someone looking to help her or do anything except seduce her.

With no good excuse in mind, he lifted the door knocker.

The house came alive with vague sounds. A curtain at the window parted. A long pause followed. Finally, the door opened and a red-haired woman faced him.

He neither spoke nor moved for a stunned five count. Then he passed her his card while he introduced himself. All through their little greeting, his mind raced, taking the facts he knew and putting them in a new arrangement.

Mrs. Rolland invited him in. He stepped over the threshold, cursing himself silently for being so stupid.

It was all there, but you chose not to see it. You did not want to know.

Mrs. Rolland had not recognized him. She truly did not know his name until he spoke it. He recognized her, however. He had seen her once, years ago, on her back in some weeds, with despair and terror in her eyes.

Mrs. Rolland, Daphne's "sister," was not one of old Becksbridge's mistresses.

She was one of Latham's victims.

"Your Grace." Daphne shook while she made her little curtsy.

The expression on Castleford's face worried her even more than his unexpected appearance here did. He looked very much a duke today.

He entered Margaret's sitting room as if he called on a countess in Mayfair. A mask of reserve hid his thoughts. His eyes, however, told a different story to anyone who knew him well. They were the eyes of Castleford on a Tuesday, when he turns his considerable faculties to matters that he must address.

Damn his curiosity. Damn his prying. Look where it had led.

They all sat in Margaret's modest home, while introductions gave way to silence.

Margaret looked to each of them in turn. She excused herself and left the chamber.

Castleford's formality dropped then. He made himself more comfortable on his chair. He crossed his arms and regarded her as if he worked out a puzzle that had pieces he had not seen before.

Damn him.

"Summerhays returned to town," he said. "Imagine his surprise to discover that you had stolen one of his coaches and a coachman."

"I will write and explain enough, and explain more when I return."

"I would like you to share at least the *enough* part with me now. What are you doing here?"

"I am under no obligation to share any explanation with you. It was not *your* coach and servant that I stole. In fact, I think that I am the one due some courtesy regarding explanations. What are *you* doing here?"

"I followed you. Did you think I would not?"

"Of course I thought you would not. There was no reason in the world for you to do so."

"That is not true."

"Oh, forgive me. That is right, how stupid I am being. The infamous wicked rogue had not completed his seduction. Well, I hardly expected you to travel all over the realm to have your way. I had no idea you were so spoiled that you would go to the ends of the earth to have a woman who had caught your eye, if she dared slip out of your grasp."

"I do not have to have my way with every woman who catches my eye, Daphne. Just you."

Her indignation drained away when he said that. A deep ache grew among the confusion of emotions that replaced it, however. *Oh, Your Grace, we neither of us truly know what we have in the other.*

"How did you even find me?" She struggled not to reveal the poignant reactions making her melt. She had made a terrible muddle of this and would pay dearly now, with her heart if not her privacy.

"I asked Miss Johnson where you had gone. When she gave me the name of the village, I guessed the rest."

She dared not respond. She would not assume what he meant by "the rest."

His dark eyes let her wonder for a while or perhaps waited for her to explain the rest herself.

He extracted some papers from his coat pocket and handed them to her. She looked down at four pages from a pocket map, marked and noted and well creased from careless handling. She saw the one that had brought him to The Rarest Blooms and also the one with this cottage's location explained.

"I guessed that the tenant of one of those spots of land I inherited had gone to visit the tenant on another of them," he said. "You had shown some interest in the others. I thought that perhaps you had come to investigate, but I know now that you lived here, after you left Becksbridge's household, during those years when you told the world you had been married and following the drum."

"Then you know enough already, it appears."

He took the pages from her and put them back in his pocket. "Not why you came here now, at such a dangerous time. You are not a stupid woman."

"Perhaps I came because I thought it was a place where you would not find me."

She felt cruel as soon as she said it, even though he did not appear insulted. She decided to add enough so that perhaps enough would indeed be enough. "I worried for my old friend. Because of the danger. Also, I thought she might be concerned, as I was, after Becksbridge died, that perhaps her future was too uncertain. I came to reassure her and to bring her back with me if I could not."

He took that in thoughtfully.

"Is your inquisition finished?" she asked.

He looked at her, and in his eyes she saw more honesty and more kindness than she had ever seen.

"I would say that is enough, Daphne. For now."

＊ ＊ ＊

Margaret politely invited Castleford to join them for their midday meal. To Daphne's dismay, he accepted.

They ate in her tidy dining room off mismatched china plates. Being the daughter of a gentleman had mattered, Daphne had realized. Mrs. Joyes had lived better than Mrs. Rolland these last years. Becksbridge had given none of them more than he thought their birth deserved.

Castleford made conversation. He did not pry, but he managed to learn enough of Margaret's history to confirm that she had been a servant in Becksbridge's household.

"So the two of you became friends there," he said.

Margaret's smile froze.

"Yes," Daphne said. If one of them had to lie, she would be the one to do it. Margaret had not asked for any of this trouble. Nor did she feel guilty for her response. If the duke wanted to pry still, they owed him no explanations.

"Mrs. Rolland, do you have any idea how many people went to Manchester today?" he asked, changing the subject.

Margaret regarded him skeptically. "Are you asking as a member of the government?"

"I am asking as a man who finds himself in a village all but emptied of men and even women. If all the villages are like this, that would mean there is a very large crowd in the city."

"Many thousands," she said. "There will be no cotton woven today."

"Such a crowd can be perilous in itself. Why would the women go?"

"They work in the mills, don't they? They go for themselves and their men and their children's futures."

Daphne recognized the little fires in Margaret's eyes. They had been burning ever since she arrived. Margaret had a good heart and sympathized with her neighbors' plight.

"You should know, Your Grace, that I support the principles behind this demonstration. I do not work in a mill, but I know many women who do. I am very good friends with some of them," Margaret said.

"Do you know any of the ones who formed friendly societies?" he asked.

"Some. Those are only social groups, however. They have nothing to do with—"

"Mrs. Rolland, everyone in the government knows that the friendly societies are frauds, created to get around the restrictions of the Combination Acts that prevent workers organizing themselves. That is true for the ones formed by men, and presumably for those formed by women too."

"I'll not be agreeing with you in words, if that is what you want, Your Grace."

"I do not expect you to betray your friends. I am just curious about how many there are. I know of the ones in Royton and Blackburn."

"There are others. You must be very curious, if you know some of the towns with such women's societies."

"It is unusual. The unusual often piques my interest." He glanced at Daphne. "Mrs. Joyes can tell you how that happens with me."

"Mrs. Joyes thinks that a better conversation might be your inheritance from Becksbridge, Your Grace," Daphne said. "Just as you are curious about these societies, Mrs. Rolland is very curious about her place on this property. Or should she wait for Tuesday to ask you about it?"

Castleford appeared not to hear her. His attention had

been distracted. His awareness shifted away, totally and rudely, halfway through her little speech.

He realized he had done it and forced his concentration on her again. Mostly.

"Becksbridge's legacy," she prompted. "Mrs. Rolland is very interested in your intentions. Since you are here now, perhaps you will reassure her—"

She lost him again. Thoroughly. This time he rose and went to the window. It was ajar, but he opened it fully and went very still.

Margaret looked at her and shrugged. Daphne waited to learn the reason for this strange behavior.

"Excuse me, please." He strode from the chamber.

Daphne hesitated briefly, then hurried after him. Margaret followed. They found him outside in the front garden, looking west.

"Listen," he said. "Can you hear it?"

She and Margaret exchanged bewildered glances. Then she tried to hear whatever it was he spoke of.

It took a while. At first she thought she imagined it and heard only because she wanted to hear something. It seemed an almost inaudible rumble came to her on the breeze. Or perhaps through the ground.

It sounded a little like London. A chaos of people and noise. It seemed to grow while she concentrated.

They stood there, the three of them, motionless, until there could be no denying that noise because it no longer was far away but pouring down the lane.

"Damnation." Castleford glared toward the empty road. "Get inside, both of you."

Daphne hesitated.

"*Go,*" he commanded. "Bar the door and let no one in. I will be back soon."

He strode to his horse and swung up. Daphne returned to the cottage and joined Margaret at a window.

Castleford had not ridden away yet. Instead he reached into a bag and removed a pistol. He fished out powder and a ball and loaded the gun while his horse waited for a command.

It came soon enough, and the duke galloped away.

Castleford rode toward the noise, shamefully glad to have something important to do that kept him from ruminating on Daphne's history and all the questions now demanding answers. Since the only answers his mind was producing were unpleasant, it had been hell to sit there being polite when he wanted to drag her to privacy and find out the truth for certain.

With each minute the chaos grew louder until its parts finally became distinct. Shouts. Cries. Voices. And beneath it all, the low thunder of feet on the move.

Soon he faced the first of them, the ones still running even though they were miles from the city.

A young man stopped to catch his breath. He noticed Castleford and his eyes widened with alarm.

Castleford trotted his horse over. "You have nothing to fear from me. What has happened?"

"Army and yeomanry," the young man gasped, bending, hands on his knees while he caught his breath. "There's people dead and more wounded, and they are arresting who they can. Was calm enough, for all the size of it. Then the army came, and—" He shook his head. "Was terrible to see and desperate to be in. There was no place to go, there were so many. I thought we'd all trample each other before we got out."

He moved on, walking now, as if in speaking of it he realized he had reached safety. Castleford moved his horse forward.

More people now. Some angry and looking to fight, others terrified, others so dejected they wept. He kept to the side of the road and watched them file past, filling the road, aiming for their towns and villages and homes.

There were wounded among them. A woman with blood on her skirt limped amid the stream, aided by a man. The crowd jostled her and the man lost hold and she went down. The feet kept coming. Some stepped over her, but more did not.

Castleford pushed his horse into the river of bodies. "Give her to me," he said to the man.

The fellow looked up the horse's mass and at its rider and hesitated.

"Give her to me, you fool. I will get her to safety."

The man picked her up, lifted her, and helped her sit behind the saddle.

"You can follow," Castleford said.

"She ain't mine. I've no idea who she is." With that, the man joined the exodus.

"Is your husband here?" Castleford asked over his shoulder.

The woman's head lolled against his back. "He be back there in the city. On the ground. Dead, maybe. He told me to run."

"We will learn what became of him later. Hold tight now." He turned his horse and joined the fleeing workers going east.

It took longer to return to the cottage than to come from it. Eventually he turned up the little lane. He noted that the low wall surrounding the front garden did not deter people.

Some just swung over and trod through the plantings, trying to avoid the thick crowd now filling the road. Others came in and paused, looking at the cottage.

That was the danger with a crowd on the run, he thought. It turned into a reckless force with no regard for property and sometimes little for life itself. It made some feel that they could do things they would not normally do, and it broke down social restraints.

He deliberately used his horse to crowd the men who dallied and hooked the side of his coat back so the pistol showed.

He cleared the garden, but there would be more. No one would really be safe for several hours at least.

He got off the horse and helped the woman down. Daphne had been watching, and the door opened as he carried the woman to it.

He entered the cottage and saw at once that he had been disobeyed. That door had opened at least once while he was gone, and perhaps several times. Three new faces looked up at his arrival. Worried faces. Terrified eyes.

He set his burden down. "She has a wound." He gestured to the blood on her skirt. "Her leg, I think."

"I will get water," Daphne said. She walked toward the back of the cottage.

Castleford made sure the door was bolted, then followed her.

"Who are they? The other women?"

"Friends of Margaret's. They were exhausted and frightened and took sanctuary as they passed." She set about pouring water into a basin. Her hands shook while she reached for a basket of rags. "They killed a woman, they say. They killed one of the speakers named Mary Fildes.

It was as if they deliberately went after her, they say. Others died too."

His jaw had been tight for an hour now, and his anger flared. "The damned fools."

She straightened and glared at him. "Who? These poor people who bore no arms but were cut down by sabers?"

"All of them, damn it, on both sides. These workers, for thinking they could mass by the thousands and their betters would not treat it like the first move in a rebellion. The government, for sending the army out to cut down its own citizens."

Her lids lowered. "You know about the army? I pray that you did not have a hand in this."

He laughed bitterly. "My counsel was not sought. Men convinced of the need for force only listen to other men who think the same way." Of course, he did not require them to seek his counsel. Dukes could have their say no matter what. He had both spoken and written to Liverpool, for all the good it had done.

There would be hell to pay now. If the goal had been to force battle lines to be drawn, this could not have been more effective in achieving that.

He took the full basin from her. He carried it into the dining room and called for the women to move there, so they were not visible through the front windows. They filed in and moved the chairs into a circle in the middle of the chamber. Two women of middle years helped his refugee to a chair and knelt to lift her skirt to see what caused the blood.

He turned away to go keep an eye on the garden. As he did he saw the slash on the young woman's thigh. A sword had caused it. A soldier's sword.

"Mrs. Joyes, if you would join me," he said over his shoulder.

Daphne came up beside him as he positioned himself at the window of the front chamber. Outside on the road, a river of bodies still moved.

"I believe that you brought a pistol with you," he said. "Go and get it, along with any powder and balls you may have." He removed his own from under his coat and placed it on the window ledge within easy reach.

She stared at that pistol, then out at the chaotic mob. Color marked her pale cheeks. Not passion or anger caused it. Not even embarrassment. Fear was her high emotion this time. She would not reveal it in any other way, he knew. Not while those other women needed reassurance.

He admired how composed she remained. It wrenched his heart that he could not promise that there was no danger at all.

She went away and returned with her pistol a short while later. She set down little bags of balls and powder on a nearby table. Then she set the gun on the window ledge right beside his pistol and took a position by his side.

Four men ventured into the garden, eyeing the cottage, then his horse. They might have noticed it was not the kind of horse and saddle their own kind would own, or perhaps they only looked for an excuse to release the day's anger.

One picked up a rock.

If one rock flew, others probably would. It was the way with such things. Castleford opened the casement, and pointed the pistol right at the man holding that big stone.

"If you throw it, it will be the last thing your arm ever does," he called.

Four pairs of eyes shifted to the voice and saw the pistol. Four men ran and jumped over the stone wall to get away.

"You do that very well, Your Grace. Your tone implies shooting them will bore you to death, but you will do it if they insist."

"I will continue trying to hit the right notes, if you promise to continue praising me."

She smiled, but her gaze did not leave the garden.

How beautiful she looked, standing there in the golden light of the late afternoon. Exquisite. Strong and determined despite her fear. He did not doubt that she would use that pistol if necessary. There were not many men in whose courage he had the same confidence.

"There are many things that we must talk about, Daphne."

"I expect so."

Two youths entered the garden, showing too much attention to the horse. He opened the casement again. "But not now."

"No. Not now."

Chapter Nineteen

"**O**h, good heavens!" Daphne whispered.

Margaret smiled helplessly and shrugged. "It was not supposed to happen this way."

"You must have known that it might, however. You all must have known." Daphne peered severely at the other three women who had pounded on the door while Castleford was gone.

"We did," the oldest of them said. Her name was Jane Woodman, and she appeared to be close to fifty. "That was why we were made leaders of the society. We none of us have families as such. Our husbands are gone, and any children are grown. If we get transported or hanged—" She faltered on that word. "Anyway, that is why."

"You are not going to be hanged." Daphne trusted she spoke the truth, but no one knew if she did. There had been some hangings in the past when workers' actions went awry.

After two hours of vigil at the window, the stream of people on the road had thinned. Castleford had gone out to the road then and spoken with some of those still trudging by. He had learned just how bad the violence in Manchester had been.

"They are bound to blame us," Jane Woodman said. "We had no weapons and were peaceable, but it will be our fault, you wait and see." She shook her head. "They cut down Mrs. Fildes no more than twenty feet from me. Was a horrible thing to see."

The attack on Mrs. Fildes had shaken these women to their souls' depths. A horrible energy poured off them all now, and Daphne knew they would not feel safe for many days. Perhaps they never would again.

Margaret appeared shaken too. This cottage had been used for the meetings of this friendly society, it had been explained. Margaret might not be one of the workers, but she had thrown in with these women and knew she was vulnerable now too.

"There has been no indication of violence as people returned home," Daphne said. "No word of damage in the village, for example. That is something. It is not turning into a conflagration that engulfs the whole county, the way it was predicted."

"They've no reason to harm their own," Margaret said. "I am sure that all the villages are free of both violence and destruction, Daphne. The only people who have been hurt were those poor souls who fell to the soldiers' swords."

Hopefully that was true. Daphne was not convinced of it, however. She had stood at that window beside

Castleford for a reason, and he had been forced to point his pistol several times to ward off intruders with no good on their minds.

"I want to be sure," she said to Margaret. "As soon as it is quiet, we must find out about the Foresters and other friends."

Margaret grasped her hand. "Do not worry so, Daphne. This is not a fight to be made in these villages or in the countryside."

"What is to become of us?" one of the women asked, dabbing her eyes of the tears leaking from them. "What if they hear we met here and come to the door and ask—"

"A duke protects you. The prince regent would be better, but Castleford will have to do," Daphne said.

They all laughed at that, but the mirth quickly gave way to the somber mood of the evening again.

Daphne left them to go and negotiate with that duke. She found him sprawled on an upholstered chair that he had moved close to the window. The casement was open so that he could hear any sounds outside. He had moved his horse to the back of the house over an hour ago so as not to tempt the reckless.

He gazed at the garden, but she doubted he saw the long shadows now streaking the ground or much of anything from the hooded gaze he held. She made out a few heads still passing down on the road, but it appeared the worst was over.

She debated how to broach the subject she needed to raise. He might just indulge her without further ado, of course. Or he might quiz her relentlessly, if she piqued his curiosity too much.

That it was well piqued already went without question. *We have many things that we must talk about.* She could only hope that many things did not include all things. She did not think so. She doubted he would still be here if he knew everything.

She went over to him. His attention moved to her from wherever it had been. Then he looked at her in a way that suggested it had not been far from her at all.

He did not perform the courtesy of standing on her appearance. Instead he reached out and grasped her arm. She twirled and fell onto his lap.

He kissed her, first sweetly, then seductively. "Let us lock the dining room door," he muttered. "They will be imprisoned there, while I have my way with you here."

"This is hardly the place for it."

"This chair is a superb place. I promise there are at least five ways to have you here without any discomfort. I will show you." His hand teased at her skirt, making it inch up her leg. "If you smother your cries of ecstasy, no one will be the wiser."

She slapped his hand. "We need to leave here."

"I agree. An inn far away is in order. I will send for Summerhays's coach, and we will be off."

"I meant that we *all* need to leave here."

He glanced toward the dining room. "You and I need to leave, and go to an inn, then travel back to London. Where do *they* need to go to after they leave here?"

"I am taking them back to The Rarest Blooms until the consequences of this day are known and the region is safe for them."

He closed his eyes. "May I ask why all those women need such sanctuary?" His expression indicated he was already guessing.

"Since you are part of the government, it might be better if you did not ask. I am very sure it would be better if I did not answer such a question, should you pose it."

"*Hell.*" He shook his head and glanced up, asking heaven to bestow patience. "Daphne—"

"Here is my plan. There is not enough room in Summerhays's coach for all of us. I suggest that you hire another carriage for the women and we send them off in it. Then you and I will travel in the coach that brought me."

He brightened at that solution, as she guessed he would. Then he scrutinized her closely. "You do realize that I will have you alone in that carriage, and at the inns, and all the way back to London? That is suspiciously accommodating of you, after the way you have dodged me these last weeks."

"As long as you are in fact accommodated, what do you care about the how or why of it?"

Another long gaze. "Well put. What do I care, indeed? Off you go." He helped her to stand. "I will go for a ride and make sure it is quiet out there. If it is, I will find another carriage. There is usually one to be had in a village of this size, even if the cattle that pull it are not the best."

The horses certainly were not the best, but they would do. Daphne helped all the women into the hired coach that Castleford had procured. The young woman he had rescued would ride along into the village and send word from there to her family to come and help her. The others would make the long journey to Middlesex.

Margaret was the last to enter.

"Do you have the maps and directions?" Daphne said.

"Of course. Do not worry about anything. I know what to do." She embraced Daphne. "I will see you again soon. You will reach your destination before we reach ours, however. I do not expect this coach to travel very quickly. It is not a lord's carriage or pair."

"All will be waiting for you. Perhaps I will have news too. You may all stay with me as long as you like, however. Even after we are sure that the magistrates are not searching for your friends and you. There is room at The Rarest Blooms for more sisters."

Margaret looked to where Castleford spoke with Summerhays's coachman. "He was generous to give us the money to pay for inns on the way. Does he know all that you are up to with these plans?"

"He knows enough."

"By your journey's end, that may not be sufficient. Will he still be generous if he knows it all, do you think?"

"He will be good to his word about the property, no matter what happens."

Margaret climbed in with the others. Daphne watched the carriage roll away, then walked toward the duke, whose curiosity about her had led him to ride a horse across England.

He watched her come, and it was all there in his eyes, the reasons he had followed her. Lights of desire and fascination sparked in them, and a warm familiarity born of what they had shared in that tent and today. She saw something else, however, something new, and it made her breath catch in her throat.

Pity. Pity and sorrow and maybe some anger. That was what she saw, for an instant, before he took her hand and guided her inside the coach.

* * *

A long carriage ride gives a man a lot of time to search his soul. Since Castleford did not fancy perusing deserts, he much preferred traveling on horseback.

He draped his arm around Daphne and held her while the coach rolled through the twilight. Her head rested on his shoulder, and she did not speak much. Normally the lack of small talk would be a relief. This evening it left him thinking about matters he would prefer to avoid.

Resenting the inclination even as he succumbed to it, he lined up the truths he knew for certain.

At least one of the properties Becksbridge had left him did not house an old mistress of the dead duke. A woman who had been raped by Latham lived there. There could be no denying it had been rape either, since he himself had stumbled upon the scene and pulled Latham off the girl. The brutality he had seen and Latham's sneering indifference about it later had marked the end of their long friendship.

Somehow Becksbridge had learned of that crime and bought the girl off with that home.

Since Mrs. Rolland—he doubted there had ever been a Mr. Rolland—had not been a mistress, it stood to reason that perhaps none of the four properties were used by old mistresses.

Without thinking about it, more on instinct, he pressed his lips to Daphne's crown and kissed her silken fair hair. He closed his eyes and tried to contain the anger swelling in him. It wanted to become a murderous rage. He hoped he was wrong about her, but he did not think he was.

He had assumed the scoundrel preyed on servants, like too many men of his station. But of course it had been helplessness that provoked the worst in Latham, not rank or blood or family background.

If you ever have the chance, kill him, Tristan.

The coach noticeably slowed. Daphne startled, as if that woke her from a sleep. She straightened and found her reticule. She did not look at him while the inn's servants opened the door and handed her out.

The inn's yard seemed oddly empty, considering night was falling. Those who felt the need to escape the day's great events had already done so, and it appeared few people felt the need to travel this evening and would wait for another, better day.

The air smelled of autumn's approach. Not an unpleasant scent, it carried a peculiar freshness, considering it spoke of decay.

Daphne waited for him, to enter the inn. She appeared totally composed but perhaps showed a bit of awkwardness. She expected him to drag her upstairs immediately and finally have her, of course. It might be a mercy to do so. She might even be counting on that, since it would delay the conversation that had been waiting since he walked into Margaret's home.

"After hours in that cottage and carriage, the air is refreshing," he said. "Let us take a turn around the property. The coachman will procure us chambers and have your baggage taken up."

She raised her eyebrows but fell into step with him. "I did not realize you so enjoyed fresh air. I thought you could go days without leaving your house."

"Only when I was keeping very busy with whores,

would I go for days without leaving." He smiled ruefully. "It was very bad of our mutual friends to tell you about that, if they did."

"Perhaps my sisters were warning me, for the day you and I finally met."

"Quite likely they were. Oh, speaking of whores . . ." He reached into his coat and withdrew four thin letters. He handed them to her. "As promised. You must never tell anyone I went to such lengths for you. It would destroy all that I have worked so hard to build."

She looked down at the letters and laughed quietly, shaking her head. "I am remembering something Verity said, about woe unto the person who captures your curiosity. I fear all the woe has been yours this time."

More woe had been his than he needed, that was certain.

She slid the letters into her reticule. They entered a little field beside the inn, where wildflowers grew in abundance. A few sheep grazed on a hill a few hundred yards away.

"You were never old Becksbridge's mistress, were you?"

She did not miss a step. Her composure did not crack. Yet he sensed a tension enter her, then leave like a deep sigh. "I never said I was."

"You never said you were not. You knew what I assumed."

She bit her lower lip. "I felt no need to explain. I am entitled to reveal what I choose about my history." She looked him in the eyes, boldly. "Some women have good reasons to leave the past behind."

Her expression and words warned him off. She did not want to talk of it. He did, however. This conversation had become important for reasons he could not explain even to himself. Important and necessary.

He took her hand and led her to a log set out like a bench along their path. He sat her down. She kept her gaze on the wildflowers and the sunset. On anyplace but his face.

"I recognized Margaret," he said. "She was not his mistress either. She was a servant who was badly misused by Latham. I know, because I saw him do it."

Her gaze snapped to him. Her color rose. Her poise relaxed a little, as if holding her shield had become too much a burden.

"I only learned about her for certain myself when I went there this time." She spoke quietly. "I had wondered, though. Not at first, but over the years. Then, when you said there were four small properties—well, I thought we might have something in common, but not what you assumed. So I came and asked Margaret for the truth. She said that one of his friends came and stopped it. I wondered if perhaps it had been you—"

He had guessed, but he did not like hearing it. He crossed his arms, turned away, and glared at the horizon. "I am going to kill him."

She reached up to touch his arm and claim his attention. "It is not what you think. Not quite like that with me. I need you to know that."

"How was it *not like that* with you?" It appalled him that the thought she might have been willing made him more furious than if she had been forced. There it was, however, disgusting though he found it, even as black rage filled him.

"He gave me the courtesy of a flirtation first. A few stolen kisses. Allusions to marriage. My father was a gentleman, and it was not unthinkable to me. We had a clandestine meeting that went too far, he said. Farther than he intended, he said."

"Was that what it was, Daphne? A romantic tryst that went too far?" *Stop yelling at her, you ass. Stop acting as though you have a right to be jealous just because it was the wrong damned Becksbridge.*

She flushed deeply, and her eyes misted. "I blamed myself for years, Castleford, and I'll not stand for your doing so now. Becksbridge blamed me too. That insufferable man *lectured me.* I had lured his son. My character was at fault." Her eyes glinted with furious tears. "But I had tried to stop him, you see. I had begged him to stop, but he did not. Many think a woman deserves such a thing merely for allowing a man to kiss her. I discarded such ideas long ago myself, but I know it is a common belief."

Still angry, still wishing Latham were within reach, right here and now, he sat beside her. They remained there, both of them in high emotion. He looked at her exquisite profile while she fought to remain collected enough not to weep at what he had just forced her to reveal.

He imagined her being told by the old duke that her abuse had been her own fault. She was correct that it was a common excuse used by men.

"It is not my belief that women invite such misuse, if you are wondering, Daphne."

She managed a small smile. Her eyes seemed to only mist more, however. She wiped them with her hand, then gave him a little, playful poke on his side. "If it were your belief, you would have had me weeks ago and forgotten my name by now."

He forgot many names, but he would never forget

hers. He already knew that. He caught that taunting hand and threaded his fingers through hers. "How did Becksbridge learn of it?"

"I told him."

"Did you? Good girl. The ass probably could not believe a governess would be so bold."

"I thought he should know what his son had done. I had no idea it had happened before. He subjected me to that scathing, insulting lecture. Yet, remembering it later, I realized there had been little real vehemence in his tone. Only in his words. I wondered if perhaps he had given that lecture before, and had lost the heart for it in truth."

He raised her hand and kissed it. "Did you blackmail him for support after you told him?"

"Not at all. He said he must release me, but he would send me to a woman in the north, where I could live. I was to stay there. If I did, he would provide an allowance. He did not want me nearby to corrupt his son again, sinful Jezebel that I was. He did not want me returning to our home county or to London to spread rumors." She sighed a little, then shrugged. "The blackmail came later."

He had to laugh. "Why do I think that was a scene to behold?"

"Well, I was older, wasn't I? And much wiser. I had been thinking about what Latham had done, and right before I left, there had been that scullery maid. After two years of stewing about it all, I had come to a boil."

"Becksbridge must have been shocked to see how Miss Avonleah had turned into the formidable Mrs. Joyes."

"He did not say much. I told him that I did not think I should continue intruding on Margaret forever, and that I was going to return to my home county. That was when he offered the use of the land in Middlesex. If I lived there quietly and had no contact with his son and did not speak lies about what had happened, with time he might see his way clear to give me the land outright."

"No allowance this time?"

"At first, yes. I refused it after I started The Rarest Blooms. It was a type of blood money to me." She looked down at their bound hands. "So there you have it."

Her soft smile trembled. With the telling done, her courage seemed to abandon her. Her eyes watered again, and her expression turned very soft and young and almost helpless.

"I have never told anyone all of this before. It was easier than I ever imagined it to be."

She appeared so vulnerable, for all her pride. And so lovely in the silver early twilight that she mesmerized him.

There were holes in this story, and questions still remained. He cursed the way his mind found them at once. He forced his curiosity to the back of his mind. No doubt the answers were insignificant. Probably she had just skipped some things so the tale did not become overlong.

"I am honored that you have told me, Daphne." He stood and raised her by her hand. "I have long regretted not letting the world know what I saw that day with Margaret. Knowing now that it left him to prey on you and others—I will never forgive myself."

She stepped closer and looked into his eyes. "How clever he is, to arrange it so good people blame themselves for his sins. You had no way to know he made a habit of such depravity."

"I did not know for certain, but I knew the truth of him better than most."

It had been, without a doubt, the most cowardly decision of his life. He had known that for a long while now. But exposing Latham would have resulted in a duel. It could be resolved no other way.

For all of his disgust back then, he had not wanted to kill the man who had been his closest friend—the man who, but for what many would consider nuances, was so much like himself.

He should have done it, though. Then, or found a way after that tragedy with Marie.

"I will not have you blaming anyone but him," Daphne said. "Please do not make me regret confiding in you."

He pretended to accept her absolution. He kissed her lips, then her cheek where the remnants of a few salty tears had dried. He took her hand and they strolled to the inn.

Their chambers were ready. The owner hurried to assure His Grace that hot water waited too. Castleford walked with Daphne to the stairs.

"I think that seducing you tonight would be inappropriate somehow," he said.

"Somehow?"

"If I could explain it better than that, I would. I do not want you to misunderstand, however. I do not want you thinking that what you told me has changed anything. Except perhaps the seduction part."

"I would say that is a fairly significant part."

He hated having to say things for which there were no good words. "It isn't that I don't want you. I just don't want to be seducing you to do something against your better judgment."

She frowned. "This is a fine thing, Castleford. I finally allow you to catch me, and you decide to stop being bad today of all days. I do not know why everyone says *women* are the capricious ones."

Damnation. It was a hell of a thing when a man had to defend acting with uncharacteristic decency, especially when all of his body and most of his mind argued to behave differently.

"I am more than willing to be bad, Daphne. I have a list of the ways I plan to be bad with you, the result of many hours of contemplating you and badness at the same time. But I'll not be luring you into it, no matter how maddening this desire. I have wanted you since the first time I saw you. If you want me, my chamber is right next to yours tonight. You have only to open the door."

He left her there at the bottom of the stairs to go above on her own. He went in search of some port. One glass only, however. He did not want her showing up in his chamber before he got there himself.

Chapter Twenty

W hat annoying nobility the duke had shown.
Daphne found it hard to absorb that he had left
her to decide how the night went. It did not seem fair that
he now expected her to make the next move in the long
game that he had started.

She barely noticed the pleasant if rustic chamber she
had been given in the inn. It probably was one of the best,
she noted, as her mind continued to accommodate the
events of the last hour. Very clean and bright, with white-
washed walls that helped the lamp's light spread, it offered comfort and a place to settle her emotions.

She sat on the edge of the bed between two falls of the
bed's blue drapes, trying to reclaim herself. She really
could not.

She would never be quite the same woman again. She
had learned too much this last week and shared too much

and risked too much. After concluding years ago that it was necessary to leave the past behind, she had turned around and embraced it. At least now, hopefully, she might not have the same regrets in the years to come that she had carried in the ones just past.

Her conversation with Castleford still made her eyes mist when she thought of it. He had been so angry when she told him about Latham, but not for the reasons she thought he would be.

She had assumed, wrongly, that he would take Becksbridge's view and see the fault as all hers, or at least equally so. If he had not caught Latham with Margaret, would he have been so sure of her own story? Few people would be, she knew to her regret. Not with any story about a man and woman, but certainly not the one she told regarding the heir to a ducal coronet.

He had sat at Margaret's table knowing most of it. All day he had kept that inside himself until they took that walk. Now the intimacy of their conversation still filled her. Moved her. He had been very kind, even as he demanded explanations that were not his by right.

I am going to kill him. That had not been a passionate outburst by a man enraged. He had said it too calmly. Too frankly. He hated Latham, and not only because of Margaret or even herself, she guessed. It was as if one fallen angel looked at another and, because of his own sins, saw the deeper wickedness that made for dangerous evil.

Calmer now, and more herself, she prepared to wash. She undressed to her chemise and poured the warm water into the basin. A fullness in her heart had not gone away, for all her deliberations.

It was not fear or indecision, she knew. Those existed

as smaller concerns, shallow in comparison to this. Gratitude swelled her heart, and relief and an emotion so poignant that she did not know how to name it. A bit of regret stirred there too.

She dried herself and gazed in the looking glass. Should she open that door waiting for her tonight? It would be an ending even as it began something. It would be the first step to "afterwards." And there would be an afterwards, of course. Not only because he was Castleford the man and Castleford the duke. Also because Mrs. Joyes had confided more than enough to him today, but not everything.

Her hands trembled while she tied her brushed hair at her nape with a ribbon. She glanced down at the simple dress she had put on. Nervousness had owned her for the last fifteen minutes, after she made her decision.

There had been vague sounds through the wall, but nothing came to her now. What a joke if he had fallen asleep. Or become so foxed in the public room below that she abandoned her momentous choice as soon as she saw him.

That decision had been surprisingly easy once she admitted what it meant. If she were going to suffer the afterwards, and her heart's fullness intimated she would suffer it badly now, she would like to experience the now while she could. Castleford saw these things in the simplest terms, in the way of men. *If you want me.* Yet, this once, that same simple question had been what swayed her.

Hoping that she appeared more confident than she felt, trusting she would not shake on the outside the way she did in her essence, she slipped out of her chamber and walked the few feet to the door of the one beside it. The latch moved down easily. She pushed the door ajar and slid through the opening.

The chamber appeared much like her own but awash in pale, golden light from several lamps. One sat on the small writing desk not far from the door and another on a table beneath the one window. The third flanked the bed.

She stepped into the room farther and saw him in that bed, sitting with his back against the headboard. He was naked above the sheet that covered him to his waist, and no doubt beneath the sheet as well.

He was all Castleford right now. All trouble, that was certain. Little of the kind and understanding man from the afternoon showed in his eyes. The devil's fires flickered in them, as well as those of the duke who, finally, was going to have his way.

"Come closer," he said. "Don't lose your nerve now."

She walked forward, until she stood at the foot of the bed. "Do you always sleep naked, or were you that sure of me?"

"I always sleep this way. I was only mostly sure of you. I counted on your concluding it was foolish to deny us both for no good purpose, and I have known from the start that you are not a fool."

Nor was he. He had realized she had been running away so he might not delve into her past.

It had been disconcerting to be pursued by a man who seemed to have been ahead of her for so much of the race.

"You should remove that dress, unless you want it ruined."

Probably so. It was not as if she had never been undressed with him before. Still, unfastening the dress and letting it drop was harder than she expected. Since she wore nothing under it, the result was she stood there as naked as he but without the benefits of that sheet.

His gaze deepened. Amusement left his expression. "You are exquisite, Daphne. That has always been the only word for your beauty."

It touched her that he bothered with such praise now. She was not going to argue, but like most women she knew her own flaws too well. Too tall and far too pale. "Frosty" had been used to describe her appearance more than once, and she had not assumed it was a compliment.

He patted the side of the bed, all devil again. She walked around and sat on it.

"Close your eyes," he said, sitting up.

She obeyed and wondered what erotic game might start this way.

He moved. She felt him by her side, kneeling. Then a cool weight encircled her neck, and his hands worked at her nape. She opened her eyes and looked down. A necklace of fine filigree, embedded with a king's ransom in diamonds, flamed on her chest. The largest stone, in the center, surpassed the ear bobs in size by several times and rested right above her breasts.

"You mustn't. I mustn't," she muttered, while she watched the white flames glisten and spark. She poked at it. "It is very beautiful, though."

"Indulge me for now. Get your hands away from that clasp. You must wear it tonight. I have never ravished a woman covered in diamonds before." He took her hand and drew her onto the bed. "Next time you will have to wear the earrings too."

She glanced at the diamonds, then at him. He caught the look.

"There must be a next time, Daphne. Let us have a right understanding on that. Do not think to put me off after this. I will never get through that list of badness tonight. I also insist on seeing you in all the diamonds at once." His fingertips skimmed the edge of the necklace, then lower. "You have no idea what you look like wearing them and nothing else. Beguiling. Devastating."

He fell back on the pillows and pulled her to him, into his embrace and along his body. The sudden feel of his skin and warmth first stunned her. Then the sensations encompassed her senses and bound her physicality to his in a comforting, exciting intimacy.

She had made the right choice, she thought, as his deep kiss showed his serious, determined passion. He had been wise to make the decision hers too. She welcomed the pleasure with a new freedom, because misgivings had been left behind.

He flipped her on her back and propped on one arm while he looked at her. His palm brushed her hair from her face, then rested there, along her face's edge.

"We will do this carefully this time, so you do not feel helpless and that old fear does not emerge."

It astonished her that he had noticed that. She could only look up at him, surprised again on this day of so many surprises. "Not too careful, I hope. I am expecting you to live up to your fame."

His head dipped so he could gently close his teeth on her nipple. "I thank you for that, darling. The truth is I have little experience with careful and none with innocents."

She was not an innocent, but she was hopelessly

ignorant, of course. He had noticed that too, along with her fear of vulnerability.

She did not feel very innocent or ignorant now, as she luxuriated in the erotic sensitivity of her breasts. He aroused one with an almost delicate caress that maddened her, while his tongue and mouth teased the other. She grasped his shoulders and flowed on the unbearable pleasure toward abandon.

He was careful. More careful than he had been on the barge or in that tent. The pleasure built sweetly, layer upon layer. He lured her in deeply with kisses down her body, revealing unexpected spots of intense excitement. His slow caresses on her breasts and stomach, her thighs and bottom moved her surely through such luscious pleasure to impatience and then to that focused desperation that cried for a finish and completion.

He lifted her shoulder and turned her. "Kneel there."

She found herself facing the headboard, kneeling high, confused and frustrated. "I do not want to kneel like this. I want you to touch me the way that maddens me and—"

His face brushed hers as he set her hands on the headboard. "Are you scolding? Again? *Now?*" He laughed quietly, then moved one of her knees. "Heaven is but a few minutes away, I promise. It will be like the last time, only better."

"I think that unlikely," she said to the wall. "There is something to be said for staying with what is successful, especially if the results were so spectac—oh!" She looked down, shocked, to where his head now rested on the pillow between her knees.

She closed her eyes. This was too wicked. In the next moment a shock of intense pleasure shot through her, as he touched her finally. Then another and another until she had to cling to the headboard so she would not collapse from it. All of the intensity seemed to aim high and spread, then collect and sink until it centered again where he touched, making her even more sensitive.

Over and over it happened, until she could hardly breathe and almost wept. When she thought she would die, when she was close to begging him to stop, the sensation changed. No longer streaking through her but all there, all at the focus of that hot need. He was using his mouth, caressing with his tongue and playing the devil with her essence.

She did beg then, in her head and probably with her voice, she did not know. She could only relieve the relentless intensity with crying gasps until, finally, her body surrendered. That moment came, the finish she ached for. It split through her with a physical scream of joy.

Hands lifted her away from the headboard and laid her down. Hard strength covered her, and shoulders submitted to her grasping embrace. A slow fullness entered her where she still throbbed, and the scream echoed, stretching her until no void remained.

For a moment nothing moved. Not him and not her. She opened her eyes. He braced above her, his shoulders taut, his face severe. He looked, she knew, to make sure that odd little fear had not fluttered to life.

He must have seen enough to know it had not, or else he could wait no longer. He lifted one of her legs and hitched it over his hip, and entered even deeper. Then the fullness withdrew, and entered again. Carefully at first, then somewhat less so. She did not mind that. She still pulsed where they joined, still ached with a quiet need, and it felt good and right to have him in her.

* * *

He realized, as the stupor thinned and Daphne lay in his arms afterwards, that he had not used the condom tucked in the book on the table beside the bed.

Careless, that. Physicians insisted they were only to prevent disease, but any fool knew they served another purpose too. Both purposes should have been tended to tonight of all nights, for her sake and reassurance.

He considered his peculiar lapse and what it could mean, which led to considerations of what he did or did not owe this particular woman. He resisted the fullness of it but forced his mind down that path anyway. He had not gone far before he realized that, in a manner of speaking, precautions against pregnancy had been unnecessary.

The reasons why struck him as inescapable. So did the inevitable consequences. It was perhaps a tribute to just how contented he felt right now that those consequences did not seem nearly as dire as they should.

"When we get back to town, I will get a special license," he said. "Our mutual friends can attend, and your Rarest Blooms if you want, but I would prefer to keep out all of the tedious relatives."

She had been playfully twisting the hairs on his chest, but now she froze so totally she might have fainted dead away. She had not been so still since that first night in the greenhouse.

Finally she turned and looked at him oddly. It could be the lighting, but she appeared annoyed.

"I am being thoughtless, aren't I? My apologies, Daphne. You can of course invite *your* tedious relatives if you want. Mine will not be allowed, is what I meant."

"What are you talking about?"

"Our marriage. The wedding. That is what special licenses are for."

She sat up and pulled the sheet around her. "You are mad. I have just been ravished by a madman."

"Actually, officially, you have not been ravished yet. Trust me about this. I was far too polite this time for it to qualify as ravishing."

"Will you please stay on the subject at hand? This marriage? It is bizarre for you to speak of it." She peered at his face. "Are you asleep? Is this one of those waking dreams some people have in which they move and talk?"

"Why would you call this bizarre? It is so normal and ordinary that I astonish myself."

"Normal is bizarre for you."

"Daphne, unlike a certain hypocritical ass whom I regret to admit is a relative, I am a gentleman still. You in turn were an innocent. Hence—" He gestured at her, him, and the bed. "Marriage."

She sighed deeply in that Hawkeswellian way. He would have to discourage that habit after the wedding.

"Castleford, your adherence to at least the bare basics of the gentleman's code of chivalry is admirable. Truly. Except we both know I was not an innocent. Hence"—she gestured as he had, mimicking him—"madman."

"You were not the ex-mistress or the widow of some other man, though, were you? As for the experience that stole your innocence, I am responsible for that too."

"Dear heavens, you are really blaming yourself for that, aren't you? You want to marry me as a form of penance. I won't have it."

"The hell you won't. Look me in the eyes and tell me that you have never blamed me for what happened to you or that scullery maid and god knows how many others due to my silence about what I knew him to be."

She looked him in the eyes, brazenly. She did not speak, however. Of course not. She wasn't a fool. She knew better than to treat him like one too.

She dropped back on the pillow and turned on her side with her back to him. "I refuse your proposal, *not that you even bothered to make one*. There is no need to start planning the ritual accompanying your execution. We will not marry."

Of course they would. He had no interest in having a row about it now, though. "Fine. If you are sure."

She laughed. "Oh, I am sure, Your Grace."

At another time he might be insulted by that laugh. Right now he only noted it in passing. His attention had been arrested by the lovely smoothness of her back and the elegant line the side of her body made as it dipped to her waist and curved up over her hip. He traced it with his hand, from her shoulder to her thigh then up again, watching his fingertips skim that line.

She looked over her shoulder at him, a little surprised.

"Don't move. I will show you what to do." He let that line entrance him awhile longer, until her body subtly flexed from the sensation.

He turned her slightly, away from him, and pressed her shoulders so her back angled away and her bottom rounded erotically. He caressed their soft swells. The small of her back angled in more, and her bottom rose a bit. Her hand clutched the pillow near her face.

"Can you tell when you are ready yet? Can you feel it?" he asked.

She nodded.

He slid his finger along her cleft. She inhaled sharply in a wonderful feminine sound of pleasure and anticipation. He moved his touch lower and deeper. She parted her thighs, encouraging him. Her eyes closed and her mouth formed a smile that parted her lips, and her face assumed an expression of pleasure and joy.

He curved his body along hers and entered her.

He did ravish her then. He pretended no restraint. He thrust into her hard, deeper, and allowed the violent power to own him. Like a velvet glove her body held him, caressed him, then tightened until every movement increased the pleasure and drove him to seek more and more.

The end came like a cataclysm, made all the more intense by the long wait to know it.

There was a third lesson that night. Having chased her so long, it appeared Castleford had no intention of denying himself now that she was caught.

Compared to the others, it seemed almost mild. The most careful of all, it grew out of conversation and jokes. Yet there was no release before he took her, so this time all those sensations centered differently, around him. She found herself more vulnerable than ever before with him, but not in a physical way. Instead, the pleasure mixed with other emotions and never obliterated her awareness of the man controlling her and claiming her.

Sometime in the very early morning he fell asleep. Daphne listened to his breaths deepen but did not sleep herself. Instead, when she was sure he was unaware, she slowly and carefully slid out from under his embracing arm and away from his side.

He appeared very handsome sleeping there, his naked

chest and shoulders hard and defined even in repose.
With his eyes closed, his eyelashes appeared very long
and thick. She suspected that he knew that. He probably
knew everything that made him attractive to women like
her, the ones who should know better than to be dazzled
by his attention.

She guessed there was a string of broken hearts in his
history. She admitted ruefully that there would probably
be one more soon. Whatever care he had taken tonight
would not spare her that. Perhaps he just assumed she
would know to protect her heart, seeing as how she was
not a fool.

Their odd conversation from earlier in the night came
to her while she looked at him. Marriage would be hell
if a woman gave a damn about this man. Not to mention
that she really did not need such an outrageous complication. Castleford concluding he had obligations like
that to her, due to his somewhat slanted way of looking
at the world, would create havoc in both their worlds.

Aside from the chaos it would create with her own
plans—the very notion alarmed her beyond the ability to
do more than envision disaster after disaster—he was
incorrigible, wasn't he? He delighted in being so.

While she would end up a duchess if such an event
transpired, her duke would still be *Castleford.* Not the
Castleford of the last few days or even the one of Tuesdays. She would be married to the other one, whose behavior had been so disgraceful for so long that even
scandal could not be bothered to rise around him.

She touched his nose to make sure he slept very
soundly. He did not stir at all. She eased out of bed and
padded over to the wardrobe. She imagined walking into
his apartment one morning after they were married and

finding it full of naked whores waiting their turn with the notorious duke. He was even rumored to indulge sometimes in more than one at a time. Oh, yes, he was.

That would be a fine thing to see—her husband in that big bed, naked, foxed no doubt, with two other women. All the diamonds in the world would not make up for that insult. Or that heartache, if she cared a fig about him.

Stars twinkled as she passed the looking glass near the washbasin. She paused and looked at her reflection and the way the diamond necklace appeared against her pale skin and below her tumble of hair. It made her exotic, she thought. It caused her to look much more interesting than she actually was. The woman in the looking glass was a worldly and dangerous minx, not staid, formidable Mrs. Joyes of The Rarest Blooms.

She opened the door of the wardrobe. It squeaked enough that she grimaced and froze. She looked back at Castleford, to make sure it had not disturbed his sleep.

His frock coat hung on a peg. She fished in the pockets until she found what she sought. She pulled out those small, creased map pages.

Glancing to check on him again, she carried them over to the one lamp that still burned on the writing table. She smoothed each one in turn, then set aside the pages with Cumberworth and Failsworth.

Bending her head low so she could see and read clearly, she memorized the other two.

Chapter Twenty-one

"You will stay with me as my guest," Castleford said. "Summerhays's brother is returning. Their house will be very full. Nor do I fancy going through tiresome antics to be discreet. I will tell my stewards to find an old female relative of mine to bring in, if you insist on maintaining appearances."

"I agree to accompany you to your house now. We will talk about where I will stay after we have refreshed ourselves," Daphne said.

This was no time to have this conversation. Castleford was too full of himself, for one thing. That probably had to do with his having sent her into ecstasy four times during hours of badness right here in this coach. He had only raised this idea of her living in his house at this moment because he assumed she was still too dazed to think straight.

It would not do, of course. Now that they were back in London, there would be more steps in the direction of afterwards. She found that increasingly difficult, even painful, to contemplate. She knew, however, that when it happened he would regret this bold indiscretion he now planned.

He did not respond to her lack of total agreement. His expression suggested that he just assumed he would have his way. That was how the world always accommodated him.

He had not bothered to send word that he was returning home today, so their arrival at the house created some surprise and confusion. While servants ran hither and fro, they glanced at their master with concern.

The butler took Castleford aside right there in the reception hall to have a private word. Initially Castleford listened with bored forbearance. Then a deep frown formed. Suddenly, in the next instant, he looked as if this were a Tuesday.

"**D**amnation, I did not tell him to return, let alone with a guest."

"The situation has been most distressing, Your Grace. He has been giving orders as if—well, as if he were *you*."

"Where is that insubordinate cub?" He glanced at Daphne, twenty feet away. There would be hell to pay now. What was Edwards thinking, bringing Miss Johnson here? That was who this nameless woman would turn out to be, he assumed.

"He is in the corner chamber, sir. The solar." The butler's lips folded in on themselves, and he permitted himself a momentary expression of disapproval. "And, sir, he has a pistol with him."

Castleford sighed, but it did little to relieve his irritation. The drama of chasing after a few trespassers in the country had clearly gone to Edwards's head. Left to his own judgment—a mistake, that, quite clearly—he had dug up the worst judgment possible.

He strode toward the stairs. He sensed a shadow and looked back to see Daphne following him.

"Stay here. Or on the terrace. Or"—he threw up his arms in exasperation—"or anywhere but up there."

"Why?"

"Because I command it."

That amused her so much that she giggled.

The butler had not moved, and now he raised a hand to garner attention. "Your Grace, I forgot to mention that yesterday Mr. Edwards sent a letter by messenger to Lady Hawkeswell. She immediately came here and visited Mr. Edwards and his guest."

Daphne's mirth dissolved into a curious, worried frown.

"How good of you to shout that through the house, you fool," Castleford said. "Display such indiscretion again, and you will be back to serving as a footman. Or maybe a dog boy."

The butler reddened and visibly shrank. Castleford continued up the stairs. Soft footfalls hurried up behind him.

"Mr. Edwards is here?" Daphne asked his back. "He called for Verity? What has happened? Since he was at my house, I think that I have a right to know."

He just kept going. There was no way to keep her out of this now. Edwards would just have to protect himself from her wrath as best he could.

He strode through the main drawing room to the door to the chamber at its end. He tried to enter but found the door locked.

"Edwards, open the damned door."

"Sir!" Edwards's muffled voice expressed alarm, then came closer. "It might be best if I do not, Your Grace."

"For your sake, undoubtedly so. You will open it anyway. *Now.*"

A long silence followed. So long that Castleford thought he might have to call up several footmen to break the door down.

"There has been an alarming development, Your Grace," Edwards's voice said. "I need your word as a gentleman that you will not repeat anything told to you, if I let you in."

"I know what has happened, and it is so ordinary that it is boring me to death already. So open the door, and we will deal with the very normal disaster that your seclusion in Middlesex has wrought."

The door did open then. Edwards faced him with a peeved expression. "You do not know anything, actually. I need your word, sir. I really do."

"You are becoming tiresome. Fine, you have my word." He pushed past Edwards, moving him aside with one arm. "Ah. As I expected. Your mystery guest is dear Miss Johnson."

"Katherine, what are you doing here?" Daphne exclaimed, riding in on his coattails.

Miss Johnson appeared most distressed. Daphne appeared astonished. Mr. Edwards appeared brave but worried.

"Permit me to explain, Mrs. Joyes, and save us all twenty minutes of wearisome dodging and euphemisms," Castleford said. "They are having an affair. My secretary made himself very much at home at The Rarest Blooms." He turned to Edwards. "Did your conscience or nature force your hand, so that now you must do the right thing? Perhaps Mrs. Hill threatened to unman you with her butcher knife if you did not?"

Miss Johnson began crying. Daphne went to comfort her.

Edwards drew himself taller. "Your assumptions are indeed ordinary and boring, Your Grace. I assure you, when I have a disaster, I can do better than that."

"It is all my fault," Miss Johnson cried. "I should have told you, my love." She looked forlornly at Daphne. "And you too. And Verity, certainly, since she was so kind to me."

Daphne suddenly appeared alarmed. "Is that why you called for Verity, so you could finally tell her what you have been hiding?" She looked at Castleford. "Verity is the one who sent Katherine to The Rarest Blooms. She was the first of us to know Katherine."

"I asked her to come here for that and so she might find a way to have the greenhouses tended after I left," Katherine said. "She said she would go herself, so my leaving would not create more guilt for me."

"How good of Lady Hawkeswell to oblige you. Now, I must insist that someone tell me what in hell is going on," Castleford said.

Daphne stood. She took Katherine's hand and made her rise too. "I will leave it to Mr. Edwards to explain what he can. If he is less than forthcoming, Your Grace, I ask that you remember that your station is such that knowing everything is not always wise. I, on the other hand, am not constrained by rank or oaths."

She led Katherine to the door. She turned before following Katherine out. "I will learn it all from her and explain it to His Grace when necessary, Mr. Edwards, so do not feel obligated to say more than good sense will permit." She stepped close to Castleford and spoke softly. "May I remind you that the first day we met, you gave your word to treat her as if she were your sister?"

She left, with him staring in amazement that she would use that fool statement about a sister in such a way, as well as give Edwards permission to dodge after all. She closed the door behind her.

He turned both his attention and his annoyance on Mr. Edwards. "I noticed that you did not deny an affair."

Edwards flushed. "This is not about that, even if it were true."

Oh, it was true. And it was about that, in some way. "Start explaining. I had intended to be doing something else by now, Edwards, so this had better be interesting." He threw himself onto the sofa and looked up expectantly.

Mr. Edwards sat without being invited. Whatever had happened, the young man had forgotten himself.

"That trespasser, the one near the house, was not interested in your investigations of the property, Your Grace. He was interested in Miss Johnson."

That was at least mildly interesting. "How so?"

"He came again, and this time I caught him. He told me he was hired by her family to find her. He had traced her to the coast where the trail went cold. When he returned some time later with a drawn portrait of her, he chanced upon a shopkeeper who remembered seeing her with Lord and Lady Hawkeswell, in Southend-on-Sea. It took him months to make the connection to The Rarest Blooms, and he came to see if he might be right about that."

"So she ran away from her family, and now they have

found her." Castleford shrugged. "She is of age, I assume, so it does not signify much. Why this run to London and your barricade behind a locked door?"

As soon as he said it, he knew the answer. Edwards's expression confirmed his conclusion.

"By family you did not mean her parents, did you? A husband searches for her."

Edwards remained stone-faced.

"You cannot keep him from her, Edwards."

Edwards's jaw tightened. "I ask permission to borrow your dueling pistols, sir. I do not have my own, you see."

"You have no standing to challenge him. It will be considered murder, if you kill the husband of your paramour."

"I must do something," Edwards said through gritted teeth.

"You must not. You cannot have her in any way other than how you have so far. If he takes her away, you must forget her. The stupid marriage laws of England decree this, not I. If he challenges you, you may protect yourself, but I fear you will see the worst of it."

"You do not understand, Your Grace."

"You mean that you are in love, and I do not understand the depths of your feeling? That is true, but it changes nothing." Not necessarily true, anymore. The thought startled him a little, but there it was.

"It is not only that." Edwards looked away, overcome with emotion. "The scoundrel beat her. I have seen marks."

That was a regrettable point, and it explained Edwards's strange behavior in seeking sanctuary here almost too well. Castleford stood, the winds of irritation suddenly gone, and walked away while Edwards got hold of himself.

He supposed the young man had done his duty as he

saw it. Edwards might even have done the same if there had been no intimacy with Miss Johnson. Had he not received orders to protect the women in that house?

"Is that all?" he asked, not turning to see Edwards.

A pause, too long. "It is enough."

Enough, but not all. For the second time in a week he was expected to accept half an explanation when he knew it was incomplete. Once again, however, it might be best to swallow his curiosity.

Probably Daphne was hearing the rest in the next room. Presumably Lady Hawkeswell already knew it. It would all come out in the end.

"You cannot challenge her husband," he repeated. "That is out of the question."

"I cannot allow him to take her back."

Castleford returned to the sofa. He made himself comfortable. "This is what is called a conundrum, Edwards. I am very glad I almost never face them myself. I leave it to you to solve it. For me to help in any way would make me complicit, as you rightly noted."

"Of course, sir. I understand. I wanted to spare you that awkwardness, and I would have if you had allowed it."

Castleford yawned and let the entire matter pass while a view out the window distracted him for a few minutes.

"I read an interesting journal article while I was gone, Edwards. I brought it back, because I remembered how you often find news of America interesting. Remind me to give it to you."

"That was thoughtful of you, Your Grace. I think I have little ability to enjoy it now, however."

"This writer commented on how that land is so vast, and the immigration so large, that most people have little knowledge of their neighbors' pasts. Nor is there any sound way to confirm whatever history might be claimed." He looked at Edwards. "Your tailor might have been a criminal in Scotland, he wrote. The wife of the boot maker might have another husband in France. Can you imagine such a thing? The entire country is probably populated by charlatans."

Edwards had the good sense to say nothing, but his gaze deepened.

"I will be sure to put the journal on your desk. Now, come with me. I may as well get some work out of you, as long as you disobeyed my directions and returned to town without permission."

He led Edwards out through the drawing room, where Miss Johnson wept into Daphne's lap. He ignored Daphne's beseeching look in his direction and went out and up the stairs to his apartment. He sent the valets away and brought Edwards to the dressing room.

"Turn your back. If you see this, I will have to kill you," he said.

Edwards turned away. Castleford opened a hidden panel in the back of a wardrobe and removed a purse heavy with gold coins.

"I need you to take this to the bank for me, to be put in my account. Take one of the carriages. It looks like it might rain."

Edwards weighed the purse in his hand. He looked first confused, then astonished.

"I advise that you obey me immediately, Edwards. You do not want me more annoyed with you, due to your recent tendency to argue."

"Of course, Your Grace." His face flushed. He struggled

with high emotion again. "If I may say, sir, I will always remember with fondness—that is, Tuesdays will be special days my whole life, I think."

"I can't imagine why, seeing as how I worked you like a slave on Tuesdays. Now, be off with you, and take care of that purse. I don't want you telling me there has been another disaster. One a week is plenty for a secretary, don't you think?"

Edwards bowed and turned on his heel. Castleford watched him go and experienced a touch of nostalgia. Then he went over and closed the wardrobe's door.

Godspeed, Mr. Edwards.

D aphne rocked slowly. Her body absorbed and released his phallus with its movements. She braced herself above him, hands on his chest, and he caressed her breasts and made the arousal coil in her even more.

It was too beautiful, she thought. The pleasure and the poignancy. Too intimate, almost painfully so. She could not separate the sensations from the heartache or the sense of raw closeness. She could only submit to all of it and hope this mood did not herald more aches to come.

He drew her down to him and held her face to a deep kiss. Then he moved her up so his teeth and tongue tantalized her breasts and forced frantic need to tighten where they joined. He held her hips so he only filled her and she could not move. She felt him so clearly, so completely, and it crazed her that she could find no relief for what he did to her.

Her mind started to darken, the way it did as fulfillment beckoned. The pleasure and her essence reached for that wonderful ecstasy. He held her hips still and took over so she could not escape the way he moved and how he made her come alive to that erotic pressure.

There was no crash of release this time. Instead an eddy of sparkling pleasure coursed through her body. No obliteration of self occurred. No escape either. She remained fully aware of every nuance of how that flow moved and affected her, until it seemed to enter her heart and soul.

She collapsed on him, spent, without any defenses to the mood now. And so she could not ignore the shadow of sadness in her, still there once the pleasure that had obscured it passed.

It was because of Katherine, she supposed. She had to smile at the way she still thought of her as Katherine, because she now knew for certain her name was not Katherine Johnson at all. She had not pressed for the real one. As long as Katherine remained in England, it would be best if none of them knew her real identity.

Castleford's arms encompassed her, as if he guessed her sorrow and knew the reason. He had not seen their parting, of course. But as soon as Mr. Edwards had called for that carriage, Daphne had known that she would never see her latest sister again.

She felt his kiss on her hair. "I think that makes it five times today," he said. "We are a better pair than I imagined. I am pleased to discover you are as insatiable as I am."

She had to laugh. She had required this fifth time. She had felt so bereft when she saw Katherine roll away in that carriage with Mr. Edwards that she had turned to a friend for comfort and initiated matters on her own. Whoever had expected her to see this man filling the role of comforting friend and in this way?

"Where do you think they are?" she asked. "How far would they have gotten by now?"

"I don't know what you mean. I expect Mr. Edwards to return from the bank any minute now."

She turned so she could see his face. "Since you may be asked questions about them, it may be best if you know what will be said so you are not too startled."

"I get to know all of it, and not only 'enough' this time? I may faint from shock at the honor."

She did not miss the sardonic note in his voice or the allusion to another "enough."

"She ran away after protecting herself from the brute. She cut his arm when he began beating her one night, and she dared not go back after that. He might only beat her worse for it, or he could have her transported by laying down information."

"In other words, you have been harboring a criminal at The Rarest Blooms."

"In a manner of speaking, perhaps."

"Unfortunately, there is no other manner of speaking about this. Still, I am doubly glad that I sent Mr. Edwards on that errand today."

"I know that I am." She kissed his chest. "I am also very grateful to you for doing this."

He made a display of looking at how they remained bound. "For this? The gratitude is all mine, I am sure. I was delighted that you insisted on dragging me to bed, even if it was not my bed. This one is much smaller. I did not even know this chamber was on this level."

The housekeeper had known, however. She had brought Daphne here to refresh herself.

They could have gone to Castleford's bed, of course. It wasn't far away. When she lured him into passion, however, she discovered her heart rebelling against lying with him in that bed where so many women had lain before.

"I favor this chamber myself," she said. "I was speaking of helping them. But, yes, I am grateful for this too. It was the best comfort for a sad heart."

That pleased him more than she expected. He turned them both so he could nestle above her. She realized, as she looked up at his face, that since that afternoon in the garden tent, a third Castleford had emerged, and she caught glimpses of him at times like this. This one had much of the two others in him, the incorrigible one and the Tuesday one, but was notable mostly for the way he instilled confidence in his—honesty, she supposed the word would be.

He toyed with locks of her hair that had come unbound. "You are not to worry about her. Mr. Edwards knows the inns where I keep all my pairs, to change off when I travel. He was responsible for sending payment for the horses' keep. They will reach Liverpool and be on a ship in good time, and even if they are followed, which I doubt, no husband will catch up."

"Liverpool? I thought they were making a run for the eastern coast."

"That is too predictable and leaves them on the Continent. Mr. Edwards needs to find employment. America probably has use for a well-educated man of letters."

America. So far away.

"I must go and tell Audrianna. She sent a messenger with a request that I come by this evening. After the carriage returned to them, the coachman must have explained his absence and where his passengers were left."

"We will go together."

That honesty showed in his eyes, and she knew what he implied.

"I welcome your company, Castleford. She will not quiz me too boldly if you are there. However, we will not return here together afterwards."

"If you return to living at Park Lane while Summerhays and his wife are in residence, it will be hellishly inconvenient. Having an affair with a married woman would be easier." He toyed with her lips and feathered his fingertips over her jaw to encourage a liberal view. "It is only for a few days that you would live here with me in sin. By the time scandal breaks, we will be wed, and that will distract the fools all the more, anyway."

There it was again, that assumption about marriage. That guilt and its necessary penance. He still had not proposed, of course. All three Castlefords just assumed it would happen as he decreed.

"I will not be living on Park Lane," she said. "Tomorrow I will return to The Rarest Blooms. I cannot expect Verity to care for the gardens and greenhouse in my stead."

He sighed in his dramatic way, as if the world's idiocy and her stubbornness conspired to persecute him. He rested his forehead against hers during a smothered moan.

Then he looked down again, too deeply and too seriously. "You know that we can hire gardeners to send there. So you leave for other reasons."

He had become curious again. He was thinking too hard on a small point.

"I belong there." A deep ache squeezed her heart, because he would hear all the rest of what she meant, even though she had not put it into words. *I don't belong here, with you. We both know it.*

"You are burying yourself there before your time. It

might as well be a graveyard covered in flowers." His gaze sharpened with his words. "Even living here in scandal would be better, and I am not asking you to do that. Living out there so long has made you too comfortable with your isolation, I think."

This time *she* heard the words unsaid. *It makes no sense for a woman to give up being a duchess and choose obscurity instead. It makes no sense even if it means marrying such as me.*

"It is not for you to decide what is best for me. Do not convince yourself to go back on your word about a place in the country where I can live, least of all to satisfy your own preferences instead of mine, in the name of saving me from my sorry fate."

He rolled off her and onto his back, thoroughly annoyed. He looked over at her. "Have you tired of me already? Was this a parting gift? How like a woman, to only admit her desire as she walks out the door."

"You are forgetting yourself, Your Grace."

"Answer me. Have you tired of me already?"

She should say she had. Only she could not lie easily when looking into eyes that were so frankly open to her.

"I need to be there when Margaret and the others arrive. I need to prepare for them, as well as care for the plants. This is not about you but about responsibilities that I have."

Coward. She should let this be the parting intimacy, the way he thought. She should accept that this dalliance was over. She could not, however, try as she might. Even this physical retreat would hurt more than she ever expected now, and, it seemed, as they watched each other across those pillows, other retreats were happening too, within him.

"It is not that far," he said, turning his gaze to the ceiling. "You will have to come here, though, unless you want me claiming my property rights while those women are in your house."

He left then to go to his chambers to wash and dress for the visit to Audrianna and Sebastian.

Soon a maid arrived with water he had sent up to her. She prepared too, while sadness weighed on her composure.

She might come back once or twice. Soon, however, she would no longer. Even if he did not tire of her, she guessed she would soon only see those other two Castlefords, no matter how deeply she gazed into his eyes. Eventually, she suspected, she would become boring and tedious and more trouble than she was worth.

Audrianna appeared ready to give birth before the night was out. Large with child, she positioned herself for as much comfort as the chaise longue afforded her. Daphne did not miss the spark in her green eyes that said this visit had distracted her most thoroughly from the awkwardness of her body, however.

Castleford and Summerhays discussed the events up in Manchester with a good many muttered curses and a good deal of shared concern. The newspapers contained lurid stories of the disaster, and already it had been dubbed "Peterloo" by voices critical of the government's role. A writer for the *Times* had been arrested during the riot, and no one expected his story to exonerate the officials.

"At least a hundred dead," Summerhays said. "Perhaps more soon, from the injuries. This was badly done."

"I doubt you will hear many of the peers agree with you. The only fair hearing will be in the Commons," Castleford said. "Let us meet tomorrow and speak of it, and have Hawkeswell come too and a few others who are not insane. We do not want to bore the ladies with it now, I am sure."

Summerhays looked amused at that. "Indeed not. I am fortunate to have you here to remind me. I know how you much prefer drawing room chatter to discussions of great events."

"I merely sought to avoid ignoring your lovely wife, who was kind enough to receive us despite her condition."

"Oh, I would not have missed this for all the world," Audrianna said. She smiled brightly at Castleford, then slyly at Daphne. "I know how rare it is for you to make any social calls, Your Grace. I am honored." She looked at Daphne again and absently felt at her chestnut curls while she tried to appear casual instead of curious as could be.

"I was very fortunate that His Grace traveled north too," Daphne tried.

"Very fortunate," Audrianna said.

"His escort out of the region was very reassuring. There was no way to know what one would find on the roads."

"You have my gratitude, Castleford, for protecting my dear cousin."

Daphne feared Audrianna would giggle soon, if she were not distracted from her all too obvious fascination with her two guests being here at the same time, after having made a journey together.

"Lord Sebastian, how does your brother fare? Will we

see him this evening?" Daphne asked, hoping to occupy Audrianna with other things.

"He has gone down to the country to see our mother. It may be some days until he returns."

"He is doing very well, however," Audrianna said. "He is walking again. I thought Sebastian would weep when he saw that."

"I was overjoyed, of course, but I did not almost *weep*, darling." Sebastian gave her an indulgent but scolding look.

"That German physician worked wonders, I am sure, but I think his body healed because his soul did first," Audrianna said. "And also his heart."

Daphne knew that Sebastian's brother, the Marquess of Wittonbury, had left England under a cloud of scandal. His return would probably stir that up again. She hoped not until after Audrianna was brought to bed. Audrianna was not a weak woman, and her pregnancy had gone well, but no one wanted her worried.

"My wife alludes to the biggest change in my brother," Sebastian said, mostly to Castleford. "He did not return alone."

Castleford had been listening politely, if somewhat lazily. Now his attention sharpened. "It does not sound as if he brought this physician back."

"No, he did not." Audrianna's expression indicated she badly wanted to share this news. "He brought back the physician's daughter, who was trained by her father in the medical arts."

"I expect that will be useful," Castleford said, his speculative tone prompting more details.

"That depends on what you mean by useful," Summerhays said a bit dryly.

"Sebastian is still accommodating the surprise," Audrianna said. "Joanna is a lovely woman. I liked her at once."

Castleford crossed his arms and speared Summerhays with a devilish look. "Enough of this polite dodging. Did he bring back a mistress?"

Summerhays shook his head. "You will find the truth of it much more interesting than that, Castleford. He brought back a wife."

"Thank goodness they left," Audrianna said. "Forgive me, but I must put up my feet or I will cry." She carefully swung her legs up so she reclined on the chaise longue. "Of all evenings for the duke to decide to make a social call."

"My apologies. I should have discouraged him. I think that he felt some obligation to deliver me safely back to you."

Audrianna opened a fan and waved it in front of her face, even though the day was not overly warm. "How chivalrous of him."

Daphne sought to move the topic elsewhere, far away from Castleford. "If you do not mind, I would like to stay here tonight and return to The Rarest Blooms tomorrow."

"Of course. We will send you down in a carriage whenever you like."

"I was wondering if, in the morning before I go, we might have Celia visit so I can see her and tell her about Katherine." She told Audrianna what had happened and that Katherine was gone.

"I will send a footman with a note to Celia this evening,"

Audrianna said, the story dimming her mood. "We can all have a late breakfast together."

"Thank you. There is another matter that I would like to explain to both of you too, and Verity when I see her. I am in need of your help."

Audrianna gazed over innocently. "A personal matter?"

"Not really. It touches on me but mostly centers on others. It concerns a little quest I have undertaken to see some old injustices righted."

Audrianna's expression fell. "A quest? In the name of justice? How . . . noble."

"You expected something else?"

Audrianna shrugged and appeared chagrined. "I will confide that Verity and Celia have been writing to me and suggesting the most outrageous things. About you and Castleford."

"So you have all been gossiping through the post about me."

"I want you to know that I was very sure that they misunderstood, and I wrote to tell them as much."

"Thank you."

"After all, I am your cousin. If you and the duke were—well, if he pursued you the way they claimed, you would have written and told me. You would have never left me to rusticate on the coast without so much as a tidbit to chew on."

Daphne hoped her smile looked like agreement.

"No, I was very sure the two of them had concocted this grand seduction scheme on his part, out of their imaginations," Audrianna said earnestly. "And even if they were correct, it went without saying that he would be on a fool's path to attempt such a thing with you, of all women."

"I appreciate your confidence."

"Well, I think I know you best, Daphne. I was sure I had got it right and they had got it wrong." She reached into her bodice. "That is, until I found these."

She opened her hand to reveal two diamond earrings.

Daphne stared at them. Audrianna began laughing in a most insinuating way.

"You appear distracted, Summerhays. I do not think it is the repercussions sure to come from Peterloo that cause it either."

"That disaster can wait a few days. It will not be going anywhere soon."

They sat in the library enjoying some excellent port. Castleford noted, as he often did these days, that when he imbibed now, it tasted better. A bit of abstinence seemed to reawaken his senses.

The same thing seemed to be happening in bed, too. One would think a man's performance would suffer from lack of practice, but the evidence proved otherwise.

"If I am distracted, it is domestic matters that do it. Audrianna's giving birth soon is enough to drive me half mad, but now my brother—" Summerhays shook his head and laughed.

"You do not care for this woman, I think. Is she an adventuress?"

"You will always think the worst of marriage, won't you? I have no opinion of her, in truth. I have just met her. He loves her very much, however, so that is all that really matters to me. No, I am thinking about where he is now and the *other* woman he is with and her reaction."

He referred to his mother. Summerhays had returned

to this house when his brother returned from the war, wounded beyond repair it was thought. He had taken his brother's place in the world and protected the marquess from the overbearing mother who would make him a child again.

It had all meant the end of a hedonistic partnership between Castleford and Summerhays. Castleford had resented the sudden estrangement for years.

"I expect there are theatrics happening that are both comical and tragic," Castleford said.

"Exactly. I have imagined my mother's face when my brother arrived and introduced his wife so many times that—" Summerhays grinned. "Hell, I don't know if I am glad I'm not there to see it or sorry that I am missing a fine show."

Castleford mimicked the wide-eyed mixture of shock and horror that probably masked their mother's face after that introduction. Summerhays laughed enough for his eyes to tear.

He caught his breath. "Of course, I also worry whether this Joanna will know to stand up to her at once. Whether he will too."

"It sounds to me that your brother is able to stand on his own two feet again. Literally and metaphorically. If he needs to lean on someone, he has a wife. Your job is done, Summerhays. He will carry the family torch now. You have enough influence of your own in the Commons, though. You still get the best of it—wealth, power, and privilege—yet you are spared the tedious parts of being a marquess. I would say your future looks ideal."

"I suppose so. I am relieved for that, along with the knowledge now that his time with us will not be too short."

Castleford stretched out his legs. "You realize this means that you can have fun again. No more need for strangling discretion either. Hell, it can be like old times, side by side."

"I think if we did some of those things side by side again, Audrianna would shoot me."

"Yes, probably so." He sipped more port. "Damn."

They drank like the two old friends they were. A comfortable silence hung. Then Summerhays looked over, with the rakish lights from years ago in his eyes.

"So?" he asked.

"So?"

"Hawkeswell wrote to me. Frequently. He could not bear that I was not here for it. A week or ten days, you told him."

"Oh. *That* so.

"Did you seduce her?"

"No."

Summerhays accepted that without comment. Unlike Hawkeswell, he did not gloat or goad.

"However, we are having an affair. You may as well know. I am not good at keeping such things discreet."

"All the same, *I* will try to."

"Once I decided I should marry her, I decided a real seduction would not be the best start. So, despite trying my damndest, in the end I didn't. I astonished myself. I hope such selflessness is not habit-forming."

Summerhays showed honest shock. "You astonish *me*, with this casual, passing mention of marriage. I never thought I would see the day when you wed, not even to produce an heir. When will this happen?"

"That is not settled yet. It might be best not to tell your wife, since it was supposed to be a secret still."

Summerhays poured more port into both their glasses. He raised his. "I congratulate you. Mrs. Joyes is an exquisite woman."

Castleford accepted the toast. He was very glad that Summerhays was back in town. For one thing, Summerhays understood that Daphne was not merely lovely.

Chapter Twenty-two

"No." Hawkeswell slammed his fist onto the table in the card room at Brooks's. "I won't have it."

He stood to emphasize his rejection of what he had just heard. "You will not marry that woman, Castleford. It is out of the question."

Summerhays laid a calming hand on his arm and urged him to sit again. "You are being ungracious. Be happy for him, as a friend should be."

"I'll be damned first."

Castleford looked meaningfully at Summerhays. "He has a protective inclination toward her. He expects me to ruin her life if I marry her. It is well-known that always happens when a man heaps jewels, silks, and furs on a woman and makes her a duchess."

"She is a grown woman, Hawkeswell," Summerhays

said. "Nor is she one not to know her own mind or to
need your interference on her behalf."

"Damnation, *she* isn't the one who will be ruined."
Hawkeswell sighed in his annoying way. "*Think*, man.
What are you doing? You were not born for marriage.
You were not educated for it either. Hell, you are *Castle-
ford*. You stand for something. Something important, and
it isn't the domesticated life."

"Such histrionics, Hawkeswell. Such touching concern for my welfare and reputation too. Have no fear.
This does not herald the end of civilization. I will still be
me no matter what."

Hawkeswell laughed bitterly at that. Even Summerhays smiled at the notion.

"You think so?" Hawkeswell said. "Let me tell you,
my friend, marriage is only a fit state for a man who finds
himself in two situations. Either he must be slavishly in
love like I am, or he must be utterly indifferent. Anything
in the middle will cause untold annoyance. Tell him,
Summerhays. Explain to him how wives are only joys
when you are so besotted that you find their little manipu-
lations adorable instead of maddening. Talk some sense
into him."

"It is past time for him to marry, you must admit."

"For anyone else, true. But not *him*." He looked away,
frustrated, like a man trying to speak to a stranger who
does not know his language. Castleford found his dismay charming.

Hawkeswell shook his head forlornly. "The best last
hope of mankind, and it comes to this." He sighed. "She
bewitched you. That is the only explanation. Caught you
in your own game."

"You were right, Castleford," Summerhays said apologetically. "I was wrong. You should not have told him yet. I should not have pressed you to do so."

Hawkeswell's head snapped around. "*Yet?* Have I been made privy to a secret? That is odd for an engagement that involves a duke." He peered over severely. "When will you publish the announcement?"

"They are being discreet still. Until it is all settled," Summerhays explained.

Hawkeswell frowned suspiciously. Dark amusement narrowed his eyes. "Summerhays, you are too good. I think our friend has taken advantage of that. I can think of only one thing that has to be settled before an engagement is announced, and that is whether there is any engagement at all."

Castleford yawned and allowed his attention to wander. He noticed that Latham was playing cards in the far corner. Latham looked up from his hand just then and nodded his acknowledgment.

"What a cynical person you are, Hawkeswell," Castleford said. "I would worry that marriage caused it and fear for myself, but it was always a tendency in your character. As for this small change in my life heralding doom the way you say, I assure you that will not be the case. Now, regarding the political crisis that brought us together here—"

"He is trying to change the subject, Summerhays. I am telling you, I am right. There is no engagement."

"Is he right? Now that I think about it, you did not tell me you were engaged last night. You only said you had decided to marry her."

"And I will."

"Did you propose?" Summerhays frowned now too, much the same way Hawkeswell did.

"She knows my intentions. I made them very plain."

"It is customary *to propose*," Summerhays said. "Women like to be asked, not merely informed of a man's intentions."

"She won't have him," Hawkeswell said. "Trust me, she has not agreed to this. If she ever does, Castleford, the price will be that you reform."

"Then mankind is safe. Its last, best hope will not fall. However, I do not expect any such demands."

"Hell, she has you almost half-reformed already."

Hawkeswell kept putting the worst possible light on everything. The man did not seem to see the obvious other side of things, which was that a person almost half-reformed was still more than half-bad. Once he and Daphne were married, Castleford assumed the balance would tilt back to the unreformed side even more again.

"When *do* you expect the announcement?" Summerhays asked.

"Soon."

"How soon?"

"A week at most. Maybe ten days."

Castleford stood and stretched his legs. One reason he did not gamble much was that the chairs at gaming tables were often uncomfortable. After two hours sitting at this one and not even having the fun of card play, he was more than done.

The men who had joined Summerhays, Hawkeswell, and him appeared very serious and sober as they also prepared to leave. More than a few other tables noted the conversation breaking up, just as the men sitting at them had noticed just who had gathered here at Brooks's and the way in which whatever was said was spoken too low to do any decent eavesdropping. Castleford trusted that Liverpool would hear of this meeting within the hour and sweat a little.

Not that much had been decided. As he expected, the Commons would have to carry the standard on any criticism of the government's role in Peterloo. The lords, with few exceptions, would choose to hear what they wanted to hear about those events, because they wanted any sign of the lower orders organizing dealt with harshly. No one had forgotten what had happened in France not all that long ago.

The affairs of state no longer occupying his mind, Hawkeswell could not resist a parting goad. "Ten days, you said. I will be watching the notices in the newspapers."

It was not the ten days that Castleford ruminated about as he bade farewell to the others. That business about Daphne demanding he reform was what stuck in his head. Hawkeswell could be unbearable at times, but sometimes he saw matters very clearly. Had he not found Daphne vague, and wondered if the "no prying" rule might be self-serving? His instincts about women had served him well there.

Was that what her resistance was about? Did she find him unsuitable? That was a hell of a thing, if so. Backwards. He was a duke, after all. During the season he almost needed a sword to go anywhere, what with all the mothers seeking to add his tail to their trophy walls.

Nonetheless, he tried to see matters through Daphne's eyes. The exercise was a novelty and not without interest. It distracted him enough that he stood by that gaming table for a spell, fascinated.

He concluded, after trying to think like a woman more than any man should attempt, that her words when they spoke of marriage might have been the honest truth. She did not fancy marrying a man who saw it as penance—and he had to admit that he did, although, if he were honest, the notion of having her around more rather than less had appeal.

She also might not want a husband who intended to continue his fun until he died. What woman would?

She had weighed the benefits against those two points, and found the title, luxury, and security lacking.

He was sympathetic until he got to that last part. Only a fool would do such stupid calculations, and Daphne was not a fool. Clearly he was missing something in his speculations on how she viewed the matter.

Unable to imagine what, he turned to leave. He almost walked right into one of the men who had joined them today, who had not yet left himself.

"You were lost in your thoughts, Castleford." Tamor Raylor, an MP from Oxfordshire, smiled hopefully, much the way a tailor does when he shows you his most expensive superfines. "I had hoped to have a word with you but did not want to interrupt your deliberations."

"We have had quite a few words already today, Raylor. I have nothing more to say on the matter."

Raylor chuckled, then glanced askance at the other gentlemen in the card room. "This is about something else entirely. The word I seek is a very private one."

The day had been too much like a Tuesday already, and Castleford thought to put him off. Then he remembered that it actually *was* a Tuesday. Reluctantly he nodded and followed Raylor out of the room.

Even the library was not private enough for this word. Raylor led him to the retiring room, with its line of commodes.

"I had no idea that you meant *that* kind of a private word, Raylor."

The man did not comprehend at first, then his eyes widened in horror. "Oh, my dear heavens. Oh, no, Your Grace. I pray you have not misunderstood—I would never—well, that is, if *you* would I am not criticizing, but I personally would never—"

Castleford sat on the lid of a commode. "Unless someone is hiding inside one of the bowls, this is as private as you can find in London, I would guess. With such care on your part, I expect this to be good."

Raylor mopped his brow with his handkerchief and collected himself. "I am speaking on behalf of a group of men. We have formed a syndicate, you see. I have been sent to offer you a considerable sum for that land in Middlesex, where you have had those engineers working."

"I had reports of trespassers there. You?"

"We are gentlemen. We do not trespass."

"But you hire men who do, perhaps."

Raylor chose not to respond.

Castleford knew he should walk out. He had other plans for that land now. It was a Tuesday, though, wasn't it? He was supposed to exercise his responsibilities today. "How considerable a sum?"

"Twenty thousand pounds."

"I am rarely impressed, Mr. Raylor, especially not by you. I will say, however, that today you have risen considerably in my opinion."

"Thank you, Your Grace. May I take that to mean you are agreeable?"

"Not at all. It is a handsome sum, but that land is worth rather more than that to me, I am afraid."

Now Raylor was impressed. "Indeed, sir? It must hold something even more valuable than we were—than we were led to think."

"Yes, it does." He stood.

Raylor followed him out. "I will speak with the other principles, Your Grace. Perhaps if you give me a number—"

"I could not be tempted for less than fifty thousand, which is not to say I could be tempted at all."

"Fifty—oh! This is very valuable land indeed! I beg you to allow me to have another private word in a few days, Your Grace. For such a prize, we may be able to meet that expectation."

"You may speak as many private words as you want, but I would be a fool to sell."

He shook off Raylor and aimed for the door and the street.

"You should not try to sell what is not yours to begin with," a voice said quietly but clearly.

Castleford did not break his stride or even look over. "I thought I saw you lurking just inside the library, Latham. Looking for sinners to save with your pompous hypocrisy, are you?"

Latham's boots passed his own, then pivoted as Latham blocked the path to the door. "You haven't been about recently. Having fun these days, are you?"

"More than you, I am sure. Pretending to be a saint probably gets very boring."

"I keep myself busy enough and find fun enough too. Recently, the busy has exceeded the fun, that is true. Besides all those meetings with the ministers, there is this matter of that damned land my father gave you. Half of London seems to be forming syndicates to buy it."

"Then half of London is made up of asses. I have said again and again there is nothing there."

"You protest too much. They don't believe you. Neither do I."

"That is because you are an ass too. Now, please stand aside. Even on Tuesdays, I have a right to be spared your presence."

Latham hesitated, like a schoolboy taunt. Castleford was deciding the delay justified a fist to the nose when, unfortunately, Latham moved.

"I know what you found there, Tristan, so do not feign bored indifference with me. One of those men you hired thought twenty pounds more useful than your good opinion of him."

"With all the idiots determined to buy something, eventually some smart fellow would make up something to sell. He probably made twenty pounds enough times over to buy a villa in Naples. I wish I knew who he was. I can always use an enterprising mind like he seems to have." He wasn't joking. He should track down the fellow. He needed a new secretary.

"If it were so empty of value, you would have taken Raylor's fifty thousand."

"You misheard. I said fifty thousand might tempt me. He did not offer it. Yet."

"I do. I suggest that you take it. I know you, and I see your game. It is time to stop this farce of encouraging other bids by pretending disinterest."

"And stop the fun? I am up to fifty thousand already, despite insisting nothing is there. Imagine if I admitted something were."

"You will do it because I will make good on my warning

to contest the will if you don't sell to me. As soon as my solicitor moves, all other offers will disappear."

Castleford frowned over the threat while Latham peered at him intently.

"I see that you have me well cornered, Latham. You really are ruthless, aren't you?"

"I only do what I know my father would have wanted."

Castleford shrugged. "Hell, if I sell at all, it might as well be to you as to one of the other idiots, I suppose. Money is money." And Tuesday was Tuesday. "I suddenly do not find fifty thousand as tempting as I thought I might, however."

Latham's eyes gleamed. He smiled smugly, confident of victory now. "I might consider a bit more."

"Put the offer in writing, and I will think about it."

Chapter Twenty-three

"We prune like this, Mrs. Palmer." Daphne showed the woman the proper use of the little knife. The climbing rose on the arbor showed the results of the artless use of that tool today, accomplished before Daphne had time to stop the damage.

She left Mrs. Palmer to try again and walked over to where Mrs. Reever hoed at some weeds in the kitchen garden. All of the women knew about growing food, and this plot had seen excellent care the last week since they all arrived. She made them take turns, however, because she needed them to learn the finer points of horticulture if the business were to thrive.

The day proved warm enough, but with the arrival of September the breeze now carried that crispness that heralds the colder weather to come. Soon the chores would return to the greenhouse, and there would have to be much more instruction.

The word from Failsworth was that indeed some men had come looking for Margaret and even entered and searched her home. Daphne wanted to believe it was due to some honest inquiry into that day's horrible events. She did not believe it, however. Neither did her guests.

They would remain with her a good long while, she suspected.

Mrs. Hill came out of the house. "Mail," she said, handing over several letters. She peered out from under her cap's edge. "I've been laying in staples and such, as you told me. I can always feed more mouths on the money we spend, but be expecting a lot of soup and bread."

"I have every confidence in you, Mrs. Hill. As long as we do not starve, all will be well."

Mrs. Hill gazed at the gardens and at the three bonnets bent to their labors. "Their trouble will pass, I am sure you know. They will not be here forever. Nor the others coming now. I've no good sense with plants in the growing, only the cooking, as you also well know. Once they all leave, and with Katherine gone now—"

"I appear to attract women who need homes, much as a light attracts moths, as *you* well know," Daphne said with a teasing smile. "I expect there to be others."

Mrs. Hill nodded. "I guessed about Katherine. I was tempted to talk to her, to reassure her. She remained so fearful, as if she expected a magistrate to show up any day. Of course, I assumed she'd had the good sense to do him in. I always say, if a woman is going to cut a brute somewhere, she may as well make it his throat."

Daphne always found Mrs. Hill's lack of contrition about one brute's neck a little dismaying. But then she reminded herself just how broken and battered the woman had been when they met six years ago.

"It was just as well that you did not talk to her, Mrs. Hill, let alone share your opinion regarding the fate due husbands who beat their wives. We would not have wanted her guessing how you came to be here, would we? It has been some years now, but there is probably a magistrate still curious about your whereabouts too."

"That be the truth of it, for certain." She bent and picked some sage from the herb row. "I'll leave you to those letters. I've still to get the chamber ready for those two who came this morning."

Daphne sat on a small bench to the side of the kitchen garden and turned her attention to the mail.

One letter arrested her attention. It bore Castleford's seal. She had received no letter since she came down two weeks ago. Afterwards had happened faster, and with more finality, than she had expected.

She tore it open and knew at once from the penmanship that the duke had not written this. He had a new secretary, it appeared. A Mr. Austry introduced himself and wrote in Castleford's stead to invite her to a dinner party His Grace was giving this Friday, in honor of the Marquess of Wittonbury. His Grace would send his coach for her on Thursday, and she would be his guest until Monday.

Once more, the duke had scrawled a short postscript in his own hand. *You must come. I insist on it. If you do not, I will come down there, as I warned I would.*

She laughed at the arrogance of those lines. Yet it touched her that he had bothered to write anything at all, let alone reveal his continued interest so clearly. A happy glow entered her heart.

The other letters came from her friends. They reported on their efforts on behalf of the little quest that she had confided in them. Audrianna also mentioned the dinner party Castleford would host and asked if she would be staying at Park Lane in order to attend.

Daphne carried the letters into the house, to the writing table in the library. She wrote to Verity first, asking her to put into effect some very special plans that they had discussed. Then she wrote to explain those plans to Celia and Audrianna.

Finally she responded to Castleford's invitation. She was grateful for His Grace's condescension and kind thoughtfulness, she explained to Mr. Austry. She would expect the duke's coach at midday on Thursday next.

"They are up to something. Our wives, that is," Hawkeswell said. He sat on a chair in Castleford's bedchamber, more into his cups than was normal these days.

All the friends visiting this afternoon had left true sobriety behind. The empty wine bottles formed a line on the writing table where the manuscript waited for its final chapter.

"Hawkeswell is known to raise suspicions without cause," Summerhays said. "This time he is correct. Something is afoot."

"We can only hope that we never learn what it is," Albrighton said. "In the meantime, I am taking advantage of Celia's efforts to distract me from noticing. I have only to mention all those letters going back and forth among them for her to drag me to bed."

A loud crash all but obliterated his last words. Castleford looked in the direction of the sound. The two men working near the fireplace froze and glanced over cautiously.

Speaking of beds . . .

"You did say all of it, sir. We've no choice but to break this piece down to do it."

"I am not complaining. Get on with it."

The men continued their labor. Hawkeswell gazed over and poured more wine into his glass.

"I still do not know why you must do this," he said.

"It is just a bed, Hawkeswell. I have bought a new one. Just as big. Much nicer and more fashionable in style too."

"It is not just any bed, and you know it."

No, it wasn't. It was the bed Daphne did not want to get into.

"This is symbolic, I assume," Albrighton said. "A rite of passage requires such rituals."

"For a man who rarely speaks plainly, sometimes you manage to baldly say what is better left unsaid, Albrighton," Castleford said.

"My apologies. I just assumed we all knew why—"

"Yes, damn it, we all know why," Hawkeswell snapped.

"See?" Castleford said, pointing to Hawkeswell. "He sees more symbolism than exists, unfortunately. As do you, perhaps. Only Summerhays here comprehends that I merely dispose of one bed because I have bought a new one."

"Actually, I am of like mind with the others," Summerhays said. "It is why you have us here, is it not? To give you courage as you send part of your old life to the funeral pyre?"

"Hell, are you going to be boring too? You are all

here because I thought it would be *fun*. Mistake, that, I can see now. Hawkeswell, stop being so tediously serious. Damn, you will probably start composing a poetic eulogy to those ropes and boards soon."

"A splendid idea, actually. Allow me," Summerhays said.

He stood and cleared his throat. "We gather here today to bid farewell to a special piece of furniture. Most beds remain nothing more than a collection of wood and hemp. They serve their purpose without complaint or praise. They know their place in the grand design, and it is a humble place. Some beds, however, most notably the one that we today send to its just rewards in the afterlife—"

"Hell, I assume that would be," Albrighton quipped.

"Would you care to take over?" Summerhays asked.

"I could never match your eloquence. Pray, continue."

"Some beds rise above the ordinary and make their marks on the history of man. Today we say good-bye to that rarity in the world, a *great* bed. A bed that saw more pleasure in a fortnight than most see in their entire existence. A bed that inspired fortitude and creativity previously unknown in sensual endeavors." He raised his glass and his voice. "Gentlemen, let us give this noble bed the honor it is due." He drank and threw the glass into the fireplace. The flames jumped high. The workers jumped back.

Albrighton's glass followed.

Hawkeswell cast his own forward. "Damnation, I think I am going to weep."

Castleford hesitated, appreciating rather suddenly the potential symbolism. He rather wished he had named the damned bed, so he could send it off properly.

He noticed the others watching him pause, Hawkeswell rather hopefully.

Summerhays smiled. "It is truly time, Your Grace. There is better to be had than you ever knew in it. Trust all of us that this is true."

Laughing at that notion, but with more trust than he would ever admit, Castleford threw his glass forward.

Daphne could not have asked to travel to London in more style. Castleford's coach rolled up to The Rarest Blooms with two footmen standing behind all decked out in their livery. Once inside she noticed that a basket with some wine and fruit waited, and a lap blanket should she find the day too cool.

Upon arriving at the duke's house, servants swarmed to serve her. The butler came out to open the coach's door himself, as if she were a duchess.

Another figure showed. Castleford himself stepped out of the house to greet her. The honor took her aback and made her pause before walking forward to join him. She looked at him intently, at how his body communicated utter confidence and how his face displayed both indifference and intense interest in her arrival.

She looked long and carefully so she would always remember him there. She suspected she would be branding her mind a lot these next few days.

The butler handed her over to his master. Castleford drew her inside. "You should have come sooner," he said, his tone very ducal and a little resentful.

"You did not invite me sooner."

"I clearly told you that you were to come here. Hell, it has been two damned weeks."

"I am here now, at least. We can have a row if you insist, but it will be a poor welcome."

He drew her aside, to privacy. "We can have the row later." He cupped her head with his hands and held her to a sweet kiss, one that made her heart shake. "I intend to make sure that by Monday, you do not want to leave."

She barely managed to hide how that touched her. She would leave, whether she wanted to or not. By Monday she expected him to feel differently on the question too.

"I told the housekeeper that you would use that chamber you and she discovered near my apartment," he said, taking her hand and leading her to the stairs.

"Was she scandalized?"

"I don't know. Are there people who worry about scandalizing servants? How odd."

They did not stop at the public rooms above but kept going. He brought her into his dressing room and immediately swung her around and began unfastening her dress.

"Two weeks," he muttered. "It has been hell."

She felt the dress gaping already. "Your Grace, I would prefer—"

"It was one thing when I had not had you yet, Daphne, but this was unacceptable torture. I do not want a row, just a right understanding. When I say you must come here to me, that means you are to do it."

She slid out of his busy hands and grasped the sides of her dress behind her. "I understand your impatience, Castleford, but let us at least go to my chamber first."

"Oh, that. Here, let me show you what I have done." He took her other hand and sped her to the bedchamber door. He threw it open and gestured. "We do not have to use that other chamber now. I removed the one here, and put in a new one."

She realized he spoke of the bed. She went over, trying not to stumble on her sagging dress's hem.

Everything was new. Even the drapes. She examined the changes, too astonished to speak.

"In case you are wondering, it is still a virgin bed," he said. "No woman has been in it."

She bit her lower lip. She had never expected him to understand that she did not want to join the spirits of his whores on that other bed. That he had not only understood but done this for her, left her undone and in danger of losing her composure.

She braved a smile, but her heart filled with a beautiful ache.

She opened her reticule. "Thank you. I am moved that you were so thoughtful." She poured the diamond necklace and earrings into her hand. "Help me to put these on, so that the first woman to use it is worthy of the honor."

He fastened the necklace at her nape while she worked the earrings. Laden with the jewels, she stepped out of her dress and began dropping her chemise.

He sat on the bed and watched, his expression severe with his attention. Thoughts that she could not fathom caused golden lights to form in his eyes. Not only desire caused that intensity while she undressed under that gaze. He was not distracted either. Those unknown thoughts centered on her.

Naked except for her hose, she propped one foot beside his hip so she could deal with her garter. He took over, loosing the ribbon and sliding her hose down, looking at all of her while his action created a caress that made her tremble.

He made quick work of the other one, then pulled her close so she stood between his knees.

"Diamonds, and nothing else," he said, tracing around her breasts with his fingertips. "They become you in so many ways. Not only your beauty. They show you as you are inside, I think. They illuminate your pride and your strength. Right now you are not a woman for a man to take lightly, that is certain. You appear capable of great danger, should you turn your mind to it."

She said nothing. She dared not assume to what he might allude. With Castleford, it could be anything.

His tongue laved her nipple playfully, then luxuriously. Powerful trembles began inside her. He must have sensed them, because his hand slid between her thighs, and he gently caressed there in ways certain to madden her quickly.

"I decided, while you were gone that you did not want to marry because I am unreformed," he said between kisses and nips. "But I also thought there was more to it. Seeing you now, I am sure there is."

She closed her eyes, because the sensations streaked through her now in a series of deep, moving tremors of pleasure.

"You are not going to tell me why, are you?"

"No." Perhaps she only answered in her mind. Her senses were being overwhelmed in a way that made it hard to know.

"So I am to have you as a mistress only, for now. I am inclined to accept the truth of that. It is in my interests to do so right now. Gentlemen are less careful in bed with mistresses than with wives, and mistresses are more willing to be wicked."

She felt quite wicked. Desperately so. His hand teased at her, stroking slowly but deliberately avoiding the touches that would also give some relief. He dazed her so badly she had to hold his shoulder to keep her balance.

He stood and had her lie down. He undressed while he looked at her. "The sunlight makes those diamonds flame," he said while he stripped off his shirt. "It is as if white fire pours out of you."

The fire was all in her, burning recklessly. When he knelt on the bed and kissed her, she reached for him and caressed his phallus, so she might make him burn too.

The scorching kisses he pressed on her neck and chest said he did. Wildness claimed them both, and they grasped and bit and clutched as if passion would consume them.

He kissed down her body, not carefully, not even very gently. He kissed her and moved her as if he had a right to do whatever he chose. His whole body turned as he did it, until his mouth could reach between her thighs and start the pleasure that unhinged her.

Her eyes blurred as the power crashed through her. His position put his hips close to her. She used both her hands to give him pleasure while she lost herself.

He stopped suddenly. She looked down, impatient and confused. He had risen up on his arm. Wicked fires showed in his gaze.

"Do as I do, if you can be so bold, Daphne."

He ensured she lost all sense then. Unbearable pleasure buried first shock, then fear, then hesitation. She kissed where she caressed him, then used her mouth as he did.

"Hawkeswell is in mourning. He thinks you are ruining me." Castleford shared that tidbit while he tied one of her wrists to the bedpost.

She tested the binding. It was not especially tight. She could get free if she chose.

"For a man besotted by one woman, he has a peculiar need to know at least one other is not hobbled," she said. "Perhaps he is not nostalgic so much for being bad but for his youth when he was bad."

He kissed her nape. "How wise you are. I am sure that you are right. We are hardly ancient, however. I think maybe he just fears he will have no one to goad. He enjoys having rows with me." He moved to the other side and went to work on her other wrist. "You understand this is only a game? I do not want you afraid."

She nodded. He could tell that the point of the game had begun to reveal itself, however, and she still accommodated it. Tied like this, hand and foot, left her very vulnerable. Which aroused him in ways not without a dark edge.

This was not a game that a woman should play with someone she did not trust, he had explained. He trusted her agreement meant she did trust him, and she was not just seeing how bold she could be tonight.

He left the bed and moved the sheet down, uncovering her. He looked at her ivory form, so elegant in its length. Facedown on the bed like that, her extended arms and legs made her back and bottom taut and perfect. She awed him and also incited a savage desire.

The waiting affected her. Slight flexes revealed her own arousal. She looked over her shoulder at him.

"Is this game ever played the other way?"

"No. It always works like this."

She frowned. "I would think it could very easily be switched."

What a rebellious notion. "It is a good thing I am here to teach you the proper way to sin, then."

She rested her head on the pillow again. "Perhaps you only play it this way because you cannot trust a woman enough."

"You are thinking too much. It is distracting you from how erotic this is."

"I promise you that nothing has distracted me from that, Your Grace." She looked back again, pointedly lowering her gaze down his body. "Nor has it distracted you at all, I see."

Not at all. He got on the bed and knelt beside her. He kissed the small of her back, and her bottom rose instinctively. Need broke in him like a storm. He clenched his jaw while he found some control and settled between her thighs.

The sensation as he entered shook his essence. He could not believe what it did to him, how good it felt. It was not the first time he had that thought with her, either. He withdrew and entered again, to know it once more.

There is better to be had than you ever knew.

Yes, damn it.

It was the last clear thought he had. The storm permitted no more as it absorbed his mind and body. It obliterated all considerations of gentility too, being born, as it was, of her erotic submission.

Chapter Twenty-four

The new Marchioness of Wittonbury was a quiet woman of small stature and soulful eyes. She wore a white dinner dress that complemented her dark hair and a strand of pearls that she occasionally fingered and admired, as if she had just received them as a gift.

She seemed an intelligent woman too. Her English was not perfect, but she contributed to the conversation at dinner in her accented speech. Sometimes Daphne caught her looking at the marquess with touching warmth. They were clearly in love, and that alone gave the party a special joy that affected the whole evening.

Daphne had not known the marquess well. She had only seen him once before he left for the Continent, and his paralysis then had affected his body in various ways. The isolation it encouraged and his reclusive habits then had caused a sickly pallor.

Now his efforts to walk had obviously given him new strength. His gait was not natural yet, and he appeared in some pain at times, but with his wife at his side he entered Castleford's home on his own and moved from the drawing room down to dinner on his own too.

They all went to the theater after dinner, except Audrianna and Summerhays, who returned home so Audrianna would not get overtired. The rest of them filled Castleford's box at Drury Lane. The drama onstage proved forgettable, and a buzz of conversation moved through the boxes as people visited each other. Daphne could hear the conversations taking place beside them and below. Peterloo was much discussed, but so was the return of Wittonbury.

Castleford moved to her side just as Joanna approached him. Wittonbury sat in the front row, looking more like his brother Sebastian in this light than he probably had in years.

"Your Grace, you have my gratitude," she said. She looked at her husband, and her gaze softened. "You have his too. This return has been—difficult. But needed, he believes. He says it is to introduce me to his family, but when he first met my father, he spoke of getting strong. Strong enough to—" She searched for the words in her memory. "Be brave outside."

"Brave it out," Castleford said.

"Yes, that was the words. It will be easier now, perhaps? After such great men show him friendship?"

"My reputation is not the best, Lady Wittonbury. My friendship is not known to rehabilitate men's reputations. Quite the opposite. However, his brother and Hawkeswell are both respected and admired."

She regarded him thoughtfully. "Perhaps you are too

modest? I thank you for whatever you have tried to do tonight."

She returned to her husband. Daphne tapped Castleford's arm with her fan. "She is correct. You are too modest. Enough people fear you that they will not slight him now."

"I assure you that most of society loathes me, not fears me."

Actually, some parts of society adored him. The very best and highest parts. "Will you invite the prince regent to dine with him, as you did with Verity?"

"Perhaps. In a few months. If it appears necessary. Do you promise to join the party if I do? Perhaps I will make it a ball, so you can wear those diamonds."

"If I am invited, perhaps I will attend." She tapped his nose with her fan and moved to the back of the box to talk to Verity, who had pointedly caught her eye.

"It is all done," Verity said quietly, her back to the wall while she watched for anyone who might overhear. "Audrianna has had the mail waylaid with no difficulty. She told me at dinner that all but two are affirmative."

"Mystery and the chance for gossip must be compelling them. It is better than I expected."

"Everyone is in place." She took Daphne's hand. "We are with you on this, but you must know that we worry for you. Even if you are successful, there will be no keeping this quiet. No living this down."

No braving it out, either. "I will be glad for it, I think. I will be relieved when all the secrets are out." She bent and kissed Verity's cheek. "You of all of us understand that."

The box door opened while Verity walked away. Daphne

was going to follow her friend, when she saw Latham slip into the box.

He stood there, searching the faces. He startled when he realized she stood not three feet away.

"Ah, there you are. I thought I saw you up here." He eased closer.

Castleford had sat and now lazily watched the play from his chair next to Celia. No one paid attention to the shadows at the back of the box.

"I heard you had left town," Latham said. "Imagine my delight in getting your invitation."

"I trust you will be discreet, as the letter asked."

"Most discreet, dear. How wise of you to let that house, so you are not tainted by Wittonbury's scandal or constrained by Lady Sebastian's curiosity. I look forward to seeing your new home." He peered at the back of Castleford's head. "Does he know? He won't like it."

"The duke could not care less about anything. Where I live and whom I entertain does not signify to him."

Latham laughed lowly. "Lost interest already, did he?"

"He could not lose interest he never had."

"I know him as well as I know myself, Daphne. We were inseparable as boys, and I can still read his thoughts, for all his pose of indifference. You caught his eye, my dear. But as I think you have learned, his gaze never rests in one place long." His eyes narrowed on Castleford. "Pity that you bored him so quickly. Having bested him on that land, I would not mind seeing his face when I stole you from him too."

His voice made her skin crawl. She hid the shiver and feigned confusion. "Land? Are you being clever again?"

"He thought to be clever, not me, and enrich himself

even more, through a spot of land my father left him. But I have got what was rightfully mine back. It cost me much more than it should, but that will be a pittance once I start bringing out the silver that is in the ground." He grinned like a naughty boy. "He'll be out hundreds of thousands before it is over."

She glared at Castleford's head. Latham was talking about The Rarest Blooms. Castleford had *sold her home*. To Latham!

"He can be too clever by half sometimes, can't he?" She turned to Latham. "Regrettably, you cannot checkmate him again. It is true he was briefly interested, but it was the shortest pursuit in the world's history."

"Not because you were easily caught, I hope."

"I am never easily caught, Gerome."

"Well, perhaps not anymore." He chuckled at his humor.

It was all she could do not to slap him. Instead she opened her fan so her outrage might not show. "You must leave now. I do not want my friends to notice you here."

"Of course. Until tomorrow, Daphne."

She feared he was about to try to steal a kiss. She walked forward, toward her friends, before he got the chance.

"You sold my home because *it was a Tuesday*?" Daphne glared at him across his dressing room.

He took a moment to admire her high color and note again how strong emotion became her. Ideally that emotion would not be fury directed at him, of course.

"Actually, I would have sold it any day of the week, under the circumstances."

That did not appease her, needless to say. She strode back and forth, and not gracefully.

"When were you going to tell me this?"

"Soon. Tonight. Or tomorrow. Soon, though."

She stomped her foot. She came at him so angrily that he really thought she would hit him.

Instead she just looked in his eyes, and her fury changed to dismay and hurt.

Hell, she was going to weep.

"Why?" It sounded like a plea.

"Listen to me. Can you do that? Can you call forth the sensible Daphne just for a moment?" He took her face in his hands. "I did not seek this. He got it in his head that he had to have that land. He is convinced it holds untold riches in its ground and would not hear otherwise."

"Silver?"

"Silver. Gold. Iron. The rumors abound. He was so convinced that he was ready to contest the will to block my use or sale of it. So I turned his conceit back on him and made him pay dearly for what he demanded."

Her brow puckered. "How dearly?"

"By the time negotiations were completed, we had settled on eighty thousand pounds."

Her eyes widened. "What is it actually worth?"

"No more than five, and that is being generous."

She pondered that, her indignation well gone now. Deciding the worst was over, he removed his waistcoat and went to work on his cravat.

"You are very sure that there is nothing of value there?" she asked.

"Only soil well suited to growing flowers."

"How very odd that everyone assumes otherwise."

"There is no accounting for it. I kept telling them the truth, but no one would hear me."

She came over and finished untying his cravat. She used the two ends to pull his head down so she looked right in his eyes. "Castleford, have you been bad? Does mama have to punish you?"

He pried the ends of the cravat out of her hand. "If it is bad to let an ass be an idiot, I am guilty. As for that other question—I do not care for the mother game. I have never understood why some men do. I think it is distasteful on the hearing of it, and probably perverse in the doing."

She looked startled. "There is actually such a game? How odd. Who would think of such a thing?"

"Daphne, whatever you could think of in your wildest imagination, there is a game for it and probably has been for a thousand years." He pulled off his shirt and advanced on her. "For example, there is the lovely lady taken up against the wall game. I'll show you how it is played."

She listened to his heart beat while her own blood slowed. She loved lying like this, on top of him, surrounded by his arms and listening to his life and his breaths. It was one of the best intimacies, and very sweet after pleasure's frenzy.

"You do know that I will keep my word," he said. His hand stroked through her hair. "There is a good farm just over the Surrey line. Not far from where you are now, actually. I will have everything you have built moved there. We will put that eighty thousand in trust for you too, so you are never dependent again."

"I knew that you would be good to your word. I did not doubt that."

"Then you do not mind too much? It is another ten miles out. It will be harder for you to visit The Rarest Blooms in one day."

"I will not be visiting. I will be living there." She waited for him to argue or to sigh. Neither came. *I will be living there, and very soon you will be glad for it.*

"When do you think Latham will know that he paid all that money for nothing more than a moderate-size farm?"

"When he sends in his own men to find where to mine."

"It was a good sum, even for him, I would think."

"He will miss it badly, if that is what you mean. His estate is not exactly boundless. That branch of the family got all the goodness. My branch has all the financial sense."

She turned her head and rested her chin on his chest so she could see his face. "You led him into this. I do not know how you did it, but I know that you did."

He just looked at her.

"Why do you hate him so? Not because of me, I think. It is older than that. Deeper too."

"I do not hate him. I find him irritating and boring."

She rested her cheek on his chest again. If he did not want to speak of it, that was fine, but his reactions to Latham were not those of a man merely irritated and bored.

His fingers stroked her back absently, as if he were not even aware of the movement. That touch soothed her, however, until she melted against him.

"He played a game once, and I was the pawn," he said. "It was as if he tested whether he could make me as dishonorable as he was. He made sure that the price of refusing to be so was very high."

He told her a story then of a sojourn in France and a young woman named Marie.

"She expected to get the family lands back after the war, you see," he said. "Everyone knew that the nobility would regain their estates lost in their revolution. Her land was in Gascony and produced superior wine, she said. The fools lined up to buy a share. I learned she had sold ten percent interests to at least forty different men, each of whom paid a good sum." He paused. "I could have ignored that, possibly."

But not the rest. Not once he learned the money went to the remnants of Bonaparte's followers.

"Latham counted on your ignoring that too, because of her?" Daphne asked.

"He hoped for it, I think. I would be bound to him forever, then, wouldn't I? If he knew what she was up to, which I suspected he did. I learned I was right."

"He could also take comfort in knowing you were no better than he. I think he badly wants to believe that."

"Perhaps so."

She kissed his chest and moved her arms to embrace him. This tale had deepened the mood between them, but sadness drenched their intimacy now.

"Did you love her?" She hoped not. That would make this story more tragic.

"She fascinated me, but I was not in love. I thought it would be easier since I was not. It wasn't."

"Do you regret it?"

He did not answer. She let it pass. She knew better than to pry into a person's heart and cursed herself for having done so without thinking.

"There are some things you do because they must be done, because the other choice makes you a coward," he finally said.

He had not said he did not regret it. Perhaps he did sometimes, when he allowed himself to think about it at all. Like now.

She understood his long anger with Latham better. It saddened her that it would never go away. He would never find Latham boring or be indifferent to that man's presence in his world.

He was right, though. Some things had to be done, or one was a coward. It was probably natural to hate the person who forces the choice on you, especially if he waits and watches for you to be less than you should be.

She moved up and kissed him, so that maybe thoughts of that night would leave his mind. She used what skill she had to distract him. After a while she succeeded, and it seemed to her that he was grateful that she made the effort.

Chapter Twenty-five

Daphne left the house the next afternoon to visit with her friends before going back to The Rarest Blooms. Castleford decided to pass the time while she was gone scribbling on his manuscript. Since it was almost completed, he also turned his mind to which printer to use.

He was drawing up a little list of printing houses that might be sympathetic to the subject matter when Albrighton's card was brought up. Not expecting the distraction but happy to have it, he told the footman to bring Albrighton to his dressing room.

They managed to fill an hour with political talk before the conversation ebbed. Albrighton just sat there in silence after that. Castleford wondered if the man scoured his brain for small talk that did not sound too slight.

"Are you looking to fill the time until your wife is finished with that little party the women are all enjoying, Albrighton? There are taverns and coffee shops for that purpose, but you are welcome to read a book here."

Albrighton smiled in his vague way. "Actually, I am trying to decide where the boundaries of friendship begin and end."

"That is an odd thing to contemplate. If it is my friendship you speak of, why not let me decide?"

Albrighton regarded him. "You are known to meddle in friends' lives most freely."

"Only for their own good."

"Only to satisfy your curiosity, you mean."

"Are you still piqued about that? It all worked out well enough. You should be grateful, not dragging it up again."

"And if it had not worked out well enough? Should a friend be glad for the truth, even if it is unpleasant?"

"Philosophy does not become you. You are getting irritating now. What is this about?"

"Hawkeswell was correct. Our wives are up to something." He looked over. "I think that which is afoot is afoot right now."

Hawkeswell's suspicions had carried little weight. Even Summerhays might have read more into the most innocent correspondence. Albrighton, on the other hand, was a trained investigator. If he thought something was afoot, it probably was.

"You appear concerned. Is it dangerous?"

"No, I do not think so. Not immediately so, at least."

"That is hardly reassuring. Perhaps you should confide in the husbands of those other wives."

"In the end, it is not about them, I am sure. It is all about Mrs. Joyes."

Damnation. "Then let me put your philosophical quandary to rest. You will confide in me. Now."

"I will share what I can. The first thing you should know is this. My wife is not at any party now. Not yet. She did ask me to be sure to be home by three o'clock. Very pointed on that, she was. I suspect that, at three o'clock, she is going to suddenly have to go somewhere, and ask me to accompany her."

"That is odd."

"Odder yet is that I saw Hawkeswell right before I came here. He also has been asked to be home at three o'clock. His wife is still at home too."

"It is possible, I suppose, that Daphne and Lady Sebastian are holding a private conversation, and the others will join them."

Albrighton did not look like he was convinced of that. Neither was Castleford, for that matter.

"You must forgive me for what I am about to tell you, Castleford. And for my actions, which were not requested or entirely honorable."

"Hell, fine. You are absolved, but only if you speak plainly and be done with it."

"I followed Mrs. Joyes when she left your house today."

How like Albrighton to demand forgiveness before revealing that. Castleford did not hide his annoyance.

"How dare you."

"I picked up a vague scent of intrigue two weeks ago, and it has only gotten stronger with time. I do not like smelling such things in my own home. As for why I turned my attention to Mrs. Joyes—two of the women involved are with child and unlikely to be the center of any scheme. Of the two that were left—Lady Hawkeswell's life is an open book now, isn't it? Her secrets are over. Mrs. Joyes is the only one of them who is still surrounded by questions."

So Albrighton had noticed that. Of course he had. Spotting ambiguities and holes in stories was what he did. What he was.

Castleford began forming the words to put an end to this, out of loyalty to Daphne. He stopped himself. If Albrighton was here, there was a reason that had not been explained yet.

"So I found it odd that my wife wanted me home at exactly three o'clock when she never is so precise, and I took a chance this was all about Mrs. Joyes, and I followed her. She did not go to Lady Sebastian. Or to Lady Hawkeswell. She went somewhere else entirely." He reached into his coat and handed over a small piece of paper with an address on it.

Castleford looked at it. "Who lives here?"

"I asked a local milliner, and she said the house had been to let until four days ago, when someone took it. So, having nothing better to do, I sought out the estate agent."

"Who took this house?"

Albrighton looked at him somewhat oddly. Cautiously. "A woman named Miss Avonleah. Do you know her?"

Castleford gazed at the paper. "I know her." At least, he had thought he did. "It sounds as if there will be a party at this house this afternoon, Albrighton. I trust that you will attend when your wife asks for your escort."

"I think it best if I do."

"So do I. I think that Miss Avonleah will be very disappointed if her salon is not well attended."

Albrighton left then to return to his wife by three

o'clock. He would be there at least, Castleford thought. And Hawkeswell and probably Summerhays.

That meant that the only person in their circle not invited to this party was the Duke of Castleford.

Daphne settled herself on a simple chair in the drawing room on Bird Street. The house was well-appointed and elegant enough. It spoke of gentility but not great wealth.

The street outside showed few carriages. There was only one shop on this block, a milliner's. The residences lining it did not encourage many passersby.

"He is coming, I think," Margaret said, running into the drawing room. She peered out the window. "That is his carriage stopping down there."

Daphne got up and went over to look out. She turned Margaret around, and made a display of fixing the long frill of her cap. "Can you manage? I do not need a housekeeper. I open the door myself and see him below in the morning room."

"I will do it." Margaret firmed her expression and forced the fear out of her eyes. "I will go now."

Daphne repositioned herself on the chair. She made sure no others were close by. She closed her eyes and built her composure as if she laid courses of bricks. She would do this and she would pay the consequences and even if it did not all work out as planned, the scoundrel would never have such power again.

Sounds below. Steps on the stairs. Margaret entered, her head bowed, and brought a card. Daphne nodded, and Margaret went and invited the visitor in.

Latham breezed in, smiling. Behind him Margaret shook her head. No, he had not recognized her. Of course not.

He paused in the middle of the chamber and looked at Daphne. He made a display of admiring her and being impressed. "You are beautiful sitting there, Daphne. The blue of that dress is very becoming."

He set aside his hat and advanced on her. To her horror, he did not sit like a proper guest but circled around her too closely. "It only lacks an appropriate jewel, my dear."

Suddenly a little box appeared in front of her eyes, held by his hand. A gold chain and a sapphire gleamed up at her. The box closed and disappeared as quickly as it had come.

"For afterwards, I think," he said.

He finally sat. He looked around the chamber. "This is pleasant enough. Well located. A quiet street too. You chose well."

"I would have preferred being on a park, but as a widow, my income is limited. At least I can remain in London, however."

"Where is your home otherwise? You never said."

"In the country. In Surrey. Too far to visit London by day easily."

"Is it just you and that housekeeper here?"

"And a cook."

"How wonderfully discreet." He appeared pleased. "I was very happy to receive your letter, Daphne. Our last meeting had not gone well. I thought perhaps—well, let us forget that, shall we. I think that you know that my interest in you has never dimmed. Circumstances did not permit—well, more, in the past. Neither mine nor yours did. It is different now, and you are an independent widow. I hope that I will receive more invitations to call on you in the future."

He did not speak like a petitioner but like a man who assumed that of course she would want his attentions, especially now that he was a duke.

She remained silent. He frowned above a jovial smile. "You are uncommonly cool, Daphne. So reserved now. Maturity has enhanced your beauty but perhaps not your manner. I think I need to find a way to melt some of that frost."

He stood and walked toward her. Her heart beat painfully in fear, but she did not move. She did not let him see it.

Please, please, do not delay. Come soon. Now. She reminded herself that she was not without protection. She had only to scream and she would be safe. But she was not so brave that she did not cringe when he took her hand and raised it to his kiss.

He looked at her, and she knew he would try another kiss next, and not on her hand. *He is too bold. Too conceited. Your plan will not work because of it.*

"If you are discourteous, Latham, there will be no more invitations. I remind you that I am a gentleman's daughter."

His expression fell at the scold. Then he straightened and began laughing.

Suddenly his laugh broke abruptly. A snarl twisted his face. His fingers cupped her chin, hard. He bent so his face was mere inches from hers. "And I remind you that I have already had you, like the whore you are. At least there will be no pretense this time."

Alarm paralyzed her. Just as she made the decision to

call for help, a sound stopped her. A door knocker, then voices below.

Latham heard too. He listened, frowning deeply, while his fingers still grasped her chin. More sounds now, on the stairs and even in the street.

He released her, strode to the window, and looked out. His face fell in surprise.

"Oh, my, these must be my other guests arriving. Did I forget to tell you, Gerome? I decided to host my first party in my new home today."

"You should not have come, Audrianna," Daphne said, while she helped her friend ease down onto the most comfortable chair.

"And miss this? I'll give birth in the reception hall first." Audrianna looked around. "Oh, good, the bishops came."

"I thought Latham would die when they walked in," Daphne said. She could not enjoy the show quite the same as Audrianna. The real drama had not begun yet. Its success would depend on her.

Lord Sebastian had brought up his wife, scowling with annoyance that she had insisted on this odd visit when her time was past due. Now he looked around, curiously, his gaze resting on those bishops and on several matrons known to see themselves as bulwarks of society.

He turned that speculative gaze on his wife. "Do we own this house now? Or did we only rent it?"

"Neither," she said. "Verity provided the money for the lease. Do not tell Hawkeswell, please. It is really none of our business, if you think about it."

Summerhays thought that amusing. "It is a very expensive party that you have helped Mrs. Joyes host."

"We expect it to cost someone else a good deal more than it cost us, before it is over," she said blithely. "Oh, here is Celia and Albrighton. Is everyone here now, Daphne?"

"Yes." She could be excused for hoping Celia would be delayed. She had no doubts about her course of action, but she did not relish walking onto the stage.

From across the drawing room, Verity caught her eye and subtly nodded. *All who are coming are here*, her gaze said. *Have heart. We are with you.*

Daphne walked to the center of the chamber. Latham, standing with his uncles the bishops, gave her a very private, very angry look.

She raised her voice and began a welcome of her guests. Talk drifted off and silence fell as attention came her way.

"You may wonder why you are here. The invitations from my friends hinted at a great spectacle, and perhaps some of you anticipate a virtuoso at a violin or the demonstration of some startling new invention. Those of you who read those letters closely, however, may have guessed that the spectacle would result from an amazing revelation and make for excellent gossip and scandal." She turned to the bishops. "Not you, of course."

A gentle laughter flowed at that. One of the bishops, a plump, hearty fellow, smiled. The other, thin and wizened and much older, scowled.

"Some of you know me as Mrs. Joyes. I have provided flowers for your garden parties or weddings, or greenery for your conservatories. I must tell you now, that is not my name. I am Daphne Avonleah, and I was never married. I took the name Mrs. Joyes to explain a peculiar period in my history. Of significance is that my father was a gentleman of Shropshire county named Michael Avonleah. He was a friend of the last Duke of Becksbridge, who took me into his household upon my father's death."

Her composure wobbled. She looked at Celia, Audrianna, and Verity for reassurance and strength.

"You must tell them," Celia said clearly. "There has been silence for too long."

A little rumble of voices reacted to that. Daphne noticed some white by the doorway. Margaret rose on her toes and looked over shoulders, her eyes burning.

"While I was in the duke's household," Daphne continued, "his son, the Earl of Latham, seduced me, and took my innocence despite my pleas that he stop."

"Lies," one of the bishops exclaimed.

"Nonsense," a voice on the other side of the chamber muttered.

"Believe what you will about me, but there were other unfortunates before and after me, for whom there was no seduction but only brute force."

"This is slander of the most insidious kind." Latham pretended to be much shocked and distressed. He looked to his uncles for sympathy. They nodded and speared Daphne with dangerous glares.

"Be most careful, Mrs. Joyes, or whoever you are. Accusing a man of a crime in this way is most serious, and you could well find yourself in Newgate Prison," the old, wizened uncle threatened.

"She is friends with wives of some political opponents," Latham said sadly. "That men would go to such extremes to silence my voice is the real scandal."

"Best that you be careful now, Latham," Hawkeswell

said. "There are three men here who are now justified in calling you out for that, and I am sore tempted to be first in line."

To say the company enjoyed this show would not be kind. Hawkeswell's allusion to a challenge sharpened attention that was already well honed, however.

"There cannot be slander in the truth," Daphne said. "But do not take my word alone."

She turned to the doorway. Margaret's cap disappeared. Then a scuffle of footsteps caused the people standing over there to part.

Margaret, her red hair uncovered now, walked forward. Two women followed. All were dressed modestly in simple dresses. They gathered around Daphne. Margaret held her own, but the other two cowered under the hard gazes of all these fine people.

"Tell them," she said quietly.

"I'll not stand for this," Latham exclaimed. He took two strides toward leaving, but a hand on his shoulder stopped him. The hand stayed there and appeared to cause some pain. Mr. Albrighton, to whom that grip belonged, appeared unaware that it might be uncomfortable.

"You should hear the women out, sir. You can't adequately deny what you have not heard."

Whether Latham accepted the sense of that or simply could not move while that hand rested there, he strode no farther.

"I was a maid in Lord Becksbridge's home before Miss Avonleah arrived," Margaret said. She told how Latham had grabbed her as she crossed a field and forced himself on her.

The oldest of them, Emma, lost her fear then. "He was

no more than fifteen when he held a knife to me. Threatened to kill me in my sleep if I told anyone."

The last woman was Susan. Small and frail and trembling from this attention and Latham's presence, she spoke very quietly. "I was only fifteen, and he much older by then. I was so ignorant still, I did not know what he was doing, except that he hurt me and I bled."

She hid her face in Daphne's breast as soon as it was done. Daphne held her and soothed her while all hell let loose in the chamber.

Latham was in fine form, playing the victim of a malicious plot. A good many of the company seemed inclined to agree with him.

The plump, affable uncle appeared less than convinced but not as glaring as before. "There is no proof of this except their tales, of course."

"The last duke knew it all," Daphne said. "He tried to compensate them. All three were found living on lands he held until his death, at no cost. All three received allowances from him. His accounts should show the money, even if there were not leases."

That uncle glanced sidewise at Latham with a skeptical eye. "It should be easy enough to disprove, then."

"It is not for me to disprove but for them to prove," Latham said with exasperation. "If there were payments, perhaps he made them for another purpose. Perhaps he paid for his own sins. He certainly was not paying for mine."

"Are you impugning my dead brother's honor? Your own father?"

"I am saying once more that there is no proof, and these women are all liars."

Everyone had an opinion on that. Outrage, doubts, and arguments raged through the air. Daphne held Susan and Emma and prayed this ordeal she had asked of them proved worth it.

"There is more than their word as proof, I assure you," a voice said.

It had come from the doorway. Although it had not been spoken loudly, everyone turned in that direction.

Castleford stood there, managing to appear bemused at the same time as indifferent. He stepped into the chamber and looked around, both enjoying the attention he garnered and showing the potential for irritation of the same.

He greeted a few of the company, then noticed Latham's uncles. "Ah, bishop one and bishop two. How redundant. Did your older brother not come? Perhaps he is still in a melancholy that Latham survived his father."

"See here, Castleford, that is in very bad taste," a gentleman muttered. "As is this entire spectacle."

"But you are still here, aren't you?"

He had not looked directly at Daphne so far, but he did now. He did not voice his thoughts, but they were in his eyes. His displeasure streamed through the air to her.

"You say there is more evidence than their words, Castleford," Summerhays said. "It might be best to share what it is."

Castleford looked at Latham. He did not glare. Daphne thought he appeared almost sad. "There is my word as well. This woman here is telling the truth at least." He pointed to Margaret. "If she is, I would say they all are. I know her evidence is sound, because I saw him with her. I saw it happen."

The entire room held its breath. Latham appeared in shock.

"He is lying," Latham spit. "He only says this for his passing amusement. He is so depraved he thinks this is a joke."

"*I give my word as a gentleman* that I saw him with her. I pulled him off her myself." He looked at Latham. "And such a thing is never a joke. I am thinking that you never understood that."

The bishops turned to Latham, dismayed. "Have you nothing to say? Are you going to let this stand?" the short, wizened one demanded furiously.

"He is weighing it," Castleford said. "He does nothing without careful calculations." He paced over to Latham. People scurried out of his way as he did. "If you say I am lying again, you know I must challenge you. Or you must challenge me soon, for impugning your honor. Either way, I think that we will meet."

Latham stared with such hatred that if he were armed, Daphne feared something would have happened right then, in front of the world. Instead, face contorted and eyes aflame, Latham pushed past Castleford and strode from the chamber.

The noise of many conversations suddenly filled the air. Amid the tumult, Castleford came to Daphne. He looked at her in his most ducal way.

"I told you not to try to bring him down."

"I had other thoughts on the matter."

"I see that you did."

"It was all begun before I learned of your own scheme. Even so, I decided that eighty thousand pounds was not enough punishment."

"I expect not." He turned his attention to Emma and Susan. "My other two tenants, I presume. You can tell me later how you knew where to find them." He cocked his head and eyed her suspiciously. "Why do I think I will not like that story?"

Hawkeswell and Summerhays came over, sober despite the apparent victory. Castleford looked at them each in turn, then past them to the milling bodies. "Can you get rid of them? Those two over there are already laying bets on whether there will be a duel."

It did not take long. Within twenty minutes all the guests had left the house.

Which left three husbands and one lover looking at Daphne and her friends most severely, with pending scolds in their eyes.

"Do you want me to kill him?"

The question came through the dark at Daphne, as the aftermath of passion slid away and the world returned too clearly.

If she were honest, she thought, she would admit that some form of that question, and all that it meant, had been with them since they left Bird Street and returned to Castleford's home. It probably explained the way he had handled her, as if he sought to force her acceptance of his mastery.

"Do you want to kill him?"

"Oh, yes. Too much."

She suspected it was the latter statement, not the first, that caused the turmoil she sensed in him.

"Perhaps there will be no challenge."

"He either challenges me, or he all but admits it is true. A duel will not change minds, but it will keep mouths shut."

"Then I am sorry that you learned of that meeting and

intruded. It was my hope to avoid such a confrontation. I did not want to put you in danger."

His hand went to his eyes. He shook his head and groaned with impatience. "Have some faith, woman. *I* am in no danger. He was always a bad shot. I would have challenged him years ago if he would have stood half a fighting chance in it." He sighed. "I should have done it anyway. It would be best to have it over, I think. His reputation is destroyed now. No honorable man will call him a friend."

"Then perhaps killing him is unnecessary."

He shrugged and gathered her to him. "I think we should keep that house. It is well located. Discreet."

She steeled herself. She had hoped, in vain of course, that they would not speak of afterwards tonight, but just let it happen as it was sure to unfold now.

"I only took it for a month."

"Then I will speak to the estate agent and extend the lease."

"I will not be living in town. A whole house is a waste."

He looked down at her. "But when you do come, I do not want you staying on Park Lane or with other friends. Since you will not stay with me, you need a house."

She swallowed an uprising of emotion and caught her breath. "I do not think I can be happy as your sometimes mistress, Castleford. There are women who can do that, I know, but I am not one of them."

He did not move. He did not speak. She waited for the objections, the arguments. They did not come.

Nor did any talk of marriage. The absence of those words hung there between them.

He was so outrageous that scandal did not bother

with him anymore. But there was scandal that titillates, and then there was scandal that truly shocks. Today she had caused the latter kind, as she had known she would for weeks now.

The man in this bed did not care about that. He was prepared to kill an old friend because of today's events if he must. He found the notion of people gossiping about her boring at worst, no doubt. He did not blame her for the past, she was sure.

But the whole world knew now what Latham had done with her, no matter how they judged it. The taint was public, and she would never escape that. The Duke of Castleford was obligated to care about such things regarding his duchess in ways Castleford the man never would.

If they could make a life out of Saturdays and Mondays, it might not matter. Unfortunately, every week had a Tuesday in it.

He did not demand that she announce that this night was the last one. He did not say it either. But he kissed her in a way that made her heart break, and his warm breath penetrated to her blood when he moved his mouth to her neck.

She gave herself over to him as she never had before. She embraced the emotions in all their sweetness and pain, and they affected every pleasure. She would not forget any of it, she promised herself. Not ever. Not the excitement and not the sadness, and especially not the love.

Chapter Twenty-six

"You are not feeling chilled, are you, Audrianna?" Verity asked.

"I am fine. Stop making me an invalid. It has been three weeks since I gave birth, and I am quite myself again."

Verity tucked a blanket around Audrianna's legs anyway.

"I am so glad that you thought of this, Daphne," Celia said. "I promise not to cry."

"In a few weeks, you can all come to the new property, once the greenhouse is completed and the plants are moved," Daphne said. "The house is larger than the one used by The Rarest Blooms now, and the soil better, I think. The roads to London are excellent, so we can still bring the plants and flowers in one day if the wagon leaves in early morning."

"It sounds like a fine property," Verity said. "It will not

be the same, of course, but in a year's time it will seem as much like home to all of us as the other one does now."

Daphne trusted so. Denouncing Latham had not stopped the sale of The Rarest Blooms' land. Those papers had already been signed, and there was no ending it. Nor had she been as sorry as she might have been. It would perhaps be a good idea to have some distance from London for a while. And, she had to admit, eighty thousand pounds in trust put a different light on things too.

"He went to France, you must have heard," Verity said. "Latham. Hawkeswell told me last night that it was all through the clubs yesterday."

Everyone knew. Daphne did, because she had received a letter at Park Lane, where she had just spent a few days helping Audrianna adjust to both a new son and a new sister-in-law. The letter had a familiar scrawl, and seeing that hand had made her heart ache. *He has fled to France* was all it said.

No one had spoken to her about Castleford the days she stayed at Park Lane. As if by agreement, his name never was mentioned. She was too proud to ask if he fared well, lest her friends think she pined for him.

She did, of course. Privately. She held memories close to her heart and remembered his fun and the high emotions he provoked in her so easily.

"We are almost there," Celia said with girlish excitement. "Will any of the others still be in residence? Have they all moved to Surrey ahead of you?"

"Mrs. Hill will be there still, so you can see her. And Margaret and a few others. Emma has returned to her home, but I think Susan may remain with us at least for a while."

The carriage turned onto the lane leading to the house.

Daphne's own excitement built until she was breathless from it. She watched the house grow larger. Her home. Her sanctuary. The place where she had harbored and nurtured dreams that she dared not believe would come true.

She looked at her dear friends, each in turn. They had all been haunted by the past when they entered these doors, but none more than she herself. They had found their lives again, however, and their freedom from secrets. And now, finally she had too.

"There is something I must tell all of you," she said. "There is a secret I must share with you, that I dared not tell you until today."

They looked at her oddly, then at each other. She opened the carriage door and they all stepped down.

The door to the house opened. Margaret waved and came out. Then another figure appeared and sprinted past Margaret and flew into Daphne's arms.

She stroked the fair hair nestled against her, and bent down to kiss the soft face. She turned to the others. "I want all of you to meet Estelle. She is my daughter."

Estelle reveled in the attention the ladies gave. Her eyes grew wide on hearing one was a countess.

In the joy and admiration that followed the first astonishment, none of her friends asked any questions. Perhaps they just guessed most of it. Estelle's apparent age told most of the tale. Despite her fairness, she was not only her mother's child in appearance too.

Celia began a little game of flipping Estelle's curls on the back of her head. Estelle squealed and pivoted and turned to try to escape Celia's hand.

"She is beautiful, Daphne," Audrianna said quietly. "It

breaks my heart that you felt you had to keep her a secret from everyone, even us."

"I will explain why tonight, after she is in bed. It was not lack of trust in you, Audrianna. Rather a fear that if anyone learned of her, I would lose her forever."

Audrianna watched those pale curls spin. "Does her father not even know about her?"

"Latham? Thank heavens, no. The father spared the son's conscience in all things, especially this."

Estelle had gotten so dizzy that she fell to the ground, laughing. She sat herself up, giggling still, and brushed her skirt. Then she stilled and looked down the lane, distracted from her fun.

She pointed. "Who is that, Mama?"

Daphne turned her head. Audrianna inhaled sharply.

A man on horseback had stopped halfway up the lane. He watched them intently. Noticed now, he moved his horse forward.

Daphne held out her hand for Estelle. She drew her close while Castleford approached. Finally he was right in front of them, looking down, appearing every inch the duke he was.

"Your Grace," Daphne said. "Estelle, this is the Duke of Castleford, another of Mama's friends."

He swung off his horse and walked around. He looked down at Estelle a good long while, then made a bow. Estelle wobbled through a clumsy curtsy.

"Estelle, come with me," Celia said. "We will go inside, and I will dress your hair like a lady does for a ball."

Castleford and his big horse could not hold a child's attention when such fun waited. Estelle ran away, leading a string of women to the door.

Finally there were no sounds surrounding her and Castleford except the blowing leaves and the horse's occasional snort. Castleford quirked a half smile, but there was no mischief in his eyes.

"No wonder you did not want me to kill him. It would be a hell of a thing explaining that to her five years from now."

"Yes. It might be best if I did not have that to admit along with the rest."

He tied his horse to a tree. "Every day that you were at Park Lane I waited for you. I was sure that you would come to me. When I learned today that you had left and had no plans to return—" He faced her squarely. "I composed a very fine speech as I rode down here. I impressed myself with my eloquence. However, seeing that child—I find that I would rather not talk but listen, if you are willing to tell me about her."

"You are very sure that he has gone to France?"

"Very sure."

"Then I will tell you about her."

They walked down the lane at the slowest pace. The breeze conspired to dishevel Daphne's hair quickly. A tendril here, another there, and soon she looked for all the world like a woman rising from a bed of pleasure.

He tucked that observation away into the place in his heart where he kept the other memories.

"I was with child when I went to old Becksbridge and told him about his son," she said. "I stupidly thought he would tell Latham to do the right thing by me. Instead he accused me of trying to trap his son. He insulted my character and my virtue until I was in tears." Her expression firmed at the memory. "Then, when I was in despair, he offered to help me if I obeyed his instructions."

"He sent you north, to live with another woman whom his son had misused."

"Margaret was beholden to him, of course. He believed he could count on her making sure that I did as he commanded." She paced on. "He was not correct there, and I am thankful to this day for that."

"How did you disobey him?"

She stopped walking. "I was to live with her and give the child over to a family he had chosen after my lying in. I was too sinful to raise a child with his blood, you see. My bad character would poison her. As the months passed, however, my heart mourned the very thought of that day. Margaret saw my melancholy. She guessed the reason and proposed that we deceive him."

"I am liking her more all the time."

"She wrote to the duke that I had lost the child during an illness. During my last months we moved to a cottage outside Eccles. After Estelle was born, I stayed there alone for some months. I could not keep her with me forever, I felt. If the duke found out, he would cast out Margaret from her home, and me too. Mostly I feared he would take Estelle and I would never see her again."

Some of that fear was in her voice as she said it. He took her hand and pressed his lips to it. "Do you fear that still? With Latham now? Is that why you wanted to be sure he had gone to France before admitting even to me who she is? Daphne, a father has no rights to a child if he is not married to the mother."

She moved closer, so she looked in his eyes over her raised hand. "You cannot know what it is like, to be a

woman alone, with no means of support except the lar-
gesse of a family that has wronged you. If either took
her, father or son, I could never find the means to fight
them. Do not tell me about the law, Castleford. For a
woman alone, with no money, a duke's power is a fearful thing."

He wanted to say this was not true, and that no man
had such power. Except he knew all too well that he could
have a child torn from a mother's arms and arrange it so
no one would ever find the men who did it or the child
again.

"There is a good family near Eccles, the Foresters, who
had befriended me. I left her with them. I sent money, and
I visited when I could. I would take the stagecoaches there,
hold my child for an hour or so, then travel right back by
stage again. Only once did I stay longer, when Estelle was
ill."

"When did you become Mrs. Joyes?"

"When I first joined Margaret. It was obvious soon that
I was with child. I became a war widow, since there were
enough in England that one more was not notable. When I
approached Becksbridge again, I let him believe I had
married Captain Joyes, only to lose him soon in the war. I
hoped that after the duke died, if Latham should see any
documents with Mrs. Joyes's name, he would never guess
it was me. I never thought to find myself near London
again. I had hoped he would give me property near Margaret and Estelle. Instead, he gave me this." She gestured
to the land they now walked.

"So you lived here and waited for old Becksbridge to
die."

"I both waited for it and dreaded it. If he settled the

land on me the way he had implied, and if Latham remained in France since he seemed to prefer it there, I could bring Estelle to live here, and all would be well."

"Instead he gave the land to me, and Latham returned to England."

"Yes."

He drew her into his arms, as he had been wanting to do since he saw her up the lane by her house. As he had been needing to do for three weeks of separation from her.

"You are not to worry any longer. If he is fool enough to return to England and learns of her, you will not be a woman alone fighting him. He will not dare hurt you through the child, because, if he tries, I will certainly kill him this time."

Her smile trembled. "I will be sure to remember that, Your Grace, and inform you should I even learn he is aware of her. It will be good to be in fear no longer."

She did not understand what he meant. Or, perhaps she chose not to hear it.

"Daphne, I have spent three weeks—more actually—trying to understand why a sensible woman would refuse the chance to become a duchess."

"Did you conclude such a woman must be mad, and that was all there was to it?"

He laughed. "That was one possibility. Then I thought, what if this woman is not mad? What if she is most sane? What if she assumes that this duke who proposes—"

"I do not want to interrupt, but officially no duke proposed to this woman."

He looked to heaven for patience. "A small detail."

"Only to a duke. But please go on."

"What if she assumes that this duke will continue his

wicked ways, as if he were not married at all? There are some women who would not mind, who might even welcome that he occupy himself elsewhere. Then there are women who would not want to use the same bed where he had been with others before her."

"No doubt you thought that mad too."

He lifted her chin and kissed her lips lightly. "At first, perhaps. On second and third thought, I found it flattering. Charming. Perhaps—loving."

She flushed and averted her eyes. He tucked her arm around his and slowly paced back up the lane. "As I rode here, I debated what I could say to you to prove that I did not only see penance in that marriage offer. It occurred to me that I could admit that I have been with no other woman since we met."

Her head snapped around and she gaped at him in shock. He had to laugh. "Hell of a thing, isn't it? I'll try to explain why someday, but it is the truth. I am sure that I can give up that part of being bad now, if I married the right woman. She would have to agree to let me be bad with her instead, of course."

"How bad?"

"Very bad, I'm afraid."

She did not object or try to negotiate further. That was an encouraging sign.

"Then it entered my head that if a woman knew she was going to arrange the dramatic exposure of an evil man but expose herself too in the process, she might, if she were a kind and thoughtful woman, think it best not to marry a man who was not aware such scandal would surround her soon."

"You cannot deny there is sound logic if this woman thought this way. It would not be honest to—"

"I do not care if the world knows about you and Latham, Daphne."

"You will. When you turn your attention to those boring duties that you loathe but execute so well, you will regret—"

"Today is Tuesday, and I tell you I do not care."

She appeared startled and a little frightened. He drew her to the side of the lane. "After all this hard thinking, however, I realized there might be one more reason you would not consider me. I have never told you that you have stolen my heart, have I?"

"No, Your Grace. You have not." She looked down. Those two pink flags marked her cheeks and darkened. "It would be very hard to be with you and love you as I do if you did not love me, Castleford. A woman would have to be very greedy to become a duchess under such circumstances. All the jewels in the world would not ease that hurt, you see."

"There is no danger of that, Daphne. If I did not know for sure before, these last three weeks of hell have made it clear enough. I have missed you badly, and I came here today to tell you so. You have indeed stolen my heart, and I do not mind at all."

She sniffed. He thought it very sweet that she was overcome with emotion. She sniffed again and wiped her eye with her hand. "So are you going to propose officially?"

"Certainly, if you desire it."

"I think I would like you to, if you do not mind."

He took her hands in his. "Well, at least you are not insisting that I get on my knees."

She looked at him, and her unshed tears of joy made tiny diamonds in her eyes. "Actually, that would be very nice too."

He looked around. He doubted they were visible from the house. He eased down onto his knees. "You must tell no one. It will ruin me."

She laughed and cried. She bent to kiss his cheek.

"Daphne, will you be my wife, so the love we have for each other can blossom like the flowers in your greenhouse?"

She bit her lower lip, then opened her mouth to respond. However, no words came, and her expression fell. She looked toward the house.

"There was one more reason for that sensible woman to refuse to marry a duke, Castleford. Estelle. Everyone will know whose child she is. And I know how you hate him." Her brow furrowed from her distress. "I could leave her at The Rarest Blooms, I suppose. I would see her often, but—" She gazed down at him with an expression too close to sad regret. "I have waited so long to have her with me."

"I may hate him, but I do not hate the child." He got to his feet. "You can say she is Captain Joyes's child if you want. You can say she is Latham's. Do it however you want. As for having her with you, there is certainly room. You might have noticed that I have very big houses." He pulled her into his arms. "I love you. Stop thinking of reasons not to marry me and say that you will."

She looked up and touched his face. While he watched, the most beautiful expression claimed her face. No high emotion and no blush but no defenses either. Just Daphne, her pure self, as open and vulnerable as he had ever seen her.

"Yes I will. I will marry you, Castleford."

He kissed her, moved by her beauty and her exquisite self and her rashness in loving him. He swore to himself that while he might never be more than almost half-

reformed, he would never do anything to make her un-
happy with this decision.

He took her hand and they walked up the lane.

"When shall we do it?" she asked.

"Why not today? I can go to Cumberworth for the
vicar. I have a special license with me."

"You obtained a special license before riding down?
That was a little conceited of you."

"Not conceited, darling. Enterprising. Desperately hope-
ful. We can use The Rarest Blooms for our wedding party,
and your friends can be our witnesses."

"That would be very appropriate, I think. I would not
want anything more. Yes, let us do it that way, in the
garden."

He stopped short, as he remembered something. "Speaking of rarest blooms, I hope it isn't ruined."

He strode to his horse and plucked a wooden box out
of the bag there. He peered inside. "All is well. After
riding twenty miles in each direction for it, I would not
want it wilted before you saw it."

Daphne came close to the horse and looked over his
arm. "What is it?"

"Exquisite transience. A flower like none other, procured from the only man in England who I am told has
the plant." He opened the box.

Her eyes widened in wonder. Even jewels had not
impressed her like this.

"It is an orchid," he said.

"I know what it is." She lifted it carefully. "I have seen
drawings of it, from when it bloomed last year. How did
you get this?"

"I heard it had bloomed again, so I went and asked

that fellow Cattley to sell me one flower. It did not cost quite as much as the diamonds."

She lifted the flower and sniffed its scent. While she admired it, he looked at the house. The women had come out. They stood clustered near the door, watching her. Those who had lived here in the past and those who would live in Surrey in the future mingled together while Daphne remained entranced by the gift.

She stretched up and kissed him. The little group at the door broke out in claps and undignified hoots and calls.

Daphne looked back at them and laughed, then returned to her astonishment over the orchid. "You amaze me, Castleford. You have actually found the rarest bloom in England."

He looked at her. "Yes, my love. I believe that I have."

The "masterful"* *New York Times* bestselling author

MADELINE HUNTER

presents the first book in
a magnificent historical romance quartet

*Ravishing
in Red*

Audrianna Kelmsleigh is unattached, independent—and
armed. Her adversary is Lord Sebastian Summerhays. What
they have in common is Audrianna's father, who died in a
scandalous conspiracy—a deserved death, in Sebastian's eyes.
Audrianna vows to clear her father's name, never expecting
to fall in love with the man devoted to destroying it . . .

*Booklist

penguin.com

Don't miss the *New York Times* bestseller from
MADELINE HUNTER

*Provocative
in Pearls*

Their marriage was arranged, but their desire was not . . .

After two years, the Earl of Hawkeswell has located his
missing bride, heiress Verity Thompson. Coerced into
marrying Hawkeswell by her duplicitous cousin, Verity
fled London for the countryside. Now, the couple must
make the most of an arranged marriage—even if it
means surrendering to their shared desire.

M702T0510

She was trained in the art of pleasure,
but she's about to get her first lesson in love . . .

From *New York Times* bestselling author
MADELINE HUNTER

Sinful in Satin

The daughter of a famed London courtesan, Celia was
educated in the art of pleasure—destined, it seemed, to
follow in her mother's footsteps. But instead, Celia ran
away, taking refuge with friends far from society's de-
bauched circles.

Her quiet life comes to an abrupt end when her mother
dies. Celia has inherited all of her property, which in-
cludes massive debts and a small house in town. She has
also inherited Jonathan Albrighton, an enigmatic gentleman who has lived in the house as a tenant . . . a man
Celia soon admits she is in no hurry to evict, no matter
how deliciously unsettling his presence.

With mounting debts threatening everything she had
hoped to build, Celia is forced to consider embracing the
scandalous profession for which she was groomed. But
now there is only one man for whom she wants to put her
erotic training to use . . .